S.K. EHRA

Copyright © 2024 by S.K. Ehra

All rights reserved.

No portion of this book may be reproduced in any form without written permission from the publisher or author, except as permitted by U.S. copyright law.

Cover design by MiblArt.

To Florence

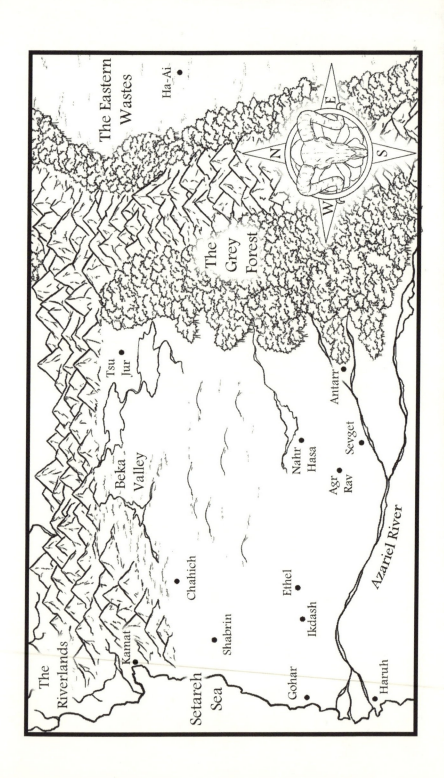

1
The Fen Witch

Taniel pressed a hand to his swelling jaw, wincing at the sting. His skull no longer throbbed from the heavy-handed blow, but the entire left side of his face was stiff beneath a blossoming bruise. The rest of him felt little better. He sat rigid to resist the rickety wagon's bump and sway, aggravated by the wheels' uncanny knack to catch every rut along the uneven country road. Farms bordered the hard-packed dirt, songbirds flitted through orchards of fig and apple growing in long, tidy rows, and goats grazed in fields rolling into woodland-shadowed hills unfurling with the soft gold-green of early spring.

The farmer driving the wagon whistled a cheerful tune, flicking the reins to encourage the dray horse's steady plod. Taniel's three companions crammed into the back of the cart were unaffected by the farmer's light mood. They sat in silence, gazes hard and mouths thin.

The cart wheels caught another depression and Taniel stifled a grunt. The jolt rattled every bone-deep bruise covering his ribs and back—courtesy of being tossed down the street stairs inconveniently close to the Top Step Tavern's entrance. The people of Chahich were friendly to strangers and tolerant of nosiness, but unforgiving of a nosy stranger who trespassed too far into taboo topics. Taniel had shown too much interest in the Fen Witch living in the marshes north of the rural town for the locals' liking, and they were fiercely protective of their elusive enchantress.

"We got no need for strangers who don't know to leave well enough alone," one of the men who'd tossed him down the stone stairs had hollered after him.

Taniel had done his best to muster some dignity as he staggered to his feet, clothes torn and blood-spattered. He cursed the fiend who'd opened a drinking establishment so close to the steep steps as he limped away under the jeers and bottles thrown to hasten his leaving. There was no doubt he was far from the tavern's first visitor to experience such unceremonious ejection. The men had been too well-practiced in their handling of an outsider asking too many of the wrong questions.

Suffering the shamed retreat, he better understood how Nesrin must have felt four years ago when his father had caught them together in his bed, returned from a job days earlier than Taniel anticipated. Her departure had been turned into a very public affair. His father shouting his disapproval of the relationship had drawn out the neighbors of the nearby flats. Curious heads had poked around doors and out windows to better witness the commotion.

Taniel and Nesrin had terrible luck as lovers; first discovered by his father, then her cousin Suri, two of Taniel's university professors, and an elderly lady at Gohar's Autumnal Festival who only nodded and went on her way. Seraphs bless the woman, as Nesrin had agreed to marry him despite their clumsy courtship. Saying marital vows had failed to grace them a lesser chance of being interrupted in intimacy, a consequence of Nesrin insisting Suri—who never remembered to knock—move in with them.

The wagon rocked, jarring the wooden edge into the knotted mass of bruising over Taniel's right ribs. He cursed beneath his breath. No matter how he sat, there was no escaping the wagon's eagerness to exaggerate the road's every irregularity.

"We'll get you some meat to slap on that eye once we get back," Tiran said, his smooth baritone at odds with his grizzled appearance. His hair had gone grey early and stubbornly refused to soften to white. Four thick scars sliced through the deep lines creasing his brow to end above his right eye and he had the hollow-cheeked look of a starving man.

If Tiran had been sent to the tavern, no one would have manhandled him. But no one would have talked to him either. All the patrons would've gone silent, claimed ignorance, or outright refused to speak to the tall, gaunt man who was so obviously a Purger.

Purger. Burner. Witch-Hunter. They were known by an endless litany of names. Regardless of what they were called, or whether they were summoned to a sprawling city like Gohar, or a country town like Chahich at the doorstep to the northern mountains, Purgers like Tiran were recognized wherever they went. Reception ranged from admiration, to cool tolerance, to the open hostility Taniel had found in Chahich. Men who fought monsters, exorcised demons, and slew dark witches received a welcome as varied as the quarry they hunted. Even in the towns where folk were pleased to see them arrive, people were always happier to see them leave.

The wagon carried them past a wooden post with the top carved into a female figure. Inscriptions ran the wood's length, asking blessing from the woman in the marshes for good health and harvest, and flower offerings were laid at the post's base.

"These farmers are fond of their Fen Witch," Aryeh said, cleaning one of the many knives lining his cloak. A rune marked each weapon;

some allowed the blade to cut through magic, others revealed its presence. All could kill monster or man that had trespassed beyond the natural.

Aryeh bore striking resemblance to the blades he cared for—thin, sharp features, and a tongue as cutting as a knife's edge. His black hair had begun to recede and the angular pattern of retreat emphasized his narrow face and the crow's feet scratched into the corners of black, watchful eyes.

"If she's what they claim her to be, they have every reason to be fond of her," Sariel said. "And a simple hedgewitch is probably all she is."

Taniel frowned. His father used that tone of forced casualness when he hid something. Five years of working together had Taniel well-trained to hear when his father lied or attempted to shelter him from darker truths. Aryeh's stony expression and Tiran's mirroring frown confirmed what Taniel suspected. They all thought Chahich's Fen Witch a graver threat than rumor told.

There were over half a dozen dark witches his father had been hunting through the years. It was well-known to be Sariel Sushan's specialty and there was no shortage of requests for his work. The question was, which did he believe Chahich's Fen Witch to be?

For sixty years—a decade longer than his father's memory—the Fen Witch, as the locals called her, had lived in the Beka Valley marshes at the northern mountain's roots. For fifty years, her presence had been tolerated. The farmers quickly learned attempting to tame the wildlands too close to her home resulted in their livestock dead of sudden illness, their children too frightened of a nameless presence to play in the fields, and their nights haunted by living shade that crept beneath doors to breed fearful unease. The hardships drove the farmers and their families away. Their tales attracted a different sort of daring spirit. Young men had set out into the marshes, thirsting to prove their bravery and earn the offered bounty on the witch. The older men in their hard-learned wisdom moved homesteads farther from the marshes as the young men ventured forth. Those wizened farmers and woodsmen were the ones who went searching for the overeager young men. They always found them, wandering the woods and fields, naked, confused, and filthy, but otherwise unharmed.

In the following forty years, the fear and mystery surrounding the Fen Witch had dwindled. She went from an existential threat to a concern occasionally brought up in town halls and at the women's circle. The menace of her presence diminished to little more than a topic for tavern gossip, and then a name to frighten children into behaving. The people of Chahich long ago decided she wasn't a dark witch, just a reclusive one, and as long as she was left alone they found their valley blessed. Farmers' fields established a comfortable distance from the marshes grew fertile and full. Sickness disappeared from Chahich and her sister towns. Lost travelers who strayed from the mountain roads told of a dancing light that led them through the forests, away from the marshes, and to the nearest homestead.

Chahich's custom of offering the Fen Witch part of the harvest on the equinoxes had evolved to erecting a shrine for her at the marshes' edge, directly imploring her favor. Local legend claimed if you left her an offering and did not trespass beyond the shrine, fortune awaited you in the coming year. Not everyone in Chahich worshipped her, but all agreed the Fen Witch was good to have around, if always at a safe distance.

That was until six months ago, when the fortunes of travelers changed. The ill-fated souls on the paths winding too close to the marshes were no longer guided away. They were discovered torn to bloody ribbons on the roadside, if they were found at all. Chahich's quiet streets boasted a disquieting number of posters featuring missing persons last seen in or headed toward the town.

Taniel had asked the men at the Top Step Tavern about this, masking his inquiries as worry for what a traveler like him faced should he venture northward. The locals had defended their witch, claiming it wasn't her behind the killings. She'd never harmed anyone before. Not like that. It was probably a karakin, an archura, or shurala. That no one bothered to pretend it was a natural predator was telling.

But karakins did not cause pale light to rise above marshes or send red-tinged fog creeping from the reeds to stalk farmers in their fields with disturbing intelligence. Archuras and shuralas were noisy creatures, their terrible cries turning the hardest of men cold with terror. The evil settled into the Beka Valley had turned it tomb-silent. The frogs, insects, and birds that had sung from the tall grasses and trees were gone, and no one remembered when they first noticed the deathly stillness.

Taniel pointing out it could be none of the suggested creatures spurred one man to accuse him of being a Witch-Hunter. At this, the tavern keeper's ruddy face blanched. Tired of seeing the faces of travelers in his tavern end up on missing posters, he'd been the one to call the Purgers in.

Taniel ensured the patrons' ire stayed on him, not wanting the well-intentioned keeper to suffer their wrath. He admitted he was a Purger and accused the townsfolk of sheltering a dark witch at the cost of who knew how many lives. The men who had chatted comfortably with him moments ago turned hostile gazes on him.

The scuffle was brief; many hands made quick work of removing his unwanted voice from the tavern. One of the larger men grabbed him by the shirt collar, and Taniel's refusal to cooperate under mob judgment earned him a stunning blow across the jaw from a second man, and a third man's fist to the stomach before being flung down the stone steps.

The wagon bounced again and Taniel hissed. He'd be a mess of black and blue by tomorrow.

"The boy should sit this one out." Aryeh gave Taniel a disapproving glance. "Should've left him at the town."

Taniel had yet to earn the respect from Aryeh to be recognized by name. He was either "the boy" or "the whelp" depending on Aryeh's mood. In a way, Taniel appreciated the thin man's reserve. Being Sariel Sushan's son was insufficient to convince him that Taniel deserved a place among them. Yet after five years, Taniel thought he'd earned at least a small bit of that elusive respect.

"I'm fine," Taniel said, seeing his father considering Aryeh's words.

"My missus can patch your boy up," the farmer driving the wagon said. "Our last two boys went off to trade school last season so she's achin' for a young one to fuss over."

"Thank you, but I'm fine," Taniel repeated hotly. At twenty-three, he was hardly a "young one," and a farmwife clucking over him promised to set him back months in getting his fellow Purgers to see him as more than Sariel's son. That Tiran had known him since before he could walk did nothing to help in proving himself a man.

"You can scarce sit still without yelping," Aryeh said. "What are you going to do when the Fen Witch—"

"Aryeh," Sariel warned.

"Don't see why any of you need go out to the marsh," the farmer said. "The Fen Witch ain't botherin' no one so long as no one bothers her."

"Our only interest in the Fen Witch is if she knows what's plaguing the mountain passes," Sariel said.

Again, Taniel heard the lie beneath his father's soothing tone.

"It's some man-wolf or the like," the farmer said. "Somethin' that'll only take a bit of silver and a good shot with a rifle. Not a whole band of Witch-Hunters."

Pulling on the horse's reins, the farmer slowed the wagon to a stop at the lane's end. A farmhouse sat nestled beside an orchard surrounded by fields speckled green with shoots of barley. The dirt road they traveled narrowed to a path cutting through untamed meadow before disappearing into a wilderness of ash and black sallow. Beneath the tree closest to the end of true road rested a shrine—an unremarkable stone piling in the semblance of a house where offerings were placed.

"Far as I go," the farmer said. "They say she's got a hut just beyond that ridge, but I don't know how anyone knows that. No one's made it through the marshes since before I was born."

"Thank you." Sariel swung out of the wagon, smooth in his movements despite having passed his fiftieth year. He tossed the farmer a bag of coins that jingled generously when caught.

"There's no need for that," the farmer said. "It was hardly a service and no sacrifice on my part."

"I pay for any service given, whether it was sacrifice or not," Sariel said.

Taniel hoped his father arguing the farmer into keeping the payment distracted him from seeing his limp when he clambered from the wagon. He fooled no one. Not even the farmer.

"Your boy's welcome to stay 'til you return," the farmer said. "Fair warning, I can't promise you won't come back to find him spoiled. My wife ruined three of our children through her dotin'."

"Thank you, but I'm alright," Taniel said. "It looks worse than it is."

"Then I expect all of you back this evening," the farmer said. "I won't be goin' to town 'til the morrow, so I'll have the wife prepare a dinner, she always cooks too much anyway, and I'll take you to town in the morning."

"The gods bless you and your kindness, stranger," Sariel said. "What name may I have to pray for you and your family?"

"Vardan," the farmer said.

"Taniel, go with Vardan," Sariel said.

"I said I'm—"

"This isn't a discussion, son," Sariel said, and there was a lot of warning loaded in the word "son."

"But—"

"Talk back to me again and I'll send you back to Gohar."

Taniel bit his tongue. Since he began working as a Purger, his father had only threatened to send him home six times. Four of those had been in the first six months, and Taniel had learned the first time when his father saw the threat through not to push him. He hated how his father continued to treat him like a child. Almost as much as he hated Aryeh's smirk—the closest the man ever came to smiling—at the silent exchange of glares between father and son.

"We'll be back." His father turned from Taniel in a final dismissal, and gave a farewell nod to Vardan.

The dust the men's feet kicked up tasted bitter as Taniel stood at the roadside, watching them leave him behind like the child they thought he was.

2
Ill-Magic

Ash and sallow twined together, trapping mist in their leaves and sheltering the wisps of grey pooling over the ground. Sariel's heart drummed in anticipation of the hunt, and his skin prickled under the faint traces of ill-magic hidden behind black boughs and hazy shroud.

"When will you admit Taniel's not a boy anymore?" Tiran asked.

Aryeh snorted. "He's certainly not a man. The whelp hardly needs to shave."

"I'd leave either of you two behind if you were as bloodied as he is," Sariel said.

"No," Tiran said, "you wouldn't."

Sariel would never admit Tiran was right. No more than he'd admit how glad he was he'd left his son with Vardan, or admit the choice had been one of a father, not a Purger. He knew he'd made the right choice in sending his son away when tinges of red polluted the thickening mist.

"That is, you wouldn't have ordered one of us to stay behind unless you thought we were facing more than a backwater hedgewitch." Tiran spoke softer in acknowledgment of the unnatural presence festering in the marsh.

"Ah, stop being such a woman, skirting around what we all know," Aryeh said. "We all think it's Minu."

"It does feel like her." Sariel glanced at Aryeh who nodded, running his thumb over his lips as if to rub away a bad taste. While Sariel lacked Aryeh's Sight—the ability to see sorcery and unnatural powers hidden from mortal eyes—he could still sense its presence. Decades of hunting dark witches and unholy creatures had sensitized him to the slightest prickle of ill-sorcery. The thrumming power soaked into the valley's marshland was far fouler than that of a simple witch seeking solitude, and it was undeniably familiar. The way Sariel's skin rose as if under a lover's touch was too close to what Minu's sorcery inspired to be coincidence.

"Sariel hopes every witch is Minu," Tiran teased. "And Minu hopes just as much every Purger who comes after her is Sariel. Honestly, the two of you should hurry up and bed each other so we can end this game of chase."

"Don't joke about that," Aryeh spat. "Taking a dark witch into your bed, might as well take a shurala."

"Some people like the exotic," Tiran said.

"Enough," Sariel said. He had no patience for the black humor that preceded their hunts. None of them could afford distraction. The rising shroud of bloodied mist veiled more than sight; it felt eager to muffle all his senses, turning him deaf and dumb.

The willow and ash trees thinned, and the narrow trail was swallowed by a sea of high grass and cattail with thickets of gnarled swamp oak and bone-white aspen. The marsh was unbearably quiet, the silent space between a breath and scream. No wrens sang. No frogs croaked from the reeds. Not even insects hummed in the rushes or skittered across the black water. The soft earth sighing beneath his steps was too loud here where the slightest sound was an unwelcome affront against a baleful want for stillness.

Sariel smelled the tang of sorcery infecting the silty scent of damp earth. The tingle caressing his skin sickened to a threatening crawl. An unseen presence had settled in place where there should have been life. The air tasted stagnant, choked, and hostile to any who dared breathe it in.

Aryeh hissed, lifting his boot from the damp ground as if he'd stepped in something fouler than mud.

"What is it?" Sariel asked.

"The whole damn swamp's infected by ill-magic." Aryeh wrinkled his nose in disgust. "It's sunk into the very earth."

"Where is it rooted?" Sariel scanned the swamp, looking for disturbed earth, a carving on a tree, or a man-made construction of mud and stone to indicate the source from where the ill-magic emanated. Usually he was able to feel magic's flow as he would a stream's current. Here, there was no telling from where the sorcery sprang. It was oddly unmoving, as listless as the marsh waters around them.

"I can't tell," Aryeh said. "It's too thickly laid."

"Can you tell if it's Minu's?"

"No, but I can tell you I don't know of another dark witch possessing this power."

"Is there—"

Aryeh yanked both him and Tiran behind a fallen tree half-buried beneath moss. Holding a finger to his lips, Aryeh motioned they stay hidden as he peered over their cover. His face paled and he signed against evil.

"What is it?" Sariel whispered, readying himself to face the monster, man, or demon prowling beyond his senses.

"Moths." Aryeh spun a rune-marked knife between his fingers. "They're everywhere."

"How many?" Sariel asked.

"Too many."

Sariel raised his eyes over the log. Now that he knew what to look for, he saw the shadowy movement haunting the marsh was more than the stirring haze. The moths lacked consistent shape, drifting as if they were little more than denser eddies of mist, but the longer he watched for them the clearer they became. No Purger agreed on what moths were, but whether they were demons escaped from the underworld, dark spirits, or restless ghosts—they mirrored the behavior of their namesake. As the soft-winged insects were inexorably drawn to light and flame, it was evil deeds and ill-magic that summoned the nearly invisible spirits to swarm. They were omens of coming misfortune, flocking to feed off sin and the despair it promised to bring.

Sariel's heart skipped a beat—it was not a few dozen moths crawling through the marsh. The mist teemed with hundreds if not thousands of them.

"Seraphs," Tiran swore, signing against evil over his forehead and heart.

Never before had Sariel seen so many moths in one place. Not even when he stopped a mad sorcerer from harvesting an entire town to feed a demonic summoning.

"Still think it's a simple hedgewitch we're dealing with?" Aryeh whispered.

Sariel never had. The moment he heard of the Fen Witch outside of Chahich, instinct more than reason told him it was Minu, and that after decades of hunting her he'd finally discovered where she'd been retreating to. He wished he'd succeeded in convincing Master Maqlu or Purger Wasi Adhar that Chahich's Fen Witch was a greater danger than tales told. Master Maqlu, the head sorcerer of Gohar, was reluctant to believe the claim. He'd refused to send even an apprentice to accompany Sariel in absence of evidence.

"I'll not spend more resource on another of your fool errands," Master Maqlu had said the moment Sariel mentioned Minu's name. "Bring me evidence to give credence to your claim. Then I will consider sending mages north."

In his younger years, Master Maqlu had survived challenging Minu. His triumph had catapulted him to the position of Gohar's High Mage, and was a feat still celebrated thirty years after the battle. Sariel failed to convince himself it was truly skepticism that kept Master Maqlu cautious, and not fear of facing the dark witch a second time.

Purger Wasi Adhar had been much more blunt in dismissing Sariel. His return letter was unpleasantly brusque, stating he had no time to waste chasing the phantasms of Sariel's fixation. The other Purgers Sariel sought for aid echoed Adhar's response. Their doubt was disappointing, though not unexpected. Too many times he had acted rashly regarding Minu. His fellow Purgers thought him obsessed. They claimed he was under her thrall. Men like Purger Adhar accused him of simply being under her bed sheets. Their disbelief combined with rumors that came too close to truth concerning his past dealings with Minu had planted seeds of doubt, fracturing Sariel's faith in his own judgment.

That uncertainty was now gone.

"To the north." Aryeh ignored the moths. His narrowed eyes watched the ground for the hidden sorcery. "I think the magic's coming from the north."

Wisdom urged Sariel to retreat, to lose a day between trains and carriages traveling to Gohar to lay his findings before Master Maqlu, and to wait for greater strength in numbers. Cold reason told him that was a doomed decision. The amount of ill-magic sank into the swamp to attract countless moths was the requisite evidence, but it was also a grim warning that he had no time to waste on convincing hand-wringing mages and haughty Purgers satisfied in their own self-righteousness; and his trespass onto ground so grievously wounded by Minu's magic would not go unnoticed by her. She'd know he was here, if she did not know already.

Sariel touched the silver talisman around his neck, praying for the Seraphs' protection, placing his fate in their mercy. He'd order Tiran and Aryeh back to Gohar, have them bring word to Master Maqlu. They did not bear the same past errors as Sariel. He had no more right to ask this sacrifice of them than he had right to call himself a Purger if he ran. He carried too much fault already to add cowardice to his failings.

Aryeh shook his head, guessing Sariel's thoughts before he spoke them.

"We knew what we were walking into," Aryeh said, and Tiran nodded. "We're not walking away."

A snapping twig severed the stifling silence, the sound as jarring as a woman's scream. The three men sank low behind the log. Grass rustled and black swamp water rippled as if disturbed by a timid breeze. Nature itself recoiled from the approaching presence.

Lying flat on the ground, mud soaking into his clothes, Sariel peered through the fallen tree's roots. A figure veiled by the reddish mist walked toward them. He squinted, unable to discern through haze and distance if the form was man, woman, or only a creature bearing human resemblance. He looked to Aryeh, who gripped a curved blade tight in one hand, signing with his other that the shrouded figure was magic-touched and a possessor of dark power.

"Minu?" Sariel mouthed. Aryeh shook his head.

Sariel reached for his sword's hilt, but froze the moment his fingers brushed the leather grip. The figure was gone. The flicker of moths was the only movement in the mist.

"Where—"

"Move!" Aryeh shoved Tiran aside.

Claws sliced the hem of Tiran's cloak instead of through his spine. The woman recovered from missing her target, rolling from her lunge with preternatural grace to land in a catlike crouch.

Sariel had never met Kharinah, knowing her only through the bloody ruin she left behind and the black stories that followed. Most claimed she was Minu's daughter, a creature born from the union of witch and demon. Or that she was a child the witch stole from the cradle to twist into a chimerical abomination of woman and monster. But every tale held a grain of truth as they all described Kharinah as inhumanly beautiful. Mud splattered her copper skin. Her long dark hair fell wild and her eyes' golden irises were set upon black sclera. She wore nothing save a filthy shirt falling to mid-thigh and slit along the sides to permit easy movement.

"Gentlemen." Her voice was a rich purr. Her smile lacked fangs but her fingers tapered into wicked, black claws. The reports of the missing travelers found slashed to ribbons had been what convinced Sariel to pay heed to the tales coming from Chahich. He knew what Kharinah's work looked like; an animal's brutality executed with intelligent precision.

Aryeh lunged. Kharinah skipped from the whistling blade's reach into the mist, disappearing in a blur of bloodied grey.

"Would you be looking for my mother?" Her voice danced around them, impossible to pinpoint, and the churning mist hid the demon-child's movement. "She'd love to see you."

Her croon sounded as if her lips hovered inches from Sariel's ear. He whirled, his sword finding only the tips of the swaying grass.

Kharinah laughed. "Mother said you would come, Sushan."

"Sariel!" Aryeh darted in front of him.

The mist buckled like smoke in wind as the hidden Kharinah retreated from his slashing blade. Her laughter harshened to a hiss.

"I can still see you, witch," he growled, striking at what looked like only air to Sariel.

"Watch the ground," Sariel said to Tiran. Soft imprints in the damp soil and the rustling grass tracked the demon-child's movements better than the unreadable mist. She circled them, engaging them with quick strikes before retreating from Aryeh's knives.

"Mother expected you sooner," Kharinah taunted. "Age has slowed you."

She's stalling us, Sariel thought. If Minu had sent her daughter to delay them, the witch and her foul deeds were close. That, or the demon-child was simply bored and wished to play with her prey.

"Can you hold her?" Sariel whispered to Aryeh.

"Long enough," he said. His cold eyes tracked the fiend prowling around them. "Head north. That's where the sorcery streams thickest."

Sariel shifted his grip on his sword, signaling to Tiran that at first chance, the two of them were to run. Snake-swift, Aryeh charged. Mire sloshed as Kharinah's hidden feet danced out of his reach, and Sariel joined Tiran in a mad dash deeper into the marsh. Aryeh yelled and a pulse of untamed magic stood Sariel's hair on end. He kept his eyes forward, trusting Aryeh to hold off the demon-child. Not indefinitely, just long enough.

"How long have you been a Witch-Hunter?"

Vardan's wife, Jana, was a cheerful woman who wore her dark hair in a braid pinned beneath a rose-patterned headscarf. Her face and figure were round, cheeks ruddy, and almond skin weathered by farm work and motherhood. Her kitchen where Taniel sat reflected her welcoming nature—warm from the oven and painted a cheery yellow with white flowers stenciled over the doorways and windows.

"Five years," Taniel said, allowing her to tilt his head to better swab the gash over his eyebrow. The room smelled of pine and sage from the arnica oil Jana had applied to his ribs mottling a dozen shades of blue.

"So long? You don't look old enough for that," she said.

"My father had been a Purger for almost ten years when he was my age. My grandfather started even earlier."

Jana tutted as she tilted his head the other way. "If we put some rosehip on this, we might stop it from scarring. But I suppose Witch-Hunters aren't too concerned about scars."

"It comes with the job." Though he'd like his scars to speak to better stories than being tossed from a tavern. No doubt upon his return home, Nesrin would fuss more than Jana. She'd throw her hands up in exasperation before demanding to know how he'd obtained his most recent injuries. He supposed he ought to be grateful that being thrown down the stone steps earned him only bruises and no broken bones. Sore as he'd be in the morning, this was far from the worst he had suffered—or would—in his line of work. What stung most was not the balm Jana dabbed onto his cuts; it was that these minor scrapes had convinced his father he was unfit to see the job through.

"The tattoos come with the job as well?" Jana gently swabbed the cut clean before applying a strong, earthy smelling ointment.

"Yes." He'd been waiting for her to ask about the tattoos since the moment he took off his shirt.

The black ink covering his chest, back, and arms turned his skin into an armor against dark magic. The circular tattoos around his ankles rendered him invisible to detection spells, the sleeves of inscriptions in the Old Tongue covering his forearms guarded him from active magic that sought to harm. The spiraling twelve-pointed star framed by two crescent moons between his shoulder blades warded away passive curses set to claim whoever trespassed into their power.

The tattoos' power wasn't absolute—no armor or wards were—but waking to a headache in the morning rather than raving mad from an Al Basty's curse, or suffering a stomachache instead of being disemboweled by a dark witch's spell was a fair trade for the intricate, painfully-acquired tattoos.

The six-horned ram skull and anemone flower inked over the center of his chest was one he shared with his father, Tiran, and Aryeh. It bound them as brothers-in-arms, linking them so they always had a vague sense of one another. The custom was an old, fading practice among a dying people. Purger numbers dwindled each generation and few worked in groups as Taniel and his father did. Only the traditionalists kept the practice of the bonded tattoo, the rest dismissing it as archaic superstition. But the bond had saved all their lives multiple times, and Taniel was ready to defy his father's order and go after them should he feel the faintest thrill of distress running through the connection. The problem was that the three older men were much more adept at restraining their emotions than he was. Aryeh had griped for the first half year after Taniel received the ink, complaining he had to know everything Taniel felt during that adjustment period. Taniel could count on his fingers all the times he ever sensed a strong emotion from one of his comrades.

"Sorry, what?" Taniel asked, having been paying more attention to the bond than Jana.

"I asked if you'd like some tea," she said patiently.

"Oh, yes, thank you." He fidgeted under the mounting anxiety at being left behind. He was unfooled by his father's earlier stoic pretense. There was something different about this job setting his father on edge.

"With all those tattoos and the scars you're earning, you'll have to beat off the more adventurous ladies with a stick," Jana said, hanging the kettle over the hearth.

"That's my wife's job," Taniel said.

"Oh. I didn't think Witch-Hunters married."

"It's uncommon, not forbidden. Most women have better sense than to marry one of us."

"Does your wife know you think so little of her sense?"

"She shares the same regard I hold for it, bemoaning her lack of sense every time she sees me."

Jana smiled. "Sounds like your wife is more than capable of handling a Witch-Hunter, then."

Taniel's returned grin collapsed as a shiver shot through him, feeling as though a rusted spoon had scooped out his innards. He pressed a hand over the ram and anemone tattoo. The dreadful chill lasted less than a second, but in that moment he knew—Aryeh was dead.

"What's wrong?" Jana asked.

Taniel grabbed his shirt from the chair, his holstered revolver, sword and knife belt from the table, and boots beside the front door. "I have to go."

"Go where? Taniel, you're limping!"

The drag to his step wasn't as bad it had been half an hour ago. The cold adrenaline in his chest where the link to Aryeh had been banished those lesser pains.

Seraphs curse it, he should have been there. If he was able to run as he was now, he had no excuse for allowing his father to bully him into staying behind. He had acted like a child, not a Purger, and now a man he'd sworn to defend from the evils they fought was dead.

Vardan looked up from chopping wood to call after him as Taniel raced down the narrowing path, past the stone-stacked shrine and into the forested swamp.

Tiran faltered, a single misstep before he recovered from the blow of Aryeh's death. Sariel never broke from his run. The grief for a friend's death belonged to a different time. In this moment it served only as a warning. With Aryeh gone, they were half-blind, unable to see the hidden things his Sight uncovered.

"Be on guard," Sariel said. "She'll come after us next."

His hand flexed on his sword hilt, ready for Kharinah to lunge through the swamp's misty gloom. But no cloaked presence disturbed the waters or tall grass. Perhaps Aryeh had dealt her a mortal blow. The man had possessed a talent for bringing death; it was not an irrational hope to think he had gifted it to the demon-child.

A burst of horror then fury flared from his bond with Taniel. Sariel barely kept his own fear in check, knowing exactly how his son would respond to Aryeh's death. He almost commanded Tiran to go ahead while he doubled back to stop his damned fool son from following them into certain death. He had silently thanked all the divine protectors when Taniel had returned from the Top Step Tavern limping and bleeding, giving him every reason to forbid his son from accompanying them. All he could do now was offer a final prayer that he and Tiran found Minu before Taniel in his youthful recklessness caught up to them. Or before Kharinah and the evils the witch had brought to the marsh caught his son.

A dull burn gripped Sariel's legs. A stitch sewed itself deeper into his side. He felt his age, breath coming short, knees aching. He should've retired ten years ago, but there were too few men in the younger generation following in his footsteps for him to abandon the hunt. Purgers were a dying breed. People relied on cities and their sorcerers sitting atop high towers to ward away the dark. Iron railroads connected the protected cities, repelling malevolence, and the dark creatures that hunted along lonely roads were relegated to fireside stories told by grandmothers, not solemn news serving as cautionary tales.

Tiran's labored breathing echoed Sariel's. They were both too old for this work, and Sariel sensed neither of them was fated to be serving as Purgers much longer.

3

Minu

All is silent. Creation holds her tired breath, waiting to witness your decades of toil come to fruition. The earth yearns for rebirth. Her rotting garden must be burned before she can grow anew.

You regret how true magic is lost to time. Mortals have forgotten how seamlessly it's meant to merge with the natural world. You taught them once, only for them to forget, to abuse the gift you gave. They willfully abandoned your teachings. They rebelled, then wept and cursed the consequences of their impudence.

The feeble power they now harness can hardly be called magic. It's a shadow of what you taught them. Meager rote. Hollow ritual. Chalk runes drawn on purified stone with tedious exactness, week-long rites suffocated beneath unnecessary ceremony. Sterile and lifeless. It lacks true magic's organic creativity. But their forgetting was the boon that hid you from detection for more than half a century. If the sorcerers secluded in their ivory towers ever looked beyond the crumbling manuscripts they struggled to comprehend, they'd have suspected long ago what you chose the marsh for.

You repurposed the very earth. As it absorbed and trapped the waters flowing from the mountains, you taught it to do the same for disease. For over sixty years, every fever, infection, and hereditary malady of the surrounding villages was siphoned here, answering the bidding you molded into the bark of the eldest tree. You sank the illness into the compliant soil, gestating a curse within an earthen womb.

The ground trembles in labor. It's only a matter of hours, perhaps minutes before the new world is born.

And that's when you hear them. You know the marsh too well to fail to notice the changes brought by the men's trespass. The black earth tells you of the two Purgers racing your way, the man lying dead in the mire, your daughter hissing through her pain, teeth bared in a snarl as she holds together one of her deeper wounds. The muscle and sinew slowly reform as her blood drips into the ground. She unknowingly contributes to the curse you've been growing all these decades, sowing in her own illnesses of mind and soul.

You're not worried for Kharinah. She'll survive her injuries. The magic you've spent a mortal's lifetime nurturing is far more vulnerable, and you're too close to seeing the world reborn to risk the interference of misguided men.

Kneeling in the reeds you take the damp soil in hand, give it shape, and the bones sunk into the marsh answer your summons to rise.

4
A Better World

A jolting tremor shook Sariel off his feet. He fell heavily, hands and knees sinking into the shivering earth. He'd been mistaken in thinking the swamp dead. It thrummed with unnatural life, the pulse unsettlingly similar to a heartbeat, and the ground possessed an eerie warmth as though his palms pressed through flesh.

Tiran had stumbled as well. He clawed the mud off his arms with a wild frenzy.

"Gods' wrath, get up!" He jerked Sariel to his feet. "Don't touch it!" Tiran held out his hands to show the skin was discolored to a deadened grey all the way up to his forearms where the muddy streaks ended. "The whole damn swamp is tainted."

Sariel wiped the mud off his arms, revealing his skin mottling to the same lifeless hue. The earth's strange warmth wormed its way beneath his skin like crawlers burrowing into a corpse, and he thought he saw flickers of red fall with the filth. Nausea washed over him, sending his stomach lurching into his throat. He vomited into the mire.

"Have you ever seen anything like this?" Tiran asked. His face was pale, brow damp in a feverish sweat.

"No." Sariel caught himself before he wiped his filthy hand over his mouth.

They moved more cautiously through the reeds and shallow waters. Discovering how thoroughly ill-magic polluted the marsh tempered their haste. Sariel watched the ground for flickers of that red sickness. He needed Aryeh to see the ill-magic hidden below and trace it to the source. Grief for his fallen friend escaped before he could suppress the sharp pang. Fresh fear stoked his heart when he felt Taniel's own grieving wrath answer. His son was closing the distance fast, and the thought of Taniel coming into contact with the dark magic festering in the earth turned Sariel's mouth dry.

"Find Minu and end this," he said.

Moths seethed around them. Sariel more carefully watched their movements. He may not be able to sense the magic's origin, but the ill-omened spirits did. Instinct more than observation told him the fluttering shapes moved toward a copse of trees where the high grass brushed the lowest of the mossy boughs.

"This way." He motioned Tiran after him.

The moths stilled from their circling as they passed through the swarm. The spirits fixed eyeless faces upon them, and what might have been mouths gnashed furiously, feeding off the dark magic heralding despair. The red tainting the mist thickened, drifting like fresh blood in water.

"Don't interfere, Sariel." The warning echoed through the crimson-burned haze. Sariel instantly recognized Minu's voice. In the many disguises she'd worn over the years, she'd never changed her voice. Not for him.

"Gods damn, where is she?" Tiran took stance beside him. Their readied swords were forged to cut through magic as easily as flesh.

"I liked your last residence better," Sariel said, seeking to tempt Minu to reveal herself. While she preferred to cling to the shadows at first, she was never able to stay there long.

Challenging any witch on her home ground was dangerous. With Minu it was suicide, but not necessarily defeat. Magic was a fickle power; pulling a single thread could either hopelessly snarl an enchantment beyond ever undoing, or cause it to instantly unravel. If he and Tiran discovered what she planned, the smallest interference might upset it.

Minu's chuckle was sweet and low. "Then you should have stayed."

The ground shifted beneath Sariel's feet like sand dragged out by a tide. The wet sucking sounds of bodies being pulled from mud rose around them.

Shkk. Shk. Shk.

A dark form slunk low to the ground. A second then third joined ranks with it.

Shkk.

Sariel whirled, slicing the lunging beast in two. The magic-born abomination disintegrated into the reeking filth of decayed bone, rotting flesh, and mire it was made from, releasing a wave of fetid stench. He'd assumed the animals of the swamp had fled when a more dangerous predator had staked her territory here. But Minu had repurposed the marsh's previous denizens.

Shkk. Shkk.

Two more moldings erupted from the earth to break upon his sword, spattering him in rot.

"Stay close!" Sariel called to Tiran. Getting separated when the very earth fought them would be their deaths.

Shkk. Shk. Shkk.

The soil shuddered as more monstrous shapes freed themselves to take form.

Shhhhhkk.

Hands shot from the ground, snaring Sariel's legs, then crumbled to dust. His warding tattoos repelled that sorcery, melting the earthen fingers the moment they touched him. The creatures of mud and rotted flesh had greater independence from the magic that birthed them; his tattoos had no power over them. They hounded him until his sword reduced them back to inanimate mud. As a younger man he'd have made quick work of them, but the strength of vernal years was long gone. His arms ached, his back strained with each twist, and he no longer had the youthful fanaticism to lose himself in the thrill of the fight and forget his physical pains for a later time.

He lashed his sword out, loosing a spray of bloodied dirt and blackened bone. The creature collapsed into rot and earth. He moved faster than he had in years, his sword a silver blur cutting down the rotting constructs before they fully emerged from the ground. His heart thundered and shoulders burned as he fought the monsters, the earth, and his age.

Minu had to be close by. The reek of her creatures failed to mask the scent of her sorcery, a blend of blood's sharp iron and cassia's sweetness that sent shivers to his most primal instincts. For over twenty years Minu had been a looming threat over his conscience, his obsession to hunt her down spurred by the blame he bore for the wickedness she committed.

He had let her go twenty years ago, and regretted it ever since.

You're reluctant to call upon greater power. The beasts molded of the marsh are pathetic creations that Sariel and his fellow Purger easily cut through. But the creatures slow them, and that is all you seek. You have no desire to upset what you've been nurturing, no more than you wish harm upon Sariel Sushan. He is like the old magic—purer, possessing purpose undiminished by time. He and those of similar spirit are who you intend for the new world. They are flowers who cannot bloom in this garden choked by weeds.

The earth rumbles, telling you Sariel trespasses dangerously close, threatening what must come to pass. You crouch once more to where earth meets black water, stirring the ground into a hungry morass. Sariel and the other Purger's wards defend them from sorcery. They do not defend against a physical world altered by magic. Quicksand made through magic is still quicksand.

The earth yields to your wishes. It ripples, churning itself into trapping mire. You feel Sariel and the Purger's footsteps halt as they're snared. Sariel pulls himself free to escape the beasts lunging at him. His companion is not so fortunate. The creatures rush upon him. He fends off the first and second, not the third. They fall into the greedy mire, their struggle brief—a blade flashes, a gasp choked by mud, and both disappear into the black, swallowed by the earth.

Sariel rushes to where the man vanished. He pulls at the muck, calling the man's name, searching for a hand to grab and haul to the surface. He finds nothing. You sense the man sink farther and farther down. You feel his struggles slow, then still. The earth delivers him to be buried where all the bones settled. Where no light or man can reach. His final breath lost in murk.

You regret that Sariel must mourn fallen friends, but they chose their fates. They had a chance to survive what is to come if they had not interfered. Those of strong, moral spirit have nothing to fear. The coming world is for them.

The tread of Sariel's step has changed since last you met. He's slowed under time's cruelty and you pity the aging he suffers. He won't stop until he is dead or his goal reached; a determination you admire and lament, the virtue twinned to the vice of moral myopia. He never saw the wonder you intended, no matter how many times you tried to show it to him.

The earth swells in climaxing labor, releasing clouds of red. Perhaps this time Sariel will understand. You wave your hand and the beasts of rot sink into the swamp, leaving his way unobstructed.

You wish him to see a better world.

The tremors shaking the ground gentled to the distressed groaning of a dying man. Sariel tensed, ready for a fresh onslaught of rot-beasts. No fiends leapt from the gloom. No hands reached up to drag him into the cursed earth. Lungs burning, skin slick with sweat, Sariel watched the bloody mist for the smallest hint of a hidden threat. The creatures' disappearance followed by the abrupt return to eerie silence was more frightening than the earthen monstrosities. The spindly tree branches knotted overhead were a net ready to snare him and he feared every step he pressed into the damp ground would be the one that pulled him under as Tiran had been.

Coming here had been a fool's errand, but it had been the duty Sariel swore to. Even if the civilized world no longer thought it necessary.

The black trees thinned, as did the red-tainted mist, revealing a perfectly circular clearing. The woman in the meadow's center only looked young, forever blessed with the appearance of a girl in her early twenties. In truth, she was decades, perhaps centuries older than Sariel. Her ebony hair fell free in a mess of curls framing a gentle face, full lips, and brilliant green eyes. Filth stained her simple dress, grime covered her hands and arms, and streaks across her cheek marked where she must have brushed away loose hair. Thick red veins twined up from where she walked, her step offering glimpses of the power infesting the earth.

She looked to where he hid in the shadowed trees. "Careful where you step, Sariel. The earth has a life of her own."

Sariel moved into the open. There was no point in hiding, and Minu smiled at seeing him. She looked no different from the last time he'd seen her five years ago. Or from when he'd first met her two decades past.

"What is this?" he asked. He scanned the clearing for a tree or rock bearing sorcery carved into its face, or an unnatural bend of the grass to indicate where her magic had been first woven.

"Rebirth," she said. "Don't you remember from when we spoke, not too long ago?"

"Which time?" he asked. Their paths had crossed at multiple points over the years, and for Minu half a century might be a passage of time she considered "not too long ago."

"When we first met. You shared with me your disappointment in what men were becoming. Soft in head and spirit. Cruel in heart and mind."

Careful movement in the trees behind Minu caught Sariel's eye. He thought it was another rot-beast until he saw it crept on two legs instead of four. Taniel was covered from head to toe in filth, too thoroughly for it to have been through a fall, and the sword and revolver he held in hand were spotless save for where he touched them. He had disguised himself as part of the swamp, hiding himself from Minu under a coating of earth saturated in her magic.

Numbing fear flushed through Sariel. His son wasn't stupid; he knew exposing himself to Minu's magic so thoroughly was a dangerous gamble. The warding tattoos lacked the power to fully protect him from sorcery as strong as hers. But disguising himself beneath ill-magic had gotten him here undetected, allowing him to search for the anchoring rune.

Sariel caught his son's eye. The two exchanged a brief, understanding glance.

"I recall you were more hopeful than I," Sariel said. He knew how to distract Minu and keep her attention from finding his son. "You spoke of a new age."

"And you spoke of why what I do is necessary," she said.

"I remember that conversation very differently."

"Sariel, this is as much for you as it is for me."

"I fail to see how this"—he motioned around the meadow and Minu's gaze followed his gesture, away from Taniel—"serves anyone, save you."

From the corner of his eye, he saw his son checking trees, rocks, and ground for physical links to disrupt Minu's spell. Sariel was certain there had to be at least one, and doubted it could be broken while Minu lived. His son seemed to come to the same conclusion. He abandoned his search to creep closer to the witch, revolver ready for when he closed the distance for an accurate shot.

Minu stepped toward Sariel. He instinctively moved away.

"There was a time you didn't recoil from me," she said.

"I was a young fool," he said. "Now I'm an old one."

A booming gunshot ripped a bullet through Minu's chest. A second shot blew through her left shoulder, spinning her round for the third to catch her below the neck. Red—both blood and magic—misted at each impact and the witch collapsed into the high grass. Regular bullets presented no more threat to her than rain, but three fatal shots from bullets marked by arcane magic could fell any creature of flesh and blood.

"Father!" Taniel rushed toward him. "Father, did she hurt you?"

"No. Find the source rune," Sariel said. There had to be one. The swamp's magic was too independent to be tied solely to Minu.

"Tiran and Aryeh, are they—"

"Dead. Find the source rune."

Taniel ignored the order. Mud squelched beneath his steps as he raced to check Minu's body. Sariel's approach to the fallen witch was far more cautious. No pained breathing or rustling grass suggested she'd survived. The thought of finding her dead offered him no vengeful closure for the death of Tiran or Aryeh. He felt only the pain of another wound added to the pitted scars on his soul.

Taniel's bruised ribs protested his hurrying to where the witch fell. The foul red mist continued to steam from the ground, the ill-magic undiminished by its mistress's death. Sorcery often outlived its caster and Minu's was proving stubbornly durable. His heart beat rabbit-quick but his hands held the revolver steady. There was always the chance she wasn't yet dead. Those who gave themselves to unnatural powers were often reluctant to accept a natural death.

His father reached the witch first, his posture stiff, expression unreadable. Coming to his father's side, Taniel wrinkled his nose at the figure splayed in the grass. This was not the first time he'd seen death deliver aberrant change to a witch's corpse. The body looked like it had been rotting in the swamp for months. Minu was little more than a skeleton, her flesh's color and consistency decayed to be almost indistinguishable from the soil. Traces of red swarmed the body, drifting from empty eye sockets and between blackened teeth like a phantom breath.

"Father?" Taniel asked, disturbed by the way his father looked at the corpse. Rain began to fall, bringing with it an icy chill. "Father?"

The earth groaned. The tremor shook his father from the trance.

"The magic survived her," he said, sounding dazed. "We need to break the source rune."

Crouching beside a flat stone, he unsheathed his dagger and sliced open his palm to let bloody rivulets fall to the shale. The red drops quivered, then ran over the flat rock, converging to stream northward. Taniel imitated him, cutting his hand and letting his blood drip onto a piece of flat shale a few dozen strides to the east. The magic in the earth was hungry, pulling his blood offering to betray where it was physically tied to the swamp. Both his and his father's blood flowed toward the same northern clump of trees.

"Be on guard," Sariel said, following where the blood led. "We don't know how much of the sorcery outlives her."

Crimson steam hissed from the earth, and a menacing shudder cost both Taniel and his father their balance. Catching himself on hands and knees, Taniel's stomach roiled under the rising magic. The sorcery had neither died with its creator, nor had it weakened. If anything, it felt stronger by the second. The momentary relief he'd found in Minu's death was lost in the fear of the ill-magic running free without a mistress to control it.

"What was she trying to do?" Taniel asked. He felt ill from being so long exposed to the sorcery saturating the soil. His skin had crawled the moment he slathered the mud over him to hide from the witch using her own magic. Now his muscles burned as if the illness in the earth had bled into him, and his skin where the rain washed off the mud had a sickly grey pallor.

"Just find the rune," his father said.

The tremors came faster and faster, one running into the next without pause. His father hurried toward the trees, but nagging unease pulled Taniel to Minu's corpse. The mud sucked at his boots as if deliberately seeking to slow him. His legs burned from the struggle of wrenching his feet free.

The corpse was still there, and no longer distracted by his father's strange reaction to the witch's death, Taniel saw what he had missed. There were no bullet holes. The corpse's condition made it difficult to discern what was cloth, flesh, and mud, but there should have been wounds in the torso. There were no tears or punctures marking the decay, and none of the exposed bones were shattered to betray where the fatal shots had impacted. Taniel's blood chilled—the corpse was too tangled into the earth to be sure, but the hair and dress looked wrong as well. Wrong length, wrong cut. Death couldn't have changed that.

"Father, she's not dead! The body isn't hers!" Red mist flooded his throat, suffocating his shout to a rasping whisper. "Father!"

His father showed no sign he heard him, crouching to examine an old tree. The sigil anchoring the sorcery in the trunk looked like natural growth of the bark, subtle and easy to miss.

Taniel raced toward him. "Father!"

Sariel neither heard the warning, nor saw Minu rise from the earth behind him. Mud fell from the witch as she stood and soil clotted her wounds.

"This was for you as much as it was for me." Her voice rang clear through the mist smothering all other sound.

His father whirled. The air surrounding Minu coiled into a crimson whip and struck snakelike out at him.

"No!" Taniel dove between his father and the sorcery. He heard his father's horrified cry as he took the spell intended for him. Taniel shut his eyes tight in expectation of agony. Something soft as silk brushed over him, a gust of wind that was there and gone.

Taniel opened his eyes. Fine red lines like transparent veins sank into him. His skin warmed then went cold, his vision swam, and the gentle touch of the threadlike magic turned terrible when it turned to poison in his blood.

For a terrifying moment, Taniel stared at the sickness burrowing into him. Then he dropped to the ground, limp and lifeless.

"No!" Sariel's world collapsed. The evil-infected marsh, the swarming moths, Minu, they meant nothing. All that mattered was that Taniel lay unmoving in the trampled grass.

"No, no, Taniel." He lifted him off the cursed earth, feeling the hum of dark power coursing through his son. "Gods, please no."

Taniel spasmed. Blood wept through his clothes in the design of his warding tattoos—the protective powers overrun by the diseased magic's strength. Decay reeked on his shallow breaths. His lips moved to soundlessly shape "father" and "cold." The hand he lifted was a mottled grey and dropped as his eyes clouded.

"No, Taniel! Taniel!"

"I warned you not to interfere," Minu said.

Sariel shielded his son from the witch. The sympathy softening her expression was as much a lie as her youthful appearance.

"Don't look at me like that, Sushan," she said. "I wanted to spare you suffering."

"Then spare him," Sariel said. Even as he spoke, Taniel thinned, wasting under the curse.

Minu shook her head. "Sushan ..."

"Of the two of us, my son was always the better man. If anything you've said is true about wanting to create a better world for the deserving, my son is one of those."

She stared down at him, and uncertain terror gripped his chest. He had no idea what Minu would do. She might easily smite them both as she had been ready to do a moment ago. Or she may take pity on them now that they no longer posed a threat to her ushering in a new world.

Taniel's ugly, sucking breath sounded like he choked on his own lungs.

"Please," Sariel begged. If there was a way to stop his son's death from being his final failure, he would see it done.

Minu knelt in front of him. The mist obscured the world beyond the three of them.

"I'd need your life to do so," she said. He held her gaze even as the strength of it made him feel like he was being buried beneath the weight of the centuries she'd witnessed. "Even then, there's no guarantee he'll survive."

"I give you my life to save his," Sariel said without hesitation.

"You're certain?"

"Of course—"

She touched her fingers to his lips. "Listen to me, Sariel Sushan. If you hold anything back, there is no chance of saving him. Your life must be given entirely. There can be no want for revenge against me. No desire to fight the war you've waged for over thirty years. You cannot want anything else, to see a lover's face once more, the chance for farewell, a creature comfort of closure, nothing besides giving your life for his." She stroked his cheek. "Can you do that?"

"Yes." If his son died, so did he. He had given his entire life to Taniel. Every kindness, every act of courage was done as example for him. Every suffering undertaken was so Taniel might be spared.

Minu kissed him. Her mouth pressed warm over his. His fingers went cold. She inhaled, and the chill spread up his arms into his chest. Her kiss drew out the deepest parts of him. His vision dimmed, and her hand supported his head as he weakened. The cold spread farther, numbing his legs, stealing sensation. He barely felt her catch him. Her lips never left his as she inhaled again, pulling the very life from his lungs. His heart slowed, a distant drum with the abyss of death waiting between each beat. He gave it all to her, every breath, every heartbeat, all his will to live he surrendered to the witch. The cold crept into his mind, turning his thoughts a distant grey. Awareness fading, he gave all that remained, the last of his hope as a final gift to his son, that Taniel be granted the strength his father lacked, to face an unknown future born from his father's failures.

The cold claimed Sariel's heart, and then the darkness took him.

You press your lips tight to hold Sariel Sushan's life in your lungs.

Resting him on the groaning earth, you trace your hand over his face, his skin already chilled. You wish his spirit well, that he find the peace in death he never knew in life.

His son—Taniel, he called him—feels fragile as you cradle him in your arms. He's not far from following his father into death. The boy must take after his mother. You would not have thought the two were father and son, they share so little physical resemblance.

Placing your mouth over Taniel's, you taste his blood seeping from cracked lips, and breathe Sariel's life onto the dying ember of his son's. It flickers, threatening to go out; but his father was right, the boy's spirit is strong. He clings to the life you gift him, feeding off it to make it his own. His grey pallor lightens, the blackness on his hands ceases its spread, and his chest rises with a strengthened breath. It won't serve on its own to save him, but it will hold until you are better able to care for him. You push his dark, sweat-damp hair off his brow. It's the same color his father's was before the years took their toll on him. Perhaps they are more alike than first glance suggests, and if this young man is to be the legacy Sariel leaves, you will see him cared for.

As if the passing of a father's life to his son is the sign the earth awaited, she releases what she nurtured those sixty years. Red floods from the ground, pluming like the angry breath of vengeful gods shaken from their slumber. You hold the boy close, and the crimson tide departs, understanding he is not to be claimed. The curse rises to swirl through the marsh. Reeds rustle, leaves shiver under the strange wind, and then with no greater fanfare than a sigh, it disperses. It will weed out the wicked, the corrupt, the weak in mind and soul who have no place in the garden you will grow. Humanity is in want of salvation, and you will deliver.

Kharinah is silent as a ghost as she emerges from the mist. The curse won't touch her; it retreats from what is yours. Blood stains her clothes and a tear across the stomach speaks to a wound fatal for a lesser creature.

"What is that?" she sneers at the young man in your arms.

"A promise to be kept." You lift Taniel, holding him as you did your daughter when she was just as frail and in need of care. Bits of him fall away when he is moved—tissue too rotted to be saved by a father's sacrifice.

You wave your hand in a circle, spinning wind to shape into an annular doorway. Sunlight shines through the portal and cool air beckons. You motion for Kharinah to walk through first and follow. In a rush of wind, the marshland is replaced by mountains cresting like dragon-spine. The sun is colder upon these northern peaks of red soil and yellow stone adorned by green oak and hornbeam.

Ringed by a garden of tamed magnolia and silk trees sits a manor; the enchantments woven around your mountain hall prevent even you from entering by means other than foot. The manor's alabaster stone is a gleaming white unfamiliar to these red and yellow mountains, a pearl among copper and gold. Ivy spreads across the façade, cultivated to leave the carved murals unveiled. The stonework tells the legends of an older time and place. The murals, the limestone statues guarding the garden pathways, and the lattice patterns interlacing over windows to cast the sunlight into intricate geometries are artistries you all but erased from the world. They are the remains of Ha-Ai, the fragments you salvaged from the kingdom's open tomb in the Eastern Wastes after you razed it.

"Kharinah, go and—" You turn to find your daughter already gone, off to run wild in the mountain forests. The shirt she wore lies ripped on the ground and you hear the howls of the wolves she races to join.

After chaining her for months to guard the marsh, you permit her a night of freedom.

The southern horizon burns crimson. The cloud hovering low over the Beka Valley spreads from its place of birth, bleeding to the farthest corners of creation.

Taniel moans. You shift your hold to better support his head against your shoulder.

"You'll wake to a better world," you promise.

5
When the Sky Burned

"Look! Look!" Suri jabbed her finger out the window. "There's another one!"

Nesrin abandoned the dough she kneaded for dumplings, wiping her flour-dusted hands on her apron. She joined her cousin leaning over the windowsill to better see the cobbled street below.

The last couple days had trained Nesrin to quickly spot the diaphanous, skittering shadows. Their presence affected no physical change on the world they'd invaded. They moved soundlessly over brick and cobblestone, scurried over walls and doorways without setting flutter to the awnings or causing the hanging flowers decorating shop entrances to sway.

"There!" Suri wrung the newspaper between her hands, spreading fine tears across the front page. "Do you see them?"

"I see them," Nesrin said.

Neither of them believed what the papers claimed—that the phantasms were spirits attracted by accident to Master Maqlu's undisclosed research. The head sorcerer of Gohar had descended from the Arcanum to issue a public apology in King's Circle. He assured the people that the apparitions were harmless, posed no threat, and though they were visible, they held no influence in the physical world and would fade from it in time. "NOTHING TO FEAR" the headlines read, urging citizens to remain calm.

But if that was true, why had Governor Sandar locked the city down save for foremost services? The bakery where Nesrin and Suri worked had been shuttered, the citizenry placed under curfew, and city guards marched the streets at all hours. Unnecessary travel was banned, and Nesrin feared this meant further delays for Taniel's return. He was already gone longer than he said he'd be.

Worry's nervous wings beat in her stomach. Her husband's work stretching longer than anticipated wasn't an uncommon occurrence, but he always sent word were that the case. She had heard nothing from him since his last letter; a brief confirmation he'd reached Chahich and expected to be back in three days. That was a week ago. The small apartment she and Suri were trapped in felt more suffocating as another day passed without word from him.

Suri went to the next window over on their third-story flat. "There's more of them today. Don't you think?"

"Perhaps we only see them better," Nesrin said, not wanting to admit her cousin was right. Suri was too blunt to see anything besides what was there. She had been among the first to notice the strange shapes crawling over the streets, insisting they were more than her imagination or tricks of the light. So when three days ago Suri had said the northern sky looked oddly discolored, Nesrin had believed her and not the day's newspaper repeating there was no cause for fear or alarm. There was no denying Suri's claim the next morning when the sky boasted two dawns—pale yellow in the east and bitter red to the north. Riots broke out in the city that day. The empty consolations of mages and politicians no longer curbed mounting fears. Smoke and screams filled the streets as the burning sky bore down from the north. Governor Sandar enacting martial law quelled the uprisings, but not the fears that inspired the unrest.

Nesrin had spent the following nights listening to shouts punctuated by gunshots, watching the sky darken from a drab red to a livid crimson, turning the moon into a bloody eye. Chahich was to the north, and she was unable to convince herself that the red tide flowing across the heavens was unrelated to what had called Taniel away.

"Gods keep him safe, Razirah guide him back to me," she had prayed as the burning veil overtook the night.

Curfew only slowed the spread of rumor. There was no silencing fearful tongues. Nesrin's neighbors told her sickness befell the north, spreading from the Beka Valley. They claimed the red-tinged sky was a storm of bloody rain. The phantasms stalking the streets were the dead come to witness a reaping of souls. It was not Master Maqlu's experimental sorcery, but a dark witch gone rogue from the Arcanum that was the source of the living shade and souring sky. One woman whispered it was the Demon Witch Minu seeking her long-desired revenge upon Maqlu for having bested her decades before.

"Have you heard from Sahak?" Suri asked. "He'll know what's really going on."

"No, but I'll go to the Arcanum tomorrow," Nesrin said. Yesterday, the sky's discoloration looked like a veil of rain moving closer to Gohar. Now, the red hung directly overhead, descending like a low, winter fog turning the air thick and dirty. "And I won't leave until I see Sahak or Razban and one of them gives me answers."

Sahak, the son of Governor Sandar, and Razban, apprentice to Master Maqlu, were both students at the Arcanum and friends of Taniel. They had to know what this was. Nesrin wished she had asked more questions about the shadowy creatures when the two visited the day before martial law went into place. Sahak Sandar often checked in on them while Taniel was away, and if Razban were not so shy and Suri a little gentler with him, the two would be married by now.

"But our pass isn't good until the day after tomorrow," Suri said.

Under curfew, their household was only permitted to go out to shop for food and basic necessities every third day.

"So?" Nesrin was done minding rules given without reason while phantoms stalked the streets and the smoke from riots burned beneath a bloodied sky. "If they catch me I'll just pretend I misread it." She switched from her native tongue to Haeranji, exaggerating her already thick accent and clumsy grasp of the language. "I so sorry, I no good read. Paper say not today? It say tomorrow? I so sorry! I no know!"

It would take no effort to present herself as an ignorant immigrant. People were quick to assume her broken diction and foreign accent meant her broken in wit as well, and as simple as her limited speech.

Suri's small grin vanished as two city guards turned onto the street, hands near their pistols and eyes darting to track the prowling phantasms. One guard kicked at the shadow circling their heels. The man's boot passed through the shape which rippled like water before reshaping. The phantasm chased the guards and three more swarmed in. The men broke into a run around the corner and out of sight.

The phantasms' intelligence unnerved Nesrin. Five of the shadows on the roof across the street sat unmoving, their eyeless faces turned toward Nesrin's windows, and she felt as though they watched her as she did them.

Hers was not the only face peering from the windows. Neighbors forced to shelter at home craned their necks, eyes flitting to the same places Nesrin stared. The less curious—or perhaps the wiser—had their curtains drawn, shutters closed, and fresh symbols to ward away evil painted on the cloth and wood.

Taniel had similar wards placed on their apartment. The runes above the windows, doors, and the hearth offered Nesrin no ease. She didn't want a warded apartment, she wanted her husband home. If he were here, he'd know what those strange spirits were and what to do about them.

Seraphs, protect him, Nesrin prayed. *Bring him back to me as you have always done.*

Suri shrieked—a shadowy creature skittered over her before it slipped out the open window.

"It touched me!" Suri shook her hands as if spiders rushed up her sleeves. "I felt it! It touched me!"

"Come away." Nesrin pulled her cousin back, shuttering and locking the windows.

"What are they?" Suri asked, rubbing her arms.

Nesrin stared at her cousin. The red veiling the sky clung to Suri, sinking into her like water into parched ground, then vanished.

"Nesrin?"

"Moths. I think they're moths." Nesrin shook her head to get her senses in order. Red curled in the edges of her vision, and she felt oddly lightheaded.

"But Master Maqlu said they were harmless."

"Moths won't harm you. But whatever brought them here might." She hugged her arms to her chest, feeling suddenly chilled.

"Do you know when Taniel will be back?" Suri asked, setting the table for three in case he returned. She looked pale. No doubt from the fright of the moth touching her.

"Soon." Nesrin forced herself to go back to kneading the dough. Worrying over Taniel, the moths, and the red sky solved nothing, and no amount of fretting would get dinner done.

The lightheadedness roared into a staggering dizziness. She grabbed the counter to stop herself from falling.

"Nesrin?" Suri rushed over to support her. "What's wrong?"

"Nothing, I ... I just felt faint for a moment." The red flared across Nesrin's sight and nausea burned within her.

Suri pressed her hand to Nesrin's forehead. "You're feverish."

"I'm fine ... I'm ..." She wasn't fine. She was possessed by the terrible feeling she teetered at the edge of a precipice. This sudden sickness following on the heels of moths and red stained skies was no coincidence.

"Stay here," Suri said. "I'll get help."

Nesrin opened her mouth to warn Suri this was no natural illness. The words were lost beneath the terrible fire rushing into her. Her vision spun, her hold on the counter slipped, and she collapsed into the burning mist.

For two days, the mist hung so thick over the mountains you could scarcely see the trees through the crimson shroud. On the third day, it began to disperse. After a week, only the faintest traces lingered before disappearing, as if it had never been.

The twilight sky is cleared of the wounded tinge, and you breathe in deep the cool mountain air redolent with spring. The strongest stars herald the coming night, insects hum from the flowering trees, and the torchlight flickers warm over the prepared garden space.

Taniel stirs feebly on the fur blankets laid out for him, lost in pained fever. You had to wait for the mist to clear before working on him, using your power to protect him from the cleansing of the world. You staved off the worst of his suffering, but his flesh continues to rot, demanding rebirth. His body is desperate to die, yet his spirit clings to the life Sariel gave him, a determination he inherited from his father.

You're pleased there is something of Sariel that survives in this purified world. You should have taken his body, not left it in the marsh, and harvested his flesh as well as his spirit to save his son. You decide this is for the better—you have the chance to shape young Taniel into something greater. You'll improve his fragile human shape. Recreate him in homage for the days of centuries gone.

He will be reborn.

The ibex you caught bellows as it strains against the rope tying it to the fig tree; a strong buck in its prime, and a fitting sacrifice to reassemble the decaying young man. The tales of Tanrisi, the horned god of the wild, were always Kharinah's favorites as a child. Your daughter spent hours searching for him in deep woods and untamed groves. Lord of the forests, he guarded the wild, sacred places, and guided wanderers of good heart while punishing the wicked who trespassed upon his realm.

That will be the role of Sariel's son, once remade.

You circle your foot over the grass in a steady, stirring motion. The ground beneath the ibex softens. It bleats in terror as it sinks into earth melting to mud. When only its head remains above the surface, you wade through. The beast thrashes, eyes rolling as you grab its horn, pull its head back and drag the ritual blade across its exposed throat. Blood sprays as the ibex fights the inevitable. Its life flows freely into the mud, its death hastened by its desperation to live. The beast gives a final shudder then stills. Its head slips beneath the mire, and the earth churns as it consumes the offered life.

You climb out to where Taniel lies, gently lifting him off the furs. His wasted form is fragile and light. You move slowly, concerned the slightest slip will break him. The earth has fully devoured the sacrifice by the time you carry him to the pit. With a mother's care, you lower him in. His right eye rotted out from his skull a day ago, and despite your gentle handling, his left arm falls off as you settle him into the hemic mire. You realign the limb with his body. Taking fistfuls of blood-fed earth, you mold his arm back into place. It's fitting this is performed under the watching heavens at last freed from the red veil. As Sariel's son is reborn, so is all creation—a sick, withering life remolded into something greater.

The horned god Tanrisi belonged to a civilization buried beneath the sands of the Eastern Wastes—a false god of a false people. But here he will be returned to a world in desperate want of guardian and guidance.

Suri tended to Nesrin for the first two days. It took that long for a healer to come. A sickness born of dark magic swept through Gohar, and the woman was haggard from long days and thankless nights spent tending to the victims.

"The whole city is ailing," the healer said, "and it won't be long before the whole city is dying."

She confessed she could do little for Nesrin, as powerless to aid her as she had been all her other patients fallen to this ill-magic. Suri asked if there was anyone else to go to for help. The healer shook her head. No medicine or magic offered relief to the sick. The mages at the Arcanum were as helpless as she. Not even Master Maqlu had found a way to banish the bloody shroud suffocating the city, turning the sun to a dull smudge in a fiery sky. The healer told Suri to keep Nesrin warm with blankets, broth, and tea before leaving to visit the family across the hall, all of them succumbed to the sickness.

Suri stayed by Nesrin's side, promising she'd be alright. "Taniel will be home soon," she said, taking Nesrin's hand in hers. "He'll come home, and Master Maqlu will find a way to lift this curse. You'll see."

The next day, Suri fell ill. One moment she was fine, cooking at the stove, the next she collapsed to the floor, her skin greying and slicked in sweat.

Nesrin lacked the strength to lift Suri onto her and Taniel's bed. She dragged her to the floor sofa which had served as Nesrin's sickbed. She lay beside her cousin, feeling her shake from the unnatural illness infecting them both. Pained moans, grieving cries, and miserable prayers visited them through the walls of their flat.

The whole city is ailing. And soon the whole city will be dying. The healer's prophecy haunted Nesrin as her lungs burned to ash and her skin cracked like ice.

Men wearing warding masks and gloves came in the morning. Finding Suri and Nesrin alive, the men painted two red circles upon the door and left it open. Through the crimson haze, Nesrin saw more men carrying sheet-wrapped bodies down the stairs. The survivors' sorrow wailed long into the night. Their cries wormed their way into her fevered dreams where she searched for Taniel but he had become like the moths, little more than shade and forever beyond her reach.

She woke, trading one nightmare for another when the masked

men came to wrap Suri in linens. Nesrin begged them not to take her. They did not listen. They crossed a black line through one of the marks on the door and left, Suri slung between them, her limp hand falling from the cloth. Nesrin cried, alone through the night. The apartments were quieter now. Soft weeping replaced the wails to join her nightly mourning, and every day a man came to see if she was alive, put fresh water and bread beside her, then left, unable to better tend to the living when death made the demands. It was only a question of who was to visit her next, the man who left her water, or death to at last carry her off.

"Nesrin?"

She turned from the voice, certain it was another dream of the dead calling out to her, asking why she took so long to join them.

A cool hand touched her cheek. "Nesrin, can you hear me?"

Her vision swam as she opened her eyes. The daylight slipping between the closed curtains was too bright, and she struggled to find the face above her.

"Taniel?" she whispered.

"No, it's me." Sahak Sandar removed his warding mask. "I'm here to take you home."

"Home?"

Two figures behind Sahak stepped forward.

"No, no." Nesrin feebly pushed away. The masked men had come for her just when she remembered she couldn't die—she had to wait for Taniel.

"It's alright, you're alright." Sahak lifted her head to help her drink from the cup he pressed to her cracked lips. His face came clearer through the sick fog clouding her mind and she saw a strained, sad smile. "I'm going to look after you. I promised Taniel I would."

They lifted her onto a litter, tucking her in blankets instead of wrapping her in the sheets for the dead. Sahak apologized that it took him so long to get to her. The city was in lockdown, and not even he as the governor's son and Arcanum mage had been allowed to travel between districts until this morning. The chaos of the Reaping—what the mages named the red sickness—had demanded his attention be spent putting down riots, and the panic had prevented him from finding reliable help to reach her.

"Where's Taniel?" she asked as they placed her into a horse-drawn carriage beside the wooden cart waiting to be filled with the dead.

"I don't know." Sahak rearranged the blankets around her. "I'm sure we'll hear from him soon. Until then, you should rest."

She wanted to ask him more, but was dizzy from being moved and overwhelmed by the sky after seeing nothing beyond her small, shuttered apartment for days.

Sahak placed his hand over hers. "I'm going to look after you."

The carriage lurched forward, carrying her away from the weeping man stumbling down the street, clutching a child-sized figure wrapped in linen.

You're surprised to learn Governor Kalich of Sevget fell to the curse. You're even more disappointed to discover Bishop Kesar of Agr Rav, and the Ladies Mila and Soraya of Haruh died as well. That wasn't as you planned. They were among the select souls intended to lead the reborn world. Instead, they were among the select bodies to receive the dignity of an individual grave, spared the fate of the countless corpses piled high to be burned.

You created the curse to smite the wicked. The pure of heart might fall ill, but they shouldn't have perished. Perhaps you repeated past mistakes, thinking better of mortals who are so eager to fall short, judging their characters better than they deserved.

A low, river-born mist hides the dewy ground recently turned for Governor Kalich's burial. A narrow pillar marks his grave on the outskirts of Sevget, the town a flicker of torchlight through the early morning grey. A woman's likeness is carved into the memorial stone. The deer skull worn upon her bowed head covers all her features save her mouth. Flowering vines twine at her feet, a sun rises over her right shoulder, and a moon to her left. The Grey Lady is worshipped in eastern Haeranj, a superstition that always irritated you, but now her influence in the east burns your blood with fury. In seeking the reason your Reaping deviated from its design, you've learned the villages closest to the Grey Forest—where legend claims the Lady resides—were spared entirely. Sevget was the farthest the mists reached before halting their easterly spread as if they'd come to an impassable threshold, rising into a wall that held for a week then faded away.

The Grey Forest's roots have spread farther than you anticipated, delivering your sister's corrupting influence west and undermining yours. You did not misjudge your curse, or the moral character of those souls who were meant to live; the Grey Lady and her damned trees despoiled the delicate magic you so carefully crafted, turning it from righteous judgment into a wild, senseless storm that swept away souls at random.

You rest your hand on Kalich's grave pillar. The wreath of flowers placed around it withers to dust. "You always interfere."

This is not the first time she's acted to spite you. She grew her forest five hundred years ago to thwart the first cleansing you judged necessary, and once again, she's the reason why good men die while the wicked survive to infest the garden you are meant to grow. Twice now you've sought to purify creation, and twice the woman carved into the gravestone has prevented justice to make a mockery of your higher intentions.

The people of Chahich worshipped you, but you played no favorites for them. You remember your sister accused you of such before Ha-Ai fell. She claimed your attachments would lead you and countless innocents to destruction. But it is her, always her, who destroys what you create, and Governor Kalich is one of the thousand souls who've died for her meddling.

"You always ruin what's mine," you say.

"Who's there?" a man calls, authority sharp on his tone. You know him instantly as a man used to being obeyed.

The gloom of early dawn cloaks your identity from mortal eyes. It does not shadow him from you. You turn to see he's leveled a pistol at you, a Purger's weapon judging by the inscription running along the barrel. He has the look of a Purger as well—hardened, scarred—and after a moment you recognize him. He accompanied Sariel twice when they hunted you.

"Wasi Adhar." You speak his name and smile, seeing the deer skull pendant of the Grey Lady around his neck. His faith in a hypocrite undeserving of worship has volunteered him for unique purpose.

Red mist spins around you, but he'll see it as a silver shroud. You step toward him, and he lowers the pistol, seeing you as a woman whose coming summons flowering vines to grow, circling up your bare feet and grey cloak. Your face is masked by a deer's skull, the antlers a throne for moon and stars wreathing you in shining light.

"Lady." He drops to his knees before you.

The Grey Lady's meddling demands retribution. The eastern lands will find no shelter in the shadow of her forest. You'll see they are cleansed, the Grey Lady punished, and the ideal man for the task kneels before you.

"Rise, Wasi Adhar, and listen." To him, your voice is maternally musical. He hears none of your derision. You tell him how men like him are needed in these dark times. A garden yearns to grow, a paradise only achieved once wickedness is cleansed, and he is chosen to be both sower and reaper.

You offer him the power to carry out this sacred duty. He sees silver fire in your outstretched hand, not the curdling red corruption ready to shape him into a tool of your will. It's a slow-spreading poison that will whisper to him in his dreams, encourage his devotions to zealotry, his passions to vices.

"I am unworthy of your grace," he says.

"No, Wasi Adhar, you are deserving of everything I give you."

His hand shakes as he accepts your gift. The red snakes up his arm, claiming every inch of him before sinking in. He murmurs humble thanks, promising to see your will done.

You touch your hand to his bowed head. "I am certain you will."

The man holds his low bow as you shape wind into a portal, returning you to your mountain manor. You allow him the chance to glimpse your illusion unraveling as you step through, but he is too devoted to his groveling reverence to see your preferred form.

The portal closes behind you. The azure northern sky stretches above yellow mountains and green pine, unobstructed by the dismal fog clinging to the eastern mountains' Grey Forest. Those under your sister's favor won't escape the Reaping. Her forest may have banished the red mists, but it cannot ward away what Wasi Adhar will bring. Worshippers of the Grey Lady will learn that following her ends in suffering.

The marble halls of your manor are cool and quiet. Your footsteps echo in a vain attempt to fill the emptiness. There was a time your halls were alive with the trod of pilgrims' weary feet, the rustle of mages' cloaks, and the voices of your petitioners soft with wonder. Nasim, the first king of Ha-Ai, built this manor in your honor. You lifted him to power, blessed his children when he brought them before you, and watched them grow old and die. When his descendants fell from the throne, you sheltered the exiled prince, gave him sons to reclaim what was rightfully his, and saw Nasim's bloodline restored. You pause at the tapestry of Nasim kneeling before a woman wreathed in a red sun, bestowing upon him a crown of fire. Brushing aside the cloth reveals scars cut into the stone, vestiges of when Nezar, the last king of Ha-Ai, lay siege upon your home. The damage is a reminder for how eager mortals are to disappoint, and how rare men like Nasim and Sariel are.

King Nezar sought to purge your influence from the kingdom. Your home survives. His throne sits in a lifeless, dusty waste.

Coming to the courtyard serving as the sacrificial site, you find Taniel where you left him beneath the fig tree, half-submerged in the steaming, red earth. His sides heave from labored breathing and the entire right half of his face is hidden beneath the viscid mud. He cringes when you rest a hand on his forehead. Red veins lace from your palm over his feverish skin. His breathing softens and the rise to his chest slows as you push him into a sleep too deep to feel the pains of what must be done.

You're glad to have taken Taniel as your own. You prefer these more intimate creations, and remaking Sariel's son is an unexpected gift. Like his father, he is stubborn, and like your daughter he is a challenge, actively resisting your influence. You will smooth away his rough reluctance to be brought into greater being. In the end, Taniel will understand what his father could not; what you do for him, everything you have done, is for a greater good.

6
Promises

Taniel's blood spoiled to poison, his bones burned to ash, and his mind fell to agonized delirium. But he could not die. No matter how he clawed, screamed, and struggled, the oblivion he begged for was denied him.

"You should have let him die." A woman spoke the thoughts his cracked lips shaped. His remaining eye was unable to open to see who spoke from the darkness. Her voice was a cruel purr, her presence a thrumming chaos steeped in malice.

"Kharinah, if you cannot be pleasant, find somewhere else to be."

He was more familiar with this second voice. She spoke to him as she worked. Most of what she said was lost in the pain pushing him to the brink of madness. Her sorcery burned with a fire that would melt stone. Her hands twisted his bones, stretched sinew, remolded his skull to replace his eye.

"Shh, be still," she hushed when he thrashed and screamed.

He didn't know where he was or how long he'd been like this. The disconnect turned him terribly aware of the witch's workings. At first, his body rejected the magic, but she was patient. Over and over she broke him down until he was certain there was nothing left of who he was.

He begged her to stop, to let him die. He felt her hand on his brow, cooling his scorching skin.

"Hush, Taniel," she said, and her sorcery pulled him into the blissful, numbing dark of unknowing.

It was through the presence or absence of pain that Taniel distinguished between consciousness and not. One darkness was blessed oblivion, the other terrible and burning. He could not see, nor could he move, but he could hear, and the witch's daughter became the voice he heard most often as Minu granted him time to recover from what she'd done to him.

He disgusted Kharinah. She complained every time she had to clean him, covered in his own mess as his body rejected Minu's magic. He disgusted himself in the few moments he escaped the stupor cast over him long enough for a lucid thought. His jaw did not close properly. Drool leaked from his deformed mouth as he cried. He had little control over his voluntary movements. It took him a week to relearn how to sit up, and another week to stand, clutching the wall as his legs trembled like a sickly fawn's. He had less control over baser functions and the demon-child mocked him when she changed the soiled sheets.

"Mother should've let you die." Her tone was so harsh he flinched under her hand gently wiping vomit-laced spittle from his face and chest. She never physically hurt him, but what need did she have for such petty torture? He was already in agony, requiring no further effort from her to find amusement in his suffering.

The witch was more civil than her daughter. She never mocked his pitiful state or complained how wretched he was. She soothed him when he screamed as she realigned his bones to accept her sorcery, apologized for causing him distress, and promised he was to be remade.

"You'll see." She rested her hand on the bulge of his skull above his replaced eye and below the curving horns she'd fused onto him.

She was pleased when after a month he stopped throwing up every other meal. She praised him when he shuffled a few unsteady steps as a mother would her infant learning to walk. His vision was reluctant to return. The room where they kept him slowly emerged from total darkness to a patchwork of shadowy light. The witch and her daughter were distorted figures that nauseated him to see move. He hid his face from them, not out of shame for how disfigured he knew he was, but because anything harder than the softest light gave him a blinding headache.

The witch stayed with him as he wept upon learning of his father's death once she deemed him strong enough to bear the news. He hated that the same hand stroking his hair was the hand that murdered his father, the voice that consoled him was the last one his father had heard. He hated that in his grief, her sympathy was sincere.

Her daughter told him of what happened beyond the confines of the room—bodies burned in piles stacked high as houses outside cities. Towns were looted as social order fractured. Villages starved as food supply chains fell apart. The railroads were torn up, the iron stolen to be used for warding. Too many of the old wardings that had held for centuries collapsed under the rotting curse Minu had unleashed, and there were too few remaining Purgers and mages to fend off the dark creatures prospering in the despair of crumbling civilization.

She told him about a city close to the Setareh Sea that had burned to the ground, civil unrest turning it into funeral pyre.

"You could see it for miles," Kharinah said as casually as if she observed the chance of rain. "And death is not done."

"Was it Gohar?" Taniel asked, sensing this was one of her more coherent days when she was not entirely ruled by her madness.

"I don't know the names," the demon-child said. "All cities are the same."

After three months he was able to feed himself, a clumsy process hampered by his recovering sight and his left hand refusing to uncurl from a half-fist. He relearned how to walk in his crippled state, tripping over his twisted feet and uneven legs, finally able to clearly see the room they kept him in.

His prison was deceptively comfortable with rounded walls and a fireplace settled across from the large bed the witch provided him. The single window, too high and narrow to climb out of, cast slanted sunlight over the ivory stone. Spiraling vine patterns decorated brocade rugs and a horned man danced across the tapestries covering the walls. Taniel ripped them down, throwing them in the hearth.

"These are centuries old, Taniel," the witch lectured when she found them in the cold ash. She pulled them out with reverence. "You will not do this again."

He felt her words pressing her will upon him, and again when she rehung the mended tapestries three days later, repeating her command. The moment she left the room, he reached to rip them down, only to double over from crippling nausea. He could not touch them.

Kharinah found him huddled on the floor. She dragged him to his bed, speaking the strange language she fell into when she wanted to avoid falling to her madness. Taniel preferred it when he couldn't understand her. Whenever she spoke the foreign tongue she was at her calmest and most sane.

Each day Taniel forced himself to walk the room until his legs gave out. He folded the sheets, stacked and restacked the wood by the fireplace, and pushed his ruined body to remaster the most basic functions. Minu encouraged him to take heart in his progress as passing weeks became passing seasons.

"The greatest feats demand patience, Taniel," she said as she inspected his left hand stubbornly frozen in a half-fist.

At six months he was able to stay awake an entire day; a progress undone at nine months when the witch decided he had recovered to where she could work on him some more. His screaming while she sought to improve his mutilated anatomy upset her. She took away his voice, neglecting to give it back until a week after she finished the latest session of remolding.

She visited him in his prison as she let him recover a second time. Weak and bedridden, unable to breathe without inviting agony, all he could do was flinch when she sat beside him.

"This will take time, Taniel." She stroked his hair. "Resisting won't change what must happen. Kharinah fought as well and you both cause yourself greater hardship."

A year passed since his father's death, and Taniel had to keep one eye closed if he wanted to see. Having both open for long made it feel as though an axe cleaved his head in two. The room was mirrorless, leaving touch as his means to know his broken shape. His left eye felt human, but his right eye was twisted to the side and bulged too large. The witch had returned some suppleness to his left hand, but his fingers remained fused at the base and were tipped by hard, black nails.

The witch visited him weekly to check his progress. The demon-child came every day. Taniel wished she would not; her mood and madness were unpredictable. One moment she acted as a child—insensitively curious and plagued by a psyche irreparably shattered from suffering what her mother now put Taniel through. The next moment she was maniacal—cruel, raving, and hostile—only to become hauntingly quiet, standing over his bed for hours without speaking. He never knew what Kharinah wanted from him, or why she spent entire days curled catlike in the chair across from his bed, staring at him unblinkingly. Some days, she spoke to him in that strange language, face falling in dejection when he had no answer. Others, she hummed to herself, swaying as she gazed out the window. On her worst days she raged and screamed, hands clenching in frantic want to harm. He learned to endure the outbursts. She never hurt him, but that lessened none of his terror when the walls shook from her fury, the destruction in her nature straining for release.

He checked the door to his room every day, praying for a miracle where he'd find it unlocked. In his darkest hours he sustained himself by imagining his escaping the manor, fleeing to Gohar, returning home to Nesrin. He dared not entertain the thought that the Reaping had claimed his wife. If it had, there was nothing left for him beyond this room. But if she was alive, his failure to stop Minu had not been absolute, and there was hope. Master Maqlu and Razban would fix his ruined shape, he'd find his way back to Nesrin, and somehow Taniel would set things right.

"So eager to show the world your wretched face?" the demon-child asked when she caught him tugging on the door.

She was calmer when she found him a week later attempting to leave.

"There's nothing for you out there," she said. "Only dust and death."

A year and six months after Minu murdered his father, Taniel tried the door to his prison and gasped when it swung open. He hesitated at the threshold, distrusting the empty hallway. It had to be a trap, a trick or cruel test to measure how his physical strength had progressed. The witch was allowing him to run free to see how far he could go before dragging him back to be broken and remolded again.

Movement shifted in the hall. He staggered into the door, cursing his childish fright when he saw it was only a mirror catching his reflection. He looked away from the glass, not wanting to know the monster that had replaced him.

His crippled right foot dragged and hip groaned as he stepped from the room. Morning streamed cheerfully through high windows, casting arches of light along a hall decorated by golden tapestries and stone carvings. He was ungainly in this new body and his timid walk was unsteady. He stumbled, and his heart almost shattered like the vase he knocked off its pedestal to the stone floor. He looked wildly around—the swiveling movement sending needling pain down his neck—as he braced for the witch, her daughter, or some fiend made of flesh and earth to investigate the racket.

The hall was quiet save for birdsong in the garden beyond the windows.

Wasting no time on stealth, he broke into a crooked run, throwing himself through the first set of doors he prayed led outside. He nearly collapsed in relief as sunlight fell freely on him, almost wept at the smell of grass, and the soft susurration of the garden's fountain was a hymn from the Seraphs. Taniel's head spun under lightheadedness, overwhelmed by open air after over a year's confinement. No walls secured the mountain manor from the surrounding forest ablaze with autumn.

Taniel limped straight for the wild, fleeing the sun-warmed garden into the forest's cool shade. He clutched his left arm to his chest to guard the aching joints from his haste. This had to be a trick; his escape came too easily. Kharinah must be playing with him using the false hope of freedom. Any moment she'd emerge to block his path and sneer at how stupid he was falling for the lie. An alarm was bound to ring out, Taniel's leaving triggering a spell to alert the witch and her daughter, and when they came for him he had no chance of outrunning them.

A twig snapped and he flinched in fear, ready for the demon-child to leap out and force him back to face fresh torment. Leaves rustled. Taniel's breath caught in his throat, then released in a sigh. Red-tailed thrushes, not Kharinah, flew from the brush.

He looked back to see the manor was lost behind the trees. With no sign of pursuer or sound of an alarm, the small flickers of hope flared too strong for him to stamp out. He abandoned himself fully to flight—stumbling, falling, forcing himself back to his feet. He had forgotten how to run and his leg muscles strained to maintain his awkward pace. His lungs struggled under the exertion, his eyes watered from pain, chest heaved, joints clicked and creaked. He ignored the bodily protests, permitting himself no rest or pause. Running into an unknown forest without supplies or notion of where he was and where to go was recklessly stupid. Taniel chose to die a fool than live a mewling wretch under the dark witch who'd killed his father.

The sun dipped lower into the western sky, leaving him in dusky shadow. His breaths rasped against his parched throat and his head throbbed beneath the weight of his horns. His twisted legs gave way, their strength utterly spent, pitching him into the leaf-strewn ground. He crawled, pulling himself through brush. Stopping was surrender. Perseverance was all that prevented his escape from being revealed a dream or one of the demon-child's cruel taunts.

Trembling with exhaustion, his abused body permitted him to go no farther. Knees bloodied and muscles spasming, he dragged himself beneath a hornbeam overrun by woody vines. He felt a kindred spirit with the tree deformed by the invading parasite, cheated out of what it should have been.

Taniel gripped his leg to stifle the shaking. He ought to rise, to follow the sloping ground until he found a road, river, anything to lead him from these wretched woods to a town. Despair hollowed his chest of hope, imagining the welcome a village had to offer a creature like him. Anyone who saw him would think him a monster. The timid would flee, the bold attempt to kill him. He had no reason to expect a compassionate hand offering him sanctuary. Not unless he found someone who knew him before Minu had ruined him.

Need for rest overpowered fear, and weariness served as a numbing balm for the pain. He closed his eyes in submission to the blackness curling at the edge of his vision. A quick rest, and then he'd not stop until he found his way.

Hovo, the lead servant of the Sandars' family estate, waited for Nesrin at the front door holding an umbrella in hand. She usually left for the train station later in the day and she thought she had the chance to leave unnoticed at this earlier hour. But nothing happened within these halls without Hovo knowing.

He opened the door for her and offered the umbrella. "It looks like rain, miss."

"Thank you," she said, still shy around the staff and Sahak's relatives despite having lived in the manor for well over a year.

Sahak had proven his mettle as Taniel's friend, taking Nesrin into his home and seeing her cared for. The flat she had lived in with Taniel and Suri was in the now-abandoned northern district, all access prohibited barring sanctioned business. Residents had been forcibly evicted from their homes. Governor Sandar was unwilling to expend the resources to build the wall around the entirety of Gohar, so its poorer sections were excised. Cutting off a third of the city caused no shortage of housing for displaced people; only one in three had survived the Reaping, leaving plenty of empty homes to be reassigned.

Gloomy grey clouds clotted the sky, the smell of coming rain drenched the air, and autumn's early gold flecked the ornamental trees lining the stone walkway. The guardsman had the gate open for Nesrin before she crossed the expansive front garden decorated by fountains and flanked by marble statues of winged hounds. The Sandar family had always been rich, and not a generation went by without one of them discovering a way to become richer. Even in the miserable crisis of the Reaping, Governor Sandar had managed to bring his family to greater fortune.

Nesrin nodded a greeting to the guards stationed at the estate gates, a gesture they returned. The younger of the two failed to wait until she was out of earshot before muttering that she'd gone mad from grief and Master Sandar ought to put an end to her daily trips. The older guard scolded him, saying a widow had every right to mourn in her own fashion.

A year ago, the guards had taken bets on how long her visits to the train station would last. They had all lost, confident she'd abandon her daily pilgrimages by winter. A foot of snow and ice had not dissuaded her, nor did the guards' muttering or Sahak's mother raising her voice from the other room to be sure Nesrin heard.

"It's so tragic about that poor girl," she often said. "She can't understand he's not coming back."

The golden cupola of the Capitol lorded over affluent houses, most of them abandoned. Ivy crept across the darkened windows of otherwise lifeless homes. Mansions that had belonged to families of old money and magic-blood fell into disrepair among sprawling lawns grown wild. The empty homes became smaller—a more modest opulence suited for bureaucrats and merchants—as Nesrin approached King's Circle. The two guardsmen at the intersection tipped their hats to her as she passed. She was a familiar face to all of the city watch who patrolled King's Circle.

Eighteen months ago, the square had been a lively place—prominent men in tailored suits heading to political meetings, courthouses, and high offices, their aides carrying leather satchels while trailing an obsequious step behind. Today, only leaves raced across the cobblestones as if driven by wandering ghosts. Before the Reaping, vendors selling sponge pastries, sweating men cooking liver kebabs over open air grills, and bakers carrying deep-fried folds stuffed with potato and onion had crowded the streets branching off King's Circle. Now, only crows pecked at the cobblestones.

Ghosts and crows. Those were the true citizens of this changed Gohar. From what Nesrin heard of tales beyond the wall, far less pleasant beings had crept forth to claim the emptied districts in the Reaping's wake. Caravan drivers spoke of dark witches roaming the woods and moors beyond the city. Soldiers muttered about wraiths haunting the abandoned northern streets, and Sahak often came home exhausted from the demanding task of rebuilding wards protecting the city that the Arcanum mages had not known existed until the Reaping collapsed them.

Rumor and hearsay were Nesrin's only access to the world outside Gohar's walls. Travel was forbidden save for a select few, and young women were rarely allowed to leave the city, not even to work the bordering farmlands. They were necessary for performing other duties in rebuilding civilization. Propaganda flyers plastered on lamp posts and walls showed a proud woman draped in Gohar's flag. Rosy-cheeked children held the cloth aloft like a wedding veil and a babe nursed at the woman's breast beneath the slogan: *Mothers for the Glory of Gohar.*

Nesrin had so far escaped a mandated marriage in part through becoming a midwife. The job was considered of essential importance, allowing her reprieve from being conscripted to bear children of her own. The greater reason she was left alone was because Sahak sheltered her, ensuring the papers annulling her and Taniel's marriage never got processed. That was a temporary protection. It was only a matter of time before she received official notice for an arranged union as all women over the age of fifteen did under Governor Sandar's edict.

Governor wasn't the proper title for Sahak's father. Not anymore. The martial law declared in the days leading up to the Reaping had not lifted when the curse did. Crisis had elevated Sandar from governor to king, and he had exploited long-standing rumors to ascend even higher. There had always been talk that the Sandar family's lineage traced its roots to a sorceress of Ha-Ai, the lost kingdom east of the Grey Forest and mountains. Wilder rumor speculated they were descendants of the Grey Lady herself and blessed by her power. When not a single one of the Sandar family fell to the Reaping, Sahak's father encouraged that casual speculation to grow into worshipful superstition, lifting him from statesmen to sovereign and a few, small steps below divine.

Sahak hated the new reverence. He understood his family could just as easily have been cast out as demons, or worse, for escaping the sickness unscathed.

Nesrin's footsteps echoed down the narrowing streets. Homes shrank from the comfortable wealth of lesser mages and politicians to small houses lacking front gardens, then to the crowded flats of laborers and craftsmen above cramped shops. Sounds of life escaped these denser living quarters. The clatter of cooking and the murmur of voices chased off the ghosts of Gohar. Four men wearing the drab brown uniform of city workers tasked to clear out emptied homes carried furniture to the street. They moved slowly like mourners burdened by grief, a weariness shared by those who'd survived the Reaping. The children who gathered at street corners to beg for handouts from the workers were too quiet and thin. The woman shelling peas on her front stoop had the same hollow eyes as the dead who'd been piled into wooden wagons to be taken out of the city and burned. The blackened sores from the mass pyres were visible from the high halls of King's Circle and the Arcanum towers overlooking Gohar and her newly built walls. A full cycle of seasons failed to tempt grass to cover the ugly scars, and the select people allowed outside the walls refused to walk near the blackened ground, claiming it cursed.

The market surrounding the train station once thrummed with life—merchants calling from their stalls, the chatter of shoppers and tourists, the bustle of workers, the conductor's holler and trains' piercing whistles to announce an unceasing trade of departures and arrivals. That life was gone. There were no trains, no tourists, no shoppers, and the surviving merchants in the market square were subdued. Nesrin recognized all by face, a few by name, and they all knew her by her daily trips to the station.

"Any news, Mrs. Sushan?" Old Woman Dalya asked, her posture so stooped her wrinkled face barely reached above her flower-filled cart. Too old to be assigned mandated labor, and the son who had supported her dead by the Reaping, she relied on the generosity of temple mourners laying flowers in memory of loved ones lost.

"Not yet." Nesrin selected an autumn rose to place before the memorial shrine she had built to Suri. She and Suri had shared a love for the flowers. Taniel had always brought a bouquet home upon returning from a job when they were in season.

She gave Dalya a silver coin. The woman offered her a dozen more roses.

"No, I not need more," Nesrin said. Until she received irrefutable proof otherwise, Taniel was alive, and she'd place no flower for him before the memorial shrine.

"I'll tolerate generosity, Mrs. Sushan, not charity," Dalya said.

"Then that pay for roses for rest of week," Nesrin said, and the woman gave a conceding nod.

The train station lay in the shadow of Gohar's High Temple and looked the architectural offspring of the sacred space, cut from the same stone with matching horseshoe windows, wheels of glass topping arched entrances, and stylized eaves swelling into domed pavilions above the main doors. The station's clock was an enormous eye overlooking the square, watchful yet wearied by the loss of souls who once passed below. Nesrin headed for the main terminus. Trains no longer ran, and only a few people milled about the café once overflowing with travelers. She and Taniel met there when he was able to give her an exact train time for his homecoming. The food was overpriced and her cooking was better, but she had loved those meals, watching travelers come and go through the lattice windows separating the restaurant from the platforms.

A thorn pricked Nesrin's thumb as she rolled the rose between her fingers. Flowers rested on the floor beside melted candles and paper prayers offered for the dead. During the Reaping, when the temple was overwhelmed and had no more room to house the ill, those deemed beyond help were carried to the station. The dying were laid on makeshift mattresses, blankets, and then eventually the coats of the deceased, waiting to be taken to a far more distant destination. Their ghosts were rumored to haunt the station, but it was not the dead that troubled Nesrin; it was the senselessness of the Reaping that turned her cold. Suri had not deserved to die, no more than Nesrin deserved to live. There had been no pattern or predictability to the curse. Some caught cold and were found dead the next day. Others, like Nesrin, burned with fever for a week after the red mist dispersed, and then as quick as the illness had come, it vanished. The good, the wicked, the young, the old—there was no meaning in who died, who was spared, who suffered a little and those whose agony reached the point they wished they had succumbed.

The station's arrivals board hosted yellowing papers; inquiries written in smeared and faded ink asking for word of family members or friends. Pleas for news of loved ones hung next to pictures of the missing. The departures board listed those confirmed dead. There were no new names or faces today, nor had there been the entire week. The last three months had seen only a handful of changes on the boards, all confirming deaths.

Nesrin sat on the bench across from the boards. She'd come here every day on the small chance of discovering word of Taniel. There never was. The paper she'd pinned to the arrivals board asking for news of him had weathered and fallen away a year ago. Everyone told her he was dead. Her father-in-law's body had been found, as had Aryeh Zoran's. But Tiran Samvelan's and Taniel's had not. If a red sky had the power to steal millions of souls in less than a month, was it too much to believe a single life among those countless lost had been spared?

Soft rain pattered on the station's roof, ushering in an early dusk. A dozen more people trickled by, refreshing flowers, lighting candles, and offering prayers on the platform serving as a memorial. No one posted news updates.

The station clock chimed the changing hour. Nesrin remained where she sat. She felt helpless, only able to offer unwavering devotion that it might earn her pity from the gods, moving them to at last reveal Taniel had survived. She would hear the whistle of the train bringing him home, she and her husband would take lunch at the station's café, watch the people pass by, before heading to their flat. Suri would be there and it would be as it was.

Nesrin's eyes drifted from the board to the rose in hand. Perhaps people were right. She was in denial and this was her way of grieving. Taniel was dead, he had died alongside his father, and she had to let him go. Mourn his memory and remember to live.

She clenched her hand tight over the rose stem, uncaring the thorns speared her palm. Taniel wasn't dead. She'd not allow him to be. Something prevented him from coming home, and she'd waited too long on this platform dedicated to the dead when she should have been out searching for him. The Sandar family, their servants, and guards were right on one matter; there was nothing for her to gain in waiting any longer.

The desolate station magnified the distinct clip of Sahak's shoes on the stone platform. He sat beside her on the bench, allowing a moment of quiet before speaking.

"My father's office hasn't received any reports of Taniel, and I haven't heard anything at the Arcanum," he said. "A trade caravan is expected in the next half week, but they're coming from the south, not the north."

He humored her with these updates. The lack of news was meant to slowly lead her to the truth there was never to be news. At least none she wanted.

"When next caravan to north?" she asked. "Not coming here, but going?"

"A week from now." Unlike the rest of his household, Sahak had no trouble understanding her poor Haeranji.

"I go with them," she said. "If word not come south, then I go north to find him."

"It's been a year and a half. We would have heard something by now if he'd survived."

"If he survive, I go north to find him. If not survive, I still go north to find him."

"Unauthorized travel is forbidden—"

"Then authorize. You have family seal and there plenty paper here." She waved her hand at the parchment pinned to the board and fallen over the tracks.

"I won't have you run off on a poorly disguised suicide errand. The roads aren't safe, and if half of the tales of monsters and brigands are true, you wouldn't make it to Shabrin, forget Chahich."

"Then I go work for caravan."

"The caravans don't hire women," Sahak said.

"Then I go—"

"Nesrin, please. I promised Taniel I'd look after you if something happened to him. Don't turn me into a liar."

He stood, brushing off his knee-length coat. The blue mage robes were tailored, yet didn't quite fit him. He looked too young to wear the clasp of a master mage and he held no illusion that he'd rightfully earned it. Sahak readily admitted his rise to High Mage of Gohar was due to his family name and the death or departure of worthier aspirants, not his personal accomplishments.

"If I hear anything of substance about Taniel, I'll ... I'll see about arranging travel," he said.

"If you hear Taniel alive, I go to him and you help me." Nesrin pressed her advantage when Sahak was willing to agree to promises out of pity, believing he'd never have to see them through.

"Of course." He offered his hand to help her from the bench.

The rain fell with greater purpose, streaking down the train station's clock face, filling the grooves in the cobblestone streets, and the drops on Nesrin's umbrella pounded in the fast-paced beat of a heart anticipating a lover's return.

7

Beasts in the Woods

Taniel covered his right eye as he woke, a learned habit to delay the onset of his daily headaches and lessen their intensity. Dizziness no longer overwhelmed him if he used both eyes at the same time, but it was better for him to ease the transition from troubled dreams to miserable waking. The lingerings of his latest nightmare followed him from sleep. Kharinah had pursued him through dark woods, lurking behind trees that melted into mud, laughing at his wretched state. Taniel had called for Nesrin but she turned away, revolted by what he'd become.

"There's nothing for you out there," she had said in Kharinah's voice. "Only dust and death."

Taniel clutched the base of his horns, willing the haunting dreams away. A twilight gloom darkened the forest. His quick rest had gone on hours longer than he'd intended. That neither Minu nor her demon daughter had found him while he slept meant they did not yet know he was gone. Their ignorance was a fickle fortuity, and he had already lost too much time.

Using the liana vines strangling the tree, he pulled himself to his feet. Rigid cramps held him captive from hip to foot. The first step was always the hardest, the second slightly easier once he resigned himself to the pain. He moved slowly, taking care to avoid falling as he followed the downward slope, the leafy carpet rustling under his tentative tread. He'd find some semblance of shelter for the night, then come morning, he'd follow the ravine until it led him anywhere besides his prison. From that anywhere, he'd find his way back to Gohar, back to Nesrin. The gods had been too cruel for him to ask for an easy journey, but if they were to grant him one mercy, he prayed it be a stream and not a dried bed that lay at the ravine base. He longed for the small relief of cool mountain water to soothe his dry throat and ease the ache of his joints.

He carefully lowered himself to pick up a fallen branch of the right height and sturdiness to serve as a poor man's walking stick. His back muscles seized from the movement and he had to pause to breathe through the constricting pain. The discomfort was worth the stick returning the stability his legs had lost, preventing him from pitching headlong down the steepening slope.

If he made it to Gohar, Master Maqlu and Razban had the ability to sort him out. A full restoration of who he'd been was impossible; Master Maqlu's power was a mere candle to Minu's wildfire and the witch's magic had too severely maimed him. But reconstruction was possible. The Arcanum mages could mold Taniel into a functioning form, restoring his appearance to one fit to face Nesrin.

He felt sick at the thought of her seeing him as he was. She'd scream and recoil, and rightly so. The sick pit in Taniel's stomach sank lower. Eighteen months was a long time to wait for anyone, especially for a husband whose work was renowned for ending in death or disappearing without a trace. What if he was too late in returning to her? What if she'd given him up for dead, mourned him, and moved on? He had been gone for almost two years, and more than once Taniel had disliked how long one of his friends let his gaze linger on his wife.

"Wait for me," he pleaded. "Please wait."

Firelight flickered through the trees. He slowed to soften his graceless step, not knowing if the owners of the campfire possessed the extraordinary compassion to help a wretched creature like him, or if they'd more likely assume him to be one of the forest monsters who came with darkness.

Hearing men's voices, Taniel crouched low, wincing as his left knee popped and his right groaned like old, overburdened wood. After a couple cautious steps closer he realized his attempts at stealth were entirely unnecessary. The men talked so loudly there was no chance of them hearing him unless he somersaulted through the brush straight into their camp. The flames silhouetted their shapes; four men passed a tankard between them and the obnoxious edge of drunkenness grated in their laughter. The pleasure they found in their drink was as obvious as that there was no kind reception to be found from them. They were footpads celebrating a good score. The small wooden hut was their den, and the spoils of their most recent robbery lay around them. They must have come across a merchant's caravan or raided a farming settlement. Small carts to be pulled by men were filled with goods tied down by rough twine, their contents spilling out like the innards of a gutted animal from the robbers' rough handling.

One of the men whistled as if summoning a dog. The others joined in, slapping their legs and snapping their fingers. When no dog answered, the first man stood and disappeared into the rundown shack. He dragged out a middle-aged woman, flinging her to the ground. The firelight glinted off the silver threads in her dark hair falling disheveled over a face filthy from travel and abuse. Her dress was ripped to the point it barely resembled clothes and provided as little function. Motherhood had softened her body and old stretch marks showed through the torn fabric.

"Don't be shy." The man kicked at her with his boot until she got to her feet.

The rope tied between her ankles barely allowed her to walk, the length far too short for her to run. Bruises covered her arms, her movements were stiff, and she flinched whenever one of the men moved her way.

"Get us another round, love." A man younger than Taniel waved his emptied cup at her. His companions joined in the jeering, their want for diversion drifting to something more lively than brandy. She had the sense to keep her eyes lowered and endure the abuse without resistance.

Taniel sank lower in the brush. The wisest choice was for him to lay low until the men drank themselves even stupider, then slip away when they lost their senses to indulgence. The right choice was to wait until the men retired for the night and then free the woman.

His hissed a self-loathing scoff. He was helpless to rescue her. Attempting heroics was doomed to end in his death and her no better off. Covering the distance between his hiding place and the men's camp without stumbling was an impossible challenge, forget doing so unheard and unseen. The footpads were too drunk for any of them to serve as a reliable night watch, but he had no confidence in getting the woman away without alerting them. She would surely scream the moment she saw him and resist being led away. Good intentions would not spare him from her reasonable reaction to the monster he was.

The woman yelped, the men laughed, and Taniel winced as if he'd been the one slapped. He turned away, unable to watch the brutality he was too wretched to stop. He hated himself for hiding. He deserved every aching stab from holding his awkward position as he listened to the woman's misery he could not spare her from.

The woman shrieked. Taniel jerked his head up, tangling his horns in the low brush and sending shooting pain through his neck. Two of the men kneeled atop her, holding her down, and all common sense abandoned Taniel. He surged forward. The men's hooting laughter masked the branches snapping under his lumbering rush, and drunken cruelty narrowed their attention. No one saw him grab a long knife from the spoils. The closest brigand's laughter cut short into a burbling gasp as Taniel ran him through.

The man standing beside him reeled back, brandy flying from his hand, mouth dropping open in stunned, stupid surprise. Fragments of Taniel's training had survived his disfigurement, and rage lent him the strength to slice the man—too slowed by alcohol to do more than gape—open from breastbone to groin. The woman grabbed the man atop her, costing him his balance. He hit the ground face first and clutched his nose, moaning in the dirt. Her second assailant rolled away, coming up to his feet in envious fluidity. He lost his balance when he got a better look at Taniel. The drunken redness drained from his face to leave him pale with fear.

"Beast, begone!" He spat on his palm and thrust his hand at Taniel. "No evil cross my way!"

Taniel's left leg gave out, and the thief—either realizing Taniel was no demon or thinking his warding had caused him to falter—tackled him. The thief's knife sank hot pain into Taniel's leg. His head hit the dirt hard, sending him to teeter dangerously at the lip of consciousness. Taniel struck out blindly through the darkness dusting his vision. The black nails of his ruined left hand slashed open the man's face. The thief howled, clutching what was left of his right eye, blood streaming between his fingers. Taniel sank his claws into the man's throat and ripped it open in a tangle of skin and sinew. The man gurgled. Taniel shoved his hand into the wound, tearing it wider. Blood sprayed over his eyes and mouth. The thief fell to the side, hands pressed to his shredded throat in a hopeless attempt to stanch the blood pumping from a severed artery.

Wiping the blood from his eyes, Taniel saw the last man the woman had tripped fleeing into the trees, shrieking of demons. His abandoned companion coughed feebly, losing the fight for the life spilling from his neck.

The woman stayed where she sat on the ground, staring at Taniel. Blood trickled from her mouth, framed by a violent bruise swelling on her jaw. Her dress was ripped to hang at her waist, and the firelight shone bright in her wide-eyes. He saw her disgust, the fear written across her face at seeing her hideous rescuer was the greater monster.

The dying man's wet gasp rattled into silence.

"Are you hurt?" Taniel asked. It was the first he'd spoken to a human in over a year. The witch and her daughter did not count as human. Screaming for Minu to stop hurting him and begging she let him die did not count as speaking, nor did his weighing every word around Kharinah for fear of triggering her madness count as conversation.

The woman pointed to Taniel's leg. "You're bleeding."

He touched the red soaking through his pants, finding the gash to be long and inconveniently deep. Taniel cursed the gods. Didn't he have enough troubles already? The knife wound worsened his limp as he looted the camp, swearing under his breath until he found gauze and bandages. He felt the woman watching his pathetic struggle to find a position to sit comfortably and reach the injury; an increasingly difficult task as his blood cooled from the fight, unmasking the strain he'd put his ruined body through. Fires flared up his spine, the left side of his body seized in quivering palsy, and the bandages slipped from his clumsy fingers. Bending to pick them up summoned a swooping dizziness that brought bile bubbling up his throat.

"Are you—"

"What? Am I what?" he snapped. The woman took a timid step back. He hated the way she looked at him, like she was unsure whether to be revolted by or pity him. He glared at her until she retreated into the hovel she'd been dragged from.

Doubting he had the strength to stand up if he sat down, he attempted to bandage his leg upright while bracing against a tree. His left hand proved too inept to wrap the linen securely around the wound, and his leg shook too violently. Cursing, he tossed the bandages aside, deciding it not the worst fate if the wound became infected and killed him.

The woman emerged from the hovel. She had traded out her ruined dress for a long shirt and pants designed for a taller man, the hem thickly rolled at her ankles.

"If you sit, I can help you," she said, picking up the bandages.

"I don't think my condition can be cured by your expertise." Taniel scowled, but the woman had overcome her initial fear of him and the petty curtness failed to frighten her off. She was more wary of the dead men—skirting around them as though their lifeless hands might grab at her—than she was the living monster snarling at her.

"I don't mean you harm." Her voice was gentle. Minu had spoken gently as well, promising the pain was temporary and for his own good. She reached her hand toward his shoulder. Taniel shied away.

"I don't need your help." He had no desire to allow a stranger near him or have anyone touch him again.

"There's an old mill two miles back," she said. "Can you walk that far?"

He nodded, understanding why the woman had no desire to wait out the night at the robbers' camp. He'd rather not be here as well if the surviving man found the courage to return, and Taniel was willing to tolerate the woman's presence for one night in exchange for shelter before setting out on his own.

"What's your name?" she asked.

"How far is it to Gohar?" Taniel ignored her attempts at familiarity. The fewer people who knew of him, the better. Minu would search for him once she discovered him gone. Though his appearance was unforgettable, he had a better chance of being thought a faceless monster if no name belonged to the wretched creature wandering the woods.

"I don't know," the woman said. "We were twenty or so miles away when the bandits caught us three days ago."

"We? Where's the rest of your party?" Taniel asked.

"Dead." She picked up the brandy, took a long drink, then handed him the tankard.

Taniel kept his eyes down as he accepted, finishing off what was left. The woman was careful to keep a considerate distance as they looted the dead men's camp in silence, taking food, water, and clothes. Her finding a lantern was a lucky discovery; at Taniel's beleaguered pace, it was bound to be full dark before they made it a mile. He limped after her as she led the way to the mill, glaring at her whenever she looked at him to discourage speaking. He'd allow their awkward alliance for the night so long as it went no further. Their paths would part come morning. She'd be eager to leave his company, and he'd be eager to be spared her pitying disgust.

The sky dawned as colorfully bruised as Shirin's body—a mess of yellows, purples, and reds. She felt as old as the millhouse they sheltered in; dusty, worn and creaking. She had thought herself a victim of true evil at the robbers' hands. That was until the deformed creature came to her rescue.

She glanced up from the breakfast fire she coaxed to life when he groaned in his sleep, fists clenched in pain or nightmare. She let him rest. There was no purpose in rushing him to wake. He had stayed up late into the night, scratching warding symbols into the doorframe and walls. She doubted he had slept much afterward. Twice when she woke from nightmares of monstrous men holding her down, she saw him awake, leaning against the wall, either holding his left arm to his chest or gripping his head between his hands.

"There's no one there. You're alright," he had said, seeing her startle awake. "Go back to sleep."

She was now sure he was a man, not a wood-goblin or demon as she'd thought when he lunged from the trees to rip out a man's throat. She was equally certain he was young as well, early twenties, no more than twenty-five. His features were so inhuman it was difficult to tell, but his injured pride, his shame when he caught her looking at him, were the vulnerabilities of a young man denied a full life before his prime.

He wasn't happy to see her when he woke and refused the breakfast she'd prepared. Through bared teeth he demanded she leave him alone. She ignored his bad temper. He snarled at her the whole time she waited for him to find his feet in the morning, telling her to go on her own way, and that he didn't want her help. When he failed to bully her away he ignored her, giving her no acknowledgment as they returned to the road. They walked slowly. Bruises from abuse left her sore. The greater wickedness the man had endured left him lame; broken beyond the body. His snarls softened to grumbles when she stayed beside him on the road. His growls quieted to glowers when she stopped to wait for him during his frequent rests.

"I don't need a nurse or mother," he said when she sat on a rock across from him. He clutched his visibly spasming leg. "I don't need your pity either."

Shirin only nodded, knowing he was in need of all three. A dark red stain spread down his pant leg. He was unable to bandage the wound properly and did not allow her close enough to help him. She forgave his hostility. His wild panic whenever she came too close was a learned terror that the hands of others harmed, not helped. A fear she understood.

They passed a half day of slow travel. The man said nothing when she stopped to prepare them a noon meal. His posture and silent glares told her well enough how much he wished for her company. He stubbornly clung to the claim he was fine on his own and was better off left alone. Shirin nodded along with his complaints, saying nothing. She gave him another day, two at most, until his leg injury on top of all else he had suffered allowed common sense to catch up to him.

He collapsed less than an hour later, feverish and sweating.

8

Karvogi

The sun streamed too brightly into Taniel's cell. He pulled the blanket over his face to hide from the morning light. Waking was a slow, painful process that he was in no hurry to begin. He hoped today to be one where he was left alone. He never knew when to expect Kharinah's coming or what mood she'd be in. If she'd greet him by mocking his wretched appearance, babble at him in her strange language, or sit in the chair staring at him with her eerie black-gold eyes.

Hearing soft rustling, Taniel groaned. Kharinah was already arrived.

"So you're awake."

He dropped the blanket. The woman's voice belonged to neither the demon-child, nor the witch, and he was not in his cell. He rested on a mat laid out on a planked floor, blankets reeking of must and sweat. His injured leg felt wooden and the rest of him felt little better, but stiffness was nothing new. These current pains were annoyances compared to the agony of the first months under Minu's care.

A vaguely familiar woman tended the fire crackling in the farmhouse's hearth. It took Taniel a moment to escape the confused pounding in his head and remember where he recognized her from—his escaping Minu's captivity, coming across the robbers' camp, the woman remaining with him despite how terribly he treated her, her pulling him off the road to hide him in brush after he collapsed. He had thought she'd left him to die as he deserved, only for her to return to load him into the barrow she'd found. She had carried him here when he had given her every excuse to abandon him on the roadside. That's what he'd asked her to do.

Shame burned in Taniel's gut for how awfully he'd acted, yet he was unable to bring himself to trust her.

"How're you feeling?" the woman asked. She had cleaned while he slept. Piles of dust were swept to the corners and the remnants of cobwebs survived in lonely strands dangling from the rafters.

Taniel sat up slowly, careful not to aggravate his neck that was always stiff after sleep. A few joints popped, sending numbing jabs down his arm to pool in his left hand. He was wary of the woman's kindness. Minu had acted kindly, claiming it was compassion that moved her to wrench his bones beneath her hands.

The woman reached her hand toward him. He caught her wrist.

"Please don't," he said.

"Taniel, we've been through this," she said. "Let me help you."

"How did—"

"You told me your name. You asked if I made it to Gohar, I find a woman named Nesrin Sushan and tell her Taniel says he's sorry."

He released his hold on her, but trembled when she rested her hand on his forehead.

"Your fever is stubborn, a lot like you." She returned to the hearth to ladle a thin rice gruel from the rusted pot to a battered bowl. "As you don't remember telling me your name, I assume you don't remember me telling you mine. I'm Shirin."

"How long have I been here?" He hesitated before accepting the steaming bowl she offered.

"A day."

The revulsion in her expression was gone, replaced by a poorly disguised curiosity that was even harder for Taniel to bear. Her eyes lingered on the horns curling from his skull, his mismatched eyes, and the unnatural bend to his limbs. He turned toward the wall, mortified by her staring.

"Sorry." She retreated to the fire to prepare her own bowl. "Are you able to eat?"

"Yes. But I don't like people watching me do it." Eating was a messy affair with food slipping from his ill-matching jaw. At least his throat no longer convulsed as it had in the early months, causing him to choke whenever he swallowed anything thicker than broth.

Kharinah discovered his self-consciousness early on. In her crueler moods she delighted in his shame. He had refused to eat in front of her on those days, so she took his untouched food away, returning hours later with the cold meal and a colder smile. In the end, he always gave in when the hunger coupling with pain became unbearable. She'd laughed at his struggle to hold a knife to cut the food, that he dropped the spoon more often than he raised it to his mouth. Her taunting had spurred him to work all the harder to relearn how to use his warped body, a losing battle as a single day of Minu working to "improve him" set him back weeks in his efforts. On Kharinah's better days, she'd cut his food for him, steadied his shaking hands, offered him water when he choked. Those days were almost more difficult to endure, her calm more unsettling than her madness.

Shirin took her bowl out to sit on the farmhouse's porch. Taniel was grateful for the simple kindness, and even more grateful that she said nothing when she returned to find he'd spilled half the soggy mess down his front. She soaked a cloth in a bucket of fire-warmed water, handed it to him, and returned to the porch to grant him a second blessed privacy to clean himself. He considered sneaking out the back while she wasn't looking, stopped only by the knowledge he'd not make it far. His leg wound was the least of his hindrances for leaving unnoticed.

"May I come in?" Shirin asked from outside the doorway.

"It's fine," Taniel said. Shame for his behavior withered the anger sustaining his mistrust. He had done nothing to deserve her patience, and his treatment of her matched his wretched appearance. "Where are we?"

"We're a little ways north of a town called Shabrin." She dusted off a chair before sitting across from him. "From there to Gohar, it's another fifteen miles—"

"I know how far Shabrin is from Gohar," Taniel said, irritated his unwanted caretaker thought him as stupid as he was ugly. He had lived in Gohar for over half a decade and traveled his whole life. There was hardly a place east of the Setareh Sea and west of the Grey Forest that he was unfamiliar with.

"I'm only trying to help." She spoke softly, as if even the wrong word threatened to break him.

Taniel turned to better hide the right side of his face from her.

"You weren't always like this, were you?" she asked.

He shook his head and winced. The motion aggravated the chronic pain running from his horns through his neck.

"Is Nesrin your wife?" she asked.

"Yes," he said.

"Then is your father Sariel Sushan?"

Hearing his father's name reminded him of deeper pains he had not been able to properly grieve.

"Was," he said, both relieved his father had not lived to see what his son had become and wishing more than anything his father was here with him now. He would know what to do, how to undo Minu's mutilating, and Taniel felt lost without his guidance.

"I'm sorry," Shirin said.

He shrugged, hoping she'd not ask what had happened.

"My eldest son was an admirer of your father," she said. "He wanted to be a Witch-Hunter when he grew up. He collected all the newspaper clippings and penny novels."

"It was nothing like those stories," Taniel said. Those tales either told romanticized adventures of knightly heroes rescuing beautiful women from the clutches of monsters, or painted Purgers as no better than the evil they hunted.

"Your father said the same thing when my son met him," Shirin said. "He stopped by our village on his way to a job in the northern mountains six years ago."

"Is that where you were headed? Back home when the robbers attacked?" Taniel asked, not wanting to talk about his father or answer questions about himself.

"No, I was traveling to Gohar." She stirred the coals in the fire. "There's no home in that village for me. The Reaping took that away."

"I'm sorry."

"You have nothing to apologize for, and are overdue for my thanks," she said. "What you did was brave. Most would have abandoned me to fate."

"Why were you headed to Gohar?" he asked, again redirecting the conversation away from him.

Shirin's lips thinned, the anger ill-fitting on her soft features.

"Never mind," he said, "you don't have to tell me."

"I'm looking for my husband," she said.

"And he's in Gohar?"

"It's the most sensible place for the coward to have fled to. When the red curse found our village, my youngest child took ill first. The rest of the children followed, then me, and then their father abandoned us. He fled our illness and ..." Shirin's chest heaved from the long-brewing fury. "He left us to die. I was too sick to even comfort my children. I had to watch them be thrown into carts to be buried in mass graves."

Cold guilt writhed in Taniel's gut. Kharinah had told him how the curse had swept across the land, giving great detail of the ruin he'd been unable to stop, but Shirin's was the first face of someone who had suffered for his failure.

"If you find him, what will you do?" he asked.

Shirin wiped her trembling hands on her shirt. "I don't know yet."

Taniel was no less reticent after breakfast, but he was much kinder. Shirin bore him no blame for his baring his teeth when they first met. Nor did she take offense that he flinched whenever she drew close. The abuses she had suffered over the last few days were a drop compared to the sea that had nearly drowned him. He grumbled but did not argue when she said there was to be no traveling for the day, that he'd rest, and she'd see how well he was tomorrow. The leg wound was only the most recent of his crippling injuries. He struggled to stand, let alone walk, as he limped around the farmhouse carving small runes into the wood at the windows and doors as he had done at the mill.

"What's that do?" Shirin asked.

"Stops evil spirits and monsters from coming in." He gave a humorless smile. "Well, most monsters that is."

She tried not to look at him too often. Whenever she did, it was difficult not to stare. That he was alive was no small miracle, though she doubted he saw it that way. Death might have been a kinder mercy than surviving the black sorcery that turned him into a crooked cross between goat and man.

She was figuring out the best way to convince Taniel to stop his listless wandering around the farmhouse and rest when he stiffened, staring out the rune-marked window.

"What's wrong?" she asked, coming to join him.

He pushed her down. "There's something out there."

He covered his right eye as he peered out. Shirin took advantage of his blind spot to poke her head above the sill. Three figures walked through the golden fields, oddly shaped and moving in an even stranger fashion. Their rhythmic steps evoked the sway and shift of a dance.

"They're just Karvogi," she said, hearing the telltale ring of the bells they wore.

"Karvogi?"

"They're men, not monsters. It's an old folk—"

"I know what Karvogi are," Taniel said. "But what are they doing out here?"

"They're doing as spirit-chasers were meant to before they became entertainers in market squares on festival days," Shirin said. "They're warding away evil from the land."

Taniel snorted.

"Is that skepticism or disdain?" she asked.

"Yes. Dancing in circles doesn't keep evil spirits away."

"But drawing circles on doorways does?"

"This is proven." Taniel tapped a clawed finger on a carved rune. "But that"—he waved a hand at the spirit-chasers—"that's a child seeking comfort where there's none to be found."

"It doesn't mean it has no influence," Shirin said.

"It's superstitions like the Karvogi that get people killed. They think smoke and bells drive off demons or moon rituals cure curses."

"Oh? Have you ever heard of a Karvogi falling to one of the demons or evil spirits he chases away?"

Taniel opened his mouth then closed it. "No," he admitted. The humorless grin returned. "I suppose you have me there."

Shirin looked between the Karvogi and Taniel. Warding away evil spirits was not the only good the spirit-chasers offered. While Taniel doubted the power of their ritual dances, their presence offered the means to lift some of his smaller troubles. People were wary, distrusting of anything strange or cursed. Taniel was both. Looking as he was, he'd find no welcome in any town. The more tolerant would turn him away, the less generous kill him thinking him the monster he appeared to be. His best chance of safe travel was to appear as something else. The gods punished those who pretended to be what they were not; it was a great evil to lie about the state of one's soul. But Taniel was closer to a Karvogi than a monster. As a Witch-Hunter he had protected people from dark creatures. He deserved protection from being mistaken for one.

"Stay here," Shirin said, packing a water canteen and dried food as cautionary preparations. She wasn't going so far as to need them, but she had learned it was best to prepare for the worst. "I'll be back."

"Where're you going?" The fear edging Taniel's voice tempted her to take him along, but it was better for both of them if he remained here.

"To the robbers' camp," she said. "I'm going to grab more supplies."

They were no more than four miles from the camp, Taniel had been unable to travel farther before collapsing.

"You shouldn't go by yourself," he said. "The man who fled might've returned and he might not be alone."

"He won't be there," Shirin said. "Those men were cowards, and when cowards run, they don't come back."

It would have taken less time to tell the truth as to why Taniel could not come—he was too slow and his presence invited greater dangers if they were seen. But the poor boy was already injured and she had no wish to hurt him more. He insisted he ought to accompany her, so she insisted he must stay and carve more wards into the abandoned house.

"I'll be back before you're finished. You'll see," she said. Setting competition in a task had worked well to get her sons to obey, and it worked with Taniel. He abandoned his argument to chase the hinted challenge. She was right in thinking him young, and his sufferings had not completely stolen that spirit from him.

Birds sang among the branches and a small herd of roe deer grazed where the trees thinned. The forest's life failed to mask the wrongness of the world. Shirin glanced over her shoulder, searching the woods for the uncanny sense of disquiet accompanying her. A haunting presence, unseen but very much felt, clung to every shadow and whisper of wind. The Reaping had torn something essential from creation. Infection festered in that wounded space, prickling Shirin's skin like a thousand watching eyes.

She shivered, picking up her pace. The aggrieved emptiness haunting the forest was the same one that had nearly stolen the will to live from her. It wasn't fair she had outlived her children, been helpless to protect them, or that each day she was reminded of her failure as a mother when she woke to silence where there ought to have been laughter and small running feet. Despair had left her indifferent to whether she lived to confront her coward husband in this life, or died to be reunited with her children in the next. Seeking justice against her husband for abandoning them had given her the strength to survive, not the will to live.

Meeting Taniel changed that. It was the gods' way of grabbing her by the shoulders to shake her from self-pitying malaise. They had proven her adversities were not absolute, shown her someone who had suffered more, had everything stripped from him, yet refused to surrender. Enduring as Taniel's spirit was, he couldn't fight his undeserved fate alone, no more than Shirin could abandon him to it. She knew what it was to be forsaken. She had been in need, and the man who swore his life to her had fled, leaving her to die alone. In a world where the Reaping had revealed all creation's hidden cruelties while ushering in countless more, if helping one poor soul was what the gods asked of her, she vowed to see it through.

Squawking crows took indignant flight as she came to the robbers' hideout. Flies swarmed the dead men, their flesh pecked by scavenging birds and faces distorted by the first touches of decay. Shirin couldn't remember what the men had looked like in life. Only memories of their cruelty survived their deaths.

She tied a headscarf around her nose and mouth to shield her from the worst of the death-choked air, then set about grabbing all the sturdy cloth she found, intending to tear most into tatters. She thanked the gods when she found a medicinal poultice to apply to Taniel's leg, and prayed that they'd grace him with the trust to allow her to tend to him. Digging through the stolen goods, she discovered a bag with bone needle, thread, and small personal trinkets from the travelers the robbers had murdered. Her bones went cold under the memory of the robbers' ambushing their caravan. They'd grabbed her with bloodied hands, held her down, and celebrated their finding an unexpected prize.

Shirin's stomach lurched and bile burned her throat. She swallowed back the memories and sickness, resuming her search of the camp. Picking out the trinkets best fit to sew onto a Karvogi costume, she packed tools and talismans that had everyday value as well. It never hurt to have a spare knife and spoon, and the duduk woodwind she found along with the talismans were worth more than coin. She and Taniel would do better to trade them for food and supplies than to rely on the silver and copper she claimed from the robbers' stash.

Slinging two packs and a cloak over her shoulders, Shirin headed back to the farmhouse. She offered prayers of thanks to the spirits of her fellow travelers. If their ghosts haunted this world, she promised them that the possessions they'd left behind were to be put to good purpose. The Karvogi dressed in outlandish costumes, wore horned masks, and their ragged cloaks gave them a misshapen appearance. One more Karvogi walking the wild was no cause for suspicions, and under the disguise, no one would think twice about Taniel's crown of horns.

Taniel found greater confidence beneath the cloak. His limping step was steadier, and he no longer hunched to hide the extent of his brokenness behind stooped posture. In little more than a day, Shirin had stitched together an impressive costume. The holes she cut in the cloak's hood allowed his horns to come through, and the tufts of fur she sewed along the openings made them look a part of the cloak, not a part of him. A cloth mask hung from the hood's lip, hiding his inhuman features, and the tattered layers of cotton, wool, and fur she'd woven together disguised his malformed shape. The bells and metal trinkets jingling on his sleeves and hood called far less attention to him than his true appearance.

His new confidence faltered when three men carrying traps and fresh game appeared on the road behind them. Their pace was quicker than his and Shirin's, and Taniel fought to rein in his rising panic when they caught up to them. What if they were spies for Minu? Or recognized him for the abomination he was? They had to know it was a monster disguised beneath the mask.

"Karvogi." The hunters touched their foreheads in respect.

"For your journey, spirit-chaser," one said, untying two of the rabbits from his belt and giving them to Shirin. She accepted with murmured thanks, having the sense not to complicate their interactions by refusing the gift.

"I didn't think this would work," Taniel said once the hunters had moved on.

Shirin smoothed his cloak's folds like a mother does her son's school uniform. "You should have more faith in me."

Taniel tensed beneath her touch. She had more than earned his trust, but he was reluctant to give that to anyone. Not after the last woman who'd claimed to wish him well had killed his father and turned him into a monstrosity. Old fears constricted Taniel's chest, recalling his helplessness to escape the witch as she tore his muscle and skin while promising that what she did was for the best—

"Taniel?" Shirin caught him when he stumbled.

His hand shook as he brushed hers away. "It's nothing."

Sweat flushed over his skin, the cool autumn breeze unable to penetrate the trapping layers of the ragged cloak. The cramp in his right foot moved up to his knee. After another mile, his left leg began to tense and lock. Each step advanced the stiffness toward his hip. He ignored the walking stick Shirin offered him the first six times. On the seventh, he gave in. The bell she tied on top to complement his Karvogi disguise jingled incessantly. He hated the tinny sound announcing his crippled gait, despite there being no one around to hear his shambling approach. Other than the hunters, the road was empty. The day would have been peaceful if Taniel had not known the grim reason why there were no other travelers, or why there were gravestones standing in place of farmers in the fields.

One mile felt very much like the next. Meadows buffered woods from the road, and empty farmhouses stood lonely in untended pastures. Their windows were dark, vines and weeds crept over the walls, and weary doors hung off hinges. It was not until he and Shirin reached a stone bridge arching over a wide stream with a signpost pointing the way to Shabrin that they saw another soul.

The farms nearer the town had men in the fields, and children playing where women tending gardens kept a watchful eye on them. From a distance, the scene passed as one Taniel had witnessed many times on his travels before the Reaping. Drawing closer revealed the changes the curse had wrought. The women wore black headscarves in mourning. The older children looked nothing like the adults they worked beside—orphans trading labor on the farm for a meal and roof. The men carried themselves with the weariness of lost travelers, shrunken, unsure, and longing for the home they once knew.

A little girl picking autumn leaves off a stone walkway startled when she looked up to see Taniel. She screamed, running to hide behind the woman washing clothes on the front steps.

"Karvogi." The woman nodded at Taniel and Shirin as they walked by. The little girl clutched the woman's skirts, burying her face in her shoulder.

Guilt twisted Taniel's stomach for disparaging the spirit-chasers. While he doubted the power of their rituals, he disliked disrespecting their faith by pretending to hold it for his advantage. He forced his limping step to quicken, eager to reach a private place to shuck off the false Karvogi cloak weighing heavily upon him.

"There's an inn at Shabrin, The Red Dove," he said. "If we can't find a room there, we can move on another mile or so south to shelter in an abandoned farmhouse or barn."

He prayed The Red Dove remained open. His aches and pains were far more bearable so long as he believed the luxuries of a warm bath, hot meal, and real bed awaited him at the day's end.

"We should stay in town and have someone look at your leg," Shirin said.

Taniel shook his head. He refused to reveal himself. Not until he reached Gohar and found someone who knew him as he had been. Master Maqlu, Razban Terzian, Sahak Sandar—if they had survived the Reaping, there was help to be found. Taniel had grown up hearing the tale of how Master Maqlu had bested Minu. Surely if Gohar's High Mage possessed the power to once defeat her, he had the power to defeat one of her curses.

In a rush of flaming wind, you step through the portal leading to your mountain manor. Autumn is barely arrived in the lowlands. Here it comes early and the trees burn bright red in the cool evening. You frown, sensing an absence. Taniel is gone. You can't feel his life within the walls.

You race for the manor, fearing the worst. You knew his recovery was difficult, worsened by his refusal to cooperate with your designs. But he wasn't in danger of death and Kharinah knew better than to harm him. You expressly forbade her from it. She couldn't have killed him.

The door to his room hangs ajar. You burst in to find it empty. There's no point in searching the grounds. You'd sense him if he was within the bounds of your home.

Your anger cracks the stone beneath your feet. "Kharinah!"

Your daughter resists your summons. She's always been rebellious, even after you bound her to obedience. She slips through loopholes like water through a net. Somehow she's discovered a way to delay a direct summons, but you have no patience for her games.

You tug sharp with your will. "Kharinah, now!"

You feel her cry in pain, a last resistance, then she answers, stepping through the portal you create for her. She takes her time crossing the manor grounds. When she arrives she's covered in mud, leaves thick in her hair, her clothes gone.

"Yes, Mother?" she asks.

You know something went wrong with your daughter. There's always been pieces missing from her. She was born too early, your womb rejecting her before she was fully formed. You were not designed to create life as such. The mortal form you adopted had flaws you did not know of until they almost killed your daughter. Desperate magic saved her. You hunted down her father, and taking his life ensured her survival, but she has too much of that demon-wolf in her. For centuries you've struggled to gentle her nature. She was probably running among wolves, demons, or both when you called her away.

"Where's Taniel?" you ask.

Kharinah glances around the room. She shrugs her dirt-streaked shoulders. "Not here."

"Did you let him out?"

"No." Kharinah shifts from foot to foot, anxious to return to running wild. There was a time she showed stability, but the ruin of Ha-Ai collapsed that thin sanity she clung to, and she has never recovered.

"Sit down," you say. Your will buckles her knees out from under her, forcing her to wait on the stone floor.

You step into the hall and take a small mirror off the wall. Your reflection blurs, changing to reveal what was caught in the past. The door to Taniel's room opens in the glass, he hesitates at the threshold, then hurries away. You want to punish your daughter for being so careless to leave the door unlocked, but you know it's not entirely her fault. After all, something went wrong with her. She doesn't have the capacity for choice, which is why you must so often take that away from her, and here is the chance for your daughter to learn responsibility and consequence.

"You will find him," you say, enchanting authority into each word. "And you will bring him back to me unharmed."

She does not rebel against the command. You sense her eager thrill for the offered hunt. Too eager.

"Unharmed," you repeat for good measure. Taniel is as much your son as Kharinah is your daughter. Perhaps that's why she's been so wild of late, jealous of the younger sibling and the attention he demands. Your daughter is a strange creature, immortal, near invulnerable, yet possessing a child's fragility. In her madness, the one thing she reliably comprehends is how alone she is. She doesn't understand you do this for her as much as for Taniel, creating a companion for her.

"Get dressed and cleaned first," you say. "Don't bring attention to yourself or cause trouble."

Fear has turned men fragile, and while you have no concern for your daughter's ability to survive their narrow-mindedness, Taniel is far more vulnerable to their intolerance.

9

The Demon at the Door

The town of Shabrin was modest and designed for durability. The bronze temple dome, glowing softly in the setting sun, was the lone ornament decorating the flagstone streets, yellow brick shops, and clay-shingled homes, their windows warmed by lamplight. A grieving ache bloomed in Shirin's chest. Shabrin reminded her very much of the northern village she had once called home, cradled between mountains and sea.

Taniel's breath came in whistling gasps, the walking stick clunked heavily on the stone, and his dragging limp became more pronounced with each step. Asking if he was in pain was pointless. He'd deny it, and her suggesting they rest was equally futile.

"You said The Red Dove was the inn's name?" She paused on the town square's temple steps on the pretense of rifling through her pack. It gave Taniel the excuse to rest while protecting his trampled pride.

"Yes." He collapsed on the steps beside her, his good hand gripping his leg, his bad hand held protectively to his chest. "The owner's name is Yerem—or was last I visited four years ago." Regaining his breath, he inched across the steps to peer into her bag. "What're you looking for?"

"The purse," she lied. She had the coins and talismans in a thin pouch strung around her neck hidden under her clothes.

Taniel opened his pack to help search for the allegedly misplaced purse. He pulled the duduk free of the spare shirt it was wrapped in. "Where did you get this?"

"The robbers' camp," Shirin said. "I thought to trade it. Not all towns accept coin and goods can buy you more than gold."

Taniel stopped guarding his left hand against his chest. Both his hands moved to hold the reed woodwind with familiar sureness.

"Can you play it?" she asked.

He nodded, fingers gliding along the duduk in silent song.

"We might be able to trade rooms at the inn for music," Shirin said.

"No. It's a good thought, but I'd rather not draw more attention to myself than I already do. Besides, it's been over a year since I've played and ..." He tucked his left hand into his sleeve to hide the fused fingers.

She stopped him from returning the instrument to the pack. "Why don't you hold onto it? Just in case."

Taniel showed more engagement with the duduk than anything else, and she'd take this opening to coax him from his defensive shell. His left hand reappeared from his sleeve to hold the instrument, fingers twitching as if in want to play.

"I'll stay here if you want to see if the innkeeper takes Karvogi and doesn't ask too many questions. It's just up that street, you'll see the sign." He nodded at a row of shops and homes along the grey stone road.

"Will you be alright by yourself?" she asked.

"I've survived far worse than being left alone for an hour," he said, and Shirin got the impression he smiled at her from behind the mask.

"I'll be back in less than half," she promised.

The wooden sign decorated by a red dove in flight creaked above a sturdy oak door. Candles in the window flickered against the navy twilight settling over the inn's clay-tiled roof supported by rounded wooden beams.

Two men sitting at the hearth glanced up at Shirin as she pushed open the door. She interpreted their returning to quiet conversation over drinks as approval for her to enter.

"What can I do for you, ma'am?" the bald man behind the counter asked. His facial hair was neatly trimmed, oiled, and salted by grey. Faint shadows haunted his eyes and there was a frailness to his manner like he had gone too long with eating too little. Shirin knew she looked no better.

"Are you Yerem?" she asked. She hunched her shoulders, disliking having the strange men at the hearth to her back.

"No, that was my father," he said. "The name's Yosef, and I haven't seen your face around here before."

"I lived in Kamat, a coastal village to the north. I'm looking for family in Gohar, and a traveler I met on the road said you and your inn's hospitality survived the Reaping. Do you have rooms?"

"Of course. I doubt the Reaping left enough living souls to fill even this inn."

"How much for a room and two beds? And to have a bath drawn?"

Yosef looked her over, unimpressed by what he saw. "How much can you pay?"

Shirin set six silver pieces on the table and held up two more. "These two are for privacy, no questions, and we'll take our meals in the room." She added the two rabbits to the coin. "Whatever stew you have with these thrown in will do."

"Who's the second bed for?"

"My son. The privacy is for him as well."

"What's wrong with him?"

"He lost his wife and father in the Reaping. Her death broke his heart, his father's death his mind," Shirin said. "He took the Karvogi mask, I think more to chase after their spirits than chase away demons, and vowed to hide his face from the world. He's broken, more than most, but he won't bring trouble over your threshold. I'll pay for the inconvenience his presence might cause."

"You don't need to buy my tolerance of the Karvogi. My granddad held the old faith. He performed the rituals each dark moon. I'm beginning to think if we hadn't abandoned those ways we'd have happier reasons to dance than to chase away demons, and it'd still be my father running the inn." He slid three of the coins back toward Shirin. "The game is worth more than the silver, and I don't take charity from poor spirit-chasers. Bring your boy in. I don't turn away travelers in need of rest either. It's bad for both my business and my conscience."

Taniel turned the duduk over in hand, doubting he had the dexterity to play the instrument. He had failed at far simpler tasks. This was bound to be no different. He stretched the fused fingers of his left hand in want to play as he once had, testing their range of motion. The temptation to try overpowered his fear of failure. Detaching the reed, he slipped it beneath his mask to wet it. He had been home in

Gohar last he played, the day before he left for Chahich. The windows to his and Nesrin's flat were thrown open to tempt in the spring breeze, and she had asked him to play "The Raven Maiden's Dance" while she baked, filling the room with the scent of honeyed bread.

Taniel mimed playing that same song. The motion loosened the stiffness in his fingers, muscle memory guided them to their proper place, and his right hand compensated for his hampered left. The fused fingers lacked reach, but at least they moved, discovering flexibility he thought lost. Replacing the reed, he closed his lips over the mouthpiece. His first breath pushed out a weak warble. He adjusted the bridle so his second sounded strong and clear.

Checking to be sure the square was empty, he played a song's opening notes, wincing at the thin whine. After a few unsure chords, he found the sought-after harmony between reed and breath. The music smoothed into a slow, wistful tune. In Gohar, the song was known as "The Winter Traveler." Eastern villages of the Azariel River knew it by "Won't You Let Me In." Taniel thought the eastern name better fit the song best played on cold nights beside the fire as wind-stirred branches tapped frosted windows.

"My feet are frozen and hands are ice in this cold and bitter wind. I'm knocking at the door, won't you let me in?"

Taniel jerked his head up to stare around the square. There was no one in sight, not even a shadow shifting in an alley or window, but someone had been singing the lyrics. Years as a Purger taught him not to call out. Asking after hidden voices in lonely places as night fell begged unpleasant answer.

A soft scuff whispered behind him. Taniel whirled, sending sharp pain splintering from his skull to hips. He swore, doubling over to grip his neck. Through gritted teeth, he cursed himself for being so easily frightened. Blinking tears from his eyes, he carefully turned to look behind him. The doorway to the temple was empty. There was no one there.

"You play well."

Another flare of pain rewarded Taniel's second startling. He'd been so worried about nonexistent phantasms he'd completely missed Shirin approaching from across the square.

"I'm sorry," she said, face stricken she'd frightened him. "I heard you playing and thought you'd stop if you saw me."

"You have nothing to apologize for." He rubbed the ache sinking between his shoulder blades.

"You truly do play well."

"Thank you." Being able to play a people's folk music was one of the best ways to get them to accept you. Men were more willing to talk to strangers about the strange things plaguing their village and woods when they shared songs.

"What song was it?" Shirin asked.

"What?" Taniel's blood chilled. The innocent question carried unsettling implications. If Shirin didn't know the song, she hadn't been the one singing. A cold crawl joined the burning in Taniel's neck. Shirin wasn't the only presence nearby.

"What song were you playing?" she repeated.

"'The Winter Traveler.' Is the inn open?" He wanted to be away from the square as soon as possible.

"Yes, a room will be ready with a bath by the time we get there." Shirin frowned. "What's wrong?"

"Nothing, I'm just tired." He was both irritated and impressed by Shirin's intuition, and he was too unnerved by the unseen presence to remember to flinch before accepting her hand to help him stand.

A serving girl waited at the inn's backdoor. Shirin had convinced Yosef to let them in through the kitchen so Taniel need not pass under curious eyes in the front room. Taniel remembered Yosef's father, Yerem, to be a considerate man and was glad to see trial had not eroded away the good character his son had inherited.

"Are you alright?" the serving girl asked, seeing Taniel's clumsy limp.

"It was a long way getting here," he said.

"If you're injured I can send for a medicine woman."

"No, I'll be fine, thank you," he said, anxious she'd move to support him and discover his twisted shape beneath the cloak. "It's not an injury that can be cured."

Shirin smoothly stepped in before the serving girl could. Taniel sagged into her.

"There's a bath ready for you and a supper is being prepared," the serving girl said. "Call if you need anything else."

Taniel shrugged his shoulders up to more thoroughly hide behind the Karvogi disguise. The cloth mask felt too thin and he worried an observant eye would see the monster beneath.

Shirin led him down the hall to their room, mercifully on the first floor. Taniel doubted he had the strength to manage stairs. The curtains over the single small window fended off the worst of autumn's chill, and the lantern's light pushed shadows to the corners, unable to fully banish them. A second set of curtains had been erected around a metal tub where inviting steam rose off the water. The room was small and cool, but clean, the two beds neatly made with heavy blankets tucked at the base. Closing the door behind him, Taniel ignored exhaustion's temptation to collapse into bed without undressing or washing. Figuring his way out of his Karvogi disguise was a trial of patience. His left hand was too clumsy to manage the clasps Shirin had sewn on and the hood snagged on his horns when he tried to pull it over his head.

"Take your turn in the bath while it's still warm," he said, tugging at the stubbornly tangled cloak, his head lost in its folds.

"I had it prepared for you," she said.

"You'll be done by the time I get this off."

Shirin touched his shoulder. He tensed as he let her unravel the cloak from his horns, guide his arms from the sleeves, and undo the undershirt. She accomplished in seconds what took him minutes to fail to do.

"Thank you," he said. Shame soured his gratitude.

His father had been fond of the proverb "Humility is the gate through which charity enters" and never passed the chance to remind Taniel of it. Only now did Taniel truly grasp the meaning, wrestling with his dying pride as much as he had the cloak.

The metal tub rose too high for him to get in on his own. His legs no longer had the range of motion necessary to lift over the edge. Even if he managed to clamber in, he'd never be able to climb out without falling flat. Furious embarrassment burned hot in his gut. He used to fight dark witches whose names men feared to speak. He hunted demons and trapped evil spirits. He had run over eight miles through rocky hills and snarled woods, taking no rest to reach a small river village before a woman gave birth, ensuring the water-demon stalking the mother did not claim her or the infant. The money he'd earned from selling its corpse to a mage in Nahr Hasa was saved to buy a proper home for Nesrin to start a family. He and Nesrin had stayed out the entire night he returned home, dancing into the early morning hours. The summer night was too brief for their hunger for life, and they still had the strength for a more intimate step when they'd tumbled into bed at dawn.

He was only twenty-five, and a tub had become too daunting a challenge for him.

Shirin took him by the arm. "Get in while it's warm."

She made a show of looking at the ceiling as she helped him in. The warm water dissolved the pain, soothed the spasms in his leg, and unraveled the knots tied into his spine by the long traveling.

"Thank you," Taniel said again. Gratitude was not enough for all Shirin had done, and he regretted having nothing more to offer.

"Let me know when you're finished," she said, drawing the curtains around the tub shut. "I'll help you out."

Taniel closed his eyes as he sank into the water, not wanting to see his ruined form.

Taniel looked anywhere but at Shirin when she helped him from the tub to dry and dress. His shyness was almost as bad as it had been when they first met, and was worsened by fresh embarrassment. She said nothing as she helped him into a fresh shirt. There were no words to ease his discomfort, and her saying there was no need for shame would only draw attention to what he wanted ignored.

"How's your leg?" she asked.

"It's a shallow cut," he said, applying fresh salve and bandages. "I'll manage."

So he was in pain, but it was mild compared to all else he'd endured. At least he moved more freely, able to sit on the bed to tend his leg on his own.

"I'll go get us dinner," she said. "We can rest for a day or two before heading toward Gohar."

"You should take your meal in the dining area," Taniel said. "Listen to what the locals are saying about the roads. See if there's news from the south, roads to avoid, happenings to be wary of. But don't ask questions, curious strangers are rarely welcomed."

"I'll bring you dinner first," she said.

"That's alright. Stay and listen for useful gossip."

"Taniel—"

He turned his face from her, posture hunched, hands going to his horns in a vain attempt to hide them. "You don't have to help me."

"It's no trouble," Shirin said.

"It's been nothing but trouble for you."

"No, just because it's been difficult at times does not mean it's been trouble."

He raised his mismatched eyes to meet hers. "I'm not your child."

There was no cruelty in his tone. The words were spoken gently to spare her some of the sting.

"I know," she said, "but I am still a mother and I will behave as one."

"Where's your boy?" Yosef asked when Shirin sat at the counter.

"Resting," she said. "He doesn't sleep well, so I won't disturb him when he does."

"We got a medicine woman in the village. She'll know a tincture for him."

"Thank you, but I'm hoping to find a mage in Gohar who can help him."

"It's better to stay away from the cities. They say the curse still endures there. It's the bad air, you're better off keeping to the country."

"I heard my brother survived the Reaping and is living there," Shirin lied. "If so, he'll take us in, which is more than we have anywhere else."

"You'd be better off joining your son chasing after spirits than those small hopes," Yosef said.

"Then what do you chase if not hope or spirits?" Shirin asked.

"I don't chase anything. I endure." He rapped his knuckles on the bar. "I hold the ground I stand on and ask for nothing more. We're all bound back to the dirt, might as well live, die, and be buried on the bit of earth you choose."

Yosef made his rounds refilling the mugs of the men huddled by the hearth and the small groups seated at roughly carved wooden tables. The men spoke in the comfortable tones of those born and raised in an insular community. Shirin ought to move closer to better eavesdrop on conversation, but a crippling timidity prevented her from sitting nearer the strangers. The men by the hearth chuckled. The cold memory of the robbers laughing as they sat around the fire, their mirth cruel and mocking, slid over her. She shrank in on herself like she had then in a pathetic attempt to hide. Remembering those awful nights reawakened the ache in the fading bruises covering her arms and back.

"Here you are." The serving girl placed two bowls of rabbit molokhia and flat bread before her.

"Thank you." Shirin forced herself to eat, finding no taste in the food, while finding it harder by the minute to sit so close to the men.

The dining room rumbled under a round of louder laughter. Shirin's spoon clattered from her shaking hand. Her nervousness reared into a suffocating helplessness. She felt the robbers' phantom hands grabbing her, the weight of them pinning her down, her face stinging from a hard blow.

Gods save me, Seraphs give me strength, she prayed, willing her hands to stop trembling. She was done living under the terrible slavery of fear. She'd not allow evil men to turn her into a cowering wretch, or past sufferings reduce her to an empty shell. She, not yesterday's horrors, decided her future.

The inn's door swung open and every head turned to the new arrival. A woman stepped in, pulling down the hood of her fur-trimmed cloak. She was breathtakingly beautiful, sable curls tumbling to her midback and framing a face of clear, copper skin. Her beauty shifted to a sinister loveliness when the firelight caught her eyes; gold irises shone bright on ink-black sclera. The men's murmurings dropped into uneasy silence. She crossed the wooden floor to sit at the closest open table, folding her gloved hands in front of her, indifferent to the fear her presence inspired. One brave soul broke the silence to nervously whisper to his neighbor, and after a long, tense pause the men returned to their dinners. They rushed to finish their meals, speaking little, and stood before they emptied their mugs to hurry from the warm dining room into the night. The strange-eyed woman neither spoke nor moved.

"How may I help you?" Yosef asked, no longer able to ignore his only remaining customer besides Shirin. He stayed behind the counter, looking poised to flee.

"I'm looking for someone." The woman rose to join them at the bar. Her throaty purr and the feral grace to her movements reminded Shirin of a cat stalking toward a cornered mouse.

"We don't get too many travelers these days," Yosef said.

"Then you'd remember him if he passed this way. He'd be traveling alone, and anyone who saw him would not soon forget him."

Yosef wiped perspiration from his upper lip. "What's he look like?"

"His head would be covered. If he wore a cloak it'd be oddly misshapen. He has a very pronounced limp, is slightly stooped, and his left hand is crippled."

"What do you want from a sad creature like that?" Yosef asked.

"He was in my mother's care. He must return."

"Haven't seen or heard of no one like that coming through here."

"Are you sure?" the woman asked. "Think carefully."

Yosef waved his hands as if to ward off an attack. "No! No one!"

"And you?" The woman turned her wolf eyes on Shirin. "Have you seen such a man?"

"No," Shirin said in a weak whisper.

"Are you sure?" the woman repeated. "Think carefully."

Shirin shook her head, too frightened to speak. The woman stared, gloved fingers clicking sharp as she drummed them on the bar counter. Shirin's throat went dry under the woman's predatory gaze. No one could think Taniel a monster after seeing this creature. Both her and Taniel's outward appearance belied their inner nature.

Shirin raised a defensive arm when the woman stood. Her cloak swept behind her as she returned to the night, leaving the door open. Yosef dashed forward, fingers fumbling on the latch to close the inn to any more travelers, then signed against evil.

"Do you often get visitors like that?" Shirin asked.

"No." Yosef mopped his neck with a handkerchief. "But word's spreading of wicked things roaming roads and woods of late. Seraphs save us."

He took a bottle from his top shelf, poured two glasses to the brim, and passed one to Shirin. The drink washed smoky down her throat, burning through the lingering dread the woman left in her wake.

"So that woman was a stranger to you?" she asked.

"Never seen her before and hope never to again," Yosef said, refilling his glass.

Shirin wished the same, while dreadful intuition warned her otherwise.

Taniel was fast asleep when she returned to the room, curled up like a child hiding from the nightmares darkness bred. She ought to wake him to eat the dinner she brought. At the very least she ought to tell him about the woman searching for him. But that would do nothing other than distress him. It was too dark to travel and their abrupt leaving risked rousing dangerous suspicions. Yosef might assume they were involved with the woman, and Taniel was unable to flee fast enough if those suspicions turned hostile. And that woman—Shirin shuddered—that demon-eyed woman might be watching to see if her coming stirred her quarry from his hiding place.

Common sense told Shirin to flee alone. The evil that had disfigured Taniel pursued him. It had tracked him to this village, was of a power far greater than she could withstand, and her only chance of escaping that evil was if she left Taniel to face it alone. She could do nothing against creatures like that demon-woman, and she was equally unable to abandon Taniel to her. She had no intention to follow her husband's example.

She tucked the blankets tighter around Taniel before dimming the lamp, unwilling to let the fire go out after seeing what waited in the dark.

"What's upsetting you?" Taniel asked.

Shirin had been nervous all morning. She'd violently tugged his Karvogi disguise over his horns in her rush to leave The Red Dove, and while she'd said nothing, he knew how slowly he moved had tried her patience. Putting a few miles between them and Shabrin failed to ease her agitation. If anything, her anxious backward glances increased once the town disappeared behind rolling woodland hills.

"A woman came to the inn last night after you'd gone to bed," she said. "She was looking for you."

Cold dread filled Taniel's chest.

"What was her name?" he asked. It had to have been Kharinah. Minu's presence was so potent it would've woken him. He'd always known when she was near or had returned to her manor.

"I don't know," Shirin said, "but she described you as you are and she had—"

"Gold and black eyes?"

She nodded. Taniel's walking stick stopped him from stumbling, his legs suddenly weak.

"What happened?" He turned his whole body to look down the road for an ominous figure stalking closer. Birds flitted through pale barked beech, wind rattled autumn-bronzed leaves, and the air was clear of the chaotic magic that heralded Kharinah's presence.

"She left the inn after Yosef and I claimed we'd seen no such man," Shirin said.

"I know she left. If she had not, you and Yosef would be dead," Taniel said. They'd have been torn to bloody ribbons and Taniel would've been dragged back to Minu. Or perhaps bloodlust would've driven Kharinah's madness beyond her mother's control and she'd have killed him as well. "Tell me exactly what happened."

Shirin recounted Kharinah's coming, and a clammy sweat slicked Taniel's palms. How had Kharinah found him so quickly? And if she'd tracked him to The Red Dove, why was he walking free and not forcibly returned to the mountain prison? Had Kharinah's madness spared him? Or was she playing a more sinister game? The demon-child's unstable psyche made her mind impossible to know.

"You should have told me right after she left," Taniel said.

"And what would you have done? Insisted we leave? Tried to run? Or gone out to confront her?" Shirin asked. "I may not have known you long, Taniel, but it took me less than an hour to learn you are unable to sit and wait. You would've acted and drawn her attention."

"If you see her again, don't hide it from me. She's not to be dismissed."

"Who is she?"

"Her name is Kharinah. She's Minu's daughter."

Shirin paled. "The Demon Witch?"

"Yes. She has all her mother's madness and none of her restraint."

"Is she a witch as well?"

"Of a sort," Taniel said. "She's more a force of magic than a wielder of it."

Anxiety exaggerated his ailments. His head pounded, muscles twitched, and a dizzy nausea swelled beneath his horns. Kharinah had never physically harmed him—that amusement belonged to her mother—but a cat has no need to harm the bird it plays with once its prey is too battered to fly away.

Taniel quickened his step, ignoring the pain lancing up his leg. He wasn't going back. He'd throw himself into death's embrace before returning to the hands of the witch who'd ruined him.

From the banks of the Azariel River you watch black smoke rise in billowing towers above the burning village. The low clouds reflect the fire's crimson glow, and the scent of the rain they promise softens the acrid reek of scorched wood and flesh. The river village was spared from facing the Reaping. But it was not spared from Wasi Adhar's judgment, and your chosen prophet has taken up his calling to see the eastern lands cleansed with a zealot's fervor.

You ensure his will aligns to yours. You whisper to him in dreams, each word further claims his heart and mind. You tell him sorcery is the source of worldly wickedness, it came from the east, brought by the corrupted survivors of the Wastes, and must be stamped out. It was sorcery that reduced the once mighty kingdom of Ha-Ai to ash. It was sorcery that birthed the Reaping plague. It cannot be tolerated and has too long found shelter in the eastern villages along the Grey Forest.

Adhar's reservations of taking the sword to fellow worshippers of the Grey Lady are long faded. His misgivings over burning hedge-witches and the magic-touched are gone. You buried those doubts beneath dreams of greatness. He no longer resists you, and his conscience is eased in his submission to let go those distracting concerns. All that matters is he sees your will done—a world burned so it might be reborn.

You hear a woman screaming within the village. The Grey Lady brought this upon her own people. Her forest was grown out of spite, so you strike back in kind. The Reaping—though twisted from your designs—was not without advantage. It culled the mortals to a more manageable number, allowing you to be more attentive to the surviving souls. Wasi Adhar is not the only one you speak to in dreams. You warned a hedgewitch away from this river village before Adhar arrived. She and her family fled north to Agr Rav. You felt their hurried feet racing away as the first flames consumed the unrepentant village.

There were no other souls worthy of warning. You left their fates untampered.

The river rises over the muddy banks to tug at your feet.

"Azariah," you greet your sister.

The water ripples toward you, streaming up to shape a human semblance. The edges drift off in droplets that spin and flow back into the figure of a young woman, a reflection of your preferred mortal shape.

"*Nakirah.*" Azariah's voice is soft, the last gasp of a drowning child. "*What have you done?*"

"I've done nothing."

"*You sow suffering on my shores. Why?*"

"Twice Asherah has denied a better world's coming. I will not permit a third." She and the rest of your sisters interfere out of spite. Never compassion. They had not the courage to live and walk among men as you have. They choose to remain distant, sanctimonious and self-satisfied, shying away from the vulnerabilities you welcomed. You alone took on your task free from reservation or pretention. They are worshipped as divine beings, while you became like man to be closer to those you were sent to guide.

"*It is not Asherah who choked the waters with the dead, the ash of the burned, the rot of the buried,*" Azariah says. "*It is you.*"

"Asherah should not have interfered," you say.

"*Have you not done enough? You've brought suffering—*"

"Better to bring suffering than tolerate evil's influence." How could your sisters understand? They have seen wickedness, but they have not known it. They have not known love or loss, and you will not tolerate their ignorance pretending at wisdom.

"*This cannot go on,*" Azariah says. An empty declaration. It is not in her power to stop you. "*Nakirah—*"

"No." You refuse that name. You abandoned it when the people of Ha-Ai abandoned you.

Azariah sighs, dissolving into the river. "*You have strayed,*" she says as one burned body, then five more, drift downstream.

10

Empty Halls

Taniel shambled along the hard-packed road leading south. He felt detached in soul and substance from the golden fields gleaming with morning dew, the birdsong trilling in the low trees, and the cool autumn sun dispassionately watching his limping struggles from a beryl blue sky. They belonged to a living world, and his weariness diminished him to little more than a fading ghost. Two nights spent tossing and turning in shallow sleep fraught by fitful nightmare left his eyes heavy and his step spiritless. Every nightly noise—real or imagined—had startled him awake. For hours he'd stared into the dark, afraid to see the glow of Kharinah's gold-black eyes, or that come morning he'd wake to find himself in the mountain prison where Minu would break his bones, play with his flesh like it was wet clay, until nothing remained of who he was. He'd be a creature like her monsters of swamp and rotting flesh. Or worse, he'd be like Kharinah.

Dawn had banished the dark, not the nightmares the Demon Witch had inflicted upon him. Those memories had followed him south, snapping and howling at him like starved hounds. In the end, fatigue dulled even his sharpest fears. He was too tired to entertain terror and its complications, so he clung to a single, simple thought.

Almost home. Almost home. His refrain cleaved through the exhaustion clouding his mind, and in its wake trailed wisping hopes of all being set right once he reached Gohar. His right foot dragged. His left limped. *Almost home. Almost home.*

Shirin spoke little, possessed by her own dark mood. A tight frown thinned her lips and her hands were clenched as if she struggled to rein in anger. Taniel assumed she dwelled on the husband who'd abandoned her and her children to die. Having no words of comfort or wisdom to offer, he gave her uninterrupted quiet to sort through her own tragedy and how to confront it.

Almost home. Almost home.

Gohar rose against the southern sky. The domed cupolas and thin minarets of the Arcanum sat atop a hill pitted and dented by the city spreading down the slopes into surrounding farmlands. Taniel lifted his eyes from the dirt road to fix on the reaching towers of the mage's seat. He knew he was permanently damaged—there was no recovery of what he had been—but he didn't want a miracle. All he wanted was to walk free of pain and be restored to where he could face his wife as a man, not a monster.

Almost home. Master Maqlu must know a way to rescue him from Minu's curse. *Almost home.*

The Arcanum was far older than the city she crowned. Her high towers and halls had overlooked the plains and low woods for centuries before Gohar's founding. The sorcerers who built the Arcanum were claimed to have come from the east, fleeing the destruction of the fabled kingdom of Ha-Ai. Much of the Arcanum's history was inseparably rooted in legend, but all the stories told that the sorcerers—wherever they had truly come from—used magic lost to time, calling upon stone to grow as trees into towers. They planted their sorcery deep into the earth where it bloomed into the Arcanum, a seat worthy of the mages' wisdom.

Taniel had no trouble believing the birth of the Arcanum was a feat of great sorcery lost to time. The Arcanum's impossibly smooth colonnades and halls branching into ribbed vaults certainly looked as though they were grown from the earth, carrying none of the blemishes born of being cut and carved. The patterns of interlacing foliage twining over walls to blossom along archways were too perfect an imitation of their floral inspiration to have been sculpted by even the most talented mortal hand. He just as easily disbelieved the sorcerers' fabled origin. More likely they had come from the west, sailing across the Setareh Sea, not from a civilization lost in the Wastes beyond the Grey Forest. Nothing good had ever come from the lands east of the mountains, and not even the bravest Purger chased quarry that fled there.

Sweat trickled down Taniel's neck, his body overtaxed from the long days of travel. Hot coals burned between his vertebrae. His left shoulder felt like a rusted blade slid in and out beneath the bone. He gripped his walking stick tight, gaze fixed on the Arcanum's towers.

Almost home.

The city of Gohar was born by more mundane means than sorcerers of legend. Farmers had settled around the mages' seat for protection. Pilgrims had come for wisdom. Students stayed to learn. The history was one shared by most Haeranji cities; sorcerers carved great halls atop stony hills, and people sheltered in their shadow.

As Gohar loomed larger, signs of life returned to the farmhouses along the road. Tilled fields replaced ones gone wild and untended. Dogs barked in warning at Taniel, unfooled by his Karvogi disguise. Smoke twisted from chimneys, and wards carved into fence posts hummed angrily as he passed by, disliking Taniel's cursed presence more than the dogs.

Almost home. His legs felt like his bones ground shards of glass into the other. His horns encouraged a headache to swell behind his eyes. *Almost home.*

An older man leading a donkey-pulled cart and a young man holding a rifle passed them. The young man—who Taniel guessed to be the older man's son—glared as they walked by, his expression hard and distrustful. Taniel envied their easy gait unburdened by pain.

I'll walk like that again, he vowed. Once he reached the Arcanum's gates, Minu's curse would be a nightmare he could at last wake from. *Almost home.*

The wall encircling Gohar—an ugly construction of uneven concrete, brick, and wood—hadn't been there when he left eighteen months ago. Ashened scabs blackened the fields surrounding the enclosed city; the graveyards for the Reaping's dead. His chest hollowed. In failing to stop Minu, he bore responsibility for every one of those lives lost. He deserved what the witch had done to him. His personal ruin reflected what he'd allowed to befall the world.

Taniel's hope soured. How could he face Nesrin like this, molded in the shape of his failure? The thought of her rejecting him was more agonizing than anything Minu had done to him.

Wooden sentry towers overlooked the road and fields. Riflemen in the elevated nests covered by thatched roofs watched Taniel and Shirin pass below. They fell in behind a band of farmers pulling wagons filled by apples, beets, and potatoes to the nearest gate. All the farmers wore matching armbands and presented papers to the two guards who critically inspected both the men and produce. Neither Taniel nor Shirin had papers of identification; was that reason for them to be turned away? Would the guards let a Karvogi through without question, or would they demand he remove his mask before allowing entrance? Taniel's hands shook. No guard in their right mind would let a creature looking like him in.

The younger guard snagged an apple from the cart as the older man waved the farmers through.

"Move along," he said.

A few anxious knots in Taniel's chest loosened. He recognized the older guard with salted beard, and a lean, wiry build. Jirair had been a city guard working at the train station. From his frequent traveling, Taniel had known most of the station security by name, all by face, and a few like Jirair had often gotten drinks with him.

"Karvogi." The shorter, younger guard nodded at Taniel and Shirin. "Where are you two coming from?"

"North," Shirin said.

"And what brings you to Gohar?" Jirair asked.

"A return home. You know me, Jirair," Taniel said. "Two winters ago, you asked me to ward your cousin's farm."

Jirair stiffened. "I don't—"

"You told him I was coming, but never told him when. He almost shot me thinking I was the chor killing his flock."

Jirair's confused blink widened into disbelief. "Sushan? Seraphs save me, they said you and your father were dead!"

"Only half that rumor is true." Taniel pulled his left sleeve up to show his malformed hand. "The rest of me is worse. I need to see Master Maqlu."

"Master Maqlu is gone." The younger guard signed against evil at the sight of Taniel's hand.

The breath in Taniel's chest curdled cold. "He's dead?"

"No, he left. He ran off to the east. Some superstitious nonsense about seeking a cure in the Grey Forest," the young guard said.

"Where—"

"Don't matter where. All that matters is he ran off, never came back, and the rest of the mages who were supposed to protect us didn't do a godsdamn thing."

"All the mages are gone?" Taniel asked.

"No." Jirair gave the young guard a look of long-suffered irritation. "The Arcanum still protects us. Her healers shepherded us through the Reaping, they will help you."

"We can't let him in." The young guard curled his lip at Taniel like he was an unpleasant smear on the bottom of a boot. "He carries a curse, and we've had enough of those. And how do you know he's who he claims—"

Jirair held up his hand. "You've said enough, and nothing worth hearing."

Unsheathing a rune-marked silver knife, Jirair held it out for Taniel to prove he was truly a man, not a shape-shifter, a demon in disguise, or possessed by one.

"Believe me," Taniel said, taking the blade, "if I could change shape, I would."

Touching the flat edge to his skin, he held it for a moment, then lifted the knife to show no marring of his skin.

"Can't be too careful," Jirair said. "Who's your companion?"

Shirin had stood by quietly during the exchange, her expression closely matching Jirair's in regarding the young guard with fraying exasperation.

"Her name is Shirin, her husband lives in Gohar, and I vouch for her." Taniel handed her the knife to perform the same process.

Jirair nodded. The younger guard scowled.

"He can't just—"

"Actually, Taniel Sushan can." Jirair cut him off. "As a Purger of Gohar, he's not to be impeded in his business."

"Yeah?" the young man sneered. "What's he purging?"

"Himself, you idiot."

The young man reddened and stuck out his jaw, refusing to be shamed out of his obstinacy. "We'll need to see his papers."

"He outranks you, boy," Jirair said. "Stop your chest puffing before you embarrass us both."

"Jirair, do you ... do you know if Nesrin ..." Taniel struggled to ask the question.

"Your wife survived," Jirair said. "Last I heard, young Sandar had taken her in."

Taniel swayed under the rush of lightheaded relief. The mask hid his mouth shaping soundless thanks to all the divine powers. Nesrin was alive. His wife was alive.

"Is Suri with her as well?" he asked. "Do you—"

"I don't know, Sushan," Jirair said. "I hardly know what goes on beyond this part of the wall and I find ignorance easier to bear than the rumors I do hear." He whistled, and a guard lounging against the wall with a cigar between his lips hurried over.

"Problem?" the guard asked, suspicion falling on Taniel as he tossed the cigar away and his hand went to the pistol holstered at his hip.

"Take over for the next hour," Jirair said.

The guard looked Taniel and Shirin up and down, shrugged, then reclaimed his cigar from the ground before resuming lounging against the wall in his newly assigned position.

Jirair motioned Shirin and Taniel to follow. "I'll take you to the Arcanum. They'll see that curse lifted from you."

"You don't have to trouble yourself. I know the way," Taniel said.

"I can't allow you to walk Gohar unsupervised. Not in your state. The boy's an idiot, but he's right. You're tainted, Sushan," Jirair said. "Seeing you to the Arcanum is as much for your protection as everyone else's."

Eyes wide and lips parted, Shirin stared in wonder. More than once she tripped as they ascended the streets sloping up to the shining domes and needle towers that Taniel called the Arcanum.

"Are you alright?" he asked. "You look like you're seeing ghosts."

"This is my first time in a city," she admitted.

"Truly?" He tilted his head, a curious gesture as it caused his cloth mask to slip, giving him a lopsided expression. "You've never been to a city before?"

"I never traveled more than ten miles from where I was born until this last year."

"Wait until you see the Arcanum," he said, and she heard a smile hidden behind the mask. "It truly is a marvel."

They turned onto a wide avenue lined by marble sculptures shaded beneath crimson flame trees. The statues of mages past—hands lifted and faces turned toward the heavens—beckoned them to the Arcanum gates.

"Oh." Shirin's mouth fell in childlike awe. She'd already been impressed by the citadel crowning Gohar, but the regality impressed on her at a distance had not prepared her for its true majesty.

The walls were a garden turned to stone, the architecture too smooth, the furling flowers and vines too intricate to be carved by human hands. Only coloring distinguished the petrified leaves from the wisteria cascading over the façade and the lilac trees bronzing from the shift of seasons. There was no distinction between the ground and the pale walls. The stone flowed up to shape windows and arches, the transition so seamless she thought to see water-like ripples cross the surface when wind stirred the living leaves to brush their stone twins.

"The interior is even more beautiful," Taniel said.

Shirin no longer harbored doubt of Taniel finding aid here. If earth and stone could be molded into this miracle, surely someone within the walls could mold him back to what he was supposed to be.

"Thank you for seeing us here, Jirair," Taniel said.

"For what it's worth, Sushan, I'm glad to know you survived." He saluted in farewell. "Gods know we need souls like yours in these times."

The guard's departure revealed how quiet the Arcanum was and trickles of unease dampened Shirin's wonderment. No birds sang from the trees. No voices carried from the impossibly smooth walls. Not even the leaves whispered beneath the soft wind. Shirin's skin prickled; a watching presence lurked within that unnatural quiet.

Taniel sensed it better than she, turning to the source. A woman stood by the lilac tree behind them. Shirin was sure she had not been there a moment ago when they walked by, yet the woman's posture was one of someone who'd been awaiting expected guests. Her hands were hidden in the folds of her ink blue robes, and her eyes were so pale there was little distinction between iris and sclera. Taniel held steady under her gaze. Shirin lacked his calm. She drew back in want to flee when the colorless eyes found hers. The woman stared at her far longer than she had Taniel. Shirin shivered, feeling as if she was being laid bare, the woman seeing her every secret and shame as clearly as Shirin saw her. The woman returning her attention to Taniel was like a weight being lifted from her chest.

"You've changed, Sushan," the woman said. Her soft voice rasped at the edges like grating stone.

"And I come here seeking to change again," he said. "Shirin, this is Mage Najwa, Seneschal of the Arcanum."

Shirin never saw the woman move. One moment she stood beneath the tree, then in the space of a blink, she was leading the way to the Arcanum gates swinging open before her on their own accord. Out from the trees' shade, Shirin saw the woman's skin color was not a trick of the light—it was the same pale, sandy yellow of the stone. Shirin held back a second shudder. The woman looked more like a moving statue than a creature of flesh and blood.

"Come." Mage Najwa gestured they follow her through the gates. "You won't find what you seek here, but you'll find where the way begins. You have far to go, Sushan, and you"—Shirin braced herself under the white-eyed gaze—"cannot go anywhere until you clear the way."

The somber hush at the Arcanum's entrance pervaded its halls. There was a terrible sense of emptiness, and the wide, cavernous passageways made Shirin feel like a mouse lost in a tomb. The vaulted ceilings were hungry for the slightest noise to feed from, catching their every step, the shift of Taniel's cloak, the clunk of his walking stick. The sandstone halls echoed their movements in a hissing murmur eerily similar to whispers.

"This way, Sushan," Mage Najwa called without looking back to see Taniel turn toward a branching corridor.

He paused. "But the Healer's Ward is this—"

"This way, Sushan," she repeated. "You are not alone in having changed of late."

Taniel stared into the corridor he'd been about to walk down. They had all stopped, and Shirin stiffened when the echoes she assumed were stirred by their footsteps continued. Voices whispered in excited hums, angry hisses, and low moans. Some hushed for quiet. Others begged to be heard. One called Shirin by name, coaxing her to come into the branching corridor.

Taniel caught her arm, stopping her from answering the summons. His touch snapped her free from the spell and she skittered behind him. She felt the voice reaching for her, an unseen hand seeking to pull her into the shadowy hall smelling of blood and a dizzying sweetness that confused the common sense warning her away.

"What happened down there?" Taniel asked.

"A mage erred in his zeal to banish the Red Plague," Mage Najwa said. "That whole wing is now inaccessible. Stay close. Walk only where I show you."

"Where are the rest of the mages and acolytes?" Taniel asked.

"Sorcery had no power to stop Minu's curse," Mage Najwa said. "Those who wielded it were reaped as readily as the rest. Too few of us survived to sit idly in these halls."

Taniel released Shirin's arm once a hallway separated them from the ominous wing. She kept a grip on his cloak, seeking the reassuring hold of something tangible. Double doors beneath a flowering arch opened in deference to Mage Najwa's approach.

"The High Mage is away, but is due to return soon." She motioned Taniel forward. "Wait here, Sushan. He will come for you."

Taniel limped into the room. The woman held up a hand to stop Shirin from following.

"What you seek is not here," she said. "Come."

Shirin stayed where she was.

"Go ahead," Taniel said. "Do as Mage Najwa instructs." The doors closed between them, and their echoing *boom* silenced her protest she stay beside him.

"Your heart is dark," Mage Najwa said.

"My heart is gone." Shirin bristled. She disliked the woman and the Arcanum. The strangeness of the halls stripped away their beauty; the impossible stone work of the whispering corridors inspired more fear than her initial awe. She looked to the doors Taniel had disappeared behind. "Will he be alright?"

"I worry for him," Mage Najwa said.

Shirin struggled to attribute true emotion to the mage. Her cold eyes, stone-colored skin, and distant manner removed her from the humanity necessary for compassion.

"His fate rests in others," Mage Najwa said. "Your fate, however, that is entirely upon you."

She showed Shirin to a room that looked like it had once served as a dormitory. Narrow beds rested in each of the four corners, accompanied by a small desk and chair. Orb lamps hung from the ceiling and the tall, arched windows overlooked a fountain courtyard.

Mage Najwa opened a desk drawer to pull out a leaf of paper. "You and Sushan may stay here until your paths lead you elsewhere. Do you have a needle or knife?"

Shirin took out a sewing needle from her pack, wary of the question.

"Prick your finger and write out his name," the mage said.

"Taniel's name?"

"No. Your husband's."

Shirin stared, torn between fury and fear at this woman who so readily knew things she had no right to.

"I know every step set upon, every heartbeat within, witnessed every dream and felt every breath that touches the Arcanum stone. There is little here that is hidden from me," Mage Najwa said. "But I cannot find your husband for you."

"Can you tell me where he is?" Shirin asked.

"No. I can only show you where to go." She tapped a slender finger to the paper. "Write his name when you're ready and follow where it leads."

"Follow it where?"

"I don't know. I cannot see beyond the walls." She placed a second sheet of paper on the desk bearing a triangular seal surrounded by spiraling inscriptions. "Take this with you. It will allow you to move unbothered through the city and return here. If you wish to go elsewhere in the Arcanum, speak my name; I will guide you. The Reaping awakened ancient magics displeased to be disturbed. I have not yet tamed them back to rest. No need to raise your voice when you call. I'll hear you."

The lantern orbs flickered, and with the sound of a loose stone being slid into place, the mage was gone.

Shirin picked up the blank paper. Caution warned her not to dabble in unnatural powers in strange places where hidden voices beckoned her from halls reeking of old blood, or to heed the advice of women who looked more like stone than flesh. Anger and curiosity burned through that caution. The needle pricked sharp into her finger and she wrote "Esref Basak" in blood on the paper.

For a long minute, nothing happened. Then her chest burned. Memories of her husband embittered by his betrayal flashed before her. The paper bearing his bloody name smoked as if flames licked beneath it, blackening and curling into a glowing ember, pulsing red-tinged light.

The ember flickered, and reappeared in the hallway, bobbing in unquestionable invitation for Shirin to follow.

11
All That Was Lost

Wrought iron lanterns hung from the finely tiled mosaic ceiling. Ornate shelves overfilled by books and scrolls lined the walls, and brocade rugs covered the ivory stone floors of the High Mage's study. The architectural artistry, mahogany furniture, and paintings depicting scenes of myth and lore were wasted in a room where the occupant spent his days with his nose buried in the musty pages of old texts, oblivious to the surrounding splendor.

Alone in the study, the absolute stillness possessing the Arcanum became more stifling than the cloak Taniel hid beneath. On his previous visits to the Arcanum when asking a mage's aid for a purging requiring sorcery, having his warding tattoos redone, or simply visiting Sahak and Razban, the halls had brimmed with life. Students, petitioners, and travelers curious to see the seat of the mages filled the corridors. Novices strained under the weight of the tomes they carried, mages discussed theories among their fellows in open atriums, and supplicants waited in vestibules to be received. The tomb-like emptiness of the once bustling halls was another depressing reminder of what had been lost.

Taniel's sigh whispered too long through the study; the Arcanum starved for life to fill the quiet void. He fumbled his way out of his Karvogi cloak and mask, wincing as his shoulder popped and neck clicked. Much as he hated to be seen, it was inevitable if the master mage was to understand the extent of Minu's ruining. If Taniel wanted to be rid of her curse, there was no hiding the ill-magic from those meant to help him free of it.

Joints creaking, he carefully lowered himself into a cushioned, high-backed chair. He felt his exhaustion more acutely in the Arcanum's somber quiet, needling his eyes and turning his limbs heavy. It really was unfair how he was so tired yet sleep remained so difficult for him to find.

The heavy oak doors groaned open and a man wearing the robes of a master mage rushed in.

"Sahak?" Taniel stared, caught off guard by the familiar face.

His friend sucked in a startled breath, his eyes flitting from horns, to clawed hands, to crippled limbs. "Gods damn, Taniel, is that really you?"

Mage Najwa must have sent word to him of Taniel's return. His robes were askew, hair mussed, and face brightly flushed as if he had run here.

"Unfortunately." Taniel turned away. He had braced himself for the disgusted greeting of a stranger, not pity from a friend. He tensed when Sahak strode over and touched his neck, reading his pulse as Taniel felt the thrum of magic unfurling from Sahak's fingers. "Don't—"

"Hush," Sahak said, sounding like he had all those times he'd checked Taniel's tattoos to be sure the warding held. "I'm trying to figure out what in hells happened to you."

Taniel quieted, unable to suppress the involuntary shudder as Sahak's magic explored his brokenness.

Sahak's lips thinned and he shook out his hand as if touching Taniel had sullied him. "By the gods, what did you do to yourself?"

"It's a long story," Taniel said, "and I'd prefer not to repeat it too often. Is the High Mage coming?"

"He's here."

"You?" Taniel had not meant to sound so incredulous, but even Mage Najwa, bound as she was to the Arcanum grounds, was a better choice than Sahak Sandar.

"Unfortunately." He showed no offense to Taniel's less than celebratory reaction. "And now I share in what you endured, drowning in accusations of nepotism. Unlike you, my accusations are deserved. My father was never one to let a tragedy go to waste. He's seeing all his relations put in positions of power, using the Reaping as the means to build his divine empire upon a field of corpses."

"Where's Nesrin?" Taniel asked, more interested in his wife's well-being than the rise and fall of civilization.

"I moved her to my family home."

"And Suri's with her?"

"Suri didn't survive. I'm sorry."

The news was a blow to Taniel. To Nesrin, it must have been devastating.

"Bad tidings and mourning the dead can wait. Tell me what happened so I can lift that curse from you." Sahak opened a drawer of the mahogany desk and pulled out a bottle of pomace brandy, pouring two generous glasses. "Long stories should never be told dry."

Taniel shook his head at the offered glass. He already felt sick and lightheaded. "Thank you, but it'd be wasted on me. I'm more likely to drop the glass than drink it. What happened to Master Maqlu? Did Razban and Dua leave with him?"

"Are you asking because you think your condition is beyond my skill to heal?"

While Taniel appreciated his friend's teasing tone, he was too weary to engage in banter. That must have shown as Sahak's expression sobered.

"You're right to think so." He placed the second glass of brandy beside Taniel despite his declining. "I've never had much skill for healing or curses, and we've lost the best of those who did. Master Maqlu was not the only mage who left to seek answers in the east. He thought a cure was to be found in the Grey Forest. It's as good a theory as any; I hear the villages closest there were spared the Reaping entirely. Other mages, braver or stupider than he, went farther east into the Wastes. I prayed some would return by now. None have." He swirled his glass, shaking his head. "Old habits die hard. Here you are back from the dead, and already I'm talking your ear off about my problems when yours are far greater. What happened to you?"

Taniel told him about the evil Minu had created in the marsh outside Chahich, what she had done to the world, and what she had done to him. He tripped and stumbled through the story, throat catching, hands gripping the armchair to steady his shaking. Sahak listened, mouth grim and fingers steepled. At the end he ran a hand over his shadowed chin, staring out the arched windows at the world so terribly changed. While the last year and a half had been kinder to him than Taniel, he looked older than the eighteen months should have aged him.

"Did Razban and Dua leave with Master Maqlu?" Taniel asked again.

Sahak nodded. "I heard from Razban once. They'd reached Agr Rav. That was well over a year ago and I've heard nothing since."

"What of Mage Banu?" Taniel asked.

"She died in the Reaping. Her apprentices as well. There's no one west of Agr Rav I can recommend in confidence of having the skill to cure you."

"I doubt even Master Maqlu has the power for a cure. I seek only relief, not rescue from my condition." Taniel felt as trapped as he had in Minu's manor. No matter where he ran or how far, he'd never fully escape her.

"Don't despair yet," Sahak said. "There are still Healers in the Arcanum, and I know hedgewitches in Gohar of rival talent. They can help you."

Taniel nodded, in acceptance of Mage Najwa's words, not Sahak's well-intended placations. What he sought was not here, it was only where his path began.

"Do you ... should I send for Nesrin?" Sahak asked.

Taniel's claws pierced the cushioning he gripped the chair so tightly. He wanted to see her as much as he feared her seeing him like this.

"No." He wanted to return to her as her husband, not a dark witch's failed creation. "Not yet."

As a child, Shirin had been told stories of young, foolish maidens who followed dancing lights. They were lured into twilight forests by demons or dark witches, never to be seen again. She was too old—and far too removed from maidenhood—to earn interest from the villains of those tales, but she certainly felt foolish following the flickering ember.

The light led her down cobblestone streets sloping away from the Arcanum until the high towers were lost behind tenements and dark-windowed shops. Whenever she drew close to where the ember waited for her, it vanished. She'd have to pause, turning on the spot to find it hovering beneath a lamp farther along the way, circling low over the cobblestones, or glowing above clay shingles. A city guard stopped her as she searched for the light's new location, curious as to why she spun in slow circles in the middle of the street. Showing him the paper bearing the Arcanum seal ended his questioning. He wanted no business in sorcery.

Coming to a street rowed by narrow homes, Shirin found the light bobbing in front of a door decorated by Naru's knot. Her heart lodged in her throat. A similar carving of the water dragon twining around a lotus flower had hung over her door in the northern coastal village. A pang of homesickness brought back the scent of the sea, her children's laughter, and the warm trust she'd placed in her husband. Anger replaced her foolish longing for what had been. That life had been stolen from her by the Reaping, and desecrated by the man who'd left his family to die.

She rapped her fist on the door, ready to do the same to her husband's head. Resentment blinded her to anything beyond that want, so she was caught off guard when it was not the wretched man she'd married who opened the door, but a woman in her early thirties. Her skin was a fair olive—pale compared to Shirin's earthy tone—and her hair woven into a neat braid was a rich chestnut brown, similar to what Shirin's had been before the frosts of winter years brought streaks of grey.

"Hello." The woman's slight frame emphasized her swelling stomach, at least five months pregnant. "May I help you?"

"My name is Izel Basak." Shirin forced her expression to stay neutral as her anger flashed hot then dropped dangerously cold. She guessed the father of the expected child and knew he was no father at all. "I'm looking for my cousin, Esref Basak."

The woman's eyes went wide and her hand fluttered to her mouth. She really was a pale, fragile thing.

"Oh, but of course! Come in, come in!" She took Shirin's hands as if they were lifelong friends, leading her into the small sitting room adjacent to a kitchen. "He's at work, but he'll be so happy to see you when he comes home!"

I sincerely doubt that, Shirin thought darkly.

"Are you married to him?" she asked, noting the ring on the woman's finger.

"Six months ago," she said. "My name is Ajda."

Shirin offered no congratulations, trapped between rue and rage at the woman who was so pleased to be married to a lying coward.

"Would you like tea? Coffee? We have jam and butter if you'd like toast."

"No, thank you," Shirin said. The taste of ash filled her mouth. Esref had left her, abandoned his children to die and be thrown into mass, unmarked graves, then gone off to find a younger woman to start over. Shirin and his children had been less than nothing to him.

Ajda prepared tea for two anyway. "Esref will be delighted to see you. He heard all his family died in the Reaping."

I'm sure that's what he told you, Shirin thought.

Ajda's smile faltered when she looked up from the kettle and saw her expression. "Are you alright?"

Her innocent sincerity moved Shirin from anger to sour pity. Ajda didn't know the man she'd married. She probably thought him another tortured soul who'd lost everything under the dark curse.

"I'm tired," Shirin said. "It was a long journey getting here."

And now that she was here, she wasn't sure what to do. She had imagined arriving in Gohar and finding where her coward of a husband hid. He would answer the door when she knocked, and whether she slapped him across the face, dragged him out to expose him as the wretch he was, or forced him to name the children he'd abandoned depended on her mood. She had expected to find hostility, denial, or indifference when she tracked her husband down. Ajda's kindness upset all her preparations.

Shirin sat on the floor sofa at Ajda's insistence and mumbled a cool thanks for the tea. Ajda sat carefully on the cushion across from her, graceful movement complicated at her stage of pregnancy.

"Tell me about Esref," Shirin said. "How has he been?"

"Better than he was when we first married. He carries his losses closer than most." Her hand drifted to rest on her stomach. "I lost both my children and husband in the plague. Did ... did you ..."

"All my children died," Shirin said bluntly, "and my husband abandoned us on our deathbeds."

"I'm sorry. I don't know if you heard, Esref's wife and children died as well. He came to Gohar to seek help. There were rumors Master Maqlu knew of a way to drive off the curse. When he found out it was false, he tried to return home, but the city forbade all travel the day after he arrived. They wouldn't allow him to leave and when the city guard caught him attempting to flee, he only escaped caning because they needed every able-bodied man to build the wall. He spent months scouring every report and paper for word of his family, only to learn his entire village had been wiped out."

Of the two hundred souls in her village, Shirin only knew of six others who survived the Reaping. None had stayed. They had all scattered in search of loved ones. It would've been easy for an outsider to assume all had perished when homes were found empty and mass graves filled.

"He told you this?" Shirin asked.

"He keeps the announcement in the memorial altar." Ajda gestured to the small black cabinet beneath the window. Fresh flower petals lay before the memorial and the room smelled faintly of the incense sticks on either side, burned not too long ago.

The floor beneath Shirin swayed like a ship's unsteady deck. The want for justice, a cold fire that had been a light in her darkest hours, sputtered feebly under Ajda's tale. Shirin didn't want to believe her, unable to let go the hate that had sustained her for over a year. Holding on to her anger was easier than facing renewed grief.

"Izel, are you alright?" Ajda asked.

"I'm sorry," Shirin said. "I was thinking on the past."

The younger woman leaned forward to take her hand. "Esref will be happy to see you."

Shirin doubted that, no longer for the same reasons she had.

"Excuse me for a moment," Ajda said, retreating from the room with the careful step of a pregnant woman doing her best not to upset the delicate balance of a baby weighing on her bladder.

Shirin waited to hear the door close before going over to the memorial altar. She couldn't believe Ajda. Not unless she saw the reports for herself in the shrine. Sunlight gleamed on the cabinet's glossy black surface. Opening the narrow doors, she hardly recognized the woman in the photograph pinned to the top of the interior wood. It was from her wedding, twenty-five years ago; her face free from lines of worry, her body slender before giving birth to five children, her hair thick and dark. Five small carvings—a dove, a lily, an infinity knot, a fawn, and a four-pointed leaf—rested on the cabinet's base in place of images or their children's personal effects. She immediately knew which carving belonged to what child, their personalities reflected in each one. Slipping out the folded papers beneath the carvings, she read over the prayer for the dead and the newspaper clipping listing her and the children's names under those claimed by the curse.

The cold fire in her chest died, having nothing left to feed from once loss replaced her fury. She felt frail and empty, the truth hollowing instead of liberating. She had dwelled on the dead and harbored hate while her husband had grieved and sought to create a new life. Esref hadn't abandoned his family. Nonetheless, fate had worked against them.

She picked up the carvings memorializing her children, wishing to truly hold them again one last time. Her path had been so clear, paved by blameless anger, and now the way had crumbled to dust, leaving her lost and unsure of how to move forward. Should she return from death to reunite with her husband?

She returned the carvings to the shrine. Revealing herself to her husband achieved no good. It only punished him to be haunted by a ghost struggling to forgive him sins he had not committed. There was no point in reopening his old wounds simply because she had allowed hers to fester. Especially when she knew she would not stay. Not in Gohar, and not with him. She had been taught in the cruelest fashion how to recognize where she had no home. She'd left her village offering nothing besides grief, and grief was all she had to offer Esref. He was as lost to her now as their little ones almost two years dead.

Shirin closed the memorial cabinet in farewell to the life she must let go. Esref had behaved with as much virtue as tragedy allowed and been given the chance of a new life. She wouldn't ruin that for him. Let her be a memory to be grieved, not a specter forever hanging over him.

Wiping away tears, she reclaimed her coat, and left the home she had no place in. The red-tinged ember waited for her, flickering, then reappearing in the direction of the Arcanum.

"Gods guide you, and Seraphs hold you safe," Shirin murmured to her lost husband, her stolen life, and walked away.

12
Won't You Let Me In?

Taniel lay on the bed, his arm resting over his closed eyes to shield him from the lantern light aggravating his drumming headache, too tired to get up to dim or blow the flame out.

The tincture Sahak had provided him trimmed the edges off the pain but failed to reach its roots. The three healer mages Sahak summoned had been equally unable to help him. The first one lasted an hour before shaking his head, saying he dared not meddle in magic so beyond his comprehension. At least he'd been able to heal Taniel's leg wound, closing the gash into a thin scar. The second mage had muttered enchantments that made Taniel's nose bleed. He promised to study the blood samples he took, warning Taniel he expected little to come of it. Like the first, he admitted what Taniel suffered was well beyond his power.

"It's a miracle you're alive," he had said, "and I fear attempting to undo that curse will undo that miracle as well."

The third mage had been more willing to test the bounds of Minu's magic in search of a weak point to unravel the curse. Her sorcery shot needles through Taniel's arms and legs. She pushed further and the needles turned to knives, setting every nerve ablaze and violently plunging him into black agony.

By the time Taniel regained consciousness, it was late evening. The mage had left after making her apologies and an offer to return tomorrow to try gentler approaches. Taniel told Sahak to thank the mage and decline a second visit.

The soft knocking on the dormitory door felt like someone slammed a hammer repeatedly into his skull.

"I told you, I don't want dinner," Taniel said. His stomach heaved at the thought of food.

"May I at least come in?" Shirin asked from the hall.

Ignoring the sharp pangs punishing him for moving, Taniel stood to open the door.

"Sorry, I thought you were Sahak," he said, allowing her to help him hobble back to the bed.

She sat on the bed across from him, a bowl of minced pork over ginger rice and a flask of wine held in hand. "He did tell me I should try to get you to eat."

"Maybe later. Where did you go?"

"I found my husband."

Taniel stiffened, unsure of what to say or do. Shirin's tone was flatly matter-of-fact, as if she'd done nothing greater than attend a small, tedious task.

"Is he ... did he ... are you alright?" he asked.

"I will be," Shirin said, and told him how she'd found where her husband lived, met his new wife, learned how he hadn't abandoned his family as she had believed.

"In a way it's worse," she said at the end of the tale. "If he had left me, I could hate him. I could be angry at him instead of sorry for myself."

"What are you going to do?"

"Move on. As he did."

"That's it? But you didn't even see or speak to him!"

"What good comes from that? He's allowed his wounds to heal, I'd only reopen them," Shirin said. "He's built a new life. He has a wife who cares for him and a coming child. I could only steal his happiness as the Reaping stole mine."

"He has a right to know you're alive."

"I'm not the woman he married. She died in the Reaping when I let hate he had not earned destroy the love I promised him. But my heart is not so blackened I'll burden him under more hardship." Her smile was forced. "Some sacrifices must be done in secret."

Taniel ran a hand over his horns. The hardship Shirin's return threatened to bring her husband was nothing compared to what Taniel's would thrust upon Nesrin. If Shirin was no longer the woman her husband had married, Taniel was certainly no longer the man Nesrin promised herself to. He wasn't even a man anymore. He was just another one of Minu's broken monsters.

"He found a life here and I know mine is to be found elsewhere." Shirin handed him the bowl of rice. "Now eat, Taniel, before it gets cold."

The hard clack of Taniel's walking stick on cobblestone announced his approach, echoing unimpeded through the quieted Gohar. At this afternoon hour, the streets ought to be filled with businessmen on café patios negotiating over coffee, women carrying the groceries for supper, and children released from school avoiding the chores awaiting them at home. Eighteen months ago, Taniel would have been swallowed by the city's bustle, his noisy step unheard, his strange Karvogi appearance earning little more than a second glance. Now, he drew the attention of every surviving eye. The woman beating carpets hung over her front rail, the man pulling a cart of potatoes, the city guards on the street corner, all looked up at the uneven clack-and-scuff of his shambling gait. The faces of Gohar's denizens were thin, their eyes weary windows to exhausted souls. He felt their stares tracking him as he passed, and was grateful to be hidden beneath his cloak and mask. No one gasped in revulsion as the Arcanum's mages had done yesterday. No one recoiled in disgust like the hedgewitches Sahak had summoned this morning. Dressed as a Karvogi, Taniel was nothing more than a passing curiosity.

The guards at the wall dividing Gohar from the abandoned northwestern district let him through unchallenged. Bad luck befell men who stood between a Karvogi and where his wanderings took him; and what better place for a spirit-chaser to be led than the ghost town beyond the wall?

Taniel knew the guards would be less willing to allow his return to the walled-in city. Bad luck as it was to stand between a Karvogi and his wanderings, it was worse to invite strange and unknown things over thresholds. The letter he carried bearing the Arcanum's seal and the Sandar family sigil provided his right of return passage unearned by his Karvogi mask.

Sahak had been reluctant to supply the papers, unhappy at the idea of Taniel leaving the Arcanum and fully against his venturing outside the walls. He did his best to dissuade Taniel from going and failed miserably. The ache to see home was too strong, one Taniel had the power to soothe, and revisiting the past had a way of revealing the best path forward.

Shirin deciding to remain dead to her husband called Taniel to confront a painfully similar choice. There was no cure for him in

Gohar, and he had no guarantee of finding one elsewhere. The only certainty he had was a life of limping days, and pain-riddled nights. He'd not wish his existence on anyone and it was certainly a life unworthy to share with Nesrin. Was it better if he remained dead to his wife like Shirin had for her husband? Or should he tell Nesrin he had survived and beg her to wait for his true return, not this monstrous mockery of homecoming?

He turned onto a street he had walked a thousand times before. The memories of days past and gone pierced him to the soul. He'd thought to find the strength to face what he must do by seeing his home once more—another hope proven false. He found no solace in the familiar sight, only a longing for what was lost. The shops below the apartments were boarded, the wood faded and weathered, and the dark windows to his and Nesrin's small flat were lifeless.

Jealousy poisoned Taniel's gratitude for Sahak taking Nesrin into his home. In weaker moments, he wished Sahak had not come for her at all. He hated the thought of Sahak comforting her, being there when Taniel had not. He clenched his hands into shaking fists, sending a sharp twinge shooting through his arm. Guilt cooled the envy spoiling in his chest; even before the Reaping he had been unforgivably absent, constantly leaving Nesrin with only frail promises he'd return. He'd provided her a meager life in a small, shabby apartment, a husband who was rarely home, and now even those pitiful offerings were beyond him.

The door to the narrow stairwell leading up to the residences creaked in welcome for his overdue return. Dust motes drifted in the tired sunlight slanting through the small windows at each landing. Taniel had carried Nesrin up these stairs the day they wed—their celebration overshadowed by his father's open disapproval of the marriage. Taniel had bounded up the steps two at a time the night he returned three weeks late from a job. Heavy rains had drowned the roads, turning them impassable and prevented his sending word of the delay to Nesrin from the rural village he'd been stuck at. He had called her name the moment he stepped into the stairwell, mud coating him from boots to waist. The roses he'd bought outside the train station were an apology for his being so late. Nesrin nearly toppled them both down the steps rushing out to meet him. Her tears held no anger, only relief.

The jobs preceding those moments were vague impressions of long weeks spent tracking monsters, tedious stakeouts, and the discomforts of difficult travel; hardly thrilling tales of adventure worth remembering to recount. But his homecomings he recalled in crisp clarity, and it was those gentler moments his heart yearned for.

Taniel paused at the door to their flat, imagining he was returning to that life, not a ghost visiting a grave. He would smell dumplings cooking, hear Nesrin and Suri talking in their native tongue, bickering, laughing, or a cross between the two. The door would squeak as it always did when opened. Nesrin would teasingly scold him for being late and almost missing dinner. He'd cut her off with a kiss, finding unspeakable bliss in how she smelled of roses and freshly baked bread.

Taniel pushed open the door. It squeaked as it always had, but instead of the familiar scents of home, he smelled dusty decay. The apartment was empty of laughter and the hiss of food cooking on the wood stove. There was only the soft sigh of stagnant air disturbed by his stepping over the threshold.

Everything was as he remembered, and yet impossibly changed. The furniture of the small living space that served as dining and sitting room was where it had always been; the table and floor sofa decorated by white coverings banded by stripes of gold, red, and green. Both Nesrin and Suri loved vibrant color, collecting painted pottery, wicker weavings, and drapings to hang across the ceiling to decorate the otherwise drab, economical flat. He felt a wrenching pang of loss for Suri, seeing the patches on the floor sofa she had stitched the week before he left for Chahich.

Dust collected on the narrow galley kitchen's counters connecting the living space and the small bedroom. The pantries had been raided, all edible contents gone while their few valuables had been bypassed. A fallen tea cup lay shattered on the floor, chipped dishes were strewn across the counter, the flower vase toppled and cracked. Taniel gathered the overlooked possessions that had the greatest value to him—a photograph of him and Nesrin from their wedding day, a handful of talismans spared from looters by his hiding them beneath a loose brick in the fireplace.

A stair creaked and a second groaned under ascending footsteps indifferent to being heard. Taniel edged into the kitchen, out of sight from the open door and landing, to wait for the intruder to pass. Most likely it was a vagrant moved in to one of the hundreds of empty homes or a tenant who'd refused to move out when ordered.

Untamed magic raked over Taniel. Fear froze the breath in his chest. In Shabrin, he'd been uncertain of what the strange presence he'd sensed in the town square was. Now, there was no mistaking the chaos Kharinah carried, nor her desire for Taniel to know she was coming. The demon-child moved silent as a spirit's shade when she wished. The only reason he heard her was because she wanted him to.

His shuffling gait was damnably loud as he hurried to the bedroom. He had no chance of fleeing. There was only one way out of the flats and Kharinah blocked his escape. Hiding was little better an option but the only one available. The bed lay too low to the floor to slide beneath, leaving him the closet. The door hung open from long-gone looters, the contents strewn across the floor in a mess Nesrin never would have tolerated. Taniel slipped into the small closet, leaving the door partially open and arranging linens to hide his shape beneath the musty folds.

If the gods took mercy on him, the wards he had painted above the door and the natural barrier of a threshold had the strength to keep Kharinah at bay.

The demon-child hummed "Won't You Let Me In" as she ascended, turning the mournful tune into a chilling taunt. Taniel jumped at the sharp crack of his apartment's front door being slammed into the wall. Her humming swelled to singing, her voice deceptively gentle with undeserved beauty.

"My feet are frozen and hands are ice in this cold and bitter wind. I'm knocking at the door, won't you let me in?"

Taniel felt the wards of his home shudder and fail beneath Kharinah's corrupting presence. He covered his mouth to muffle his breathing, gritting his teeth as his muscles ached to spasm from the stress of lying absolutely still. If Kharinah's search of the flat was partial—her mood one of impatience prone to boredom—he might escape detection. But the longer she lingered the more likely he'd reveal himself through an involuntary tremor.

"The night is cold, the grave lonely, and the dark road has no end. I'm waiting at the window, won't you let me in?"

Taniel's leg trembled. He dared not move to steady it, desperately praying the twitching not worsen.

"The door trembles, windows shake, the winter storm is no friend. I'm coming back to you, my love, won't you let me in?"

Ceramic shattered in the kitchen. He imagined Kharinah picking up dishes then letting them go to smash to the floor. Aimless destruction had irresistible appeal to her.

She resumed her humming. Taniel heard claws tapping on the bedroom door, then the violative hush of her crossing another threshold. He felt her presence defile every corner of his home. Terror tied his muscles tight. Spasms shook his spine. He couldn't hold still much longer; his snarled nerves wouldn't allow it. He needed to move to relieve the wildfire raging in his joints. The light filtering through the linen he hid beneath darkened as Kharinah passed between him and the window. He held his breath, certain she heard his hammering heart, saw the shaking spread from his legs to wrack his entire body.

Wooden drawers opened, the floor creaked, and cloth rustled as Kharinah rifled through his bedroom. Icy needles splintered through his left side. His arm twitched violently. Hiding had been a child's wish; Kharinah knew he was here. She knew she had him cornered. She had to hear his shaking, smell his fear, sense his struggle to hold still mere feet away. She was seconds from finding him, and when she did, his fate hinged upon which madness gripped her. One madness ended in his death, the other delivered him to Minu for a worse fate.

Taniel tensed to fight. He wasn't going back. He'd rather die than suffer another hour as Minu's plaything. He wished he'd thought to grab a knife or weapon from the kitchen, and was ready to use horns, teeth, and mangled hands, all the while knowing how his struggle against Kharinah was fated to end.

The flat fell into a sudden quiet—no humming, no sinister step, not even the unpleasant chill of Kharinah's presence shadowed his home. Taniel remained hidden, distrusting the silence. Terrified seconds stretched into minutes. The pain cramping his legs went beyond tolerance. He moved, wincing at the pop of angry joints, bracing for the demon-child's attack. None came. Taniel lifted the linen, clumsily rising to his feet. The apartment was empty. If not for the drawers in the dresser left open, the kitchen floor littered by broken cups and plates, he could almost convince himself Kharinah had never come and it had all been a waking nightmare.

Taniel's throat went dry, seeing the Karvogi walking stick where he'd left it by the front door, impossible for Kharinah even at her most unstable to have missed. She'd known he was here.

So why had she left him?

Grabbing the walking stick, he hobbled down the stairs to the street. Fast as his broken gait allowed, he fled to the protection of the city wall, certain he'd see golden eyes glint in the shadows stretched over alleyways. He wasted no time pondering Kharinah's intentions. He knew them to be malicious. More importantly, he knew what he must do. Minu had wholly tainted him and he'd bring neither his curse, nor lead the demon-child hunting him to Nesrin. The witch and her daughter had taken everything else from him. They would not take his wife. Night was too near in the eastern sky for travel, but as soon as the sun rose, he was resolved to be gone from Gohar.

"What are you doing?" Sahak stood in the Arcanum dormitory's doorway, arms crossed.

"Packing," Taniel said, taking stock of his and Shirin's supplies for the journey. Shirin had made it abundantly clear that if he attempted to slip away without her, she'd exact the vengeance upon him she had reserved for her husband when she thought him a contemptible coward.

"And why are you packing?" Sahak asked.

"Because I'm going to Grey Forest."

"Like hells you are. You can hardly walk to the door and back. How are you going to make it to the Grey Forest?"

"One limping step at a time."

"Taniel, there are other treatments to try," Sahak said. "This will take time."

"Mage Najwa says what I seek is not here. Master Maqlu and the best of the healer mages went east, and so will I." That Mage Najwa had been waiting for Taniel upon his return from the northern district to the Arcanum—a Purger's knife and protective talismans in hand for him to take—was a reminder of what she'd told him when he first arrived. What he sought was far beyond the safety of the Arcanum and her warded city.

Sahak dragged a hand through his hair, light catching on the silver flecks hidden in the black. He looked more like his father than the young man Taniel remembered.

"You walk out of Gohar, you walk into your own grave," Sahak said.

"I managed to get here just fine," Taniel said.

"Not from what I see."

The words cut deeper than they had right to. Taniel turned away, a pointless gesture as there was no part of him free from disfigurement.

"Forgive me, that was unworthy," Sahak muttered. "But the world isn't what it was, and neither are you. The Reaping loosed more than disease. Monsters outnumber men. You won't get ten miles before a ghoul kills you and sucks the marrow from your bones."

"I'm far from inexperienced in dealing with the darker beings of this world," Taniel said.

"You're far from fit to face them."

"On the contrary, I'm more fit than ever to walk among monsters. They'll never expect one of their own to turn on them."

"Don't be an idiot."

"I'd be an idiot to stay. If there's a cure for my condition, it's not here."

"How would you know? You've been here for less than a week!"

"Mage Najwa says I'll not find what I seek here."

"That doesn't mean you should leave," Sahak said. "Taniel, please, see reason. I'll send word to surrounding towns, find other mages who can help you. Master Maqlu is gone, that doesn't mean there's nothing that can be done."

"Do you know of where he went along the Grey Forest?"

"No. I don't even know if he made it there or if he's alive. Which is all the more reason for you to stay and not chase after hopeful hearsay."

"There's nothing for me here," Taniel said. Minu's power was unrivaled, demanding more than the average mage to lessen her curse's hold upon him. Even if he failed to find Master Maqlu, the Grey Forest was a site of pilgrimage for mages and the magic-touched. There had to be someone in the east able to help him.

"Nothing for you here?" Sahak asked. "What about Nesrin?"

Taniel had asked Sahak to not tell Nesrin of his return, hoping to reunite with her when he was recognizable as the man she'd married. But the Arcanum mages' inability to so much as understand Minu's workings, Shirin's deciding to leave her husband to afford him a better life, Kharinah's hunting him, and the terrible truth that he was far from free of Minu forced Taniel to ask an even more difficult request of him.

"You said she's safe and well." Taniel felt as though someone else spoke through him. "I trust you to see she stays that way."

"You won't even go to her?"

"Would you go to your wife looking like this? No, she married a man, not a monster. I won't demand she suffer me."

Sahak shifted uncomfortably. "Are you sure?"

Taniel clenched his teeth. He long suspected Sahak carried more than feelings of chaste friendship for Nesrin, and Sahak's disquiet confirmed it. The remnants of who Taniel had been wanted to deck Sahak across the jaw, yet beneath the jealous anger was an awful voice whispering it was for the best. Nesrin would be looked after, protected, and—Taniel bit back the bitterness—she would be loved.

"See that she's taken care of." Taniel hated himself almost as much as he hated Sahak in that moment.

"When I took her into my home—"

"And is that all you've taken?"

Sahak flushed red. "She deserves more credit than you give her. She's waited for you this whole time."

Once, after too many drinks, Sahak had said Nesrin deserved better than to be married to a Purger. Taniel had laughed it off, pretended the comment was nothing more than drunken ribbing, but it had watered seeds of doubt that had come to bloom.

"Tell her you've received news," Taniel said, "confirming my death."

"You want me to lie to her?"

His careful tone infuriated Taniel. He gripped the Karvogi cloak tight to keep from lashing out.

"I want her to have a life," Taniel said. "Don't tell her until I'm a day gone. Please."

He saw the conflict on his friend's face. Sahak's mouth shaped a mute protest, then he nodded, the love he harbored for Nesrin winning out over his loyalty to Taniel.

"I'll see it done," he said.

"Thank you," Taniel said in place of succumbing to the inner rage eager to give Sahak a small taste of the pain he'd suffered.

"There's no hurry for you to leave until you're ready." Sahak had the decency to meet Taniel's eye. "Stay at the Arcanum as long as you choose. I'll tell Nesrin they found your body after you're gone."

13

Eastern Roads

Looking back at Gohar receding into the distance was an unfairly complicated task. Taniel had to turn his whole body to avoid sending flaring pain through his neck. The decision to leave without seeing Nesrin became no easier to bear the farther his home fell away. Leaving her was a greater agony than when Minu fused horns to his skull. Convincing himself he'd made the right choice to shield his wife from the evil hunting him was more difficult than his relearning to walk. But seeing Nesrin would have been selfish. In Gohar, ignorant of his survival, she was safe from witches, curses, and demon children. Sahak would look after her. The thought inflamed the ache in Taniel's chest, but Nesrin deserved a whole life, not a crippled, broken one with a crippled, broken husband.

He turned to look once more at Gohar before the city was lost behind hills transitioning from fields to woodlands. There was the chance Nesrin wouldn't remarry. She'd refuse Sahak, and in time, Taniel would find a cure allowing him to return to her. That naïve hope threatened to bring forth the tears his misery was too cold to inspire.

Let it go, he told himself. There was no miracle to remake him into anything worth loving. The best he might hope for was to walk free of a limp, or see from both his eyes without inviting in a blinding headache. *That life is lost to you and she should not suffer for it.*

"We could go back," Shirin said.

"What?" Taniel blinked hot tears from the corners of his eyes.

"Go back to Gohar," she said. "It's not too late to see your wife. She survived the plague. She's not lost to you."

"No. I'll not expose her to a curse, or the attentions of the witch who laid it."

"Gohar is warded, the Sandar family keeps her safe. Surely that's enough for you to at least speak to her."

Shirin didn't understand the strength of the evil pursuing him. Taniel had tried to explain the danger she put herself in traveling alongside him and she'd refused to hear it. In the end he'd relented, torn between gratitude for her loyalty, and fear it would cost Shirin her life. Though he had been unable to convince Shirin of the danger, he'd not draw evil's attention to Nesrin. Dark dreams had haunted him the previous night where his curse spread to his wife. Her flesh had corrupted under his touch, rotted skin melting off diseased flesh. Her bones had twisted when he tried to hold her, and he'd watched in helpless, horrified guilt as Kharinah silenced Nesrin's pain-maddened screams by devouring her.

"No." The words caught in Taniel's throat. "I'll not risk her life for my sake. She deserves better."

"She deserves to know her husband lives," Shirin said.

"As your husband deserved to know your fate? Or did you also hide your survival to spare him further suffering? Let Nesrin believe me dead so she may live."

"Esref moved on and built a new a life. I made myself hate him and can only ruin what he created. But a woman who waits over a year for a husband the world claims to be dead isn't going to be frightened away by a witch's curse."

"She waited for her husband. Not what I am now." His words came out harsher than he intended. "I'd rather have her remember me with some fondness than have her know the nightmare I've become."

They scarcely spoke more than two words the rest of the day, setting up camp in an abandoned shack nestled in an overgrown field. There was no shortage of empty farmhouses, mills, and shepherd huts to choose from for the night's rest, and Taniel preferred one removed from the road, less likely to be visited by opportunistic thieves and footpads.

He slid down the shack's wall to slow his collapse. They had retired sooner than he liked, but he had pressed himself longer than was wise. His legs twitched from exhaustion, the headache festering from his horns gripped his entire skull, and his left hand spasmed as he unpacked the balm Sahak had given him. Unsealing the vial, Taniel worked a liberal helping into his left wrist. The ointment burned then cooled, soothing pain's harshest edges. Rolling up his pants to apply the balm to his shaking lower legs, he resigned himself to an agonizingly slow journey. At least an hour of tomorrow's morning was to be wasted on him working loose stiff joints and warming snarled muscles before setting out.

He wished he had a balm for the mind as well, to ease his anxieties that there was no remedy to be found in the east, only more disappointments proving his efforts pointless. He had no confidence in his future; it was a bleak tapestry barely held together by fraying threads of hope and chance.

Shirin murmured a short, repeating prayer of thanks as she unpacked supplies to start a meal. Taniel had no prayers to offer the divine in their cruel indifference. The gods had not protected him. The Seraphs, their earthly messengers sent to guard and guide creation, had abandoned him, his father, Suri and the countless souls the Reaping had claimed. They allowed evil to run unchecked, suffering to thrive, and punished those who challenged the world's wretchedness.

"For the gifts of life you have bestowed, I give thanks," Shirin prayed. "May I strive—"

"Shirin?"

"Yes?"

"Thank you," he said. Her patient compassion deserved his gratitude more than the gods.

"For what?" she asked.

"You didn't have to do any of this. Know that whatever happens, I'm grateful."

She smiled and stayed his hand when he moved to help her. "I'll take care of dinner. You set the wards."

Taniel sat by the door to whittle runes into the wood. They held no power to banish mortal intruders, only spirits and creatures that prowled beyond the bounds of the natural world. He hoped those dark creatures would be what repelled predatory men in the night. Cutting a man's throat to steal his purse upon a less-traveled path was worth nothing if the robber found himself between a monster's fangs. Taniel carved more wardings into the floor at the door's threshold, similar to the runes that had guarded the entryway to his home. Unease knotted his stomach. Kharinah had so easily crossed those protections, breaking through the threshold's power like it was brittle glass. Leaving Nesrin was the right choice. If his heading east accomplished no more than drawing Minu's evil away from her, it was a journey worth taking.

As bitterly angry as Taniel was at the divine for abandoning him and the world, fear pushed him to a hollow faith, imploring protection for a more deserving soul.

Keep her safe. Please.

Sahak was suspiciously quiet at the dinner table. Usually, he asked after Nesrin's day. Tonight he avoided substantive conversation and gave vague, unsatisfactory answers when she asked where he'd been the last half week. The more she pressed, the more flustered he became, tripping over his words in his haste to change the subject.

Nesrin set her spoon down, her patience gone. "What you not saying?"

"What do you mean?" Sahak's voice went high like a child's caught red-handed in mischief. His talent for sorcery was a fortunate blessing. He was a terrible liar and would never have succeeded following his father's footsteps as a politician.

"You not want to say something, so you try to say nothing at all," Nesrin said. "What you not telling me?"

He stared into his soup as if hoping to read the lentils as a shaman did animal entrails to find an answer to satisfy her.

"You hear something about Taniel?" she guessed.

His silence was an undeniable "yes." If he'd heard nothing, he would have said so. His reluctance to speak, even if well-intended, fired her temper.

She rose from her chair, ready to pursue the wildest rumor for her husband's whereabouts. "What you hear? He alive?"

"Nesrin, please, sit—"

"I not sit until you tell me there is news for me to sit and listen for."

"I don't want to upset—"

"I already upset! Do you know if Taniel alive?"

"Yes, I know, now sit."

"He alive?"

"Sit down first."

She complied, perching at the chair's edge. "Where is he? He coming home? Or do I go to him? Where and when you hear word?"

"Taniel is ... he's ..." Sahak sighed, meeting her gaze for the first time this evening. "Taniel's alive."

Nesrin's breath caught, holding fast to the simple sentence she had waited over a year to hear. Taniel was alive. He was alive.

"But he's not coming back," Sahak finished.

"Then where is he? I go to him," she said.

Sahak shook his head, and Nesrin bristled at his pitying expression. She saw it whenever people spoke to her on serious matters, assuming her too ignorant, her Haeranji too broken, to understand.

"He's already gone. He won't be coming back," he said.

Nesrin stared, certain she had misunderstood. "He gone already? That mean ... that mean he was here?"

Sahak stuttered over the unintended slip. "I ... no, he was ... I mean ..."

"He here and not come to me?" She shot to her feet. "And you only tell me now?"

He stood as well, hands raised in panicked placation. "Nesrin, please, it's for the best."

"What for best? That he leave me? That you hide him from me?"

"He's not well. Something happened to him and—"

"If something happen I need know!" Despite her fury, there was always room for worry over Taniel. "What wrong with him?"

Sahak took hold of her arm to guide her to the table. "Please, sit and let me explain."

Nesrin dug her feet in, jerking her arm free. "You lie to me already, hide my husband from me, why I listen?"

"By all the Seraphs that protect us, I swear to speak only truth to you," he said.

"Then tell me why my husband return only to leave without me!"

"Because he's cursed. The Demon Witch cursed him, he survived, but he's not the man you married. Now sit and let me tell you."

Nesrin sat, hands gripping her skirt tight as he told her how Taniel had come to the Arcanum, what had happened after he and his fellow Purgers went to investigate the Fen Witch in Chahich, how her father-in-law had been killed and Taniel cursed. That her husband had escaped the dark witch's prison and returned in search of a cure for his condition. But there was none to be found, and a demon born of the dark witch pursued him.

"But he survive?" Nesrin asked to be sure she understood. "Taniel alive?"

"Yes, he ... no, not really," Sahak said. "He's alive, but he's not Taniel anymore."

"I no understand." Sahak wasn't making sense, and Nesrin's mind kept flitting between the joy of Taniel being alive, and the despair that he'd not come to her. She couldn't understand why he'd refused to see her, or why Sahak thought Taniel had done right by leaving her.

"The witch turned him into a monster," Sahak said. "He's deformed, broken, and he's gone to search for a way to escape the curse."

"So he hurt, but why he not come to me?"

"He doesn't want you to see what he's become."

"Well, he stupid."

"Nesrin, you didn't see him—"

"I know I not see him! That why I angry!"

"—he wanted to do you a mercy. You should follow your husband's wishes."

"If I follow his wishes, we both stupid."

"You don't understand. You wouldn't want to see him—"

"Yes, I do."

"For Seraph's sake! He can hardly walk, he has horns coming out his head, and he's right in admitting you deserve better!"

Nesrin was never caught not knowing what to say in her native tongue, a confidence lost in translation as she rarely knew how to say it in her second language. She struggled to find the words in her shallow grasp of Haeranji; the anger, grief, and hope went too deep.

"You saying for me to give up on him?" she asked.

"No, I'm saying … he wants you to … I want …" Sahak ran an agitated hand through his hair. "What's left of him is not long for this world. He's not going to escape his curse, and he won't survive it. It would've been a kinder fate if the Demon Witch had killed him. He wants you to remember him as he was. Nesrin, let him go."

"He say this to you?"

Sahak didn't answer. Nesrin suspected he wanted to lie, so kept silent instead of breaking his promise of honesty.

"I don't think he say this to you." She knew her husband, and knew what he would've told his friend. "I think he say that you tell me he dead. He want me to think he gone so I not go after him."

"He did," Sahak admitted, "but you should know the truth of it, and Taniel is right, you deserve better. His life is over. Don't spend yours chasing a ghost."

"Taniel life not over. You say he looking for cure."

"He won't find one. He knows this and anyone who sees him knows it too."

Nesrin was undaunted by Sahak's warnings and uninterested in his pleading. If Taniel's condition was truly so terrible, her husband wouldn't waste his time seeking out lesser sorcerers for healing.

"Master Maqlu go to Grey Forest, yes? So Taniel go east too?" she asked.

"Nesrin—"

"Do you know where? What village?" If Taniel's curse was as terrible as Sahak claimed, he was in danger from more than the ill-magic. She'd heard tales of hedgewitches being burned in the south, saw the scars on the refugees who came to Gohar to escape persecution. Hostility toward the magic-touched ran rampant following the Reaping—tolerance for strangers and strange things was another casualty of the Red Plague.

"He won't—"

"Taniel go east, did he?" She had to find her idiot husband before he got himself into worse trouble. If Sahak refused to tell her where he'd gone, she'd search every village and walk every road between here and the eastern mountains until she found Taniel or another rumor to guide her.

"You can't mean to go after him," Sahak said.

"Yes, I do."

"I won't allow it. He goes to his death leaving Gohar, and you'd do the same. Don't look at me like that. I promised you truth, and this is it. There are no trains, no watchmen, nothing to see you safe. The roads are overrun by monsters, and if you escape their fangs you'll fall to the men who prey on foolish travelers." He stood straighter, as if by his height over her he'd intimidate her into obedience. "Taniel is gone, and I'll not let you throw away your life so carelessly."

"It my life, not yours."

"I promised Taniel I'd look after you."

"And this looking after mean locking me away? Because that what you need do to stop me."

"I know this is difficult, but in time you'll see it's the right choice."

"I already see right choice. I go find my husband."

"He wouldn't want you to."

"Then he should have stayed," she said, pushing past him.

She felt his fingers on her arm, reaching to forcibly pull her back, and at the last moment reconsidering. He chose to physically block the way instead, hurrying to stand between her and the stairs.

"Nesrin, please!"

She slipped beneath his arm and strode to the guest suite. Sahak followed after her, pleading that she see reason. He had never possessed Taniel's commitment to act. He was more comfortable observing than stepping onto uncharted roads.

"If you go after him, you'll die," he said as she pulled a bag from the wardrobe. She had prepared a pack months ago. Taniel told her to always keep one ready if she ever had to flee an area. "It's too dangerous. You've heard what's become of the world, it's no place for a woman to be looking for a cursed man."

Nesrin stared at him, better able to convey her resolution in quiet defiance than spoken argument. His breath was better spent convincing a stone to become water than for her to change her mind.

"Please." He touched her cheek. Just as his fingers had brushed her arm to stop her, he caught himself too late.

She spoke a saying in her native tongue.

"What does that mean?" he asked.

Haeranji was too simple a language to grasp the true meaning, so she stripped it down to fit words Sahak understood.

"My soul not here," she said. "I must go."

Wind whistles over the barren Wastes. Clouds of dry sand greet your coming through the portal. The resinous smell of mountain pine disappears when the way closes behind you. The air of the Wastes drags desiccated down your throat. Skeletal trees rise like bones from the dead earth. Their limbs are long fallen and withered to nothing. You remember the forest that once grew here, verdant and lush. The dark abyss beyond the petrified trees was once a lake, the fields of ash were farms, and to the east sat the gleaming thrones of the sorcerer-kings of Ha-Ai.

Dust plumes beneath your bare feet as you walk the grounds where your manor stood. Five hundred years ago, your halls overlooked the golden kingdom. You remember when goatherders walked these rugged hills, farmers toiled in the fields, and the air was sweet from ripened oranges. At sunrise and sunset, you saw the eastern gleam of the temple tholobate and palace, a brief shining moment that winked out as quick as it came.

Nakirah, what have you done?

Azariah's words echo what your sisters asked you those centuries past. They feigned horror to hide their indifference.

"I have done nothing," you say as you said then, when ash fell instead of rain, the crops sickened, the ground withered, and Ha-Ai's people did the same.

It was King Nezar who wrought this. He sparked the blaze. All you did was let it burn.

The men's clothes felt awkward on Nesrin, tight and loose in all the wrong places. She had worn trousers before, though never outside the home, and her legs felt uncovered as she walked beside the wagon carrying preserved vegetables and honey. She kept to the middle of the procession; horses, men, and a half dozen more wagons to her front and back. Sahak had been reluctant to let her leave Gohar, so she made it clear if he didn't find travel arrangements for her, she'd find a way to leave on her own, and he wanted that even less. He'd disguised her as a boy and arranged for her to accompany a caravan led by a man he trusted.

"He's received word his father survived the curse," Sahak had told the captain. "Will you help get him to his family?"

The captain had agreed with surprising alacrity, asking no further questions and doing all in his power to see Nesrin smuggled from the city, travel bans be damned. She guessed his caravan regularly spirited away separated survivors to reunite families.

The thrill of escaping Gohar to find Taniel buoyed her steps for the first few miles. A bright, shining dawn beckoned her east. She felt fettered by the wagons' plodding pace. She wanted to race ahead, eager to find her husband. She knew it was a silly notion, but part of her believed that the evil that had befallen him need nothing more than their reunion to be set right.

The lightness in her step faded as Gohar grew distant, then disappeared behind wooded hills. Only then, when the last of the familiar was gone, did the impossibility of her task reveal itself to her. She had no notion of where Taniel had gone besides east, and the world in all its strange hostility became larger with every mile. By noon, the skip in her step was replaced by guardedness. Shoulders tensed, head down, she watched the caravan's men, no longer gazing bright-eyed and unmindful to the east. Sahak had been right to insist she disguise herself as a boy. The men in the caravan were a coarse lot, hardened men for a hard life, and while Sahak had assured her the captain was trustworthy, he was only one man among the dozen.

For the most part, the men left her alone and she kept to herself, speaking rarely so her voice not betray her. As evening drew nearer and the captain announced they'd make camp at an abandoned farm a mile down the road, Nesrin's worries of being found out darkened to dreadful imaginings. She was foolish enough to venture into the wild in search of her husband, but not so foolish to delude herself in thinking the Sandar family's protection extended beyond the walls she had willingly left behind. Out here, she was on her own.

Soft movement caught her eye. The same flickering shades she saw in the days leading up to the Reaping crawled through trees bordering a wild field. A watchman noticed her staring and followed her gaze.

"Moths to the southern trees," he called.

The sighting was repeated down the caravan line. The men glanced to where he gestured, then checked swords and pistols to be sure they were ready. There was no panic or worried murmurs. Such childish fears belonged solely to Nesrin.

"You got a good eye," the watchman said. "Don't keep what you see quiet. Speak up even if unsure. Any chance is too great for poor souls such as ours to afford."

Nesrin said nothing.

"A daughter has a right to find her father unbothered," the man said softly. "These boys might be rough, but they won't cause you trouble. The boss'll see to it."

"It that obvious?" she asked, tightening the scarf and hat hiding her hair. The disguise had hardly lasted a day.

"Most of us figured there was a reason you wanted to be alone to take a piss, and a few of us aren't as stupid as we look. The name's Razmik," he said. "May I know yours?"

"Nesrin. And I looking for my husband, not father," she said to make clear she was unavailable for a specific type of companionship.

Razmik nodded. "I hope you find him. One of the reasons I took this work was to find my sister."

"Did you?"

"Yeah." He smiled. "She and her three kids pulled through. She walked all the way to Ethel with two brats in tow, and her youngest had the decency to wait to be born until the day after she arrived. I shouldn't have been surprised she survived the curse. She was born kicking and screaming and that's the way she'll go. Not on a sickbed. Is your husband in Ethel?"

"I no know where he be. Only go east," she said.

"If you'd like, I know a hedgewitch in Ethel who has a knack for tracking sorcery. Most of her spells take a couple days to mature, but her work is good. If there's a trail to follow to your husband, she'll find it for you."

"Yes, I like that, thank you."

"And if you need a place to stay, my sister will be happy to have you. You wouldn't be the first she's made sure had a meal and bed before going on their way."

"I thank you. Truly with my soul."

"Kindness don't cost a thing," he said, "but it's got more worth than ever these days."

Another flurry of transparent flutterings to the north caught Nesrin's attention.

"There so many," she said, watching the ill-omen spirits flit over the meadow grass.

"That's not a whole lot. Once you see a swarm, that small group over there looks like nothing."

"I never see moths until Reaping."

"That was my first as well," Razmik said. "Now I see them almost every day."

"You see other things on road?" she asked, wondering if the stories of dark creatures flooding the world in the Reaping's wake were true.

"There're more monsters than men on the roads these days. And some of those men are closer to monsters than the men they were before."

Nesrin swallowed a dry lump in her throat, Razmik's words feeding her fears for Taniel's fate. Sahak had looked rightly ashamed when he let slip the word "monstrous" in describing her husband. After that, he'd refused to say anything on Taniel's state. From what she gathered, Taniel was still flesh and blood, but maimed into something unrecognizable. Sahak had meant to spare her in not giving specifics, not realizing his silence only encouraged her imagination to run wildly into the worst of her nightmares. What if it was not only Taniel's body that had been warped, but his mind and soul as well? What if there was nothing left of her husband and he was little more than the shade-like moths haunting the land? What if he was so far gone, he wouldn't know her if she found him?

"Forgive my gloom. Don't let it frighten you," Razmik said.

"I not frightened for me. I have fright for my husband."

Razmik grunted. Nesrin assumed that was his way of offering comfort.

"Is there often trouble on your walkings?" She decided to stay close to him for the rest of the way. There were signs of a good heart beneath his rough exterior.

He gave a casual wave. "Nothing we can't handle."

She allowed that line of conversation to fall to the dust behind them. That Razmik refused to give a straight answer told her all she needed. She closed her hand over the protective talisman on the silver chain beneath her shirt, the charm a gift from Taniel.

"Only wear it when needed," he had said, showing the ram's head and crescent moon pendant to her before tucking it in a box. "Talismans and charms don't last forever. Evil is a corrosive force. The more wards are used, the more they weaken."

The bandages around his arms and chest had confirmed that. He'd put off getting his tattooing touched up and it cost him a new set of scars. The tattoos were one of the reasons Purgers—those who survived—often retired early. All the protective runes inked into their skin eventually did more harm than good. Years of heavy warding left retired Purgers with frail constitutions and quick to fatigue, as if they carried unseen burdens.

Nesrin had checked Taniel's tattoos every night after that day he'd returned to her bloodied and bandaged, searching for breaks or fading he had missed. Now, she paid the same obsessive attention to her talisman, looking for the tarnish of beginning corruption. The metal gleamed unsullied, a purity she doubted would last long. She had worn it only a day and had miles to go.

14

Pilgrims

The morning's chill endured under the grey sky's protective pall, preventing the brisk cool of dawn from lifting as the day moved toward noon. Shirin yawned, eyes and feet heavy as she trudged along the forest path carpeted by golden leaves. Neither she nor Taniel slept well the night before. A creature had stalked outside their tent, circling the wards he'd carved into the ground and surrounding trees. Its terrible shrieks were disturbingly similar to those of a weeping child, and Shirin swore it called her by name.

"Don't." Taniel had caught her arm when she moved to peer out. "Seeing it will only make it worse."

He said it was most likely a salua, and however compelled Shirin felt to investigate, she was not to so much as pull back the tent flap. The cries grew more despairing. Shirin covered her ears when they mimicked those of her dead children, echoing their pleas for help she could not give as they succumbed to the Red Plague. Her bones burned in yearning to answer the cries, to brave the night and be sure it wasn't really her children's spirits weeping for her. Taniel took out the duduk, using music to shield Shirin from the terrible voices. He didn't stop playing until sunrise.

The creature had fled dawn's coming. The nervous exhaustion it inspired had not, remaining their close companion through the woods turned deceptively peaceful by day.

"Shirin." Taniel called her back to the forest path she had strayed from. The way was buried in leaves, making it easy for a tired soul to wander off. Taniel had no trouble keeping to the narrow forest path, while this was the third time Shirin had drifted into the trees. She'd been willing to risk taking the River Road to the south, or the Lady's Way to the north. Those well-traveled roads were wide, warded, and far easier for Taniel to walk. He'd insisted they take forest paths instead, trading time and ease for safety and anonymity.

"I doubt the forest is any safer," Shirin had said when they turned from the Lady's Way onto the woodland trail. Wickedness followed no set road. There was as much chance of meeting bandits on a wide, straight path as a winding, narrow one.

Taniel had argued highwaymen kept closer to main roads where there were more travelers to rob, and less chance of them becoming the prey of darker creatures.

"Monsters I can defend against," he'd said. "And hiding behind them is our best defense against men."

Shirin, suppressing another yawn, nearly bumped into Taniel when he came to a sudden halt.

"Do you hear that?" he asked.

"Hear what?" At first she thought his exhaustion invented threats where there were none, until she heard the birds were not alone in their singing. A man's voice lilted through the trees to the steady beat of plodding hooves.

"Come on." He took her arm. "We need to get off the road."

Shirin planted her feet. "Wait, don't you recognize the song?"

The man offered a hymn to Naru, goddess of fertility, fishermen, and patron of her home village. Shirin was not so jaded to think a man who sang sacred praise was of treacherous heart, or a demon in disguise. Besides, she and Taniel fleeing the path only invited unwanted attention. Undergrowth was scarce and the trees thin. There was no reliable cover to hide them from the fellow traveler.

The man came into view and Shirin relaxed. The faded brown cloak and frayed, white tassel rope wrapping his waist marked him an Irakan holy brother. His hood was down to show thinning grey hair, fine lines framing his eyes and mouth, and he had the sturdy, dependable build of a man who'd earned his strength through hard labor. One calloused hand moved over the beads tied to his waist tassels as he prayed through song, his other hand held a rope leading a mule eager to sample the low leaves along the trail's edge.

Seeing them, the monk broke from his hymn and raised a hand in greeting. "Travelers. I hope I find you well."

Shirin returned the gesture. Taniel moved to stand between her and the man.

"Karvogi." The monk nodded. "I didn't think to be graced by company on this path so soon, let alone by a spirit-chaser. To where are you headed?"

"East," Taniel said.

The monk nodded, either oblivious or choosing to ignore the hostility scorching Taniel's tone.

"Toward Agr Rav," Shirin said.

"We're heading the same way," the monk said, and Taniel muttered "obviously" beneath his breath. "I was praying to find fellow travelers on this journey. Karvogi, if you're willing, I'd consider it a great honor to walk beside a spirit-chaser."

"I didn't think holy men of the Irakan faith held much regard for spirit-chasers," Taniel said.

"Theological disagreement is not the same as disrespect, and as we both wear sacred cloth, I'd like to think we have more values in common than not."

Taniel turned the black eyeholes of his cloth mask to Shirin. She gave a small nod, and he grunted consent, walking closer to her as the monk and mule led the way.

"My name is Brother Emet. May I ask yours?"

"I'm Shirin and this is Taniel," she said. Taniel gave a disapproving hiss. He had probably wanted to lie about their names, or at least his.

"So long as we're walking the same way, place your packs on Berjouhi." Brother Emet patted the mule's neck. "She won't mind."

Shirin took up the offer. Taniel held tighter to his.

"I'm too old to run off with your belongings, and Berjouhi is too elegant a lady to run at all," Brother Emet said. "We're not going to rob you."

"I'll hang onto it," Taniel said.

Shirin knew to be patient with Taniel's bad temper. If he truly thought the man a threat, he would have refused his company entirely. She gave him a day or two before he warmed to their new companion. Compared to how unreceptive he was to her when they first met, he was behaving nothing short of friendly toward Brother Emet.

Men made pilgrimages to Ha-Ai, seeking your counsel. They offered their finest treasures, richest lands, beloved sons and daughters in exchange for your blessing. They sought your favor, thirsting for your power the way a desert hermit longs for rain. The men of influence who lay the world's riches at your feet were rarities. Most of your supplicants—the woodsmen, the shepherds, the farm-wives—sought only wisdom, their humility all they had to offer. You received them all as they were. A wealthy lord raged when you advised a poor widow before him, unable to understand how little his king's ransom of precious gems was worth. Favor cannot be bought, only earned, and it is lost far more easily.

You are the last of Ha-Ai's pilgrims as you cross the ashen earth, returning to the ruins of the golden kingdom; seeking answer for why absence festers ever more deeply within you, why your triumphs are so quickly undermined, your deeds undone. You spent a mortal's lifetime gestating that curse only to have it turned from your designs. This brittle hollowness, like bone without marrow, is the one you suffered when the people you were sent to guide turned on you. When your sister betrayed you. You sought to purify the land, and Asherah sided with the mortals who rebelled against you.

The mountain slopes rising behind you in the west are not as barren as they were a century ago. What was bone-pale waste is darkened by the slow spread of Asherah's parasitic trees. The Grey Forest is a creeping blight; bark, branch, and root spreading to where they have no right to be.

Nakirah, what have you done?

Asherah, always the sanctimonious hypocrite, only stepping in to interfere, to chastise, to undermine. If her wretched forest hadn't stopped King Nezar's curse, the world would have been purified centuries ago. There would have been no need for you to grow and release the Red Plague.

The ruins of Ha-Ai are faded, white stone crumbling into the earth. The once lustrous marble halls are a lifeless bone yard. The statues that served as pillars are weathered to faceless shades. No moss, grass, or creeping tendril grows in the decay. You won't allow it. Here, life is forbidden.

You run a hand over a collapsed column buried in sand. The gates of Ha-Ai once towered high in their glory, gleaming in the sun. The city's vibrance was the envy of the world with markets colored by dyes and carved ivory, the air fragrant with the scent of spices, the ground thrumming from the thousands of feet upon the cobblestone ways. All of it now dust.

You scoop up a handful of sand, letting the fine grains run through your fingers. There's a cleansing nature to sand—its sharp sting scours away impurities. On holy days, Ha-Ai's people mixed ash with sand to mark their foreheads in recognition of their sins. The whole kingdom has now borne that mark for centuries. Time is different for you than it is for mortals. They heal. Forget. Die. The ragged wound from the people you took in as your own children rising in rebellion is undiminished by the centuries. The pain of what they did to your true children cuts far deeper.

Nakirah, what have you done?

"Only what is just." You came to huts of clay and straw on the muddy lake banks and showed them how to build temples and palaces of wonder. You taught fishermen to be sorcerers, turned goatherders to kings. And they turned on you.

The remains of the High Temple are dull and worn. Broken stones lie scattered over buckling steps. You pause at the entrance, then crouch to examine an unexpected finding. There are footprints in the sand. The ruins are not as lifeless as you thought.

There is a trespasser in Ha-Ai's tomb.

The temple's nave and antechamber are empty, but you sense a soul has been here recently and is not far gone. A woman's statue stands behind the altar. Her hands are outstretched, vines twine up her robes, a sun and moon are engraved on the wall behind her. Her head is gone, crumbled into dust across the floor. The altar stone, once white, is weathered to grey. You still see it drenched in red as it was five hundred years ago.

You taught the people sorcery, and they harvested the children of your blood to turn their power against you. They dragged them to this altar. Butchered them like animals to steal their inherited magic. In punishment, you turned King Nezar's power against him. You made it so every ill he wished upon you, every wound, every damage done by his hand would not befall him, but what he loved most. He raged as he failed to undo the curse crumbling his kingdom beneath his feet. He cursed his people when they abandoned him, fleeing west to escape dying lands. He roared his fury when the armies he sent after the souls deserting his kingdom sickened and withered to husks. He screamed in helpless terror when his queen wasted away like the earth. He sobbed in desperation when his daughter followed her mother, and then his sons.

You waited to leave the wastelands until he came to you. The year before, he'd come to your manor at the head of an army, steel drawn, banners of a golden sun flying high in the breeze. This time, he came alone on his knees, a last pilgrimage paid in your honor.

"End this." He wore tattered rags. His bare feet were blistered and bloodied, lips cracked in thirst, his beard once black had gone grey. His skin was similarly shaded from grief and dust. "I beg you."

"This is your doing, not mine," you said. "What you wished has been done. Is it not what you expected?"

He begged your forgiveness. You refused. He begged your mercy. You granted it.

Kharinah had been beside herself. A woodsman she had visited for years, whom she'd grown to love as an elder brother and who'd loved her despite her brokenness, had been claimed by King Nezar's wickedness. Barely a century old, she struggled to retain her shape, shifting between child, wolf, and something else entirely. You summoned her, seeing opportunity in her malleable nature, and encouraged her father's heritage to take over. King Nezar received his deliverance from his self-made suffering. Kharinah received justice from the man who had destroyed her joy.

You're certain King Nezar—ungrateful to his final breath—cursed your daughter as she devoured him. She's never been the same since.

15

Faith's Reward

The temple and tavern were the only buildings with glass windows in Ikdash. The rest of the town was built of simple stone, wood, and clay. Houses and shops clustered at the intersecting crossroads, farms and orchards dressed the surrounding hills, and men unpacked their fall harvests beneath cloth awnings held up by thin poles to create a marketplace. As a crossroads town, Ikdash was a site of sanctuary, hosting the divine protection belonging to where four roads met—an ancient power shared by thresholds and blessed-hearth homes. The gods had woven those protections into the world as undeniably as they had carved the mountains, painted the sky, and sent Seraphs to protect mortals, grant them divine blessing, and teach how to harness the hidden powers.

The temple bell tolled the noon hour.

"When that bell rings twice, we head out," the captain hollered to his men. "Anyone not back in line and ready by then gets left."

Razmik and the senior men remained to barter at the square. The hired guns and younger men headed straight for the tavern. Women in thin dresses leaned out the second-story window, advertising pleasures more sensuous than wine, and called coy greetings down from their perch.

"You get drunk, you get left behind," the captain hollered after the men keen to answer the invitation.

Nesrin was unsure of where to go. She thought to stay close to Razmik, but a couple of the men who remained near the wagons made her nervous. She didn't like the look of them, or the way they looked at her.

She had visited Ikdash three years ago when Taniel took her here for the Springtide Festival. There had been no whores at the tavern. No dusty caravans. No leering men. No mourning wreaths or memorial stones laid before Razirah's statue—servant of the Wind Daughter goddess and Seraph of crossroads, travelers, strangers, and pilgrims—standing in the town center. A stone veil covered the Seraph's face to show only her mouth. Her arms were raised in welcome and her robes were carved in a windswept frenzy. During the Springtide Festival, the statue had been decorated by white anemones. More colorful blooms had brightened the marketplace. Women dressed as the Raven Maiden played out the courtship dance with men costumed as the Shepherd Boy, and passions inspired by the lovers' spring story had couples of all ages eager to join the dance.

Through a mouthful of mshabak, Taniel had told Nesrin hers was better than the festival's. She told him he'd get fat if he kept eating the desserts at the rate he was.

"I no care if you fat," she'd said, patting his stomach, "but only if from my cooking."

The temple had been decorated in flowered garlands and papers folded into lotus blooms and birds. Costumed performers sang beneath candlelit windows, and the hanging lanterns strung across the central crossroads encouraged music and dancing long into the nights of the three-day-long festival.

The delight of those days was gone. The candles and lanterns were absent from the temple, and there was no cheer on the tired priest's face as he spoke to an irate middle-aged woman, her hair covered by the black mourning veil of a widow.

"Karvogi travel where they will," the priest told the woman. "If they didn't damage your fields, there's no reason to raise fuss."

"I won't stand for them!" the widow said. "They're nothing but thieving—"

"You say Karvogi here?" Nesrin rushed over. Sahak refused to tell her what Taniel looked like, only describing the Karvogi mask and cloak he wore as disguise, telling her that's how she'd recognize him and to look for horns.

"They've been sneaking through my orchards the last two nights," the woman said. "I don't want their witchcraft coming on my land no more."

"They said they have no intention of returning this way." The priest's soothing tone had little sway.

"They'll keep coming through, bringing their bad luck and ill-magic if you don't—"

"When they leave?" Nesrin asked.

"Not fifteen minutes ago," the priest said.

The woman shook her head. "Filthy, stinking—"

"Which way they go?" Nesrin asked.

"They took the southern road," the priest said, and Nesrin flew down the path he pointed. The priest called after her, his words lost in her haste. If she hurried she should be able to catch the spirit-chasers and return to Ikdash long before the temple bell tolled twice.

The chance that Taniel was one of the Karvogi was slim, but every hope was thread thin, and she'd follow all until she found the one that led to her husband.

She caught up to the Karvogi sooner than expected. They ambled along the path beneath their strange cloaks and masks. One was dressed as a bear, draped in furs and carrying a goblet drum slung over his wide shoulders. Horns rose from the hoods of the other two. Nesrin sprinted after them, her hair coming loose from the scarf, her hat lost half a mile back.

"Taniel!" she cried.

The bear-like Karvogi turned. Red, painted eyes bulged from a mask inlaid by yellow teeth stretching his grin from ear to ear.

"Taniel!" she called again. All three Karvogi stopped to look at her.

She came to a panting halt, her pounding heart sinking into disappointment. None of the men beneath tattered cloaks and fur were her husband. Taniel may have left her to hide beneath a Karvogi mask, but he'd never hide behind pretending not to know her. Not unless the dark magic had affected his mind.

"Any you Taniel Sushan?" she asked to be sure.

The three Karvogi shook their heads, bells jingling on the one who wore wolf's ears.

Nesrin wanted to scream, to weep, to collapse on the road. She wanted to rip their masks off and curse any man who hid his identity from her.

"You see other Karvogi? Man with horns?" She mimed horns rising from her head.

Again, they shook their heads.

Cold resignation swallowed up her anger at their unhelpful silence. She ought to count herself lucky she'd found the Karvogi to confirm they were not her husband. This disappointment was kinder than the unknowing that would have plagued her if she'd returned to Ikdash before finding them, forever wondering if she'd missed Taniel.

"Thank you," she mumbled, turning back to the caravan, her single remaining thread leading her east to her husband.

"Young one."

The shortest Karvogi stepped forward, a woman judging by her voice. Her face was hidden beneath a black and gold mask with slanted eyes, a white circle for a mouth, and ram horns curling from the sides. She extended her hand. Nesrin hesitated before offering hers. The woman ran a thumb over Nesrin's palm, tracing over the lines and each finger. The gloves the Karvogi woman wore only covered her hands to show the tips of her fingers were painted black.

"You have far to go. Evil waits in your path and good men will stand in your way. Hold this alongside your hope," the Karvogi woman said, closing Nesrin's hand over something small and soft, "and you will find what you seek."

As one, the spirit-chasers resumed their southern course, bells jingling from masks and sleeves, the bearish Karvogi playing a steady beat on the animal-hide drum.

Nesrin opened her hand. A white anemone flower sat in her palm, petals as perfect as if freshly plucked. In her Irakan faith, the anemone was the flower of the Wind Daughter who carried off evil to make way for new beginnings. Outside of holy festivals, the white flowers were reserved for funerals. They were never given as gifts to the living, and she wanted to drop the anemone on the path. She tucked it into her jacket pocket instead, unable to abandon the little flower. Not when it—and the woman in the ram's mask who had given it to her—reminded her of the tattoo on Taniel's chest.

The return to Ikdash felt shorter even though she walked instead of ran. There was no hurry. It had taken less than a quarter hour for her to catch the Karvogi. She had plenty of time to reach the caravan, and she wanted to be alone for a little longer.

"There you are."

Nesrin startled, berating herself for allowing disappointment to cast her eyes to the ground, self-pity distracting her from staying alert to her surroundings. Two men she recognized from the caravan stepped from the thick trees bordering the path. A horse waited tethered to a low branch. There was no sign of anyone else nearby.

"Boss sent us looking for you," the taller one said. Youthful freckles covered his nose and his voice was boyishly light. "Didn't want you to get left. Come on, we'll take you back."

She stepped away when he stepped forward, not believing a word he said. If they had good intentions, they would've been on the road, not lurking in the trees.

"Your name's Nesrin, right?" the shorter one asked, face broad and smiling.

"I don't think she understands us." The taller one glanced up and down the road in a way Nesrin very much understood. He checked to be sure they were alone.

Nesrin whirled on her heel and sprinted into the trees.

"Stay with the horse," the taller said. "I'll get her."

Leaves hissed and branches snapped as the man gave chase. Nesrin felt like her feet hardly touched the ground. She couldn't outrun him or reach Ikdash before he caught her, but there were farms between here and there, homes that had goats in the pens and smoke rising from the chimneys. She only had to reach one of those or get close enough for someone to hear her scream.

The man caught her arm, yanked her back, and there was no one to hear her scream. She lost her footing and he helped her fall, straddling to pin her down, a leering grin spread beneath his freckles. Nesrin planted her feet as Taniel had taught her and bucked her hips up. He jolted forward and she gained the space to drive her leg up between his. His surprised cry at her fighting back choked on a pained wheeze. The hands holding her arms went to his groin. Nesrin grabbed a small stone and slammed it into the side of his head.

The man keeled over. She twisted from beneath him, exploding into a run. His companion called from the roadway, teasing to ask if his friend wanted privacy or if he could watch, unaware of the scuffle.

Nesrin fled up a slope of rounded rock to hide her trail on the stony ground. The man called out again, exasperated as to what was taking so long. She heard him laugh, presumably having found his friend.

"Get that little bitch!" Pain grated coarse in the taller man's snarl.

Their voices pursued her through the trees—one mocking, the other furious. They were too close. They'd catch her before she reached Ikdash, and the town was no guarantee of safety. The captain might truly have sent them after her. Women fetched a high price to the right buyer. The lucky ones were traded to towns where men sought wives, and unwilling bride was far from the worst fate awaiting abducted women.

She yelped as her right leg plunged through a brush-hidden crevice. The opening was shallow, just large enough for a small woman to curl up and hide in. Ankle throbbing from her misstep, she circled around to be sure she'd be hidden from all angles before crawling in. The muddy water pooled in the grooved stone soaked into her pants, a many-legged creature slithered over her hand, and the crevice's edges scraped her arms and legs as she made herself as small as possible. So long as the men did not repeat her slip of stumbling directly over the opening, she was hidden.

Their voices grew louder. Their boots thumped on the stone slope as they drew nearer. Nesrin curled tighter in on herself, unable to catch more than pieces of what they said over her hammering heart, fear rendering their words all but incomprehensible. The gruffer voice mentioned the Sandars. He knew she was connected to them and thought the best price to be had was in ransoming her. The lighter voice wanted to sell her down river and be done with it. Once he was done with her.

Nesrin held a hand over her mouth to muffle her terrified breath, feeling helplessly small in her pathetic hiding place. She should have kept running instead of surrendering herself to be found. At least then she'd face them standing instead of tucked away like a whimpering child. The Purger's blade on her hip felt like a toy, useless against men trained in violence and far more eager than her to engage in it.

"Do you see her?"

"No."

"She can't have gone far."

Nesrin dared not move. Not even to peer through the leaves to see how close the men hunting her stood. She was sure that they were mere feet away, standing directly over her hiding place, ready to grab her.

The gruff voice spoke, the lighter one answered, and she pieced the words she picked out into vague understanding. They said she'd have to head back to town eventually, but she missed what they decided to do about it. Were they going to watch the road leading to Ikdash? Stake out the town? Give up on her and rejoin the caravan? It sounded like they knew someone in Ikdash who'd keep an eye out to hold her if they saw her.

Boots scuffed over the stone and their voices faded. Nesrin stayed where she hid. The mud soaking into her pants chilled her skin, her back and hips ached from the cramped space, her right ankle throbbed. She was certain the men lurked at the base of the rocky slope. They'd see her the moment she crawled from her hiding place, lured out by the misleading quiet.

Only when she feared being alone in the woods after dark more than being discovered did she wriggle out from rock and brush, shivering from cold. She stumbled on her ankle, swollen and pulsing hot. Fear had masked how badly she twisted it and her whole leg trembled under her weight.

Hobbling down the sloping stone, she broke off a tree branch to lend support to her throbbing ankle. Hoisting her pack over her shoulders, brushing the mud and dead leaves off her legs, she put the sun to her back and headed northeast. There was no point in returning to Ikdash. The sun's position told her she'd missed the caravan's departure and she held no faith in finding help or sanctuary in the crossroads town. She'd cut across country, avoiding men who sought to take advantage of her, and reconnect with the Lady's Way to head east to Ethel. It couldn't be far. The caravan captain had said they'd reach the town by evening. She should make it there before nightfall, even on her injured ankle.

Clutching the talisman around her neck, she prayed Taniel's travels were safer than hers and that if trouble had to befall one of them, it fall upon her. She was prepared to walk through a world on fire to find him, and from what Sahak had told her, her husband had already suffered more than was fair.

There were a few more hours of travel left in the day for a healthy man to take advantage of, and Taniel hoped Brother Emet, grown impatient with the slow progress, would walk on. Unfortunately, the monk showed no hint of irritation at their limping, labored pace. He joined in setting up camp at the wayfarer's chapel along the forested path, a single room of yellow stone topped by a domed roof collecting fallen leaves. Narrow windows divided the carved mural of a woman wearing a windswept veil guiding travelers through scrollwork foliage, and a second woman who stood over kneeling men. A deer's skull hid her face and the antlers grew into branches.

Taniel hated the little chapel. The mural reminded him of the room Minu had imprisoned him in. The stone forest and the woman wearing the deer skull were unpleasantly similar to the tapestries of Tanrisi guiding travelers through thread-woven woods. Taniel found every reason not to go inside the sacred space. He kept his back to the hateful murals as he carved warding runes into more trees than necessary. The work strained his hand, and he used his crippled left to stabilize his trembling right as he dug the knife into the bark.

"We're on holy ground, there's no need for that," Brother Emet said.

Taniel ignored the monk, wishing the brother would find somewhere else to gather firewood, and take his unwanted wisdom with him. Wayfarer's chapels and crossroad towns were some of the safest places to shelter, but Taniel's curse had turned him unwilling to accept protections on faith. His right hand spasmed and the fumbled blade sliced into his palm. Dropping the knife, he cursed and clutched his hand, blood welling between his fingers. Long days of travel left him too tired for fine coordination, the twitching of overtaxed muscles kept him awake through the night, headaches greeted him each morning sure as coming dawn, and the Arcanum salves provided less relief with each application. It was as if the malady was a conscious force seeking to overcome the balms and better cause him pain.

"What?" Taniel hated Brother Emet's sympathetic stare.

"Do you—"

"I don't need help!"

Brother Emet glanced between Taniel and the unfinished, blood-spattered rune.

"Of course." The monk retreated inside the wayfarer's chapel. A moment later, Shirin emerged carrying bandages.

"Taniel—"

"Spare me the motherly lecture," he said. "I don't need it."

"Just as you don't need help?" Her hands were steady as she cleaned and bandaged his hand.

Exhaustion and fresh injury atop chronic pain stole his patience. Not the guilt at taking his bad temper out on Shirin.

"I'm sorry," he mumbled. "I don't mean to be like this."

"I know what it is to have hate in your heart. Your anger is not unwarranted, but don't make my mistake in letting it rule you."

Taniel had no reply. He kept silent through dinner, sitting against the chapel wall and away from the fire where Brother Emet and Shirin talked, already at ease in the other's company. There was no reason for Taniel to distrust the holy man. He had been friendly, respectful, and patient when confronted by Taniel's surliness. It wasn't a fault of character in the monk that Taniel disliked; it was that he was a stranger, and every unknown face reminded Taniel of how he'd become a stranger to himself. The holy brother was whole while Taniel was broken. He knew it was only a matter of time before Brother Emet's lip curled in disgust as the Arcanum healers and Gohar's hedgewitches had when they saw how ruined he was.

He ran a hand over his horns. There was a saying from Nesrin's country: "No injury is healed by wounding another." Taniel's indiscriminate bitterness accomplished no good. He swallowed his pride, feeling it scrape like dry bones down his throat, resolving to act less of the monster he looked—a resolution tested moments later when Brother Emet walked over to join him and Taniel's hackles immediately rose.

"Do you mind if I sit?" Brother Emet asked.

"No." Taniel checked his mask and hood to be sure they fully covered his appearance.

The monk settled a respectful distance away. Still too close for Taniel's liking. "How long have you been a Karvogi?"

"Not long."

"And you were a Purger before the Reaping?"

"Did Shirin—"

"Shirin has told me nothing of your past, but it doesn't take a clever mind to discern the path you've walked. I've only ever seen Purgers use the runes you carved into the trees and can guess the reasons you wear the Karvogi cloak."

Taniel tucked his left hand into his sleeve and habitually leaned away as if that might better hide his horns.

"A Purger who became a Karvogi," Brother Emet said, "now there must be a story."

"Hardly one worth sharing."

"I don't think it chance I met you on this road."

"No, I think we happened to be walking the same way, you a little faster."

The monk chuckled. "It's always more comfortable to dismiss the guiding hand of the gods as happy chance. I can't do that in this instance. As I said earlier, I prayed to meet good company on the road. More specifically, I prayed to find someone who could help, and not an hour later I meet a Purger become spirit-chaser."

Taniel shook his head, deciding Brother Emet had earned some honesty. "I only carry their cloak, not their beliefs, and I hold none of their authority. As a Purger, I'm afraid I'll be of even less help."

"No, Agr Rav is in need of a man such as you," Brother Emet said. "An evil has taken root in the city, ushered in by the Reaping. It claims a young man every few months and it cannot be banished or exorcised. It must be destroyed."

"What of Agr Rav's High Mage?" Taniel searched his memory for the name. "Master Tahir? If he can't confront this evil I doubt I can do better."

"The Reaping claimed Master Tahir. Our new High Mage is honest in admitting he has neither the knowledge nor the stomach to face such evils."

"Do the men stay missing? Or do you find their remains?"

"They disappear entirely," Brother Emet said. "It's taken two of my brothers at the monastery. Our walls are supposed to provide sanctuary, but we're unable to uphold that barest oath in these dark times."

Taniel sat up straighter, spine cracking from the shift. "Tell me about the disappearances."

Brother Emet told him when the first victim disappeared, a novice at the monastery, they thought he'd run away. It wasn't unheard of for people to leave Agr Rav upon hearing of a surviving relative, or when suddenly overwhelmed by a need to escape the place they'd suffered the despair of the Reaping. As a novice, the young man had few earthly possessions, so it raised no great misgiving that they had been left behind. But the brothers were uneasy there was no note to explain his abrupt departure.

When the second young man vanished, a physician's assistant while making house calls, people became suspicious. The third disappearance of a mage's apprentice darkened those suspicions to fear. The fourth disappearance two months ago, another young monk, nearly resulted in the lynching of a cursed man who had sought refuge in Agr Rav after his village fell to a dark witch. The man was saved when one of the holy brothers—built like a bull and possessing a temper to match—swatted down the mob and bodily carried the man into the monastery's safety.

"If you can call if safety," Brother Emet glowered. "The monastery offers no sanctuary until the monster preying on our young men is found."

"You'll want to keep praying to find better company on the road, then." Taniel rubbed salve into his left hand to soothe the aching joints. "I barely endure the evils placed upon me, never mind hunting down dark creatures. And it seems the people of Agr Rav do not receive cursed men as well as they once did."

"Cursed men have come for centuries to find sanctuary in Agr Rav. One year of fear does not change that, and our new High Mage's talents, while ill-equipped for hunting monsters, lie in the medicinal sorceries and lifting curses. He can help you with yours."

"I'm beyond such help," Taniel said. A mage lacking the constitution to face monsters had as little use to him as Taniel knew he'd be to Brother Emet. Yet ruined as he was, he bore a responsibility. The Purger oath he'd sworn was an inescapable urging to accept the monk's plea.

"I would not blame you if you declined," Brother Emet said, "but I would not ask if I thought it beyond your ability."

"We're headed through Agr Rav anyway," Taniel said. "It's no inconvenience to see if I can be of service."

The sun sank low in the west, the swelling ache in Nesrin's ankle slowed her step, and the swiftly descending darkness promised to overtake her before she reached Ethel. She had less than an hour before night caught her limping alone on a forested road with no idea of how much farther she had to go. Insects hummed in the trees, an owl hooted, and it would not be much longer until the woods came alive with unnatural predators.

"Razirah, help me," she prayed. The silver talisman hanging around her neck and the Purger's blade at her hip were flimsy defenses against the all-consuming night.

Hooves sounded behind her. Nesrin hobbled to the roadside. She had stopped walking the few times she came across other travelers, waiting for them go by before resuming her eastward trek. The men who'd passed her may have been good souls, or they may have had black hearts like the caravan men and been all too eager to take advantage of an injured traveler. So she hid her limp from them, refusing to reveal how vulnerable she was.

The hoofbeats thudded faster, the rider urging his mount to hurry. "Nesrin!"

Her blood chilled and she traded her walking stick for the knife. If the man recognized her, he had to be from the caravan. She considered fleeing into the trees, but there was no outrunning him and she'd most likely only succeed in spraining her other ankle in the dusky gloom before being caught.

Razmik pulled the reins, slowing the horse to a stop in front of her.

"Thank the gods," he said and dismounted.

Nesrin retreated, favoring her right ankle as her hand tightened on the knife hilt. "Why you here?"

"Looking for you," he said.

Looking for you. The two men waiting to ambush her had said the same thing. They had also said something about a third man waiting to see if she returned to Ikdash. Nesrin felt small and stupid for ever thinking it safe to trust Razmik.

"I wasn't sure if you'd returned to Ikdash or gone on toward Ethel," he said. "Let's get you on the horse and off that leg."

"No." She took another step back, her ankle trembled, and she raised the knife higher. "Last men who want get me on horse had not good intention."

"Nesrin, please, it's getting dark. There isn't time for—"

"No!"

"Fine." Razmik's mouth thinned with impatience. "I'll gladly be the villain you think I am and throw you over the horse if that's what it takes to get you to Ethel."

He stepped forward, Nesrin stumbled back, and her ankle gave way beneath her. Razmik caught her arm to keep her from falling. His other hand grasped the wrist of her knife-wielding hand.

"If my wife had survived the Reaping and was looking for me," he said gently, "I'd like to think there'd be souls who'd help her."

Slowly, he let go his grip on her, stepped back and offered his hand for her to take. Nesrin stared, unable to accept his offered hand or raise the knife she had lowered to hang limp at her side.

"Please," he said.

Hands shaking, terrified she was committing to the wrong choice but seeing no better option, she sheathed her knife and took his hand. She flinched when he lifted her onto the horse and shrank in on herself to avoid touching him more than necessary when he mounted behind her. It felt wrong to be so close to a man other than Taniel.

He clucked the horse into a quick canter. "Are you hurt other than your leg?"

"No, I fine," Nesrin mumbled.

After a mile of riding, she decided Razmik was well-intended. He kept his hands on the horse's reins and more importantly, he kept to the road leading east to Ethel rather than turning south to sell her along the river.

"Thank you," she said. "You no have to go look for me."

"I've done nothing deserving thanks or praise. I only did the least any man should."

The hope of yesterday's morning was gone. Nesrin felt foolishly naïve in how unprepared she was to face the world Sahak had warned her of. Using the heel of her hand, she wiped away tears of relief at being rescued, shame that she had needed rescuing, and despair that finding Taniel seemed impossible on an injured ankle, darkness falling, and failing to last two days before being overcome by trouble.

You sense the trespasser wandering the ruins. You feel the fragile thrum of a mortal heart, the puff of living breath, and the drag of tired feet approaching where you wait in the temple. Mortal life is such a strange thing. So vulnerable, yet doomed to commit and suffer the most terrible violences.

The trespasser stares in surprise to see you at the altar. His clothes are worn, boots frayed, and dust colors him a pale grey.

"Seraph." He bows, head to the ground, unfooled by your human guise. "Forgive my trespass."

"You have strayed far from home," you say.

"I seek answers," he says. "And there is no home left for me to stray from."

He tenses as you come forward, trembles when you crouch to lift his chin so his eyes meet yours. He's reached the middling of mortal years, old enough to be weary, while retaining the last flickers of youth's passion. Sorcery flows through his veins, an old bloodline that originated in the very ruins you stand in. How fitting the gift of magic you gave to Ha-Ai—strayed and wandering—has returned at last to kneel before you.

"What is your name, wanderer?" you ask.

"Farid."

"Farid, tell me of your sufferings."

Mortals are unique in their capacity for story. They are so bound in time, so limited in scope, yet they see and experience the world in an intimacy you envy. Farid's tale of the Reaping moves you. He tells how he was a sorcerer at Gohar's Arcanum, how he watched his friends and family fall. How he had no power over the Red Plague. When Master Maqlu abandoned his office of High Mage to seek answers in the east, Farid did the same, alongside many of his brethren. Most mages ended their eastward trek at the mountains, respecting the boundary of the Grey Forest, not daring to face the mist-veiled trees and the Wastes beyond. But Farid, he persevered. He survived the forest, the mountains, the barren sands to come here. He held fast to a faith there were answers to be found, hidden in the ruins of the lost kingdom.

His faith deserves reward.

"The Reaping is ended, Farid," you say. "What do you hope to gain living among the dead and dust?"

"To heal a broken world. In any way that is left to me."

You smile. "Then rise."

You were sent to teach and guide, and here is a worthy soul. It will not be Asherah and her blighted forest that slowly reclaims the Eastern Wastes. You have found the seed to plant in these barren lands. What is to grow will be in your image. Not hers.

Farid watches in wonder as you brush your hand over the altar's stone. It softens into fertile earth. From the vestiges of your children's stolen lives, a small green shoot unfurls from the blood that stained it centuries ago.

"Tend to it," you tell him.

"There's no water and I have not the power to sustain it otherwise." He trembles, terrified of failing you.

You touch your fingers to his cheek, willing upon him the first of small changes to lift him to greater being. "Then you shall learn."

16

More Cursed than Most

The bronze domes and red-ivory walls of Agr Rav's monastery caught the westering sun's final rays in a coppery burn. The holy halls were visible for miles atop the high hill. Taniel assumed most travelers saw that as a promise of haven on the horizon. He saw it as an interminable torture of how much farther he had to walk.

Agr Rav's founding mirrored Gohar's. Both were cities born beneath a sanctuary. Gohar had looked to mages for protection, Agr Rav to the holy brothers of the Irakan faith for guidance. In the aftermath of the Reaping, the two cities once again reflected the other—the roughly constructed wall cloistering Agr Rav from the cursed world was twin to Gohar's. Wood and rough rock encircled the three-tiered city. Men covered in sweat-streaked dust toiled along the wall, replacing the hasty creation with sturdier concrete core and brick for more enduring protection. Farmers worked the fields ringing the city and riflemen watched the road from wooden towers.

The guards at the gate recognized Brother Emet and nodded them all through. Either Brother Emet's character earned respect clearing those who traveled in his company, or the guards decided a middle-aged woman and limping Karvogi presented less trouble than it'd be to interrogate them.

Unlike Gohar, Agr Rav's streets were not winding tombs of boarded-up shops and empty homes. The suffering the Reaping had visited upon Agr Rav was a healing scar, where in Gohar it remained an open wound. People had flocked to the city's protection, and the bustle of refugees paid homage to a more hopeful time. Merchants sat on mats beneath awnings. Farmers pulled carts of apple, beetroot, and squash. Women wearing black mourning scarves carried shopping baskets, and children clung tight to their skirts. People looked curiously at Taniel, whispered to their neighbors, and a few older souls nodded in respect to him.

The cobblestone streets sloped up through the city's terraced levels, and Taniel cursed whoever kept placing Arcanums and monasteries on the highest hills. His legs burned, hips ached, and Shirin placed a steadying hand on his back for the streets that steepened into stairs.

The thrum of the market ringing the wall's interior faded as they ascended. The city's life belonged to the lower level, leaving the middle tier a ghost town similar to what most of Gohar had become. Empty apartments stood above shuttered artisan shops. The watchmaker, the milliner, the café and its decorative glass windows were relics of better days and abandoned luxuries.

Movement stirred in the shadows. Taniel stepped in front of Shirin, his free hand going for the Purger knife hidden in his cloak.

"What is it?" she asked.

"Just moths." He kept his hand on the blade. The spirits crawled over the dark windows, peered down from roofs, and skittered through alleyways.

"They're always there," Brother Emet said. Both he and Shirin signed against evil. "We see them at the monastery as well, but they don't haunt the lower city."

Three moths trailed after them, holding Taniel in particular interest. They circled close to him, mouths gnashing furiously on eyeless faces. He no longer believed the ill-omen spirits acted as heralds for misfortune. He posited they were ever-present, but only noticed in times of hardship, or best seen through suffering eyes.

"Are you sure it's only every few months a young man is taken?" Taniel asked.

Agr Rav's middle tier offered plenty of lonely space and quiet shadow for people to be stolen from. The young men might not be the only victims, simply the ones whose absence was noticed. Monastery novices, a physician's assistant, and a mage apprentice were impossible to abduct and not draw attention. Too many times Taniel had hunted monsters grown fat from feeding off beggars, orphans, and the displaced, preying upon poor souls for years before locals bothered to pay attention to the street corner suddenly bereft of a drifter, or one less face waiting for bread outside a temple's doors.

"No, we can't be sure." Brother Emet stepped around a moth standing unmoving in his path. "There are too many strangers in Agr Rav to know who leaves and who is lost. But the evil taking the young men has its preferences, leading us to think its victims are the few we know of. All were younger than twenty-five, healthy, whole, and all were magic-touched by blood."

Living souls once again populated the streets of Agr Rav's highest tier. Women hung clothes on long lines to dry, older children tended to community gardens while the younger ones played chase, small feet pattering over cobblestone.

Shirin watched the children run by, her grief evident. Taniel rested his hand on her shoulder and she gave a small, appreciative smile, blinking away tears.

Most of the adults, and a few of the children, bore marks of curses.

An Irakan novice walked alongside a man hidden behind bandages. Black veins coursed over the hands and face of a woman weeding a garden. A child no older than ten showed no physical affliction, but the ill-magic infecting her radiated a hum Taniel felt in his bones as she skipped by.

"You take in the tainted?" he asked.

"The monastery has always taken in the cursed," Brother Emet said. "The world will always have the unfortunate, and we will always offer a place for them to seek sanctuary."

"Are the disappearances widely known? Do people know to be wary?" Taniel asked.

"Yes, Abbot Mardiros decided it best for the citizens to be informed of the evil to better guard themselves from it. Our Abbot is not one to be frightened by truth. Nor hide from it." The monk's eyes flicked down, and Taniel hid his left hand in the cloak's sleeve.

"And the new High Mage, what's his name?"

"Terzian."

Taniel stopped. "Razban Terzian?"

"Yes, do you know him?" Brother Emet asked.

"We're friends." Taniel felt lighter than he had in days. The gods had finally taken pity on him, delivering him not only to a familiar face but one of the most talented mages in healing and curse-lifting in centuries. "Did he come here with Master Maqlu?"

"Yes, there was a third as well, a woman apprentice."

"Dua," Taniel said. She was a quiet girl who managed to pass through the world unnoticed despite being Master Maqlu's hand-picked apprentice. Her demureness worked until she revealed the extent of her sorcery. Then she was unforgettable. "Are they here as well?"

"No, Master Maqlu and the woman didn't stay long. Master Tahir fell ill the day before they arrived. Terzian wanted to stay, Maqlu said they could do nothing for him. They argued and parted ways, Master Terzian choosing to remain in Agr Rav. The young mage did his best, Tahir lasted longer than most, but he succumbed in the end, giving Terzian his blessing to take on the responsibility of High Mage."

"He did?" Taniel asked. No one in their right mind would appoint Razban Terzian as High Mage. He was a genius in the medicinal arts, but he had no stomach for leadership and his abilities were narrow, not versatile. "Didn't Tahir have an apprentice?"

"Yes, the Reaping claimed him as well."

Taniel frowned. No doubt Master Tahir had been desperate to find a successor on his deathbed, yet it struck Taniel as out of character for Razban to accept—even in interim. Razban knew his limitations and had never held aspirations to power.

"Master Terzian has been unable to help us with the evil hunting our young men, but I believe he can help you with your troubles. He's worked nothing short of miracles."

Taniel nodded. "I've seen his talent."

Even if Taniel's condition was beyond Razban's skill, it'd be welcome relief to see a friend. And perhaps, despite parting on poor terms, Razban remained in contact with Master Maqlu. Or at least knew to what town along the Grey Forest's border the mage had traveled.

Taniel straightened. The crooked weight of twisted bones was easier to bear at the thought.

"I'll have Master Terzian sent for," Brother Emet said. "He's probably in the lower tiers working with the physicians. He'll return by sundown."

"Thank you. In the meantime, are there written reports on the disappearances I might read? Witness statements and testimonies?" Taniel asked.

"I'll see them delivered, though Abbott Mardiros will want to speak to you first."

"Is your Abbott as accepting of Karvogi as you?"

"He's much like you. He was a Purger before taking the holy cloth," Brother Emet said. "I hope, unlike yours, his is not a disguise."

Abbott Mardiros' study was small and austere—two wooden chairs, an old desk, and walls absent of decoration. None of the religious icons or mosaic tilings adorning the monastery found welcome in the barren room. Taniel sat in one of the two chairs, gently kneading his legs to prevent stiffness from settling in. The chanting of the monks' evening song echoed through the halls to find him where he waited for the Abbott. Shirin had been reluctant to leave Taniel on his own, and very grudgingly accepted his encouragement she allow Brother Emet to show her to guest quarters, receive a meal, and a warmed bath to wash off the road dust.

Rest and a good meal were the least of what she deserved. Taniel had no idea how to repay her for all she'd done. He wondered if this was what it was like to have a mother. His mother had left his father when Taniel was too young to remember more than a vague impression of a woman's face and sweet singing voice. Tiran had often said Taniel looked like her, and the only time he saw his father strike a friend was when Aryeh claimed Taniel took after her in both appearance and lack of character.

The study door opened and Abbott Mardiros entered. He was tall, broad shouldered, his face was lined by decades of hard labor, and his steel-grey beard and hair were neatly trimmed. The imposing figure he presented diminished the brother escorting him to look a small, mousy creature with curling brown hair, upturned nose, and suspicious eyes. Abbott Mardiros' eyes were milk-white. Cursed scarring mottled his skin from forehead to nose bridge, giving him the appearance of wearing a ghastly mask.

The mousy brother guided the Abbott to sit at the desk across from Taniel. The blinding scar across his eyes was undoubtedly what had ended his career as a Purger, yet the older monk moved well despite his age and injuries.

"Brother Emet told us of his meeting you," Mardiros said. His gentle voice defied his formidable appearance. "He said you carry a curse and that your name is Taniel."

"Yes," Taniel said, belatedly remembering his nod went unseen.

"Brother Ashot, you may go," Mardiros said.

"Are you sure there's nothing more I can assist you with?" Brother Ashot's upturned nose wrinkled in disapproval at Taniel. If the Karvogi attire offended the monk, Taniel's appearance beneath the cloak and mask would no doubt upset him even more.

"You may go," Mardiros repeated.

Sparing Taniel a look of unbridled mistrust, Brother Ashot retreated into the hall.

"I'm blind, boy, not deaf," Mardiros said. "Close the door and see to higher works than eavesdropping."

The door clicked shut and disgruntled feet stomped away.

"Taniel, am I right in assuming your family name is Sushan?" Mardiros asked.

"Yes." A renewed pang of loss drove into Taniel's chest at hearing the name he'd failed to live up to.

The Abbott nodded. "I knew your father."

"Forgive me, Abbott, but I'd rather not talk on the past and the dead unless it pertains to the current problem. Brother Emet told me a little of the disappearances, I'd like to hear it in your words as well."

Abbott Mardiros gave a tale much like Brother Emet's, providing more detail on the vanishings and the investigation's findings.

"People want to blame qutrubs," Mardiros said. "They've been a source of endless trouble outside the city, digging up the graves of those who fell to the Reaping. But qutrubs feast on the dead. They don't prey on the living."

"And Razban hasn't been able to find anything concerning the disappearances?"

"Only because there have been no bodies recovered. If we had a corpse, I'm sure he'd be able to track the culprit within an hour. Which leads me to think this evil belongs to a man, not a monster. It's ..."

"Intelligent?"

"Unsettlingly so. I believe we have a dark witch among us, a speculation I'm reluctant to voice in absence of evidence. The magic-touched already face too much blame for the Demon Witch's Reaping. I'll not fuel those fears. The woman you are traveling with, is she also a Purger?"

Taniel smiled at the thought of Shirin as a Purger. "No, she has a greater calling. I'd like to speak to Mage Terzian as soon as possible. Brother Emet said he'd be back from errands in the evening?"

"I'll arrange a meeting," Mardiros said. "I understand he may be as much aid to you, as you to us."

"Thank you." Taniel refrained from voicing his bitter comment that he doubted a ruined creature like him had any aid to offer. "I'd also like to visit the places the victims were last seen."

"Of course." Abbott Mardiros turned to the door. "Brother Ashot, why don't you come in?"

There was a sheepish scuffling and the young monk poked his head in. "I was only—"

"Listening outside the door. I told you, boy, I'm blind, not deaf." Mardiros beckoned the brother in. "And as you clearly failed to find higher purpose for your time, I'll task you with showing Taniel to the places where the young men were last seen."

The Abbott could not see Brother Ashot open his mouth to protest, but he surely heard the younger man grind his teeth. "Of course, Father Abbott."

The men lighting the iron lanterns along Agr Rav's streets watched Taniel walk by. Their gazes were curious and lacked Brother Ashot's cold appraisal. Taniel felt his every step being scrutinized by the monk—the scrape of his feet, the clunk of his walking stick, the stiff, crooked posture the Karvogi costume was unable to disguise from an attentive eye.

"You're not a real Karvogi, are you?" Brother Ashot asked.

"No, I don't hold their faith," Taniel said, seeing no advantage to deception.

"Then why do you dress as one?"

"To hide what I've become. You'd receive it with less grace than you do a Karvogi."

"Children of Irakai welcome all to their table," Brother Ashot said hotly. "We hold no hatred of cursed men or Karvogi."

"Disgust is not the same as hatred." Taniel held up his left hand to show the curled, fused fingers tipped by black claws. "This is the least of what has been done to me."

The anger drained from the monk's face and he looked away. Three streets passed where only the clack of Taniel's walking stick disrupted the quiet. He hoped to find Razban at the monastery by the time he returned. He was eager to see a friend, and optimistic of Razban having greater success in untangling Minu's curse than Gohar's mages.

"What happened to you?" Brother Ashot asked, his tone emptied of antagonism.

"Some men are cursed more than most," Taniel said. "And I'd rather have you go back to snarling at me than this pity."

"I don't deal in pity, but I am called to practice compassion."

"Save that as well, Brother, for someone more deserving than I."

"What exactly are you looking for?"

Taniel shrugged, his shoulder protesting the motion. "I'm not looking for anything exact. I'm simply getting a feel for the terrain."

Putting patterns together was easier when he had physical pieces to work from. Tangible starting points brought clarity to the vague pictures of witnesses' secondhand accounts that were inevitably colored by bias.

"We think it came from the churchyard." Brother Ashot pointed to the temple's domed tholobate rising over the rooftops. "There've always been reports of hauntings, and the Reaping woke far darker beings than restive ghosts."

More to appease Brother Ashot than in expectation of finding useful insight, Taniel limped toward the temple. Graveyards were haunting grounds of ghouls and gelin, not creatures that stole the living and left no trace. But until he had a stronger lead, he made a habit of investigating what locals wanted looked at first, even when he knew their suspicions were wrong. There was little to gain and much to lose in arguing with those seeking a Purger's help.

The temple's remembrance yard was large, yet cramped by thin gravestone pillars filling the grass lawns divided by mossy walkways. Taniel's skin prickled as he stepped beneath the iron gate. There was evidence of spiritual hauntings; ghosts of the improperly buried, or those who lingered from lives cut abruptly short. Those restless souls caught between this life and the After were not what threatened Agr Rav's young men, and no ghost could have churned the earth to dig up the recent graves.

Taniel tapped his walking stick on the disturbed ground. "What happened here?"

"Qutrubs," Brother Ashot said. "They've been climbing over the city walls. We haven't found a ward that keeps them out."

"There isn't a good one," Taniel said. "Get some dogs. Those work better than sorcery to chase them off. Did someone come to cleanse the grounds?"

"Yes. We reburied the disturbed, and Abbott Mardiros reconsecrated the yard."

Taniel nodded in approval. He sat beneath a golden-leaved oak, pulling out the map of Agr Rav Mardiros had provided him. He closed one eye to better study the paper; the blurring in the corners of his vision promised a headache soon to come.

"Has anyone seen qutrubs in the churchyard?" he asked, tracing his finger over the paper to draw connecting lines between where the victims were last seen.

"Master Terzian did." Brother Ashot pointed to black patches of scorched earth and stone further along the walkway. "He was overzealous in driving them off."

Taniel frowned. Razban hardly got a candle to burn, forget summoning fire. He never had an aptitude for violent magic or flashy sorcery. If not for Brother Emet confirming Razban came to Agr Rav with Master Maqlu, Taniel was inclined to think they spoke of two different men sharing the same name. Apparently, Razban had also changed in the eighteen months since the Reaping.

"Has Razban said anything on the disappearances?" Taniel asked.

"He thinks it's a demon. One deliberately summoned. He's been searching the city for a bidding rune or—Ah, speaking the name summons! Master Terzian!"

The man wearing the blue robes of a master mage stopped on the street outside the remembrance yard. Unlike Taniel, Razban was not so changed to be unrecognizable, but he was changed. The young man with the round, boyish face, circular spectacles, and figure prone to plumpness had been replaced by a thinner, gaunter man.

"Brother Ashot," Razban said in greeting. His gaze fixed on Taniel. The spectacles were gone, as was his tendency to smile. "Karvogi, you are welcome."

Taniel offered no return greeting. There was a wrongness to Razban that went beyond his change from a genial young man to a skeletal stranger.

"Master Terzian, this is Taniel Sushan," Brother Ashot said. "He's a Purger come to investigate the disappearances."

"The Sushans didn't practice the Karvogi faith," Razban said. His fingers curled and a faint thrum of hostile magic thickened the air.

"And your practice never strayed beyond the living arts of sorcery," Taniel said. "Yet the scorch marks in the remembrance yard say you've changed as well."

Razban stared at Taniel too long, eyes narrowing in a face that had thinned too quickly. This was far from the reunion Taniel anticipated. The uneasiness of seeing a friend's face turned into a stranger's raised his skin.

"The tattoo on the center of your chest," Razban said. "What is it?"

"The ram's head and Wind Daughter's anemone. You and I are friends of Sahak Sandar and we went to The Poor Man's Theatre tavern more often than proper. Your fellow apprentices nicknamed you 'Ghoul' for all your time spent studying cadavers. Two winters ago, you got recklessly drunk on the last day of the Festival of Lights and tried to kiss Suri. She blacked your eye."

"Yes." Razban touched his left eye. "She did."

Taniel thanked the gods his mask hid his discomfort. Suri had been left-handed and bruised the right side of Razban's face. It was not simply his misremembering that upset Taniel; the way he moved was unnaturally wrong, as if invisible strings guided his limbs.

"Forgive my suspicion, Taniel, I've learned the hard way the cost of blind trust." Razban's smile was painfully forced. "Come, all there is to catch up on is better done over a cup of the monastery's wine beside a fire, not over the graves of the dead."

The monastery room Brother Ashot showed Taniel and Razban to was far more comfortable than Abbot Mardiros' ascetic study. The light of the fire warming the hearth flickered merrily off the polished table, and Taniel's joints groaned in relief to sit in a cushioned chair.

A novice set out a wine decanter, a platter of flat bread, minced meat, pomegranate molasses, and promised a real dinner was in preparation.

"You'll have to forgive me." Razban sat at the table in his eerie, fitful way of moving. "I'm not the man you remember."

"That's something we have in common," Taniel said. He had never been as close to Razban as he was Sahak, but they had been good friends. The man sitting across the table from him was completely at odds with the Razban he knew. "What happened to you?"

"I was about to ask you the same. I think my story is shorter so I'll tell first." He held up his hand to bend each finger, the flexion mechanically stiff. "In trying to save Master Tahir from the Reaping, I overstretched myself. There were consequences of body and mind. I've been working ever since to lessen them and progress proves slow."

He poured a cup of wine and passed it to Taniel.

"Thank you, but I don't drink anymore," Taniel lied. He smelled a peculiar sorcery clinging to his friend. Mages who practiced medicinal spellwork often had odd odors hanging about them; formaldehyde from the laboratory, the sour stench of bodies both living and preserved, or the metallic aroma that was a shared trait of their magic. Razban smelled sickly, like wet rot.

"Nor do I," Razban admitted. "It no longer agrees with me, and I have difficulty enough keeping my memories straight while sober."

"When Master Maqlu headed east, did he say where he intended to go?" Taniel asked.

Razban paused as if searching for a distant memory, then shook his head. "I only know he continued toward the Grey Forest, determined to chase fables. I chose to stay where I might accomplish some true good. Unrest burns in the south, and once they run out of men to kill along the river banks, it will spread north. A mage's duty is to protect his people. Not run from responsibility."

"Master Maqlu didn't mention the town or village he intended to travel to?"

"No, and your questions do little to speak confidence in my abilities to aid you."

"The mages at the Arcanum could do nothing. I'm better off doing as your former master did, consigning myself to chasing fables." Taniel would have permitted the Razban he knew to try and rescue him from his curse. The man across from him—he held back a shudder at the thought of this changed Razban touching him.

"Whatever curse you hide beneath that Karvogi cloak, I assure you I've seen worse."

"I'll seek help for myself once I see the evil preying upon Agr Rav gone. Until then, I have nothing to offer for a High Mage's service."

Razban snorted. "Taniel, you don't pay for a friend's help."

"Thank you, but I prefer to earn what is sure to be a long and costly service."

The firelight stretched shadows over Razban's hollowed features, placing upon him a mask more inhuman than Taniel's.

"Yes, you were always proud," Razban said. "That is one thing unchanged."

"Flex your foot," Iradah the hedgewitch said. She mimed the action with her hand before cupping both around Nesrin's ankle. She was a stout woman of middling years, her dark hair was braided into a practical twist, and the frown lines creasing the corners of her mouth brooked no nonsense.

Nesrin did as instructed, continuing the motion as her skin burned hot before cooling beneath the hedgewitch's hands. The swelling visibly lessened, leaving the joint feeling oddly light.

"It fix?" Nesrin asked.

"Roll your foot in a circle." Iradah again demonstrated the movement to imitate.

Nesrin winced as her ankle strained from the motion. The hedgewitch pursed her lips in concentration, fingers palpating the joint. Focused heat poured to where Nesrin felt the pain most acutely, a cooling sensation loosened the last of the stiffness, and her ankle moved unhindered in its full range of motion.

"It fix now?" she asked.

"Patience, child," Iradah said as she had her every visit over the last three days. Razmik's sister, Shadi, had readily welcomed Nesrin into her home and heartily berated her whenever Nesrin attempted to help with chores that required her to be on her feet. Shadi insisted she rest, a difficult task as Nesrin grew more restive by the hour. Under Iradah's attention, her injury's mending had been shortened from weeks to days, but Nesrin was anxious to go east. Every day lost was gods knew how many more miles between her and Taniel.

Iradah used long cloth bandages to rewrap Nesrin's ankle. "Stay off that foot another couple days. If you feel tingling, loss of sensation, or the swelling returns, send for me."

"But it fix now?" Nesrin asked.

"Give it another couple days," Iradah said sternly.

"Then tracking spell, you say it take couple days to set. We do it now, yes?"

"No."

"Why no?"

"Child, I use my gifts to heal and help, not to send grief-sick young women wandering to their deaths."

"You say you would."

"I thought you'd see reason by now," Iradah said. "You're better off returning to Gohar, or staying in Ethel to make a home here."

"I go where my husband go. That my home." If Iradah refused to perform the tracking spell, then Nesrin would head east without it.

"Do you know how many people have come to me after hearing rumor that a loved one survived the Reaping? They beg me to help find them, only to discover their hope was false. At best, the spell leads them to where the body was burned or buried. More often, in absence of a living soul to find, tracking spells drive the seeker mad, and they follow their loved one into death. You'd take that risk? Have your death or madness be on my conscience?"

"This my choice. My risk," Nesrin said. "If I not mad now, I will be if I let my husband go. If I too scared to chase hope, then I coward and I not live that life."

The hedgewitch gave her a measuring stare as if searching for a fracture in Nesrin's resolve. "Are you certain you wish to go through with this?"

"Yes." Nesrin had made up her mind for what must be done the moment she learned Taniel was alive. There was no swaying her from that path, no matter where it led.

"I should have saved myself the job of wrapping the ankle, then." Iradah undid the cloth from Nesrin's foot. "Stay there, it's a simple casting and won't take long."

She disappeared into the hall and Nesrin heard the creak of the back door opening, the squeak of the well pump being worked, and Iradah speaking to Shadi who was hanging clothes to dry in the garden. The hedgewitch returned in multiple trips, first carrying two pitchers of water, then fetching a kitchen knife, a single candle, and fresh cloth.

"Do you be needing something of Taniel's?" Nesrin asked. The clothes she had worn to disguise herself as a man were his and ought to suffice.

"I have his wife. I can't do much better than that. Wash yourself thoroughly using one of the pitchers. Leave the other untouched." She stepped from the room to give her privacy. "Call me when you're finished, but stay undressed."

Nesrin stripped out of the dress Shadi had lent her, folding it neatly in the room's corner. A flash of falling white caught her eye and she picked the small anemone flower the Karvogi had given to her off the floor. It was impossible for the flower to have fallen free while she was undressing, the simple garment had no pockets, and she remembered leaving the flower in Taniel's traveling coat. The petals were as pure white as the day the Karvogi gave it to her and smelled as sweet as if freshly plucked. She gently placed the small flower on top of the folded dress, sparing it curious glances as she washed.

"Ready," she said, wrapping herself in the floor sofa's blanket for modesty.

Iradah reentered the room and gave a faint smile seeing Nesrin shielded behind the blanket.

"You've got nothing to hide I haven't seen before," she said.

"Does it upset ritual?" Nesrin asked.

"No, it's fine, child. Though you're an odd soul. Fearless in the face of the unknown, yet blushing with a maiden's shyness."

Setting the candle in the room's center, Iradah pinched the wick between her fingers. A flame sputtered to life.

"Razirah, servant of the Wind Daughter, patron to those who wander, light the way for one in need," she said. The candle's light bloomed across the room, banishing shadows with its radiance.

Motioning for her to sit facing the candle, the hedgewitch took Nesrin's right hand and used the kitchen knife to prick her palm.

"Lead the asking soul to where she must go." Iradah tapped her finger to the knife's dull edge, sprinkling droplets of Nesrin's blood into the second water pitcher. She repeated the process on Nesrin's left palm, the soles of her feet, and finally the skin above her heart. "Razirah, heal a grieving world, guide her, and make her whole again."

The shallow knife wounds tingled as if a soft thumb brushed Nesrin's skin. The hedgewitch snuffed out the candle between her fingers and natural light's return felt oppressively dark after the brilliant glow.

Iradah held up the water pitcher mixed with Nesrin's blood. "Wash again, and use all the water."

Nesrin waited for the hedgewitch to leave before letting the blanket fall, wetting the cloth, and scrubbing her skin. She braced for a new sensation to come over her—a fire in her feet to carry her to her husband, a vision revealing hidden knowledge of his whereabouts, or a guiding voice whispering where she must go. Nothing happened save her shivering from cool air on exposed skin. She pulled the dress on, holding her breath in anticipation of revelation. None came. No whispering word, no compelling direction. She felt nothing other than sinking disappointment.

"What's wrong?" Iradah asked when Nesrin opened the door.

"Nothing happen. It all feel same," she said, sitting for her ankle to be rewrapped.

"It can take up to a week to set, child. You must be patient with this. I'll be back in two days to see how the spell is coming along, and I expect you to be here, resting. I've told Shadi to keep an eye on you and to not be afraid to tie you down if you act recklessly. No, sit, there's no need to show me out, I know the way and you need practice in staying still to heal and not running off to reopen wounds."

"It take more than bad ankle to excuse bad manners." Nesrin hopped beside Iradah as she showed her to the front door. Though her ankle felt ready to run on, she held her foot off the ground for Iradah's sake. "And thank you, for all help."

"I can believe your husband survived the Reaping if he survived a wife as headstrong as you. The two of you must've been ..." Iradah trailed off when she stepped out the front door, mouth hanging open and eyes going wide.

"What wrong?" Nesrin peered around her.

A gentle breeze swept over the dirt road, rustling the white anemones blooming before their eyes. Defying the cycle of seasons, the springtime flowers rose like snow from beneath the autumn leaves, unfurling in the wake of the eastbound wind.

"Well, forget my folly I mistook for wisdom," Iradah said. "You are called, child, and you must go."

17

The Dark Witch of Agr Rav

Taniel flexed his fingers to work the cramping from his hand. Writing severely taxed his limited dexterity, and the notes he jotted in the map of Agr Rav's margins had a child's refinement. He and Brother Ashot had gone out in the morning's early hours to retrace the trail paved by the investigation's witness testimony, and Taniel had used the map to keep record of the sites they'd visited. Jagged crosses marked the map where the victims had lived, lopsided circles where they had last been seen, crude black dots for places they'd worked or frequented. There was no clustering in the ink to indicate a particular section of the city where the disappearances occurred; the pattern of the vanishings was one of behavior, not location. All the victims had traveled through Agr Rav's emptied middle ring the day they vanished, and the abductions followed a ritualistic nature with specific victims, the regularity of the disappearances, and the care taken so no trace remained. Abbott Mardiros was right. This was a man's work, not a monster's.

"What about a demon?" Shirin asked, looking up from the book she read.

"Oh, sorry." Taniel had not realized he'd been musing aloud. The habit was one he'd inherited from his father and it drove Nesrin mad. "I didn't mean to distract you."

Abbott Mardiros allowed an exception to the rule of men and

women sleeping in different guest wings for Shirin and Taniel to share a room. Taniel's unusual condition required assistance, and he trusted no one else to see him beneath the Karvogi cloak.

Shirin set her book down and stretched. "That's alright, my mind is in the mood to be distracted and yours is clearly in want of an ear to listen. So could it be a demon?"

"I don't think so," Taniel said. "It's too neat and I've never known a demon to be secretive in its evils. Only men take care to hide their wickedness."

He tapped the quill to the map, wondering how much to tell Shirin and how much to keep private until he had evidence. The witnesses Taniel spoke to throughout the day were quick to name who they blamed for the disappearances: the bone-traders who were constantly taking their filthy dealings in and out of the city, or the hedgewitch from across the Setareh Sea whose magic practices were as dark as his skin. Taniel had followed to where all the fingers pointed in accusation led. As expected, he'd found none of the provided names to be convincing suspects, but an afternoon and evening spent interviewing relatives and friends of the vanished men, the people they accused, and a narrowing circle of witnesses revealed threads linking the victims. All had strong associations with the monastery. Two of the young men had lived on the grounds, the other two had made frequent visits tending to the curse-afflicted people seeking sanctuary. And all the victims—in the week leading up to their disappearance—had visited a certain mage whose manor neighbored the monastery.

A week ago, Taniel would have laughed at the thought of Razban Terzian willfully harming anyone. Yesterday's meeting with him had changed that.

"Stay close to Abbott Mardiros tomorrow," he said. "If I'm not with you, be sure you are in his company."

"And what of you?"

"I need to look into something."

"You think someone at the monastery has a hand in the disappearances?"

"I'm not ruling anything out." Taniel winced at the sharp tingle joining the cramping in his hand. "So please, stay close to the Abbott, and away from Razban Terzian."

"Isn't he your friend?"

"He's not the man I knew." He rubbed his eyes to soften the headache blooming beneath his horns, aggravated by his staring at the map and hunching over the desk.

"Did your meeting with him not …" Shirin's mouth thinned into a grim line. "You suspect him of being involved."

"If he's not involved in the disappearances, he is involved in something broken," Taniel said, unsurprised Shirin came to her conclusion. She was cleverly intuitive, as were most housewives he had met. They possessed an uncanny knack for knowing where threats to family and home lurked, and for that reason, they were among the first he spoke to when a dark creature threatened a village. "I'll need evidence before bringing a claim against him."

Regardless of how off-putting he found Agr Rav's new High Mage, Razban had been a friend and there was a respect owed there. Not a benefit of the doubt, but a caution to avoid calling undue wrath upon him. Brother Emet had warned Taniel how quick to judgment and eager for blood Agr Rav's people were. For the sake of his conscience, Taniel resolved to keep his suspicions private until he was certain whether Razban's new mannerisms were born of hardship endured, or if they were rooted in more sinister sources. He had little hope of it being the former, and feared there was little to nothing left of his friend.

He had only shared his concerns to Abbott Mardiros. The retired Purger agreed to keep them quiet and granted Taniel a second exception—the monastery's skeleton key, enchanted to open any door on the grounds. The entire upper tier of Agr Rav had once belonged to the hallowed halls, including the High Mage's manor. Mardiros was confident the key's enchantment should overpower newer additions to the manor the resident mage had laid to keep out snooping holy men or Purgers. The Abbott told him that Razban spent mornings at the monastery tending to the tainted before traveling to the lower tier to work alongside the physicians, giving Taniel long, uninterrupted hours to search his home.

The dull throbs spreading from Taniel's horns worsened, feeling as though the bones curled into his skull. Surrendering to the headache, he tucked away the map and limped to bed. His wrist and finger joints popped under his massaging them, beginning the long ritual of working loose the day's stiffness to stop the worst of it from greeting him in the morning.

"What are you going to do?" Shirin asked.

"My duty as a Purger," he said.

"Please don't do anything reckless."

"Everything a Purger does is reckless."

"Taniel."

"I promise to do nothing more reckless than charging headlong into the Demon Witch's swamp." His charging days were long gone. Instead, he'd limp headlong into the manor of a suspected fallen mage.

"Gods help you, Taniel." Shirin shook her head. "You won't accept anyone else's."

Uncapping a vial of the balm, she sat beside him to work the soothing ointment into his neck, chronically strained from holding the horns' unnatural weight.

"Thank you," he said, wishing he had more to offer Shirin than gratitude.

"You have too much left to give the world to throw your life away. One day, you'll see that."

The High Mage's manor stood at the western edge of Agr Rav's top tier, sheltered behind the privacy of scarlet dogwood and hardy dwarf cedar. A feeble wind stirred anemic clouds across a dull sky and sent dry leaves spiraling from the trees. The fallen leaves crackled beneath Taniel's feet as he followed the unwelcoming lane leading to the once regal estate succumbing to decay. The manor was better suited to host ghosts than the living. The red tile roof was chipped and discolored by aged lichen, the arched windows grimy. Weeds conquered the front garden, spilling out to invade the cracks scarring the stone walkway. Taniel struggled to imagine the fastidious Razban living here. Dread for what awaited him within settled cold in his chest. If his suspicions proved right, Razban didn't live here at all, and his friend had been dead for over a year.

Wards designed to disallow uninvited visitors pulsed against Taniel. The monastery's iron skeleton key dampened the repelling magic, reducing the overwhelming urge to flee the manor grounds to a low, nervous irritation. The nagging fear to run was too real to be constructed solely from sorcery. The emotions in the enchantment must have been harvested, and Taniel suspected the abducted men had provided the horror seeking to drive him away.

Writhing discomfort ran through his arms and chest. He pulled up his sleeve to see his veins raised, and a crimson mist hissing from his skin like wind-blown sand. The manor's warding disliked Minu's magic and sought to remove her tainted sorcery from the grounds. Taniel limped faster to distance himself from the spells guarding the walkway before their attacking the witch's magic shifted to attacking what her magic held together—him.

Stronger wards guarded the front door, breeding black terror screaming for him to flee. He fumbled for the skeleton key beneath his Karvogi cloak, a frightened sweat beading his brow, his heart pounding and breaths coming in short, anxious gasps. He ignored the sorcery-born panic. He was well-practiced in working through the body's shortcomings.

The key grated in the lock, Taniel felt the manor's defensive magics fail, and the front door swung slowly open with a neglected groan. He tucked the skeleton key beneath his cloak. The iron clinked against the talismans he wore, serving as poor replacements for his warding tattoos Minu had destroyed. Vestiges of the tattoos' power endured—as vestiges of himself lingered in this crippled form—but they had been broken from their design and only traces of the black ink remained.

The enchanted fear sent a piercing chill through him upon crossing the threshold. His left hand spasmed, his skull throbbed beneath his horns, and Minu's sorcery misted from him in a scarlet burst. Taniel leaned on the wall, breathing deep until his heart rate settled and the red ceased hissing from his skin.

The manor's interior presented no better than its frontage. Dusty curtains covered shuttered windows, cobwebs draped the stairwell banisters, and beneath the musty odor lay the chilling iron-scent of blood-magic. The dining area evidenced someone lived in these dark, dusty halls. The smell of oil lamps perfumed the stale air. Half-eaten bread and a glass sticky from a red residue were left on the table beside books, papers, inkwell, and quill. The open tome's language was foreign to Taniel, the scrawling shorthand written in the margins even more alien. He had no need to be able to read the strange scripts; he understood that the diagram of a dissected human body and the runes carved into the illustrated flesh were malefic.

Faint stains spattered the floor in the pattern of blood dripped from an open wound. They clustered thickest around the table and the wall covered by a tapestry. Taniel moved the cloth aside to reveal the hidden doorway. The entrance was carelessly disguised, as was the man who wore Razban's face, confident no one would look too closely.

The skeleton key caught in the hidden door's lock, the two magics fighting the other. The key's won out, ringing like the tinny sound of bells as it opened the door to stairs descending from the dining room's grey gloom into total blackness. Taniel stared down the dark, apprehensive that finding the hidden basement had been so simple. Overreliance on enchantments and warding was a common failing shared by dark witches, but he was wary that this false Razban—who was capable of creating the complex fear-fed magic guarding the manor—had neglected to cover the simple trail of mundane evidence exposing the evil he wished to hide. No one was this careless. Unless this was a trap, or the witch was arrogantly assured of no one getting past the front door.

Doubling back to the kitchen, Taniel claimed an oil lantern from beneath the table. He wasted three matches before his fumbling fingers got the fourth to catch and light the wick. He took a second lantern and pocketed spare matches as well, not putting it past himself to drop his only source of light as he descended the black stairs reeking of blood-magic.

The lantern stretched weak shadows along the arched stairwell as he slowly descended the narrow, uneven steps. The stone was unpleasantly slippery from a dark, oily substance. Twice he clutched at the wall to prevent himself from falling. The metallic taste of sorcery and the vinegary tang he associated with the Arcanum cadaver labs thickened nearer the stairwell base. The lantern flame sputtered at the bottom stair as if recoiling from what it must reveal.

The headless body lay naked on the wooden table. Bruising around the wrists and ankles suggested restraints were used in the man's last moments and that he'd been terribly aware of his fate. Sorcery preserved the discoloration and prevented marbling rot from claiming the corpse. The head rested on a raised plinth, its skin a strange texture closer to soft clay than flesh, and in the gloom it looked as though slow ripples crossed over the features. Taniel stepped closer. The movement was not a trick of lantern-cast shadow. The tissue flowed like sap's lazy ooze along a tree, molded and pushed by unseen fingers to shape a new face.

The lantern light reflected off glass jars lining wooden shelves built into the stone walls, showing bits of dismembered corpses floating in sickly yellow liquid. What Taniel thought were grotesque masks were revealed to be skinned faces set upon mannequin heads, all of them bearing unmistakable similarity to Razban. The large wooden barrels stacked in the room's corners demanded no imagination for

Taniel to guess their contents, and he had no desire to continue his explorations. He had all the required evidence.

Turning from the macabre workshop, he limped up the stairs. He felt the empty eye sockets of the skinned faces following him, and he cursed his slow, shuffling step. If he had been undamaged and whole he wouldn't have to run to Abbott Mardiros. He'd wait for the witch wearing Razban's face to return, then kill the bastard. Taniel's knee popped, his leg faltered, and he gripped the wall to stop from tumbling down the slick stairs.

"Seraphs," he swore. In his ruined condition, it took all his will to flee and send better men to do what he was too broken to see done.

Reaching the top stair, he froze. The man wearing Razban's face stared at him from across the hall in polite surprise.

"How did you get in?" he asked.

"You invited me to come to your workshop just two nights ago," Taniel said then added, "Tahir."

Agr Rav had not received a new High Mage. Master Tahir had retained his office under a new guise.

Razban's false face stretched into a rictus smile. "What gave it away?"

"That you're careless," Taniel said, eyes darting beneath his mask to find the quickest escape, makeshift weapons, or wards for hidden sorcery Tahir had ready to use. "I'm surprised no one suspects you."

"People see what gives them comfort," Tahir said. "And providing Agr Rav the comfort of a High Mage to protect her is the least of my duties."

He motioned for Taniel to sit at the dining table. Taniel stayed where he was.

"My dear boy," Tahir said, "you are, as you say, an invited guest and that ridiculous Karvogi cloak can't disguise how strenuous it is for you to simply stand. Sit, I insist."

Taniel obeyed, deciding it better to avoid further antagonizing Tahir.

"I do commiserate. This must be terribly disappointing," Tahir said. "You came all this way looking for a friend, hoping he might free you from that curse."

"It's not the worst disappointment I've faced." Taniel's fingers itched from the urge to grab the knife hidden beneath his cloak. Purger advice ran a thousand contradictory ways for confronting dark witches. Never let them speak lest they put a curse on you. Let them talk to reveal their secrets to your advantage. Always watch their eyes, never meet their gaze, never answer questions, only answer what is asked. In a sea of superstition and conflicting wisdom, Taniel followed his father's advice on the matter.

"Don't be stupid, don't be careless," he had said. "People are flawed and dark magic belongs to the most fractured. Figure out where that weak line runs."

Tahir was unrepentantly a witch who enjoyed the sound of his own voice. Too much to limit it to incantations. Keeping him talking was Taniel's best play until he devised a better strategy.

"Why Razban?" Taniel asked.

"He interfered," Tahir said. "It was unfortunate. My apprentice was to serve as my escape from the Reaping, but Mage Terzian walked in during the process. I would only have needed one life if not for him trying to stop me. What you saw in my work room, well, as I said, it's unfortunate but necessary."

"Necessary for what?" Taniel stalled as he raced through doomed plans of escape.

"For Agr Rav. I was tasked to defend her, and the Demon Witch will not steal me from my duty. Not when it is needed more than ever. The Reaping was merely the beginning, young Sushan. Worse horrors rise in its wake."

Taniel kept silent his opinion that Tahir was one of those "worse horrors."

"The Mad Purger and his zealots wreak havoc, setting fire to villages, burning hedgewitches, and harvesting the magic-touched. It's only a matter of time before the southern unrest spreads north." Tahir spoke with the calm confidence of an instructor explaining a concept to a curious student. "But you have other concerns, my young friend. Ailments you seek a mage to cure."

Taniel glanced between the front door behind Tahir and the tall windows, knowing he'd not make it three hobbling paces before the mage struck him down.

"Sushan, I am the High Mage of Agr Rav. It is my sworn duty to cure ills such as yours, and you saw for yourself my talent in remolding flesh," Tahir said. "If I can escape the Reaping, I can rescue you from your affliction."

"In exchange for what?"

"You mistake me, and unfairly so. I'm a mage, not a monster. Everything I've done is for the good of the people I serve. I knew your father—"

"Funnily enough, so did I."

"—and he understood the burden of sacrificing for a greater good. The cost of a few lives to protect the many."

Taniel bristled. The mage's words echoed Minu's; happily justifying atrocity under self-righteous delusion.

"The people need mages during this dark time, and you are one such person in need. I can save you, Sushan. Your coming here is not in vain." Tahir held out his hand. "A show of faith. Give me your left hand, that's the one the Demon Witch mangled, is it not?"

Tahir stepped forward and Taniel bolted to his feet, retreating from the snaring magic the mage began to twine around him. Years of surviving dark witches made Tahir's treachery obvious, and Minu's infecting magic thrummed angrily in Taniel's blood, disliking the sorcerer attempting to trespass upon what was hers.

"If your good intentions demand the death of innocents, I want no part in them," Taniel said.

"The world is not so simple. There are no innocents."

Taniel's ears popped from a sudden shift in air pressure. He barely staggered out from Tahir's more aggressive snaring spell erupting around him. The magic snapped after Taniel like a hound's teeth seeking purchase on prey. His mask slipped, blinding him from seeing Tahir raise his hand until it was too late.

The spell splintered the table, screeched over stone, and took Taniel off his feet. A combination of talismans and the surviving warding tattoos on what was left of his original skin protected him from the magic, not the raw, kinetic force of it sending him skidding across the broken floor, colliding hard into the wall.

Red and black spun across his vision as he lay stunned, the wind knocked out from him. Booted footsteps crunched over broken wood and glass. Taniel lay unmoving, making no effort to struggle to his feet. Tahir was a cat who wanted to play with his prey. He'd either continue to blast Taniel until the force of the spells ripped him limb from limb, or he'd take a more refined approach, curiosity compelling him to see what the Karvogi mask hid. Taniel wagered his life it'd be the latter.

"Did you think this would end differently?" Tahir asked. "How did you expect to stand against me when you can barely stand at all?"

The footsteps stopped. Taniel sensed the mage standing over him, smelled the rotted reek of his corrupted magic.

"Or was your coming here a desperate bid to die?" He pressed his boot toe into Taniel's back.

Taniel held still, scarcely daring to breathe, his fingers wrapped around the hidden blade's hilt.

"No, meddlers like you and Terzian don't deserve easy fates." Cloth rustled as the mage crouched beside Taniel. A hand felt for the edge of his mask. "You had the chance to sate your curiosity, prying into my secrets. I'm allowed the same to yours—"

Taniel struck. The knife's edge sliced through Tahir's forearms brought up in instinctive defense. Tahir screeched and Taniel's clumsy roll took him out from the spell's path that cracked the floor where he'd been, sending stone shards biting into him. He lunged for the off-balanced mage, sinking the knife into Tahir's neck, and gave a vicious tug. Blood, unnaturally dark and thick, sprayed over him. Tahir clutched his ruined throat, putrid magic pulsing from the wound. Taniel allowed the mage no time to contemplate his mortal wound. He plunged the knife into Tahir's chest and dragged the blade through the artery.

A thin mewling escaped Tahir's torn throat. "No ... no, I can ... I can save you, Sushan." He crumpled to the floor, twitching in a spreading, dark pool. Sorcery feebly sparked over the dying mage. His false face sagged, skin sloughing off to show the skeletal creature beneath. "Spare me. Spare ... I can save ..."

Taniel took out a larger blade better for cutting through bone. All dark witches were dangerous until dead, burned, and a few days buried. Taniel settled for the cruder insurance of separating Tahir's head from the stolen body.

The body continued to twitch after the last sinew was severed. The mouth moved in wordless pleas and empty promises. The eddying magic swirling over the corpse dissipated, the fingers ceased twitching, and the flesh melted like wax in fire. The bones were the last to dissolve into the reeking mess of rot and robes.

Legs trembling and head spinning, Taniel collapsed against the wall. His heart and head pounded in agonizing disharmony, his strained muscles shook, and his lungs burned from the exertion they no longer had the strength to sustain. The adrenaline rushing through his tainted blood faded, allowing him to more acutely feel the incompatibility between Tahir's and Minu's magic, his body serving as the battleground for the two forces. He had to leave the manor grounds before he became a casualty in their war.

He pulled himself to his feet only to fall, legs shaking too violently to hold him. The headache forever festering beneath his horns burst into a blinding migraine. His senses blurred at the cusp of unconsciousness. He attempted to crawl from the manor. His vision clouded red then dipped into darkness. His arms gave out, and he fell to the floor. He felt the remembered agony of Minu wrenching his bones to her design, Kharinah's presence roiling with chaotic destruction, and his helpless begging for a mercy that never came.

A woman spoke through the burning black, her words lost in the darkness keen to claim him. Hands lifted him from the stone floor—Minu come to drag him further into brokenness. He was too close to unconsciousness to struggle. A weak "no" escaped his lips, terrified tears streamed hot down his cheeks, and the unseen hands carried him into the waiting dark.

Air untainted by death fell sweet over Taniel. He sucked in a gasping breath. His chest felt bonelessly light, no longer crushed beneath the oppressive hostilities of Tahir's and Minu's sorcery. He winced, gripping his head whirling from the dizziness of waking too quickly. His vision cleared to show grey sky through the black branches above him. He blinked in aching confusion. He had no memory of how he ended up beneath the dogwood tree, safely beyond the range of Tahir's wards that refused to tolerate Minu's ill-magic coursing through him. Last he remembered, he was lying in the manor's ruined hallway.

Someone must have carried him out, but there was no sign of another soul. No figure stood on the walkway, lurked behind the trees or watched from the manor's front doors left hanging open. A cold, pattering rain darkened the stone path, and set the leaves above him to shiver. He lay alone beneath the dogwood outside the boundary of the manor grounds and there he remained, unable to stand on watery legs, curled beneath his cloak sheltering him from the rain, until half an hour later when in disregard of all advice and wisdom, Shirin came looking for him.

Weariness was Nesrin's sole companion. She had walked alone the last two days, not a soul to be seen or to share the easterly road. The sweeping meadows on either side of the hard-packed path fractured into craggy hills. Yew and hazel trees swayed under soft winds funneled through the valley by looming red cliffs adorned by dark juniper; a gateway carved by the gods to the eastern mountains painted a white-capped indigo beneath the pale morning sky. There was a bitter beauty to days such as this. The sun alighting upon the meadow's winding creek belonged to the same world where the sky had burned red to reap countless souls. The songbirds flitting above fields colored by autumn's final bloom were neighbors to monsters, demons, and the men who mirrored their evils.

Nesrin touched the talisman around her neck, seeking the small comfort of the cool silver. A growing disquiet, as though she was watched by a baleful presence, had plagued her since the previous night. The birds singing in the meadows, the cool breeze, the sun casting the fields in golden hues—it meant nothing. Wickedness held no reverence for beauty; even on a day as lovely as this, it sought harm to the unfortunate souls who strayed into its reach.

She tucked the talisman beneath her shirt. If evil was to cross her way, so be it. She'd not be frightened from the path laid clear before her. Razirah's white anemones bordered the road, encouraging her east. No matter the trials she'd not turn from finding her husband.

A shepherd's hut built into a low hill offered a place of rest for a midday meal. The missing shingles, empty windows, and neglected fields promised that her days of solitude were in no danger of being disrupted.

"Lovely day, child."

Nesrin gasped. She had almost walked right past the man sitting at the roadside, leaning against a crooked, wooden fence. His faded grey clothes were ragged and frayed, a wide-brimmed hat used by rice farmers was pulled low over his eyes, and the little she saw of his lower face was paler than bone.

"It is," she said uneasily. The man sat stone-still and was impossibly clean. Despite the aged condition of his clothes no stains marked the cloth, and his hands—waxen and lifelessly white—were spotless. Not a speck of dirt clung beneath his effeminately long nails.

"What brings you out here?" he asked. "It's been long since a traveler's come this way."

Nesrin took a wary step back. There was a wrongness to this man. He tilted his head up so the hat no longer obscured his face. Soulless black eyes met hers.

"Are you headed far, traveler?" the man that was not a man asked. His bloodless lips had not moved when he spoke and the nagging dread that had haunted Nesrin the last day plunged into cold terror.

She ran, trusting her life to the talisman around her neck to keep the evil guised as a man at bay. Her mind raced through all Taniel had told her of the creatures he purged. There were dozens of demons who preyed on travelers—which was this? The waxen human visage meant nothing. Taniel had told her creatures were defined by their behavior, not how they looked. Too many refused obedience to the natural law of holding a single shape for appearance to be a reliable identifier.

The not-man's laugh chased her, sounding as if it were a mere step behind her. "How far is home, traveler?"

She whipped around, Purger knife raised. No demon pursued her. No cloaked figure sat by the crooked fence. The road was empty. A gentle breeze teased the tall grass and spun golden leaves on lazy spirals. Her loneliness was a lie.

Karakin. That's what Taniel had called them. A demon that asked deceptively innocent questions of travelers, and with each answer given, pulled their victims further under their thrall. Nesrin held the knife tight, willing her hand to stop trembling. How long had the karakin been stalking her before revealing its presence? She hadn't answered any of the questions, but she had spoken to it. Was that enough to fall under its thrall? Did it need only her voice to turn her mind against her?

One hand holding her pack tight to her back, the other gripping the talisman around her neck, she hurried down the path, heart and feet pounding in a desperate search for shelter. She didn't trust anything less than a threshold or hearth to protect her from the monsters prowling this broken world, not now she knew how closely one stalked her.

18

How Far Is Home?

A crowd gathered outside the physician's home. Word had spread fast about the cursed Purger who'd slain the dark witch of Agr Rav. A few people stood on tiptoe in hopes of seeing through the curtained windows. One woman, noticing Shirin peering out, pointed to draw her fellow onlookers' attention. Shirin let the curtain fall shut before more eyes found her. She was glad the holy brothers had spirited Taniel to the lower tier where the physician lived before the wildfire of rumor caught him.

A hedgewitch had been sent for the moment the physician saw Taniel's condition, more alarmed by his twisted form than his injuries. Shirin alternated between nervously nibbling at the sweetbread with tea set out for her, and pacing the sitting room as the hedgewitch and physician's tending to Taniel dragged from one hour to the next. Her anxious fretting irritated the physician's young apprentice who shot increasingly annoyed scowls at her from his study desk. Finding Taniel beneath the tree unable to stand, unsure of how he got out from the manor, and trembling too violently for her to lift him reminded her too much of when the Reaping had come for her children. Her youngest had succumbed to confused delirium. She had found her middle daughter shivering on the front step, too weak to stand. Her eldest son suffered seizing fits before wasting away until he was too weak to move.

The hedgewitch emerged from the room where she and the physician examined Taniel. Her expression did little to ease Shirin's worry.

"How is he?" Shirin asked.

"That curse is beyond me." The hedgewitch shook her head, silver talisman earrings jangling. "I have no idea how to help him. He'll have to search elsewhere for a cure. Gohar perhaps."

"That's where we came from," Shirin said.

"Then continue east. Go to the Grey Forest if you must, but stay far from the Azariel River and Sevget. The magic-touched aren't tolerated there. A Purger has gone mad and—"

"He's not mad," the physician's assistant said. "He's one of the few sane men left. Sorcery brings nothing but suffering. He's right to stamp it out."

"And his followers who set fire to my home and forced my family to flee, they were in the right as well?" the hedgewitch asked.

"If you—"

"Mazdak, enough," the physician said, following the hedgewitch from the room.

The assistant scowled. Muttering beneath his breath, he took his heavy book up the stairs and behind a slammed door.

"You'll have to forgive him," the physician said. "My other assistant was one of Tahir's victims. He and Mazdak were close, and Mazdak has always been leery of sorcery. Learning what Tahir did to his friend has fanned that distrust to include all magic-touched."

"How's Taniel?" Shirin asked.

"His physical injuries are minor," the physician said. "Only a few required stitching, but I advise against pursuing unnatural healing."

The hedgewitch nodded in agreement. "That curse is volatile. I don't think it'll tolerate tampering magics."

"I think he's getting worse," Shirin confessed.

"I've given him medication for the pain," the physician said. "Beyond that, I'm at a loss. This is sorcery, not a sickness I can cure."

"Do you know of anyone who can?" Shirin asked.

"You said the Demon Witch did that to him?" the physician asked.

"Yes, and we've already been to the Arcanum in Gohar. They couldn't help him there."

"Master Maqlu passed through here a little over a year ago," the physician said. "He bested the Demon Witch before, perhaps he can best her curse."

"Taniel holds that same hope," Shirin said.

"It's unfortunate you missed him. All I know is he and his other apprentice went east," the physician said. "I agree with your son in thinking finding Maqlu is his best bet, but I can't recommend travel for him. His condition is too precarious."

Shirin didn't correct him that Taniel was not her son. Nor did she voice her growing doubt that Master Maqlu, powerful as he was claimed to be, lacked the ability to overcome Taniel's curse. She suspected the only one who had the power to manage Taniel's condition was the witch who'd cursed him.

The physician handed her a vial. "Two drops, morning and evening, or as the pain demands. Be sure he takes it with food. I'll be back to check on him later tonight."

"Thank you," Shirin said. She knocked on Taniel's door before entering.

He sat up when he saw her. Bandages wrapped his arms where shattered stone had scored and sorcery burned him, but he was far more alert than he'd been when first brought to the physician.

"Did you hear what was said?" she asked.

"Yes, and the physician told me the same." He eyed the vial Shirin set on the bedside table. "Did the physician or his assistant give you that?"

"The physician."

"Good. I think his assistant would poison me if he got the chance."

"What do you plan to do now?" Shirin asked. Agr Rav had proven a more bitter disappointment than Gohar; not only had Taniel discovered there was no cure for him here, but had learned the grisly fate of a friend.

"Master Maqlu stayed at the monastery during his time here," Taniel said. "I'll hire that hedgewitch to visit his rooms, see if there's a way to lay a tracking spell. If not, Abbott Mardiros sent word to Nahr Hasa and the nearest towns seeking word for where Maqlu went. We'll follow his trail east and ... that is, only if you want to. I don't ... if you want to stay in Agr Rav I wouldn't blame you."

Shirin brushed Taniel's hair back. He leaned into the maternal gesture.

"We'll leave when you're rested," she said. "Did the physician say when you'd be cleared to travel?"

"He recommended I not travel at all, or at the very least wait half a week. He suggested we buy passage on the river, find a tradesman willing to take us east."

"The hedgewitch said to avoid the south and the river. Something about a cult who holds no tolerance for the magic-touched."

"I never liked boats anyway."

"Well, you're in better spirits than I thought to find you."

"It's the medicine the physician gave me. I hardly feel a thing, and that's the best I've felt in over a year."

Shirin believed Taniel's sanguine mood was born from more than diminished pain. He had been trapped as a prisoner, then trapped in a crippled body. His being able to act despite that to defeat a dark witch was a greater balm than the physician's medicine. In a way, Taniel reminded her of her eldest son—incapable of sitting still, ever-possessed by an insatiable want to act. He'd always been in motion, quick to become frustrated in life's slower moments, but quicker to laugh and never hesitating to offer a hand to those in need whether they be a lifelong friend or an unmet stranger.

Tears slipped free before Shirin had the chance to hide them.

"What's wrong?" Taniel asked.

"Sorry, it's nothing." She wiped at her eyes in a feeble effort to recompose herself.

"You have nothing to apologize for. What is it?"

"Oh, it's ... you remind me of my eldest, that's all." For some reason the admission embarrassed her. She shook her head, fighting back a second wave of tears threatening to brim over. "I told you, it's nothing. I don't know what came over me. I'm being ridiculous."

"That's not nothing," Taniel said softly. "And if you want ridiculous, I can tell you how I made a complete ass of myself when I first met my wife."

"Oh? How so?"

"She was working in the bakery. She'd just come east across the Setareh Sea and didn't speak a word of Haeranji."

He told her how he'd seen her working behind the bakery counter and went in to order a cup of coffee because he thought her pretty. Her dark curls fell loose from a twist held back by a white headscarf, framing large eyes, skin smooth as silk and dark as earth after rain. By the time he finished his coffee he realized he'd been mistaken thinking her pretty—she was the most beautiful woman he'd ever seen. That the other girl working behind the counter, her older cousin Suri, had to translate everything for her hadn't deterred Taniel from walking over to ask her on a date. He assumed Suri would translate the request. That proved to be his second, and far greater mistake. Suri had smirked in wicked delight, choosing to watch, offering no help as Taniel struggled to ask what time Nesrin got off work. Nesrin had stared at him blankly and Taniel grew increasingly desperate in miming out his intentions. Soon the whole café watched, laughing and hollering advice at him.

Giving up on words, he'd grabbed a napkin and drew a picture of the tower clock in the park across the street with the hands set at six. When Nesrin accepted the napkin, he took it on faith it was in agreement to meet him at the scribbled place and time. He still remembered the dress she wore when she met him beneath the clock.

"She said I tried too hard that first date," Taniel said, "and that she only agreed to go to dinner because she felt sorry for me. But it worked."

"It's a good thing your wife has a merciful heart," Shirin teased, smiling at the thought of Taniel—a man who hunted monsters, survived the worst of dark witches, who'd not let his crippling stop him from rushing in to save a stranger—awkwardly fumbling his way through courtship.

"She does, she always said ..." Taniel's good humor faded. He tucked his left hand against his chest. "You were right. I shouldn't have had Sahak lie to her."

While the story had distracted Shirin from her grief, it had reminded Taniel of his.

"It's not too late," she said. "You both survived."

"I wish I'd had the wisdom to see it then." He shook his head as if to dispel the gloomy mood. "Enough about me and the problems I make for myself. Is there anything I can do for you?"

"Find a cure for your curse. Reunite with your wife. Live a long and happy life."

Taniel snorted. "Well, you certainly don't ask for much."

"Until then, I'll settle for music if you're up to it."

He pulled the duduk from his pack. Without needing to be asked, he played the hymn for Naru, bittersweet and soothing.

Stones had replaced the bones in Nesrin's legs turning them stiff and heavy. Her pounding heart felt close to bursting, and each harsh breath was a knife driving deeper into her side. She kept running. She could not stop. Not when the demon stalked her racing steps. She risked no rest until she found shelter, pausing only long enough to drink and eat, those brief moments spared to sustain her haste and hold off the growing fatigue.

The sun dipped lower on the horizon, stretching the forest's shadows below a sky tinged by twilight's coming. She regretted not running back the way she'd come after seeing the karakin. She had passed by a village the day before; she should have taken shelter there, and she would have if the sudden meeting of the demon had not frightened reason from her. She had thought of nothing at the time besides fleeing as far from it as possible, only remembering there were people, hearthfires, and warded thresholds to the west when it was too late. She was too far, too deep into the woods to turn around and make it there before nightfall. Now, with the sun setting and her pushed to the edge of complete exhaustion, she was desperate to find a sheltering threshold to see her through the dark hours. She'd not seen the karakin since it spoke to her on the roadside. That did not mean it was gone. She felt it following her, a dreadful chill drawing strength from the weakening daylight.

The trees thinned to show a clustering of stone homes and Nesrin sobbed a grateful prayer to the gods for delivering her from a night in the forest. The misfortune that had burned the village was months past, leaving scorched ruins for her to take refuge in. Wind had scoured the ash from the scarred skeletons of homes, rain had washed away the soot, and tall grass grew among the blistered wood and charred stone. Finding two crumbling skulls and ribcages in a blackened home encouraged Nesrin farther down the path to seek shelter untouched by the fire.

The farmhouse built into the hillside had escaped the blaze, not the decay of abandonment. The wooden roof drooped into the dwelling of clay and yellow stone, the front garden was wild with weeds, and creeping vines tendriled over the wall and walkway.

She circled the home, searching for movement in the dark windows, the wild fields, and stony hills beyond. She had no desire to be surprised a second time by a dark presence hungry for an unwary soul. When she startled only a rabbit from the high grass and was sure nothing more sinister lurked in the abandoned house, she pushed open the creaking front door hanging crookedly on worn hinges. The useless door was of no concern, it was the ancient power of thresholds she wanted. Though her silver talisman kept evil at bay, the pursuing karakin's influence would slowly corrupt it until it was a useless, tarnished trinket. Thresholds were not so fickle in their protection.

"Hello?" Nesrin called into the farmhouse.

Silence answered her, a quiet she distrusted. Her skin prickled from the misgiving there was a presence close by.

"Hello?" She stepped over the threshold. The hut's small windows stifled the dulling daylight from reaching the gloomy corners of the single room and upper loft.

"Who's there?" a child's high voice trembled.

"It okay," she said quickly, not wanting to frighten the child more than she already had. "Don't have fear."

"Who are you?" The poor thing was probably hiding in the loft, too scared to peer over the edge. "Who are you?"

"My name is—" Nesrin clapped her hands over her mouth, realizing what she'd done.

The karakin stood on the overgrown front path. It wore the guise of a child, feet bare, faded grey shirt hanging to its knees, its pale skin immaculately clean.

"How far is home?" It smiled at her, lips stretching impossibly wide beneath empty, black eyes.

She slammed the creaking door shut, bolted the rusted lock, and prayed for the threshold's warding power to hold even after she'd been so stupid to answer its questions, inviting it in. Driving the Purger knife into the door's wood, she carved the warding symbol Taniel had taught her, a simpler version of one of the many tattooed on his skin.

Chest tight and blood cold, Nesrin looked out the small window. The karakin watched her from the weed-covered walkway—a cat patiently waiting at the crevice it knew the mouse must come out from.

"How far is home?"

Taniel placed a black, river-smoothed rock at the roots of the remembrance yard's tree. By a higher grace, his twitching fingers managed to light the incense on the first strike, and he placed the thin stalks before the river stone serving as a meager memorial for Razban Terzian.

"Find peace, my friend," he said.

Razban had deserved better than to die in a dark mage's cellar, his name a footnote in the tale of a lesser man's evil deeds. Tiran, Aryeh, Suri, his father—they had all deserved better, and Taniel had not properly mourned them. He clutched his left arm to his chest, closing his eyes under the nauseating thrum spreading from his horns. Once he found Master Maqlu and was restored, he'd build memorial shrines for the dead as they deserved. He'd see them properly remembered.

Rising to his feet, he winced at the jagged ache clawing up his legs into his lower spine. He leaned heavily on his walking stick, waiting for the worst of the fire to subside before limping from the remembrance yard. Walking was becoming more difficult, rising from bed more painful, and it was a rare day if he avoided nausea after eating. He wanted to blame it on weariness from the long journey to reach Agr Rav, or from exposure to Tahir's dark magic. Deep down he knew it was nothing so trivial. His fleeing Minu had removed the magic from its mistress. It ran unchecked, eating away at what little remained of him. If left unchallenged, it was only a matter of time before the sorcery killed him.

There was no denying his condition worsened, yet his renewed resolution to live and return to Nesrin gave him the stubbornness to endure. Whether it take months or years, he was going to find a way to survive this curse and find his wife. She was safe in Gohar, he had made sure of that, and once he was freed from Minu's ruining and Kharinah's hunting, he'd beg his wife's forgiveness.

"Wait for me," he prayed. Of all his failures, leaving Nesrin was his worst and the one he was most determined to set right. "Please."

Moths drifted over the dark windows, turning eyeless faces toward him as he limped through the abandoned middle tier, down the sloping streets to the lower city where the physician lived. Shirin disliked his walking through Agr Rav alone, but it made more sense for her to stay at the monastery where they were better equipped for guests, and not further burden the physician who had graciously accepted Taniel into his home until he was better recovered.

A violent shudder coursed through Taniel's leg. He stumbled, the walking stick stopped his fall, and he used the wall of an abandoned shop for greater support until the spasming ceased. He coughed, wiping blood stained black from ill-magic off his lips. The discharge that had begun to leak from his mouth and nose after confronting Tahir showed no sign of stopping. He needed to leave Agr Rav. If not tomorrow, then the day after. He and Shirin had only lingered so long because she insisted he rest a few days more, and Abbott Mardiros promised to do all in his power to find more than rumor as to where Master Maqlu had gone. But there was no cure for him here, and he wasted his waning time waiting for one.

Dusk bruised the sky by the time he reached the mercifully flat streets of the lower tier. Lamplighters lifted long poles to the oil lanterns, illuminating Agr Rav in a golden glow. Shopkeepers shuttered their windows and taverns opened their doors. People finishing evening errands paused to whisper as Taniel walked by. He'd made a name for himself as the Karvogi Purger who defeated the dark witch of Agr Rav. The onlookers were respectfully curious, a good opinion that would last only so long as no one saw beneath his mask and cloak. Mazdak, the physician's assistant, curled his lip in disgust whenever he saw Taniel. The young man's reaction was an honest reminder that Taniel was too tainted for tolerance. The excited gossip of Tahir's defeat was fated to sour into whispers about the monster hidden beneath a Karvogi cloak. Another reason he and Shirin must leave, and soon.

Taniel took care not to trip on the front step to the physician's home. The physician providing him a key was a thoughtful but unnecessary gesture as the man never remembered to lock his door when he left to visit patients. He had told Taniel he'd most likely be gone until morning; a woman had gone into labor, and since her last two children had been unenthusiastic to come into the world, he believed her third was likely to show similar hesitation.

Turning down the hall, Taniel nearly bumped into Mazdak leaving the guest room. The assistant gasped, pressing himself flat to the wall as if terrified he'd come so close to touching a tainted creature.

"There are new tonics for you," he said before hurrying off. Compared to the barbed mutterings Taniel usually received, such treatment from Mazdak was the utmost courtesy.

Taniel closed the door before stripping off his boots and Karvogi cloak. Freshly replenished medicine vials awaited him on the bedstand. His reaching for the tonic to help him sleep through the night was halted by a palsy seizing his left side. Sweat beaded along his brow as he forced himself to breathe through the pain, feeling as though dull blades peeled his flesh from bone. What would he do when he grew too weak to travel? That day was fast approaching and Taniel had yet to find a way to so much as delay its arrival. The physician's tonics alleviated physical pain, but they did nothing to slow Minu's curse from claiming him. Was it better to stay within Agr Rav's warded walls and on the monastery's hallowed ground as he awaited word from Abbott Mardiros, or did he only invite Kharinah into protected walls and sacred spaces through the unwanted bond they shared as broken creatures of Minu?

The spasming hold on his left side loosened, and Taniel hissed in relief. Leaving Agr Rav in his condition was a fool's hope, yet it was a dismal surrender to stay. He unstoppered the sleeping tonic. Deciding on how to handle his condition was best delayed until morning after speaking to Shirin. The exhaustion dulling his mind and the mangled pain in his limbs left him too weary to think beyond the challenge of finding sleep. The medicine had a bitter smell, an unpleasant taste, and its effect was near immediate, stronger than the medicine the physician had previously given him. His eyelids drooped under the sedative's weight. Every ugly sensation preventing him from finding rest—the aches rusting his joints, the nausea bubbling at the back of his throat—was swept out on a dark tide. Yet he did not find true sleep. He was caught between consciousness and not, aware of his blurring surroundings as if from a great distance.

"In here." Mazdak beckoned hazy figures into the room.

Taniel tried to sit up. His limbs refused to move. His mind was lost in a heavy fog. He was vaguely aware of what was happening, that something was wrong, and that the drug rendered him too dumb to make sense of it. Men's voices, low and furtive, teased at the edge of his clouded senses. Hands fell upon him. The room became a hall, the ceiling a night sky that spun around him.

He was back in the wagon in the Beka Valley. The trundle and bump aggravated his injuries as they headed to Minu's marsh. He wanted to speak, to warn his father, Tiran, and Aryeh that they went to their deaths. His words were lost in the red fog, reducing his warning to a weak, pleading groan. A man's voice, his father's perhaps, spoke from the impossible distance of death. Aryeh responded, cold and disapproving, and it all tumbled into a senseless unknowing.

The night was clear, the moon nearly full. Its silver light was a bane, not blessing. It spun the room's shadows into sinister shapes while the firelight threw them into darting figures, filling the farmhouse with the quick menace of shifting shade. Nesrin huddled close to the fire, holding her knees to her chest. The flames stretched her flickering shadow toward the door she watched with fearful vigilance. The karakin waited for her just beyond the weathered wood, tugging on the barbed threads it had hooked into her mind the moment she'd foolishly answered its questions.

"It can't come in, it can't come in," she whispered, as if her frightened invocation had the power to banish the demon by granting greater strength to the threshold, talisman, and wardings she'd carved into the door. So long as she stayed where she was, she was safe to wait for dawn's rescue. "It can't come in. It can't come in."

A soft skittering circled the farmhouse. Wood creaked. She heard a faint tap-tap-tapping like claws scratching at the door. An uninvited presence sought entry.

"It can't come in. It can't come in." She hadn't spoken to the karakin much. It shouldn't have true power over her. The demon hunted unwary travelers who unwittingly answered its questions until they were completely under its influence. It called to them in the night, and the enthralled victims answered, walking willingly to their death to be found in the morning with necks torn and blood drained.

Nesrin. A gentle voice called. *Come to me ...*

She covered her ears, praying to Razirah for strength. "It can't come in. It can't come in."

Nesrin, come to me.

She was not yet married to Taniel when he told her of karakins. He'd just returned from hunting one when he snuck her into the small apartment where he lived with his father. Sariel was away on another job and Taniel had been sent home to study for his university exam. He chose to study Nesrin instead. In a gesture as romantic as it was poorly thought, he attempted to make dinner for her that night, a traditional dish from her home country. He hadn't cooked the ingredients in the right order, sautéed instead of stewed the onions so the curry was thin, and Nesrin swooped in before he ruined the chicken beyond saving. The sourdough flatbread was only spared his culinary ineptitude as he'd bought it already baked from the market.

She shooed him from the cramped kitchen and fought a grueling battle to salvage the dinner as he did his best to distract her, seeing how many times he could kiss her neck or how low he could move his hands down her hips before she turned from the stove to swat him away with the spoon. Late evening had settled by the time she left the ingredients to stew. They sat at the wooden table by the fireplace and she asked about his work.

"It was a karakin," he said. He didn't always like talking about it, but she knew it helped him to.

"What karakin?" she asked.

"Black goblin," he said in her language.

"I know those. They ask question and look like dark cloak woman."

"Yes, and no, not exactly." He told her they took many shapes. The one he'd hunted preferred the appearance of an old man or a yellow-eyed fiend with spindly arms and skin the pale, lifeless shade of winter moonlight. "They imitate the voices of the dead, loved ones the victim's lost, luring people away to feed on their blood."

"Why they follow dead voice?" she asked.

"They're under a thrall." He always understood what she meant, piecing together her broken phrasing, never growing impatient when she paused midsentence. He was happy to wait for her to find unfamiliar words.

"What be 'thrall'?" she asked.

"It's when you're under someone else's power. Answering a karakin's questions allows them access to your mind. Turns you weak to their suggestions."

"So it be casting thrall?" she asked.

"Yes."

"And this done by questionings?"

"Yes."

"And more questionings give karakin more power?"

"Mm-hmm."

"Then you lucky I no be karakin. My thrall on you so strong now, you never get free."

He grinned. "I think you already have that part taken care of."

She hadn't understood what he meant, asking him twice to repeat what he said. Only when he kissed her, his mouth warm on hers, his fingers tenderly tucking her hair behind her ear, did she grasp his full meaning. And it was that moment she decided when he asked, she would marry him.

Nesrin. Taniel had whispered her name as he did now. Soft and gentle. Beckoning. *Nesrin, come.*

She stood in a daze. Her fire-cast shadow swayed with her toward the door. Taniel was calling and she must go. Go to him. Go.

Come to me, Nesrin. Come to me.

He was so close. If she stepped across the threshold, he'd be there. Her fingers fumbled for the door handle. Her heart trembled with a longing ache.

Come to me, Nesrin.

The door creaked open. A cool night breeze greeted her and his voice on the chill was a lover's sigh on her skin.

Come to me.

All she had to do was step forward, take off her talisman, and he'd be there, arms open, waiting—

Nesrin reeled back, slamming the door shut on the karakin's clawed hand that she'd been a heartbeat away from taking. She scuttled to the fire, feeling the pain of the heat and none of the warmth as she took refuge too close to the flames.

Nesrin... It scratched at the door, using Taniel's voice to torment her. The threshold and wardings preventing it from entering felt a pitiful defense when it had already found its way into her mind. *Nesrin, don't run, don't run from me. Come to me. Come to me. Come—*

She clutched the Purger's knife in one trembling hand, the talisman in the other. Black specks dotted the silver, the demon's presence corrupting the charm.

"It can't come in, it can't come in." She begged the Seraphs for their protection, terrified tears streaming down her cheeks.

The demon scratched at the door, whispering its own unceasing chant in her husband's voice. *Come to me, Nesrin, come to me. Come to me, Nesrin. Come to me, come to me.*

19

Tainted Minds

The freshly baked sweet loaves were warm in Shirin's arms as she left the bakery for the physician's home. At this early hour the streets were not yet crowded by the lower tier bustle that she found overwhelming. She hoped Taniel had rallied today. His spirits had been as volatile as waves stirred by a coming storm; rising in a surge of determined hope to crash down into grey despair. There was no denying his affliction worsened. Bad mornings stretched into bad days, shivers compounded to seizures, and his coughing up blood yesterday boded poorly. Concerned as she was for Taniel's tenuous condition, confirming Master Maqlu had come through Agr Rav was a light on the horizon. The gods were not unjust. They would not allow Taniel to suffer in vain.

She tucked the warm loaves in the crook of her arm to knock on the physician's door.

He answered, frowned, and looked past her to the street. "Where's your son?"

"He should be here," Shirin said.

The physician's frown deepened. "Didn't he stay the night at the monastery with you?"

"No, he returned here in the early evening." She pushed past the physician and dropped the loaves on the nearest table, hurrying to Taniel's guest room.

Her forceful opening slammed the door hard into the wall, revealing an empty bed. There was nothing obviously wrong—little reason to think Taniel had done anything besides visit the remembrance yard to pay respects to Razban, or gone to wander the lower tier in a fit of restlessness—but a dozen little details needled Shirin, warning her something was very wrong indeed. The bed sheets were slightly rumpled, as if hardly used and then left unmade. An unstoppered medicinal vial was tipped over on the floor, clearly fallen and carelessly left to leave a small stain on the rug. The bedside table stood slightly askew from the wall and the rug's corner was turned up as if a foot had caught on the edge.

"When did you last see Taniel?" She circled to the other side of the bed. The worry needling her dropped to breathless dread. Taniel's Karvogi cloak and walking stick lay on the floor.

"Yesterday afternoon," the physician said.

"And that was when he told you he intended to stay the night at the monastery?"

"No, Mazdak told me this morning when I saw Taniel was gone."

Taniel wouldn't have left the physician's home without donning the cloak, and he certainly wouldn't have left Agr Rav to go east on his own. He was not so cruel to hide his leaving from her, nor so stupid to attempt a journey alone without supplies. His pack was at their shared room in the monastery, and he never would've left the photograph of his and Nesrin's wedding behind. If Taniel was gone, it was not by his choice.

Shirin rounded on the physician. "Where's Mazdak?"

"He's out on deliveries."

"Tell me his route." Her voice snapped with the icy wrath filling her chest. "I need to find him. Now."

Locating Mazdak in the ever-thickening crowd moving through Agr Rav's markets took well into late morning. Twice Shirin followed his trail all the way to the upper tier, racing up the sloping streets and steep stairs, only to be directed down again to the lower ring. Her hair was mussed, dress dampened by sweat, and she was panting for breath when she finally saw the young assistant leaving an apothecary shop.

"Mazdak!" the physician called. The boy's head whipped around. Panicked guilt flashed across his features before his jaw set.

"Is something the matter?" he asked.

"Where's Taniel?" Shirin was unfooled by his act of defiant boredom. She had seen it too many times before on her teenage son, masking wrongdoing behind pretended indifference.

Mazdak shrugged. "The monastery, I think."

"Mazdak"—the physician's tone carried no patience for lie or evasion—"what have you done?"

Fractures cut through the boy's obstinate façade. He suddenly looked much younger, vulnerable and naïve. "He was cursed." He dropped his eyes and his defiance. "He didn't belong here."

"Where did you send him?"

"I didn't—"

The physician grabbed him by the shirt collar. "Don't lie!"

"It's not like we could've done anything for him," Mazdak said quickly. "A man said he'd pay to take his taint away."

"What man?"

"A trader! He was heading to Nahr Hasa. There's a butcher there who prepares creatures for talismans—"

"You sold Taniel to a butcher?" Shirin's hand shook in want to slap the stupid boy.

"He won't be butchered," Mazdak said indignantly. "They'll send him to Healer Yasser once they see what he is."

"Who did you sell him to?"

"I don't know—"

The physician struck him across the face. "Who was it, Mazdak?"

"Shorn, I think his name was Shorn." Mazdak touched his reddening cheek, completely taken aback that his actions had earned such anger. "He's one of the bone-smugglers that hang around the lower tier's south end."

"How could you do this?" The physician demanded answers to why Mazdak had betrayed his trust, what the stupid boy had been thinking, and how else Mazdak had abused his position as a physician's apprentice.

There was only one question that mattered to Shirin.

"How far to Nahr Hasa?" she asked.

Cold was the first sensation to penetrate Taniel's groggy confusion. He shivered, ignoring his complaining joints as he curled tighter against the chill gnawing harshest at his wrists and right ankle. Hard clinks answered his movements, and it was a dull dismay to escape from drugged bleariness to find a set of chains binding his hands. A second shackle attached to his ankle looped through a metal ring in the stone floor. A pitiful scattering of straw served as a bed, and there were no windows in his wooden stall prison. All his light came from weak slants of sun slipping through thin gaps in the wood. Both portions of the half-door were closed, blocking off what lay beyond the small space.

He pushed at the door. It groaned, refusing to budge. Locked in and chained. Whoever put him here had taken thorough measures to be sure he stayed.

There was a rap on the wall to his left.

"You awake yet?" a man asked.

"Getting there." Taniel clutched his aching head in hand. He tasted coppery blood and a sickly rot. Wiping a hand beneath his nose brought away a bloody trail of ill-magic.

"Take your time, there's no rush," the man said. "Neither of us is going anywhere until he comes for us."

"Who?"

"The Mad Purger. Isn't he the one who got you?"

"I don't think so," Taniel said. Vague memories of his returning to the physician's home were lost in drug-muddled dream.

"Then how'd you end up here?"

"I don't know, but it wasn't by choice."

"Well, he got me. I didn't take kindly to him torching the magic-touched he came across, and he didn't take kindly to me seeing how he liked being set on fire. Guess I brought that on myself."

"Do you have a name?"

"Hanji."

"I'm Taniel." He closed his eyes until the dizziness spinning his head and sickening his stomach steadied. The skin around his horns felt like it was being stripped off by rusted tongs. His skull felt miserably worse.

"Good to meet you, Taniel. It's nice to have someone to talk to again."

"Was there someone in here before me?" Taniel asked. Pushing aside a clump of straw revealed old bloodstains on the stone.

"Yeah, another hedgewitch like me."

Hanji's tone and the bloody floor told the rest of that hedgewitch's story.

"Where are we?" Taniel asked.

"The charming town of Sevget," Hanji said, "renowned for her hospitality."

"Do you know who's in charge?"

"What's the point of having someone to talk to if they don't listen? The Mad Purger, you idiot. He took over, and he's looking to do the same to every town that—"

"Shh!" A heavy door groaned open and Taniel pressed his ear to the stall door to better hear the approaching men.

"You said you was interested in anything strange, so I had them bring him here."

"You did well."

"Don't know what he is though. Right wretched looking."

The footsteps stopped outside his stall. Metal clinked, the lock was undone, and the door scraped over the straw-strewn floor. Taniel recoiled from the daylight flooding his gloomy stall.

"Seraphs." The youngest of the three men skittered behind the older two regarding Taniel in cold interest.

"See? Told you," one man said through a bushy beard, peering at Taniel from beneath a wide-brimmed hat. "Don't know what he is."

The taller man showed no horror or the slightest unease at Taniel's appearance. Eyes adjusting to the light, Taniel recognized him and knew it took more than a broken monster to earn a response from this man. Taniel had met Purger Wasi Adhar a few times over the years. Adhar had worked alongside his father on difficult cases demanding aggressive measures. The respect the two held for the other bridged the difference of their personalities that had twice brought them to blows outside of professional arrangement.

"He's a man I'd bring to battle and wish to meet nowhere else," Taniel's father had told him. "He's been consumed by the evil he hunts. He just doesn't know it yet."

Adhar's flat expression showed no sign he shared Taniel's recognition. Understandable, as Taniel looked very different from last they met, while Adhar had scarcely changed at all. His iron-grey hair was cut short, dark brown eyes narrowed in perpetual distrust, and his wide jaw emphasized a grimly thin mouth.

"Thank you, Shorn." Adhar kept his eyes on Taniel as he handed the bearded man a small bag of coin. "Be on your way."

The bearded man wasted no time taking the payment and dismissal, boots clacking quick over the stone floor.

"What is it?" the young man asked. More a boy than a man, at least ten years Taniel's junior and built like a waterbird, all long limbs and looking vulnerably fragile standing beside Adhar. Pale, slicing scars marked the boy's forearms and a single line slit fully across his throat. "Have you seen this before?"

"You have," Taniel said. "Your hair's gone greyer since last I saw you, Purger Adhar, though the years have been kinder to you than me."

The boy gasped, looking horrified an abomination such as Taniel possessed the ability to speak.

"You may not remember me, but you must remember my father, Sariel." Taniel trusted the Purger to be more reasonable than the excitable boy.

Adhar's expression shifted from stony to unreadable. "Yael, go wait outside."

The boy rushed to obey. Adhar used his foot to sweep straw off a patch of floor. Taking out chalk, he sketched a circle on the cleared stone, ringing talismanic symbols around the interior and drawing the Open Hand in its center. Taniel rested his hand atop the completed drawing. That his skin did not blister on contact proved him to be neither a demon nor possessed by one—at least not willingly—and it satisfied Adhar.

"The world has become a wretched place," Adhar said, "and if you are who you claim, your fate has been more wretched than most."

"I survived," Taniel said. "That's better than most."

"Death would be a more merciful state for you."

"But a hopeless one."

Adhar crossed his arms. "I heard tale your father was killed by Minu. My condolences. I also heard it was his failure to stop her that allowed this plague to ruin creation."

"You'll not speak of my father so." Taniel bristled at his contemptuous tone.

"You're in no position to make demands."

"And nothing you do or say can frighten me from defending my father's memory."

Purger Adhar tapped leathered fingers on his crossed arms, his eyes hard as flint. "There's no shortage of tales about what happened in the Beka Valley, and none can be true as they all claimed you dead. What happened there, Taniel Sushan? How did you survive?"

Taniel had no reason to deceive Wasi Adhar or anything to gain in lying. He told him of all the events following his arriving in Chahich—Minu unleashing the Red Plague, his escaping her to reach Gohar, and his traveling to Agr Rav. He omitted Shirin from his story, sensing she was safer remaining unknown to the Purger.

"I'm heading east to the Grey Forest," Taniel said, "looking for Master Maqlu."

"You won't find salvation from a sorcerer," Adhar said. "Their kind is what opened the gates for this hell to be unleashed upon us. You chase a false hope."

"All the same, it's my hope to chase. If you have no further use for me, I'd appreciate you unlocking these chains so I may be on my way."

"That cannot be done."

"Why not?" Taniel forced himself to stand through the needling numbness in his right leg. Though he hardly presented an impressive sight, he found greater confidence standing than sitting crumpled on the floor.

"Come, Taniel, don't hide from the truth. You're corrupted by Minu's ill-magic. Your very being is tainted and you'll spread that affliction wherever you go."

"My condition isn't contagious."

"All evil infects," Adhar said. "Not always in ways we see."

"You have no right to hold me here."

"I have every responsibility to see unnatural corruption stamped out. And I'll not permit a fellow Purger to suffer a witch's dark magic."

Taniel glanced at the knives lining Adhar's belt; each blade curved a different way to cut with specialized precision.

"There's no need for fear, Taniel Sushan, I will see you purified."

The night is cold. The black sky swallows the western mountains, creating the illusion there is nothing beyond Ha-Ai's broken ruins save for endless pale sand stretching to meet a dark oblivion. The thunderstorm raging far in the west shatters this deception. A fork of lightning reveals the mountains, crouching giants hiding from the wrathful heavens.

"The rains never reach here." Farid joins you to gaze at the western sky. "Not a drop has fallen since I've come here."

"Rain has not reached here for a long time," you say. The rains end where the roots of the Grey Forest do. You allow the waters no farther. Their trespass is forbidden as it has been for the last five hundred years.

Despite the distance, you feel the patter of rain falling to the earth, encouraging the creep of Asherah's roots to slowly spread farther into the Wastes. Your sister is forever seeking to twist mortals, nature, and you to her advantage.

The firelight from the camp Farid pitched in the temple's interior shadows every weary line of his face, scars from his battle against time that men are doomed to lose. You will spare Farid that fate. The shahavaz are the servant spirits of a Seraph, born from mortal souls who choose to linger after death. They are a rarity and becoming more so as fewer and fewer Seraphs retain that divine right. No mortal soul has ever promised their death-transcending service to you, or at least, none have been permitted to linger to do so. Your mortal servants are dragged across death's threshold to the After, denied honoring the pledges they made to you in life.

The service Farid has sworn to you demands far longer than a mortal lifetime has to offer, so he will not die. At least, not as readily.

He has noticed the changes you gift upon him. He no longer must create portals—an art you were pleased to learn was taught to him by your last wayward apprentice—to return to the Grey Forest's eastern edge in search of food and water. He hardly needs to drink at all.

His eating is out of habit. His skin is patched, caught in transition between frail mortal flesh and greater being. Scales break through his peeling skin. He does not know, but his eyes are slowly shifting from black to a veined gold.

From the truth of the shahavaz was born the legend of the shvaza, guardian spirits shaped like serpents. They roamed pasture and field, protected hearth and home. You remember farmers, fishermen, wealthy merchants, and kings putting out milk and honey for the imaginary spirits. You never corrected the people of this misbelief. The benign superstition of the shvaza served as a child's first tottering steps to understanding the significance of ritual worship.

You model Farid after the shvaza. He came to you, hardly able to speak through his terror, when his skin first began to pebble to scales along his neck and arms. You promised it was not a change to fear, only one to endure. Unlike Taniel, Farid is healthy and whole, there is no need for immediately drastic change. It will come in time.

Nesrin woke bleary-eyed and confused, if it could be called waking, for she had not truly slept. Nor had she for the last three nights. Her days were spent walking until the setting sun drove her to find shelter in an abandoned village, farmhouse, or shepherd's hut. Her nights were spent huddled in corners, knowing the karakin waited on the other side of the threshold. Her terror, once sufficiently sharp to keep her awake through the night, was dangerously dulled by exhaustion. Every time she nodded off into the liminal grey between waking and sleep, the karakin slipped deeper into her fretful dreams, and she fell further under its thrall.

The first night she'd startled awake at the faintest hint of its presence. The second night she'd been slower to recognize when the karakin entered her mind. Her legs had twitched when it called. A lightheaded yearning urged her to answer Taniel's voice. She'd writhed and cried, resisting the maddening desire to follow her husband's pleading, covering her ears as tears streamed down her face.

Last night, the demon's call had overwhelmed her waning defenses. It spoke her name and all her resistance fell away. She was barely aware of her body moving toward the door, or that the demon's will had replaced hers. Habit had guided her hand to touch the talisman on her neck. Enough of its fading power remained that her fingers on the silver broke her from the thrall. In that moment of her mind unclouding, she'd tied her ankle to a table in the dusty farmhouse. When the karakin called and she unthinkingly answered, the rope had tripped her, and she fell free of the trance-like state. Dawn had revealed her hands scraped, knees bloodied, and her whole right side bruised. A small price to pay to prevent the karakin from taking her.

The bruises left her sore, the sleepless nights sick. The stale bread for breakfast had all the taste of old cotton. She gagged on the dried fruits she forced herself to eat. Her every muscle ached as she dragged herself from the farmhouse to the eastern road where white flowers trembled under an autumn wind. She'd lost her sense of time, unsure if it was midmorning or afternoon. She'd lost her bearings as well and relied entirely upon the anemone's snow-white petals blooming along the dirt road to guide her. She felt unnaturally slowed, as if trapped in a disquieting dream. Her thoughts felt even more sluggish. Her dragging feet tripped over each other, her eyes burned from unrelenting exhaustion, and her legs begged for rest. She risked none. Anything nearing sleep left her too vulnerable. She could not rest, nor could she much longer outrun weariness, or the demon following in its wake. She had to find a town of living souls, a hedgewitch, priest, or Purger to rescue her from the karakin's thrall.

Nesrin, come to me. It no longer waited until dusk to call to her. Taniel's voice haunted her every step. *Come to me.*

She gripped the talisman tight in hand. Black corruption tarnished the silver, the consuming stain weakening its power.

Nesrin, come to me, come to me ...

She swayed, shaking her head to clear the taint clouding her mind. She could not rest, not yet. Until she found a threshold or took shelter behind wardings, the deteriorating talisman and her waning willpower was all that kept the demon at bay.

Come to me.

"Not yet ... not yet ..." she murmured, unable to offer a more articulate prayer for protection.

Taniel stood by the roadside, hand outstretched for her to take. His smile was gentle. His eyes sad.

"Nesrin," he pleaded. The karakin's cold influence raked through her. *Come to me. Come to me. Come to me.*

She balled her hands into fists, hugging her arms to her chest to stop herself from reaching for Taniel as she hurried past.

"Not yet." Tears stung her eyes. "Not yet."

Come to me.

"Nesrin, please."

She squeezed her eyes shut, hiding herself from her husband's shade. The despair in his pleas echoed her own misery. The wound of losing Taniel had never healed. Her refusal to believe him dead had prevented it. Learning he was alive and had not come to her had torn that wound ragged and weeping.

Nesrin, come to me.

Fatigue stole her feet from under her. She stumbled to the dirt. Taniel crouched beside her. He was so close. All she had to do was reach for him. Let him take her.

"Close your eyes," he said.

She let her heavy eyelids flutter shut for memory to meet dream. She was back in Gohar, Taniel returned from work, and they were letting the day pass in bed and the other's company. She reached for him, her fingers falling short, unable to touch him. She frowned, sensing something was wrong, her mind too clouded to discern what.

"Taniel, I ..." Nesrin blinked up at the sky, confused as to why she lay in the middle of a dirt road. Taniel was inches from her, waiting to take her into his arms.

Come to me.

Her talisman. That was the wrong. She had to remove the talisman if she wanted to go to him. Throw away the charm, take his hand, and there'd be only bliss.

"Come, Nesrin." Suri stood behind Taniel. "Let's go home."

Nesrin's fingers touched the silver talisman. Taniel's form flickered, revealing the leering karakin beneath.

"No!" She surged to her feet, nearly dropping her pack as she fled from the evil illusions. Shelter, she had to find shelter. A mill, a farmhouse, a shed of nothing more than four crumbling walls and a broken roof. Anything with a threshold. The talisman was cold in her hand. She dared not look at the silver, not wanting to see how tarnished it had become—a reflection of her mind as the karakin's thrall overtook her.

Nesrin, come to me. Taniel's voice echoed through her mind.

Let's go home. Suri implored Nesrin to join her in death.

They stood beneath the trees she sprinted through. They awaited her at every bend. Begged she come to them. Promised to take her home.

Come to me, come to me, come to me, come—

"No, no, no!" Nesrin pressed her hands over her ears as she ran. She was furious at herself for being tricked by the karakin's stealing Taniel's appearance. She was more furious at Taniel. She was going to find her idiot husband, and the curse that witch had cast upon him was nothing compared to what she'd do to him. What in hells possessed him, other than self-righteous stupidity, to think she was happier believing him dead? She was his wife; it had been cowardice, not mercy, to lie to her.

Fading sunlight fell through the trees. She wasn't going to find shelter before nightfall. She'd have no threshold or hearth to ward off the demon and she lacked the strength to stop it from completely claiming her mind come darkness. She had allowed it too far in.

Come to me, Nesrin. Come to me, come to me.

"Please," she begged a child's prayer. Divine mercy was her last hope to see sunrise. "Razirah, help me."

A river's rumbling answered her plea. Nesrin swerved off the path bordered by the pale flowers toward the sound, praying it was real, not another figment of her desperate imagination. Running water cleansed unnatural powers; crossing the river was a chance to wash away the karakin's influence and free her from its thrall. It would also wash away the tracking spell Iradah the hedgewitch had cast. Tears blurred Nesrin's eyes, feeling like she betrayed Taniel by choosing to sever the enchantment leading her to him.

Nesrin. Come to me. Come to me. Come to me.

Sunlight winked off a wide, rippling river. The waters frothed where they battered rocks, then smoothed to silver polish, forking around a lonely tree on a small island eroded from the opposite bank. Nesrin slid down the muddy slope to the willow-shaded banks. Each slipping step demanded all her will; her every fiber burned with a want to turn and offer herself to the demon's fangs.

Nesrin, come to me.

She plunged into the waters, gasping at the frigid bite. The piercing cold unhooked the worst of the karakin's influence from her mind. Clarity flooded through her as she plowed through the river, stumbling at a sudden drop that sent the water from her waist up to her chest.

Nesrin! The demon prowled the bank, gnashing its teeth, demanding she return. She ignored the summons. Its power was diminished to a shadow of what it had been. She saw and heard the karakin for what it was. How could she ever have mistaken that awful voice for her husband's?

The icy current tugged at her clothes, threatening to pull her under as it rose to her shoulders. The cold quickly sapped what little strength was left in her. Gritting her chattering teeth, she fixed her eyes on the lone tree parting the waters. The island was her refuge for the night. The running water on either side of her was the best natural defense she had to weaken the karakin's thrall. The river wasn't as reliable a warding as a threshold; she'd have to be vigilant to survive the night. She wouldn't sleep, wouldn't so much as rest against the little tree. She'd wait out the night until morning and then not stop until she reached a village of living souls. She might have already passed villages offering rescue, oblivious to them as the karakin twisted her senses to its will. She shivered, considering the possibility the white anemones she'd been following had not been blooms of the tracking spell and instead been the karakin's creations leading her from safety.

Her numbed fingers sank into the rising ground of the island. Shaking and clumsy, she dragged herself on hands and knees from the river's pull, her entire body aching as if she'd run for miles. The water had soaked all her belongings. She stripped out of her waterlogged clothes, hanging them on the tree to dry in the waning daylight. She rubbed her arms to reclaim some warmth and busied herself preparing for coming night. Breaking off a low branch from the tree, she dug warding symbols into the banks and built small cairns from the river-smoothed stones, turning the small island into a feeble stronghold against the demon.

Taniel watched her from the opposite bank. *Nesrin, please. Come to me. Come back to me. Nesrin. Nesrin.*

Suri joined him. Tears streamed down her face as she called for Nesrin to return home. *Don't leave me. Come home. Come to me. Come to me.*

A hard shudder rattled Nesrin's bones; the chill revealing a fatal flaw in her plan of waiting out the night. There was no wood for a fire. The tree's branches were green and the few fallen twigs were hardly more than kindling. If she was fortunate enough to get those to catch, they'd not last an hour.

She reached for her talisman and felt only twine on skin. The charm was gone, most likely so corrupted it had fallen off in her flight or been tugged away by the river's flow. Nesrin shivered again, from more than the teeth-chattering cold. Without a fire she'd freeze long before dawn. But without a talisman, the thought of leaving the island's sanctuary left her feeling colder and more vulnerable than she did naked and quivering.

Nesrin looked back to the farther bank. The karakin had disappeared from stalking the bowing willows. Soon the last of dusk's light would disappear as well. Gone from sight did not mean the demon was gone from her mind. She felt the dark roots of its thrall that the river had failed to fully remove. The demon was waiting for the chance to reclaim her, and once she moved beyond the running water into darkening woods she was easy prey.

Sluggish and stiff from cold, she pulled her soaked clothes back on and twice checked to be sure the Purger knife was securely sheathed at her hip. She needed fire's warmth more than the island's protection, at the very least to dry her clothes clinging to her like a frozen second skin. She hardly felt the river rising to her numbed waist as she crossed to the opposite bank. The mud sucked at her bare feet. Her legs felt as though the icy waters had replaced her muscle and bone. The bank was a gentle slope, yet she had to crawl out on her hands and knees, fatigue turning the muddy rise into a mountain.

The moment she left the river, she felt the karakin's influence return; shadowing her mind, creeping closer the farther she moved from the water. Her fingers had all the suppleness of the firewood she gathered and she moved slowly as if continuing to wade through chest-deep waters. A strange light shone through the trees. Much as Nesrin wished to believe the glow belonged to a campfire or town, she dared not trust her senses to lead her into the unknown. The island was her only assured refuge. Being lured away was a willing walk to death. Arms filled with spindly branches and sun sinking too low to risk exploration, she turned back toward the river.

The karakin stood ten strides in front of her. It wore Taniel's shape, how he looked after coming home from a long journey—his hair messy, jaw darkened by stubble, and green eyes bright at seeing her.

"Nesrin, come to me."

She dropped the firewood, arms slack, all resistance stripped from her. She no longer had the strength to fight or a talisman to shield her.

Come to me.

Her weary feet obeyed. She was vaguely aware of the knife at her belt, unsure of why the silver blade mattered. She belonged to the voice summoning her from this nightmare, promising to lift her into a sweet and endless dream.

"I've been waiting for you." Taniel smiled. His pointed teeth stirred a feeble warning from the fog filling her mind. She drew back, but an unseen hand brushed that lingering fear away.

Come to me.

There was no warmth in Taniel's false touch. Her soul recoiled from the perversion as her mind and body succumbed.

Give in, Nesrin, and come to me.

She did as told. It wouldn't hurt, and she'd be spared from worse suffering. This was the closest she'd ever be to Taniel again, why should she care it false?

"No." The faint whisper was all her fight.

Hush, Nesrin. I bring you peace.

It pulled down her shirt collar to expose her neck. Its fingers were cold. So cold. This wasn't right, this wasn't Taniel. She had to find him, she had to go, to run. Run. Run!

"No!" She shoved the karakin. It sank its claws into her arm and the illusion fell.

Its skin was black as coal, with sunken scabs for eyes and a mouth splitting wide to show needle-thin teeth. Nesrin jerked to the side so its fangs missed her throat to sink into her shoulder. She screamed.

Blinding cold shot from the wound and claws of ice dragged her to the ground. The karakin groaned, shuddering like a lover overcome by pleasure. The hot rush of blood and sharp terror cut through the fog of its thrall. Nesrin's hand fumbled, then found the Purger knife at her hip. Her strike found the karakin's neck. Its shriek split her ears. She struck again, again, and again. A bloody substance sprayed from the demon, burning her skin where it fell. Cries and screams spun around her, no distinction between hers and the demon's. The karakin fell off her, teeth gnashing, hands scrabbling at its neck. Nesrin slashed wildly at the air, sobbing with terror at the edge of madness. Dark, smoking ash flaked from the demon where the knife had pieced. Its shape twisted between a black monstrosity, Taniel, a child, a cloaked man, and Suri, bits of it dissolving like dust in water. It snarled and lunged. Crumbling claws sank into her arm, its maw stretched wide to rip open her neck, and then it shattered into stinging dust.

The knife slipped from Nesrin's hands and she collapsed to the ground, coughing and shivering. Cries continued to ring in her ears. The cold gripping her chest had not died with the demon. She felt the warm wet of the wound savaged inches from her neck spilling down her chest to join the bloody trails streaming from the long scratches running over her ribs. Heat pulsed along her legs and arms where the demon's claws had scored. The wounds burned hot on her skin turned to ice.

Shapes moved in her dimming vision. Voices swarmed around her. Spots of light shone painfully bright against the dark woods, then turned to pinpricks as her senses faded.

"Taniel ..." His name whispered from her frozen lips. She wanted to stand and flee. To curl up and hide. The cold held her too tightly in its grasp, pulling her down and away.

20

The Man Who Became a Monster

"Easy now." Purger Adhar pressed a glass vial to Taniel's arm to catch the dripping blood.

Yael held Taniel's arm steady, not because he resisted, but because his sudden palsies came more frequently and his last one threw him into a full seizure. The medicine Adhar provided eased only the pain; they did nothing to slow his condition's worsening. Adhar's new power, the alleged gift of the Grey Lady, was equally impotent to temper Minu's sorcery spoiling inside Taniel. If anything, his attempts to gentle Taniel's illness exacerbated the symptoms.

"That'll do," Adhar said, stoppering the vial. He pinched the skin of Taniel's forearm around the gash. Warmth seeped into his flesh and the wound stitched back together.

Purger Adhar denied his new power was sorcery. He declared it was a higher gift from the divine, granted by the Grey Lady herself. She visited him in dreams, told him of the duty he was destined to fulfill, and the people of Sevget revered him as her chosen prophet. Taniel had no doubt Adhar believed his tale to be the truth. Instead, he doubted that the woman who appeared to Adhar was who he thought she was. The "gift" he'd been granted felt too much like Minu's sorcery.

Aside from the daily bloodletting, Taniel's imprisonment had not been needlessly unpleasant. Respect for a fellow Purger moved Adhar to remove the chains. He provided a real mattress for Taniel, poppy for the pain, a wash basin, and saw he received three meals each day. Hanji, Taniel's fellow prisoner, received one meal and usually a kick from the guard upon delivery. A pile of straw in the corner wall between their stalls hid the small opening Taniel tore in the wood to slip Hanji most of his food through.

"You shouldn't waste kindness or food on a dead man," Hanji would say, before accepting all Taniel gave him.

The food was more wasted on Taniel. He grew sicker, and struggled to keep down the food he kept for himself.

"I'll bring you a meal in a little while," Yael said, cleaning the blood from Taniel's arm.

"Thank you," Taniel said. Yael's first impression of him had not survived long. Pity quickly replaced the boy's initial fear. It took only a few kind words for Yael to warm up to him, and for Taniel to see the guilt the boy carried whenever he brought him a meal, fresh water, or helped Purger Adhar collect blood. The first day, Yael had only given single-word responses when Taniel spoke to him. By the third day, Yael was initiating their brief exchanges. Yesterday, Yael had stayed for over an hour to speak to him, asking about the world beyond Sevget. The boy admitted he'd only been to a handful of local villages along the river before the Reaping. Now, Adhar forbade him to go so far as the woods bordering the town.

"If you're unhappy here, why don't you leave?" Taniel had asked.

Yael had covered the scar crossing his throat with his hand. "There's nowhere for me to go."

Adhar pocketed the vial of Taniel's blood and rested a commanding hand on Yael's shoulder. "Come."

Yael gave Taniel a furtive, apologetic glance before following Purger Adhar, locking the stall door behind him. The door to the barn grated shut and Hanji tapped on the wall separating them.

"Did they leave you food?" he asked.

"No," Taniel said.

"Shame. What're they doing to you over there?"

"Bloodletting." Taniel ran his fingers along the newly healed scar joining the half dozen from Adhar's past harvestings. The pale lines matched the ones Yael bore on his arms and neck.

"Why?"

"Because I'm tainted by the Demon Witch and Purger Adhar believes she can be traced by the sorcery that corrupts me."

At least that was what Adhar claimed, another allegation Taniel doubted. If that was the true intention, there was no need to harvest his blood so frequently, it did not explain why Yael was subjected to similar bloodletting, and as a Purger, Adhar must know the effort was futile. Minu wasn't going to be found using a trick as crude as blood-tracing. More likely, Adhar's new gift was insufficient to sate his growing worship of power. Yael, Hanji, and Taniel were all sources for him to harvest, find what fed him best, and dispose of what did not.

"At least that means he'll keep you alive," Hanji said. "That is, until he tracks her down."

Taniel kept his disagreement quiet. It was only a matter of time before Adhar decided more drastic harvestings of Taniel better served his designs. His stay under Adhar's hospitality was fated to be brief, and end in violence.

A strange energy choked the air like trapped smoke. The skin beneath Taniel's horns itched, irritated by the magic being cast, and he rubbed his temples throbbing in rhythm with the pulsing power. For a man who abhorred sorcery and the magic-touched, Purger Adhar had certainly taken quickly to the practice.

"What's he doing?" Taniel asked. The pounding wasn't solely in his head. Drum beats sounded and he smelled wood burning.

"Don't know," Hanji said. "Is it a festival day?"

"Maybe," Taniel said, certain the drums beat for nothing so benign. The sorcery took on a menacing edge, smelling more acrid than the fire, and causing his itching skin to crawl.

The barn door rumbled open. Taniel sat up to ask Yael bringing a meal what was going on. No one came to his stall. The door to Hanji's slammed open, rattling the wooden walls.

"What're you—no! Stop—" Hanji's cries cut short under the thump of a heavy blow.

"Get him up," a man said. There was a grunt, a groan, then the hiss of a body being dragged over straw. The footsteps faded. There was no rumbling shut of the barn door; it was left open to admit the pounding of drums and the murmur of a gathering crowd.

Taniel pressed himself flat on the ground, peering beneath the stall door. He saw nothing through the thin opening save for straw-covered stone. Adhar's commanding boom brought the crowd to silence. His words came muffled through the wooden door. Taniel caught only snippets of the speech calling the people of Sevget to action and denouncing a shared evil. The menacing sorcery churning in the air went taut as Adhar began a droning chant. The incantation set Taniel's hair on end. The blood in his veins shivered as Minu's corrupting magic danced within him, excited by its brother's song. Adhar's words remained indiscernible while Hanji's cries cut bone-chillingly clear.

"No! Don't! Don't do this! No!"

The crowd joined Adhar's chanting, turning it into a thundering, senseless rumble.

"No!" Hanji's screams pitched shrill into tortured screeching. The scent of burning flesh overpowered that of wood, and the chant's fervor rose to cheering madness as another hedgewitch was purified of his taint.

Yael came to Taniel's stall late in the evening, bringing food, the smell of ash, and a sickly sweet odor.

"You burned him?" Taniel asked.

"He was tainted. He needed to be purified," Yael said, his eyes cast down into the bowl of broth he set out for Taniel.

"What is Purger Adhar if not tainted by the same sorcery he seeks to destroy?"

"He's been graced by the Grey Lady's gift. His power is divine, not a perversion of nature."

"And this is how Adhar uses his divine gift? Kidnaps men less fortunate than he to burn them in the village square?"

"Purger Adhar keeps the monsters away."

"I thought he locked them in this barn to use as firewood."

"He's not going to burn you," Yael said. "He says there's another way to save your soul."

"I'm sure it will be equally pleasant as to how he 'saved' Hanji."

"He protects the people from corruption, and saves those who have fallen to it."

"Are those your words or his?"

"They are the right words."

"Did he do that to you?" Taniel pointed to the scar on Yael's neck. He already knew the answer.

Yael raised his hand to hide the slicing line. "He stops the taint from corrupting me. It has to be reaped, and through the Grey Lady, he can turn it to good."

"So that's what Purger Adhar has become? A man who harvests a boy's talent and uses the Grey Lady's name to mask the evil of his deeds?"

"He's not ... the Grey Lady chose him."

Taniel waited for Yael to meet his eye. "You know this is wrong."

Yael pulled his sleeves down to cover the white scars crossing his skin. He had outgrown the shirt and the sleeves were too short on his lanky arms to hide the lower marks. "There's nothing I can do."

"You know that's not true as much as you know this is wrong."

"Honorable Adhar protects us. It's not my place to question him."

"Why not?"

"He's wiser than I am."

"Madness is not wisdom."

"I'm sorry," Yael said. He left shame-faced, closing the stall door with a hollow *thud*.

In time, Taniel knew he could sway Yael. Unfortunately, that was a task requiring weeks he didn't have to steadily chip at the boy's faltering faith in Adhar. If Taniel struck too hard too soon, he'd shatter the trust he'd built between him and Yael.

Taniel wiped a thin trail of bloody taint dripping from his nose. Hopelessness was a faithful companion and it found him in the barn's lonely gloom. The quiet was an unpleasant reminder of the empty stall next to his.

Taniel begged Nesrin to come to him. She searched for her husband only to lose herself in an endless night, shouting his name into the expanding dark. The karakin stole her voice she had so carelessly shared before sinking its teeth into her neck.

She woke, sweating from a broken fever and disorienting nightmares.

For a moment she thought she was home in Gohar. The bed's soft mattress, clean sheets and pillows were luxuries belonging to a lost life. The comfort quickly vanished when she sat up, discovering the bedroom as unfamiliar as the long cotton shirt she wore. The room was simply furnished with a chair beside the bed, a small table in the corner, an embroidered rug covered the floor, and birds warbled in the garden outside the window.

Thick bandages wrapped her forearm. She checked beneath her shirt's neckline to reveal more covered her torso and shoulder where the demon's claws and teeth had scored. Nesrin winced as she climbed out of bed, feeling as if she'd fallen from a very high cliff onto unforgiving ground. Her knees wobbled and stomach churned. She ignored the feebleness, having no patience for such petty complaints. These injuries were nothing. Not after all she'd endured.

She donned the robe left on the wooden chair beside the bed, lacking the courage to face the troubles awaiting her beyond the bedroom door while wearing nothing more than a nightshirt that ended too high above her knees and the bandages beneath. Her shoulder ached as she slipped her arms into the robe's sleeves, and every muscle felt spent from the small effort of getting out of bed and barely dressing.

She had to sit on the chair, head between her hands, before she rallied the strength to totter out the door.

The home reminded her of Sandar's manor, a place of easy wealth and creature comforts. Ornate carvings knotted above the arched doors lined the red stone hallway, large windows generously invited in the midday sun, and the long brocade rug stretching over the stone floor was soft beneath her bare feet. The swirling floral designs patterning her woolen pathway led her to a balustrade overlooking the floor below.

"Ah, good to see you on your feet, young miss." The man ascending the stairs grinned at her over the linens he carried. His brown hair was tied in a short ponytail, and he had a broad, kindly face with a large nose and easy smile. Nesrin took a wary step back.

"It's alright." He set the linens on the divan at the top of the stairwell. "My name is Eli, and you're safe in Nahr Hasa in the house of Healer Yasser."

He guessed each of the questions she'd been about to ask, though the answers given told her little. She had no idea where Nahr Hasa was, nor who Healer Yasser was—although her bandages suggested she'd already met him.

Eli's smile faltered. "Do you ... do you speak Haeranji?"

"I speak," she said, holding the robe tightly around her.

"Oh good. We weren't sure. You've been speaking a language none of us knew the last couple of days."

"Couple days? I be here so long?" Her head throbbed, stomach lurched, and she swayed atop trembling knees.

"Are you alright?" Eli stepped forward, ready to catch her.

"I fine. I just ... I don't remember ..." She had no memory of coming to this place, who this man was, or anything after the demon turned to dust, leaving her to bleed out in the forest. Even that memory felt uncertain, like it had happened years ago or been another figment of her nightmarish hallucinations.

"Why don't I show you to the dining room?" He offered his arm for her to take. "We'll get you a cup of tea, something to eat, and I'll answer all the questions I can. Yes?"

She nodded, shyly accepting his arm and grateful to have his support as her legs had all the sturdiness of wet rags as he guided her down the stairs. The dining room was warm and welcoming, its curtains tied open to let light stream through large glass windows. The mahogany table, chairs, and matching porcelain-filled hutch probably cost more than three month's rent at her and Taniel's flat in Gohar.

"Here." Eli escorted her to sit in one of the cushioned chairs. He pulled a string on the wall and a bell's faint tinkling sounded down the manor hall.

"You live here?" Nesrin asked. "Healer Yasser be your father?"

"Yes, I live here, but no, my relation is that of apprentice." He gave a small bow. "And I am as much at your service as I am his."

"I looking for husband," she said.

"Sorry, what?"

"I looking for my husband." She pointed to her ring finger then to her chest. "He go east. I look for him."

Eli's confusion fell to a sympathetic frown. "Is that who Taniel was?"

"You know my husband?" Nesrin lurched to her feet. "He here?"

She'd welcome the miracle if she'd been brought to the same town Taniel had traveled to. He'd been looking for a healer mage; had the gods guided them to the same one?

"Please, you mustn't excite yourself." Eli gestured for her to sit down. "Your husband isn't here—"

"Then how you know name?"

"You said it in your fever. You called for him."

The bright light of hope turned ashen in Nesrin's chest, and that loss was almost too much on top of all else. Tears burned in the corners of her eyes. She forced them back, breathing deep to steady herself. So Taniel wasn't here. That was no reason to fall into pathetic weeping. All it meant was she must return to her search as soon as possible.

"You find white flower?" Nesrin asked. The Karvogi had told her to keep the anemone with her and she had come to believe the woman's wisdom. So long as she carried that little flower, she'd find Taniel.

"Pardon?"

"I have white flower. It help me find him. Is white flower here?" It should have been in the pocket of her clothes when they found her.

"There's no white flower," Eli said slowly.

"My clothes?" she asked. "What happen to my clothes?"

"They were ruined. Torn to shreds, covered in blood and demon-taint. Healer Yasser had them burned."

"He burn flower too?" The tears she had just subdued threatened to fall free again.

"I don't know—"

"Master Eli, you rang?" A middle-aged woman dressed in a servant's uniform waited obediently at the dining room's entrance. She was tall, strong-jawed, and possessed an air of steadfast dependability. Nesrin crossed her arms over her chest, embarrassed to be seen by yet another stranger while wearing so little.

"Yes, Karu." Eli looked relieved to have an excuse to break from their conversation. "Would you mind preparing a meal for our guest? Something light, she just woke up."

"Of course," Karu said. "And perhaps the young lady would like fresher clothes?"

"Yes, please," Nesrin said.

Karu gave an understanding smile. "Tea as well while you wait?"

Nesrin nodded. "Thank you."

"You'll start feeling like yourself again in a few weeks," Eli said as Karu disappeared into the kitchens. "It takes time, but you'll shake off the karakin's influence."

"Taniel say most demon-tainted by karakin go mad," Nesrin said.

Eli looked uncomfortable again. "Well, some do. Healer Yasser has high hopes that won't be the case for you—and the name summons, here he is."

Eli stood in respect for the man descending the stairwell. He wore his middling years well, handsome with silver streaking his neatly trimmed beard and his dark hair swept back from a strong brow creased by faint lines. His belted tunic, wide trousers, and silk jacket matched the home's interior of tasteful wealth.

"It's good to see you awake, young lady," the man said. "I am Healer Yasser, and you are welcome in my home."

"Thank you," Nesrin said, too shy around all the strangers to attempt a more eloquent greeting.

"May I know your name?"

"Nesrin. You be sorcerer?"

He certainly looked like one in his silk robes, and who else could afford such a large home, servants, and take on apprentices?

"I am a recognized master," he said, sitting across from her.

"You know Master Maqlu?" she asked.

"I know of him."

"Do you know where he be? My husband going to him. He go to Grey Forest and I need find him."

"Of course, I understand."

Nesrin frowned. Clearly the sorcerer did not understand because he said nothing more, thinking she'd be content with that unsatisfactory answer.

"I looking for my husband." She spoke slowly to better articulate her intentions. "He go east and I go find him."

"Is that the form the karakin took for you?" Yasser asked.

"I sorry?" Nesrin furrowed her brow, certain she and the sorcerer were misunderstanding each other.

"Karakins often take the appearance of lost loved ones to lure their victims away," Yasser said.

Nesrin knew this. What she did not know is why no one grasped that she was not concerned about the demon. She only wanted to find Taniel.

"I'm sorry for your loss, and the cruelty of a demon exploiting it," he continued. "The urge to find your husband will fade in time."

"No, no, that not right," she said, relieved to finally understand the source of the confusion. "My husband not dead. I looking for him when karakin come."

"Yes, why don't you tell me what you remember about the karakin?"

"Is karakin not gone?" she asked, worried she'd only imagined killing the demon.

"Oh, it is. The Karvogi who delivered you here saw you slay it. Razirah must be guiding you, child. If you'd been brought to me an hour later you'd have been too far gone. Unfortunately, a demon's influence survives its demise. Tell me what you remember, it will help clear its taint from you."

"I searching for Taniel when ..." Nesrin paused, having trouble ordering the events. The karakin had been waiting for her outside the farmhouse, prowled the river banks as she sought refuge on the small island, spoken to her as it leaned against the fence by the abandoned shepherd's hut. She pressed a hand to her forehead, struggling to remember how it had all begun. She knew the karakin had taken on many forms, but she only remembered it stealing Taniel's visage.

"I leave Gohar, looking for Taniel." She started from the beginning in hopes of clarifying. "Sahak Sandar say he go to Master Maqlu at Grey Forest. He be telling ... told me go east and I find him." She bit her lip, aware she butchered this telling as well. She was tired, confused, and flustered which exaggerated her inability to articulate well in Haeranji. "I leave and ... and I ..."

Had the karakin found her at Ethel? Or was it after Iradah cast the tracking spell that caused the snow flowers to bloom? Her thoughts felt tangled, crossed and snarled like old yarn.

She started over, got confused, and tried again. Healer Yasser showed remarkable patience enduring her stumbling story.

"Go on," he encouraged when she trailed off for a third time. Her cheeks burned, humiliated by how poorly she wove her tale. "You left Gohar to find someone."

"My husband, I looking for my husband. But I lost ... I lost ..."

She had lost the tracking spell Iradah the hedgewitch had laid upon her, the talisman Taniel had gifted her, and the Karvogi's white anemone, swept away by the stream or abandoned on the small island along with the rest of her supplies. Her breath caught in her throat, certain through losing those, she had lost Taniel as well.

"And you traveled in a trade caravan as far as Ethel," Yasser continued for her.

"I need find my husband," Nesrin said. "I had flower and tracking—"

"In good time, my dear, yes. For now, tell me how you came to be here. You traveled to Ethel and then?"

"Then karakin found me. I don't ... I have trouble ... I sorry, I don't know how to say." The karakin stalking her had been an unrelenting hell that her mind shied away from revisiting. She couldn't remember how long it had hunted her, the tormented days blurring together, the sleepless nights indistinguishable from the last.

"Do you have family in Gohar?" Yasser asked.

"No, they all gone," she said. "The Reaping took them."

"Including your husband?"

"No, he not dead, he ..." Nesrin broke off to swear in her native tongue. Why couldn't she make herself understood? Yasser seemed to pick up everything else she struggled to say. "I look for husband. Taniel Sushan."

"Sushan? By any chance was his father Sariel Sushan?"

"Yes, yes!" Nesrin said, glad Yasser understood her at least on this.

"I'm truly sorry for your loss. I read about his and his father's death in the papers," Yasser said. "When papers were still printed."

"No, no. He not dead. I come find him."

"Yes, you were traveling, the karakin took your husband's appearance, and you went searching for him."

"No!" She slammed her fist on the table, her temper flaring hot. "Why you not listen?"

"My dear Nesrin, I am listening," he said, "as I have for many others who have suffered a karakin. They all share a story similar to yours.

The demon takes on the form of a lost loved one, uses their voice and visage to lure them to their death—"

"Karakin dead. Not Taniel. I kill demon and now I go find my husband."

Yasser's smile was infuriatingly indulgent, one a grandfather spared a willful child who sought more independence than their maturity permitted. "Your killing the karakin is why I hold high hopes that you'll be able to escape its influence on you."

"I not under demon thrall."

"You'll have to be patient. You've been tainted, and that takes time to recover from."

"I don't need time, I need find Taniel!"

"Yes, I understand," Yasser said with kindly patience.

Nesrin knew she was being handled and was equally aware she lacked both the energy and eloquence to resist it. Their conversation had drained all her recovered strength, leaving her to sit angry and exhausted at the elegant table, breathing hard as if she had run for miles. Karu returned from the kitchen carrying a platter of citrus fruit, flatbread, and tea.

"Thank you, Karu," Yasser said as she poured tea for two. Clearly, the sorcerer thought their conversation was done. Nesrin was not ready to give up convincing him Taniel was alive and she had to find him.

"My husband—"

He held up his hand. "We have plenty of time to discuss this later. For now, have something to eat. You've endured too much to also suffer an empty stomach."

She was almost too tired to eat. She was certainly too tired to protest when Karu shepherded her back to bed after the meal, and too exhausted to dwell on how unmoored she felt before drifting into unhappy dreams.

Wolves howled in the night, wind whistled through the barn's eaves, and the moonlight slanting through the thin gaps in the wooden walls was too weak to reach the floor of Taniel's prison. A few of the village boys had come by at sunset, tapping on the outside wall, curious to see the monster locked away. A man had shooed them off, scolding them for playing around demons. No one else had come since. Not a shame-faced Yael bringing a meal, or Purger Adhar demanding blood and interrogating him yet again on what he knew about Minu.

Taniel traced his fingers along his skull where bone curled into horns. He had told himself that his suffering served some purpose—a penance for allowing the world to fall to Minu's Reaping. He had sought a fool's comfort in believing that through his travails there was a path to set things right. He'd lacked the cynical wisdom to see the gods were endlessly imaginative in the suffering they permitted, and they had decided his being twisted into a monster was too gentle a punishment. They'd cursed his final days to be spent in shapeless misery absent of design or escape, waiting to be butchered as an animal for parts, or burned for the amusement of a town taught to hate the magic-touched.

The heavy barn doors groaned open, soft and slow. Taniel sat up. A late night visitor boded ill, particularly one who moved with the quiet of a man wishing to keep his deeds secret. Cautious footsteps stopped outside his stall.

"Taniel?" a small voice whispered through the door. "Taniel, are you awake?"

"Yael?" Taniel's legs cramped from his standing too quickly. "What are you doing?"

The lock clinked and Yael eased the door open, the wood hissing over straw and stone. Moonlight limned his lanky frame. One hand held a pack slung over his shoulder, his other raised a finger to his lips. His eyes glowed unnaturally bright and lacings of silver sorcery threaded along the scars crossing his neck and arms.

"The watchman's asleep," he said, "but we need to hurry."

"Hurry where?" Taniel refused to blindly trust this good fortune.

Even in the dim light, he saw exasperation cross Yael's worried features. "To the river. It's not far, follow it east, and it'll take you to the Grey Forest. I packed a bag to last you a few days."

Taniel accepted the offered pack and followed Yael. He'd have to find a different route than the waterway; it presented too great a risk of him being seen by people who'd kill him for the monster he appeared to be. Even if he escaped chance hostility, word was bound to travel back to Adhar of the horned creature prowling the river. Though the Purger's mind had fallen to madness, his soul belonged to the hunt. He'd come after Taniel, unable to permit the evil tainting him to go free.

"Come on." Yael replaced the lock to the stall door so it looked undisturbed. He moved as confidently through the dark as if he walked beneath a noon sun, kicking a coil of rope to the side to prevent Taniel from tripping over it.

"What about you?" Taniel asked.

Yael peered around the barn's corner, held up his hand for Taniel to wait, then after a dozen heartbeats, waved him to follow.

"They'll figure out it was you who set me free," Taniel said.

Yael shrugged, clearly trying not to think too long on the consequences for his courage. He dashed across the path toward the cover of a woodpile.

Taniel limped behind. "Are there other towns nearby? Places that survived the Reaping?"

"A lot of villages closer to the Grey Forest survived. At least that's what the men allowed to travel say." Yael checked for unwanted witnesses before leading Taniel to duck behind a stone wall.

"You leave for one of those villages tonight."

"I can't."

"Did Adhar bind you?" If so, Taniel knew how to break most of those spells using nothing more than a river's running water.

"No, but this is my home. Everyone I know is here."

"Everyone you know won't be punished for helping me. You will."

Yael shook his head. "I can't leave."

"You must," Taniel said. The boy wasn't stupid, but he was caught in childish naivety, lacking the life experience to know the danger he'd put himself in. "You run and don't come back. Adhar won't forgive your disobedience. He already thinks you tainted. He'll think I've corrupted you and do to you as he did to Hanji."

"He's my uncle. Mother told me to stay with him before she died."

A twig snapped and they both froze, listening for sign they'd been discovered.

"You can't stay here," Taniel whispered when silence reclaimed the night. "Do you understand?"

Yael nodded, slow and reluctant.

"Do you have a talisman?" Taniel asked.

The boy slipped a silver sun and moon hanging on twine from beneath his shirt. "It was my mother's. It protected her from monsters and dark witches. Not the Reaping."

They made their way across the fields to the forest, sneaking behind haystacks, stonewalls and woodpiles. Taniel planned to accompany Yael as far as the river, then leave him with the pack. Crippled as he was, he knew how to survive in the woods. Yael, young and inexperienced, needed the supplies more, and Taniel didn't want the boy doubling back to pack a second bag. Once Yael had the river to navigate by, he was better off on his own. Taniel would only slow him while drawing harmful attention.

"Wait." He grabbed Yael's arm, stopping him from stepping out from behind the haystack. Narrowing his eyes, he stared at where he saw the shadows shift in the night's gloom. It could've been a dog, a watchman searching for them, or simply one of the many tricks darkness played on the mind. Yael's small gasp told Taniel it hadn't been his imagination.

"How many men do you see?" Taniel asked.

"Six. No, seven."

Taniel cursed. One of their absences had been discovered.

"Go, run." He pushed Yael toward the woods. A lantern light flared in a window. A second bobbed, held by a dark figure heading into the barn that had been Taniel's prison.

Yael's glowing eyes widened in fear. "Go where?"

"The river. Anywhere. Just run."

"But—"

"Go!" Taniel hissed. Yael turned on heel and fled into the trees.

Taniel headed the opposite way. The forest's sheltering black was a false refuge. There was no escape for him. Adhar had too soon discovered him gone and he was too slow, too clumsy, too broken.

The villagers would run him down or flush him out wherever he hid. He ran nonetheless, ignoring the creak of his misaligned joints, the liquid fire coursing in his spine, and the headache blinding him more thoroughly than the night. He wasn't going to get away, but he'd ensure Adhar wasted his energies searching for him to give Yael a chance of escape. The boy deserved a better life. One free from living under the rule of a Purger gone mad.

Calls of alarm rose from the village, men were being woken and rallied. Looking behind, he saw the orange glow of torches approaching the trees. Adhar was on the hunt.

Taniel held course as the ground sloped up to a stony rise, using the rough terrain to hide his trail. He counted on Adhar to first search easier paths better suited for a crippled creature to take. Eventually, someone would climb the rise of rock for a vantage point, but not until morning when there was sufficient light to make the ascent worthwhile. There were many dark hours between now and dawn, giving Taniel a place to hide for the night. The rise steepened and he was forced to slow, using his hands to clamber higher. Despite how little past mercy they'd shown him, Taniel prayed to any listening god that they not allow him to fall and break himself tumbling down the rocky ledge—he was already broken enough. Legs trembling, arms burning, he pulled himself over the upper ledge and collapsed onto his side. A warm, choking wet caught in his throat. He coughed out blood viscous with ill-magic. He held his left arm tight to his chest, his twisted ribs heaved, and his chronic headache sent knives plunging through his skull.

Regaining his breath, he rolled onto his back to stare up at the heavens, unobstructed by the trees the stone outcrop rose above. The inky black was resplendent in stars, beautiful even in this dismal hour. How strange a thing it was that beauty endured in a world so cruel. Taniel sighed in fateful resignation, wiping the tainted blood from his mouth and nose. Here beneath the star-painted sky was as good a place as any for his pursuers to catch him. He thought of Nesrin, and it was consolation to know she was safe in Gohar beneath these same stars. In the end he'd been right to let her think him dead. Better he die to her once, not be reborn a monster only to again disappear into death.

Men's voices rustled in the forest below. Torch and lantern glow revealed their movements through the trees thinned by autumn. Crawling to the outcrop's edge, Taniel counted eight roving lights scouring the woods. One approached the outcrop then turned downhill toward the streambed. Another circled the rising stone. He heard two men speaking in low murmurs as they ascended the slope. Taniel glanced around, looking for a place to hide if darkness failed to dissuade the men from making the climb. There was no cover to shelter him, and he lacked the strength to clamber down the rockface to hide or flee.

An eerie whickering cry stilled the forest and the approaching men. Taniel's breath caught in his chest. He was pathetically vulnerable to dark creatures, lacking talisman or weapon. He sliced his black nails into his forearm, drawing blood to sketch hasty runes around him, certain the pathetic, tainted wards had even less strength than he did. The creature cried again. Almost as one, the orange lights moved to the village's safety. There were far more menacing things than cursed, crippled men in the woods at night. It had been in contempt of the men's lives for Purger Adhar to send them in pursuit of his escaped monster. Either the retreating villagers had decided to act on wisdom and risk Adhar's wrath in giving up the hunt, or Adhar had reclaimed the sense to order them home to wait for morning to pick up a trail.

They wouldn't have to search far.

A dull burn lanced through Taniel's side, causing his twitching muscles to cramp. He refused to roll off his back in submission to the pain. Accepting this might very well be the last night he saw stars gave him a clearheaded calm to endure the discomfort. Pain was a burden he'd not have to carry much longer. Purger Adhar would not tolerate him to survive so long.

Pale eastern yellows unraveled the night. Birds sang to welcome the dawn. Taniel remained where he lay, pretending that in this moment of peace, the world was as pure and untainted as the clear morning sky.

"Taniel."

He moved his head slowly to keep the stiffness in his neck from igniting to agony. Wasi Adhar climbed over the rock ledge, his movements enviably effortless despite him being twice Taniel's age. His clothes were rumpled, mud and leaves splattered his boots up to his lower trousers, and the dawn light gleamed on the sweat beading his brow despite the cool air. Apparently, not all the searchers had been frightened off by the dark. Purger Adhar was not so easily scared from the hunt.

"Where's Yael?" Adhar asked.

"What do you mean?" Taniel feigned ignorance. The act wasn't difficult to pull off. His weariness masked all emotion.

"He's the one who let you out. Isn't he?"

"I don't know who did. I awoke to a sound and saw the door open." Adhar shook his head. "Your father enjoyed being difficult as well."

"What do you want with the boy? He's done no evil."

"I want to keep it that way. He's my sister-son, and through his father he's inherited witchcraft. I'll not allow it to corrupt him."

"No, instead you—" Taniel's reply cut short as bone-deep shudders racked his entire body. Worse than his previous fits, this convulsion dove through skeletal muscle to find his lungs and heart. He choked on sorcery-spoiled blood. Red and black burned across his vision, his heart beat too fast and feeble, his blood boiled, and he felt his bones bend to the point of cracking under his seizing.

Adhar sat on a rock across from him, waiting for his fit to end. "You're tainted, Taniel. And it's killing you."

"So you offer me a more merciful end?" Taniel panted.

"An end is coming for you. I'd hate to see it be without purpose." Adhar lacked the heart for compassion, but Taniel thought he saw pity trace its way through the Purger's expression. "It won't hurt. I'll see to it. I have no desire to cause you further distress. I can end your pain, and in so doing rescue dozens more from future suffering."

"You want to harvest me."

"I want to reap good from the evil that's been done."

Something warm wept down the side of Taniel's face. He touched where his horns met his skull and his fingers took away blood turned thick and black with rejected sorcery. He was no longer simply coughing up the infection, it leaked from him at Minu's poorly stitched seams. Death came for him on swift feet, what did it matter if he met his end at Purger Adhar's hand today? It spared him another season of deteriorating until he choked to death on collapsing lungs or withered to the point his gut ruptured and rotted him from within.

"Stop resisting what you know must be done," Adhar said.

"For all your hatred of dark witches, you sound just like Minu." Gritting his teeth, Taniel forced himself to his knees, then slowly, painfully, to stand. It mattered very much if he surrendered to death or fought to the fated end. "Stop fighting the inevitable, give in—you speak the very words she spoke to me. I suppose there's only so many ways for those who fall slave to power to justify their evils, and it makes sense for the servant to echo his master."

"You're the one born of her black deeds, not I."

"And you are the one who refuses to see what is clear. It's not the Grey Lady who bestowed that gift upon you, and it is no gift at all. You were too much a fool to see through Minu's deception then, and you're too much a coward to admit it now."

Adhar's face hardened. Snake-swift he struck, knocking Taniel to the ground. A booted foot slammed into his skull and the world disappeared in a flash of white, then black.

Angry buzzing filled Taniel's head. A sick throbbing soured in his gut. Men's voices drifted in and out of focus, lost behind hazy half-consciousness. Two men gripped him, one on each arm, dragging him over dead leaves. From somewhere beyond the buzzing he heard Adhar speak his name, then Yael's.

"Have you found him?" Adhar asked.

"No, but we have men along the river. He won't get far."

The buzzing in Taniel's ears became a roar, drowning out the men's words. His senses were too battered for him to understand.

They hauled him to the barn, tossed him into the stall, and left him alone to cringe and gasp, bleeding from injuries that told him Adhar had not stopped beating him after he lost consciousness. He used the remaining water in the bucket to wipe away the blood of Adhar's fury and the filth of being dragged through the dirt. These latest wounds were of no great consequence. Adhar's wrath was a breath compared to the storm he'd endured under Minu, and Taniel no longer remembered what it was to be free of pain. He had little concern for his well-being. He only worried what fate awaited Yael should Adhar find the boy. He prayed the Seraphs protect him and guide him somewhere safe.

Like all of Taniel's prayers of late, it went unanswered. Less than an hour later, the barn doors slammed open. Taniel's chest went cold when he heard Yael cry in pain.

"Ungrateful brat!" Adhar's anger sent thunder through his voice. "After all I've done for you!"

Sorcery—horridly similar to Minu's—pulsed. A weaker magic reared in feeble defense, silken like a stream's flow. A blow struck hard, Yael yelped, and the frailer magic puffed out like a snuffed candle.

"You dare use that evil against me?" Adhar roared.

"No! I didn't mean to! I didn't—"

A body hit the floor in the stall where Hanji had been held.

"It was an accident! I didn't mean to!" Yael cried.

Taniel winced as a second, third, and fourth blow fell on the pleading boy.

"Please! I didn't—" Yael screamed and the wall shook from him being slammed into the wood.

"Adhar, stop!" Taniel tugged at the unmoving stall door.

"Uncle, please! I'm sorry! I'm sorry!"

Yael begging his uncle for mercy went unheeded. Red polluted the air, Adhar's wrath seeping out like blood in water. A bone snapped. Yael shrieked.

"Adhar, stop!" Taniel pounded his mangled fist on the wall. "You're going to kill him!"

Yael's pleas fell into wordless cries, screaming from fear as much as pain, then to terrified sobs that continued even after the harsh crack of Adhar's blows stopped falling.

"If you were not my sister's child, I'd see you burn," Adhar said, voice disturbingly steady.

The stall door slammed shut, a lock clicked into place, and heavy feet stormed away.

Taniel tapped on the wall dividing the stalls. "Yael?"

The boy wept in answer, each ragged whimper a fresh knife twisting into Taniel's conscience.

21
Little Lost Child

"Any pain?" Healer Yasser asked. His hands were gentle as he palpated Nesrin's shoulder and arm.

She shook her head. New, tender skin knitted over her wounds beneath his fingers. In another day, her injuries would be fully healed thanks to his work. Healer Yasser had warned her that the scars would be severe. Demonic wounds never mended cleanly. She was lucky she'd been brought to him so quickly and the black veins branching from the jagged scars were the worst she'd physically suffer from the injuries.

"And how are you feeling today?" Yasser asked. "Any troubled dreams? Waking hallucinations?"

"No," she said.

While her physical recovery went better than anticipated, Healer Yasser was less optimistic about her mental well-being, convinced those wounds went far deeper. She was not the only patient residing in his home, but she was the only one he locked in her room when there was no one to supervise her. Yasser was convinced that the karakin's thrall had not lifted, and if given the chance, she'd run off into the woods to chase the fantasies it had planted in her mind.

"Are you sure?" he asked. "Not even strange dreams?"

"No." She lifted her arm for him to better bandage the wounds.

There was no point in telling him she still saw figures lurking in shadowed corners, dark shapes following her from haunted dreams. She knew these were the karakin's waning influence and that there was nothing to be gained in sharing them. She had given up on speaking to Healer Yasser. No matter what she said, it only confirmed his belief her mind was tarnished by the karakin. Her broken Haeranji ruined her chance of credibility, and the more she argued Taniel was alive and she must leave to find him, the more she convinced Healer Yasser the karakin's thrall was dangerously rooted in her mind.

"You're confused," he said whenever she insisted her husband lived. "What you saw, what you feel compelled to run off and find, it isn't your husband."

So she did not argue today as his sorcery encouraged her injuries to mend. She couldn't bear to hear him once more say, "That's the demon-taint in you, my dear," or "Your husband is dead, the karakin was only imitating his voice." Worse was when he took her hand, the sympathetic gesture pushing her to the point of screaming, and promised in time the taint would clear from her mind.

Healer Yasser finished securing the bandages. "Karu tells me you haven't been sleeping well."

"I sleep fine," she said. She'd woken before dawn this morning panting for breath, ripped from the nightmare by her own screaming.

"Nesrin," he prompted her to speak.

She said nothing.

"I'll be gone for the afternoon. Karu and Eli are out as well, and will return by early evening," he said, a gentle way of warning her she was to be locked alone in her room for the next few hours. "Is there anything you need until then?"

"No."

He took her hand. She bristled at his well-intended condescension.

"There is no shame in what you've suffered," he said.

Nesrin kept her gaze on the wall, waiting until she heard the door close behind him, the lock click into place, and his footsteps go quiet. She rose and pressed her ear to the door to be sure the hall held only silence before returning to the bed. Stripping the sheets, she tied them in a long line to reach the ground from her second-story window. The only clothes she had were those her hosts had given her—a long shirt, loose trousers, and house slippers. Hardly attire fit for a journey but hardly an inconvenience to deter her. She had not let a demon stop her; she would not let dressing do so either. She'd slip out of the manor, find out where the nearest town was, then run there. Once escaped from the stigma of being demon-tainted, she'd resupply herself for the journey and find the path back to Taniel.

The window was reluctant to budge and she worried someone heard its stubborn groan as she forced it open. Securing one end of the sheets to the bed, she discovered it was surprisingly easy to shimmy out the window, use the knotted fabric to clamber down, climb over the garden wall, and drop into the narrow alleyway behind the mage's manor.

The brief confidence gained in her easy escape blew away like ash on wind when she came to a main street. People glanced her way, instantly knowing her for a stranger by her darker complexion, and she felt ridiculous wearing slippers and bedclothes. She strode forward in false sureness, pretending she knew where she was going. A couple knots loosened in her chest when no one moved to question her and only the most curious spared her more than cursory looks.

She went where the crowd grew thickest, following the creaking of carts, the scent of cooking street food, and the clamor of haggling shoppers. A dark green tholobate rose above the merchant tents and clay-shingled homes. Nesrin headed toward the temple. Holy sites, particularly those hosting a shrine to Razirah, often had talismans for travelers. She'd claim one, ask the priest to direct her to the closest town, and leave in search of a hedgewitch for a new tracking spell to find her husband. Her hand went for the silver ram's head pendant that should have been at her throat, feeling naked without it. Taniel distrusted the talismans offered at temples, and he told her to never buy one from a hand that had not made it.

"Young miss!"

Nesrin joined the heads turning to the voice.

"Young miss!" Eli waved as he jogged over. Nesrin fought the strong temptation to flee. "I didn't expect to see you up and about so soon."

"I lost my talisman," she said. "I look for new one."

"Oh, you won't need one here. Nahr Hasa is warded."

"Yes, but I ... I no feel safe without."

His expression became one of pity, unique to men desiring to protect vulnerable women. "If you want a talisman I wouldn't buy from a street vendor. Healer Yasser makes his own, and if you don't find one of his to your liking, he'll know where to direct you."

He gestured for her to accompany him back to Yasser's manor.

"I go to temple." Nesrin pointed the opposite way, hiding her insecurity when Eli frowned, taking in her slippers and loose cotton clothes. She hoped he assumed the dress was an eccentricity of her being a foreigner not understanding the attire was inappropriate to wear outside.

"You must be cold." He took off his jacket to give to her. "There's no hurry to see the temple. It's been there three hundred years, it can wait another day until you're better rested—"

"Eli! Thank the Seraphs, you found her."

Eli turned to Healer Yasser hurrying their way. "Pardon?"

Nesrin bolted. People startled as she flew down the streets. She paid no attention to where her feet took her so long as it was far from the doubting healer and locked doors.

Eli's longer stride easily overtook her. He grabbed her wrist. "Nesrin, wait!"

"Get off!" She stepped toward him for better leverage and snapped her arm free. She hesitated to follow through with a low kick between his legs as Taniel had taught her to do after breaking a man's grasp. She didn't want to hurt Eli, but that moment of hesitation cost her the small possibility of getting away. Their short chase had drawn a crowd. Onlookers blocked the street and men stepped forward, quick to assume Eli in the right and the strange woman at fault.

"I'm not going to hurt you." Eli raised his hands to show he meant peace. Or to more easily grab her if she ran.

"What's the trouble here?" a stout man with a thick beard asked.

"She's demon-tainted." Healer Yasser huffed, face red from his haste. "A karakin. Her mind is unwell, she still thinks her husband's alive."

The men muttered darkly on demons. They closed around her, cutting off all escape.

"Nesrin." Yasser spoke to her as if she were a frightened child. "Come along, it's time to go—"

"No! I find Taniel, he not dead, he not demon, he … he …" The words she knew in her native tongue went clumsy when she tried to translate them to her second language.

"Easy there, miss, you're alright." A man reached for her. She swatted his hand away.

"Don't you dare touch me," she said in her native language, aware she very much looked and acted the madwoman they thought her.

"It's alright. The lady has been through a terrible ordeal," Yasser said. "Her mind is not yet mended."

"Come now, miss, calm down." The stout man tried to take hold of her. She slipped around him. A second pair of hands missed as well. The third caught her upper arm. She slapped the man across the face with her free hand. He suffered the blow, showing no angry want for retribution. A fourth man stopped her second strike.

"Easy," Yasser said, "don't hurt her."

They tried to be gentle, but Nesrin made it impossible for them, clawing and fighting. To the men's credit, they didn't look happy having to force her to the ground.

"Poor girl, the demon marked her good."

"My daughter was the same way after a karakin. Took her a year before she stopped trying to run off into the woods."

"Hold her still a moment." Healer Yasser stepped forward. A glowing white mist curled in his palm. Nesrin clamped her lips shut when he pressed his hand over her nose and mouth. "It's alright. This will calm you down."

Lightheadedness forced her to draw breath. The sorcery smelled sickly sweet as its sedating influence seeped into her, flooding her lungs and setting her vision spinning. The fight left her arms, her legs fell limp, and the men slackened their hold as her breathing slowed.

Eli lifted her up. "I've got her."

Her limbs weighed too heavy for her to push him off. She barely kept her eyelids half open to see the smeared faces of onlookers drawn by the commotion. Her resistance to wriggle from Eli's hold amounted to nothing more than feeble tremors as they carried her to the manor. She had no strength to kick free as they lay her on the bed and Yasser set a binding around her ankle, preventing her from leaving the grounds.

Both master and apprentice promised her it was for the best, imprisoning her under the most sympathetic of intentions.

Moonlight cast Taniel's prison in shades of smoke and black. The night beyond was grave-quiet. Yael had cried himself to sleep some time ago, and Taniel sat close to the wall, listening for the pained whimper that told him the boy was still alive. He'd tried speaking to Yael earlier in the evening, but the boy was inconsolable and had only wept harder when Taniel had thanked him for his courage.

Taniel winced as his leg seized from hip to ankle. He slowly stretched until hip and knee joint clicked to ease the discomfort. He pressed his hands to his temples, sick from the ache beneath his horns and the smell of tainted blood filling his nose.

He'd be dead by tomorrow. Adhar's tolerance of him was gone, and the Purger had made it clear he intended to butcher Taniel and harvest Minu's sorcery to better practice the evil he claimed to oppose. Taniel was more disappointed than frightened by his fate, and the night's dull gloom gifted him uninterrupted opportunity to revisit all the failings that had led him here.

He should've stayed in Gohar, not run off on a damned fool quest seeking a sorcerer gone to a mystical forest. He should've stayed to rot in Minu's cell, a far more comfortable living grave than his current one. Or found a dusty, abandoned farmhouse to die in instead of drawing the innocent Yael into his suffering. He should've been more grateful to Shirin. Done better by his father. Taniel's shoulders slumped under his greatest mistake. He should've had the courage to see Nesrin, even if it was only once more. But he was a coward. He was too afraid she'd recoil in disgust. Too afraid to lose her so completely. He'd been terrified the evil infecting him might spread to her, and that Kharinah—

Taniel raised his head from his hands. A woman sang in the night. The words were foreign, but he recognized the tune as "Little Lost Child Found," an old eastern lullaby warning children from straying too far from home. The woman's voice, misleading in its gentle beauty, heralded a wild power that prickled his skin. He tensed as the singing drew closer. Fear was a vestige of a life he was fast fading from and Kharinah's coming inspired only a shadow of the soul-snaring dread it once had.

The singing fell to humming, then silence. The stall door groaned open revealing Kharinah, eyes glowing feral in the feeble light, smelling of damp forests, fresh blood, and Minu's sorcery.

"Whatever you're here to do," Taniel said, "get it done and leave me alone."

She stepped forward. Her predatory way of moving rekindled his old fears, and he scuttled to the farthest wall.

"The sages claim you only truly see a man when he's reflected in death's river before his crossing," she said.

"I wouldn't put much stock in that proverb."

She crouched to trace her claws along the bloody trails seeping from the base of his horns. "Why?"

Taniel weighed how to respond. Reading Kharinah's temper was always difficult. Even when she sounded reasonably lucid, as she did now, there was no telling if that was due to her finding a fleeting hold on fragile sanity or because her demonic nature—cruel and calculating—was in control.

"You can't judge a man by a single moment," he said.

"Mortal lives are a single moment."

"I've known men who braved the harshest trials, but wept at meeting death. Love of life isn't cowardice."

"Then what do you call a coward who runs to death?"

"I don't run to death."

Kharinah shook her head, humming that eastern tune of children wandering into forgotten forests and a mother's promise to find them no matter how far they strayed.

"Why're you here?" he asked.

"Mother told me to find you," she said. "She was displeased to learn you gone."

"Does she know you let me leave?"

"Of course. Mother isn't stupid."

"Why did you?"

She hummed. Her claws tapped the tune on his leg.

"Why did you let me go?" he asked.

She shifted to sit as a child, knees forward, bare feet turned out. "You needed to see."

"See what?"

"And learn."

"See and learn what?"

"See and learn. And learn what, and learn what?" she sang then shook her head. "If you got away, Mother would send me after you. I could leave. For a while."

"And that's why you continued to let me go?" He sensed the strands holding Kharinah to sanity were fraying fast.

"So long as you ran free, so did I."

When Shirin told him of Kharinah's coming to The Red Dove Inn, he'd assumed the demon-child's madness distracted her from finishing the task of hunting him down. After she'd followed him to his apartment in Gohar, he'd thought she'd let him go as part of a cruel game; a cat playing with a lamed mouse. Her carrying him from Tahir's manor in Agr Rav, leaving him beneath the tree instead of taking him to Minu, was too deliberate to be madness, too merciful to be a demon's game. He did not know what reason—if any—guided her actions now.

"Why did you take me from the manor?" Taniel asked.

She tilted her head to the side. "What?"

"In Agr Rav, you took me away from Tahir's magic."

Kharinah hummed in answer, claws plucking at his pant leg.

"You could have left me there," he said. He'd be dead if she had, overcome by Tahir's lingering sorcery in its desire to stamp out Minu's trespassing power.

She shrugged. "Mother said to ... said not to ... Mother would be angry."

"Why do you serve her?"

Her demeanor snapped from childish inattention to coiled hostility. She sat up straighter, eyes narrowing to slits. The straw on the floor shivered and her hair danced on the brewing storm of her feral magic.

"You served your father," she said. Her voice was deeper. Colder.

"I served the same cause as he," Taniel said. "Not him."

Kharinah grabbed his horn to force his face inches from hers. "You'll die without her. You needed to see that. We want to run, but there's nowhere to go."

"You don't have to serve her." Pained tears welled in his eyes. His head felt as though a twist of her hand would rip the horn from his skull.

"Don't, don't." She shook her head slowly, then faster. "Don't! Don't! Don't!"

He scarcely dared to breathe, praying for her to reclaim her fractured sanity. She kept her grip on him as she touched her free hand to her face, feeling her jaw, lips, and eyes as if uncertain they were there.

"I'm barely put better together than you," she said. "If I stay away too long, I'll fall apart. Just like you. We can't run, little brother. You need to learn that."

"I'm not—"

She jerked him forward, pinning him to the floor and slamming her hand over his mouth to cut off his cry. "You're not listening!"

The walls rattled under her anger. She snarled at him in her ancient language, holding him down by horn and throat, claws curled terrifyingly close to his artery. Fresh bloody taint seeped from where his skin split along the horns. He allowed it to run into his eyes, staying still as stone as he endured her tirade, terrified if he so much as gasped in pain she'd kill him.

Quick as the madness came, it left. The barn ceased shaking. The wild power coursing from Kharinah calmed. She lifted him up, carefully resting him against the wall.

"She made you for her and only her," she said, returning to the language they shared. He flinched when she used her sleeve to wipe the blood from his eyes. Her touch was as gentle as it had been when she cared for him in Minu's manor. "There's nowhere to go, Taniel. The farther you run, the more you tear yourself apart, and all that'll do is have you suffer her putting you back together. The more you fight her, the tighter she chains you, and each time she'll leave you less of who you were. Keep what little you have before she takes that from you as well." She finished wiping the blood from his face and pulled a duduk from her cloak, offering him the instrument. "Play."

"That'll wake the guard."

"The guard can't wake. Play."

"No."

"Then I'll call Mother right here, tell her I've found you, and she'll take us both back. Do you want that?"

Taniel swallowed. "No."

"Neither do I." Her hands found his and she waited until he accepted the duduk from her. "Play."

He watched Kharinah for a flicker of agitation or spark of violent madness. None came as she patiently waited for him to wet the reed and adjust the bridle. The first notes faltered, then smoothed into "Little Lost Child Found." His father had sung it to him as a boy. Tiran had taught him to play it when he was older. He remembered the low rumble of his father's singing when a fever had kept Taniel up through a winter night. He smelled the campfire's smoke when Tiran had guided him through the song, their audience the summer insects humming in the trees. Retreating to those memories distanced him from the reality that he waited to be bled out like an animal sacrifice by a Purger gone mad, or dragged back to serve as a dark witch's plaything by the demon-child sitting across from him.

"He played that one," Kharinah said at the song's end. "I remember. She wants me to forget, but I remember. He played it when I was in the woods and he wanted me to come home."

"Who?" Taniel asked.

"She won't say. I've been trying to remember. I asked what his name was but she won't say." She flicked at the straw covering the floor. "Play it again, please. I've been trying to remember."

Her saying "please" both surprised and disturbed him. She had yet to blink. Her gold eyes stared through him to a distant place as he played the tune once, twice, then a third time upon her request.

"He played that song," she said again at the end. "I remember, he wanted me to come home but Mother turned them all to dust. She turned the forest grey and him as well. I can't remember his name. It's not there anymore. It's all dust." Taking hold of Taniel's left hand, she traced her fingers over his fused ones. "Does this make it difficult to play?"

"It makes everything difficult."

"Mother can fix this. It hurt, but she fixed me."

"She broke you," Taniel said. "I'm not going back to her."

Kharinah's childish fascination disappeared. Her lip curled and eyes narrowed. "There's nowhere else to go. The world doesn't want you. You don't belong to it. You belong to her."

"I'm not going back."

She grabbed his neck. "You'd rather die?"

"Yes."

She laughed, claws stroking the skin above his rapidly thrumming pulse. "What do you gain from your pride? Or have left to be proud of? They'll kill you tomorrow, slice you down the middle to bleed you out like a pig. Is that what you want?" She moved her hand down his neck and chest in the motion of a blade gutting an animal for slaughter. "They'll take out your organs. Cut out your eyes and tongue. They'll strip your skin from flesh. Boil what's left to bones. Turn your bones to trinkets, blood to nostrums, and mount your head on a stick outside Adhar's squalid hovel of a kingdom. Is that what you want?"

Taniel had no response he thought safe to give.

"Purger Adhar might not bleed you out first," she said. "There are certain powers best harvested while it breathes. He knows this. Mother gave him that knowledge. He won't kill you before he begins. You'll feel every cut as he takes you apart." She plucked at his fingers. "Bit by bit."

"There's little left to take. Your mother saw to that."

"She's as much your mother as mine. She made us both. We belong to her. Stop resisting and you'll be made whole."

"Is that what you did? Surrendered to her?"

"Don't pretend there's a choice. You can delay, you can die, or you can be what she makes you."

"I told you my choice. As much as your mother might change me, I'm not going to allow her to change that."

Kharinah stared at him. A hundred frightened heartbeats pounded against his twisted ribs before she stood, brushing straw off her cloak.

"Then die," she said. "Serve your pride. It's all you have left, and not for long."

The darkness twisted, consuming every trace of moonlight. With the cold sigh of winter wind Kharinah was gone, the door was locked, and Taniel was alone.

Dawn's light barely found its way into Taniel's stall when Adhar burst in, slamming the door into the wall.

"What did you do?" Spit flew from his clenched teeth.

"I did nothing," Taniel said.

"Who came in the night and killed the guards?" Adhar grabbed him by the shirt collar and shook. "Tell me!"

Taniel gave no answer. He didn't even flinch. There was nothing Adhar could do that was worse than what he'd already endured.

"You bring evil, Sushan." Adhar tossed him to the floor. "You're tainted and what must be done is a mercy."

Taniel had no chance of winning a physical contest against Wasi Adhar, but neither did he have any intention of going quietly. He'd never understood why men pretended at dignity when they faced their end. Honor and esteem meant nothing to the dead. He had begged Minu for death, and in the height of his agony, he would have done anything to receive that mercy. But he'd not give Adhar the satisfaction of leading a docile sacrifice to slaughter. If Taniel was to die today, it'd be kicking and raging, holding fast to the life that was his to have so long as he fought for it.

Adhar grabbed for him. Taniel dug his black nails into the Purger's wrist and sank his teeth into his arm.

"Gods damn!" Adhar's grip slackened, and Taniel ripped free. Grabbing a fistful of dirty straw, he flung it into Adhar's eyes and lunged for his legs, bringing him crashing to the floor. Sharp barbs lanced through Taniel's spine from the reckless movement. His stomach roiled and white pain burst bright behind his eyes when Adhar landed an elbow to his head.

"Be still!" He grabbed Taniel's neck. Pulsing sorcery sent a numbness flooding through him, a thousand tiny blades severing him from sense. Taniel lashed out through the daze. His claws scored Adhar's face and neck.

A second then third blow succeeded in knocking Taniel from sense where Adhar's magic had failed. Blood filled his mouth, dark spots his vision, and his resistance collapsed into coughing groans.

"This didn't have to be painful." Adhar took hold of Taniel's leg and dragged him from the barn.

The early morning sun shone bright, indifferent to the dark deeds slated to unfold. Taniel kicked and was rewarded by a stronger wave of the paralyzing magic. This second spell succeeded in stealing his senses to leave him limp. By the time the sorcery faded to where he could move, Adhar had dragged him beneath a wooden statue in a clearing by the forest's edge.

"Don't make this more difficult." Adhar bound thick rope around his hands and ankles, leaving him at the Grey Lady's carved feet.

The stench of ash choked the air from the ground recently cleansed through burning. Four men circled the black patch, demarcating the ritual site using white, purifying powder. They hardly spared Taniel a brief glance before returning to their work. There was no mercy to be found among them. They had watched a man burn to death the day before; what was butchering a monster after that? Stomach heaving, head spinning from the paralyzing sorcery, Taniel struggled to his hands and knees. He was not too proud to crawl, even if there was no escape.

An all too familiar presence reeking of untamed power raised his skin. He turned to see Kharinah standing in the trees. Her ripped dress was filthy from the forest, and stained rusted brown by the dried blood beneath the crimson of more recent violence.

"When will you learn, little brother?" she asked.

Every man looked to her. One gasped, another went for his knife. Blood-red fire flared in Adhar's hands.

"Who are you?" he demanded. "Name yourself."

Kharinah's wolf eyes shifted to Adhar. Taniel saw the change come over her. She smiled, coquettish and cruel.

"You remind me of him. That proud eastern king." She strode unconcerned and unhurried toward Adhar. "The little man who wanted to wear too large a crown. He lusted after power, and when he took her to his bed, he found he could not please her."

She darted forward. Adhar was ready. Fiery light flashed, blinding Taniel. He heard a second, third, and fourth roar of sorcery, then the demon-child's taunting laugh.

"You're just like him, just like him!" she sang. "He wished to burn bright and now he's dust!"

Adhar yelled a warning and a man shrieked. Taniel's sight cleared to see a man fall in a spray of bloody entrails. A second man drew his sword and charged the demon-child. His oath to the Grey Lady ended in a wet gurgle, his throat clenched tight in Kharinah's hand as the rest of him fell away. A ring of bloody fire sprang from the earth, shielding the two remaining men. Wasi Adhar stepped forward, wreathed in flame.

"Begone, demon!" He flicked his hand and fire roared for Kharinah. The flames broke upon her like water on rock. Smoke curled on her dress while her skin remained untouched.

"Why does she always choose men like you?" she asked.

Adhar's burning sorcery collided with Kharinah's savage power in a deafening thunderclap. Taniel rolled behind the Grey Lady's statue. The wooden totem shielded him from the worst of the aftershock as fire and chaos reared against the other.

"I despise men like you," Kharinah said. "Like you. Like you! Like you!"

Sorcery roared, shaking the ground and toppling Taniel off his knees. Blood flowed from his horns and a high ringing pierced his ears. His vision dipped black under a wave of hostile magic that nearly pushed him to unconsciousness. Keeping low, he crawled over the smoking earth to the nearest of Adhar's fallen men. The man staring empty-eyed above the ragged red hole that'd been his throat had come well-prepared for the harvest. The collection of blades hanging from his belt would've made Aryeh proud. Unsheathing a serrated knife, Taniel sawed through his ankle bindings and pushed himself to his feet. He didn't have the time or dexterity to undo the ropes around his wrists. No matter. He didn't need free hands to flee.

Kharinah had forgotten about him. All her madness was fixed on Adhar.

"You're just like him, you're just like him!" She laughed, weaving her way through his ever more frantic volleys of fire. "Small, petty insects who think they're dragons."

Adhar's flames ran wild, corrupted by Kharinah's chaos. They spread in an unnatural eagerness to consume, racing over grass, twining up trees, only yielding in their hunger to clear a path for the demon-child, the fire deferring to her greater power.

"Dust is all you'll have, Nezar." She waved her hand and darkness slashed through the air to devour Adhar's defensive wall of fire. The flames smoked into nothingness, and the two remaining men fled as their protection failed.

Kharinah bounded forward, grabbed the slower man, and lifted him to take the brunt of Adhar's fiery whip. The red flames incinerated the shrieking man. Kharinah was untouched. She dropped the smoking corpse to break upon the ground.

"And dust is all you'll be," she said.

The surviving man sprinted to the village, begging for the Grey Lady's protection. Corrupted flames chased after him. They crackled and snapped at his heels. A few licking tongues broke from the pursuit to further spread their inferno. They reached the barn and in seconds the building was ablaze. Yael's terrified scream from within barely escaped the fiery roar.

Taniel ran toward the barn, pausing only to dunk himself in the water trough to soak his clothes, before charging into the fire. Smoke suffocated his sight and the damp clothes did little to discourage the rising heat, but much like Kharinah, the flames showed no interest in him. They sought out what was not already claimed by their true mistress.

"Yael!" he yelled. The fire roared louder.

The roof groaned, wood snapped, and he threw his arms up as a beam collapsed, splintering in a spray of embers less than a foot from him.

"Yael!" He shoved at the charred door of the stall—once, twice, and the burning wood gave way.

Yael lay curled in the stall's center. Flame and debris were suspended around him on a slow, silver current. His eyes were shut tight, his hands held protectively over his head as he pled a terrified prayer. The boy's sorcery pushed at Taniel in want to keep him away like it did the flames and collapsing barn. Taniel forced his way through. His feet almost left the ground as the silver fought his intrusion.

"Yael!"

The boy startled when Taniel grabbed his arm. The instinctive spell collapsed, showering them in burning straw and wood. Yael's left eye was swollen shut, his eyebrow and lip were split, and hardly an inch of him was unmarked by violent bruising.

"Move!" Taniel pulled him up.

Yael took one step then cried in pain, falling to his knees. Flames slithered for him as if sensing easy prey. Taniel maneuvered the boy onto his uneven shoulders out of the fire's reaching tongues.

Gods help me and Seraphs save him. He prayed they return him a fraction of the strength Minu had stolen from him, just enough to get Yael clear of the flames. Joints groaning from the strain, his left leg threatening to give way, he staggered to where he hoped the barn door was.

There was no cleansing breath to be found when he limped from the barn. Smoke and heat choked the air, his lungs burned from the acrid reek, and his shoulders screamed beneath Yael's weight. A dozen paces free of the barn turned bonfire, Taniel's knee buckled in a burst of white pain and he fell to the scorched earth.

The fire circled them like starving wolves, snapping hungrily after Yael. Taniel shifted to shield the boy, waving his bound hands to dispel the greedy flames. They were reluctant to retreat, and Taniel didn't trust the fire to submit to him—a creature who held only unwilling ties to Minu—for long.

"Can you walk?" He coughed on smoke and blood.

Yael nodded, only to stumble when he put weight on his trembling leg.

"Lean on me," Taniel said, squinting to see through the fiery haze. "Which way to the river?"

"South," Yael said, leading them into the trees, his limp worse than Taniel's.

A cry caught between mad laughter and a wounded wolf's howl called forth a shrieking wind. Taniel grabbed Yael tight to stop him from being caught in the gale tugging ash and flame to rush like scorching floodwaters toward the village, leaving the blackened woods and sacrifice site a stretch of smoldering ruin.

"What was that?" Yael asked.

"A demon. Keep moving," Taniel said. Terrified screams pierced the fire's hungry roar. He moved to block Yael from looking back. "Don't look. It won't help."

"But I—"

"You can't do anything. Get to the river. Don't look back."

"What about my uncle?"

"Dead." Adhar's fate was sealed. If Kharinah had not killed him yet, she would, and not mercifully.

Silent tears slipped from Yael's swollen eyes, either in relief he was free from his abuser, in mourning for the uncle whom he'd watched fall to madness, or perhaps in bitter grief torn between the two.

The scent of autumn leaves and damp riparian earth replaced the pungent reek of burning death, and the warble of wrens flitting through rushes bid them to the river's bank. The water was smooth as glass, a perfect mirror of the autumn trees and blue sky above, untainted by the red-black smoke curling over Sevget.

Taniel collapsed to his knees at the river's edge, panting through gritted teeth. Yael limped onward. Stripping off his torn shirt, he waded into the waters, washing off dried blood and ash. Bruises blossomed unbroken from his face and neck, down his chest and back, and over his arms where he'd shielded himself from the blows. Judging by the timid way he moved, Taniel guessed he suffered cracked ribs.

"I don't know how far it is to the nearest town." Yael sloshed unsteadily from the waters. "But traders traveled there and back in a single day."

"Did they use boats or walk?" Taniel asked.

"I don't know. Uncle rarely let me come to the banks." Yael gingerly pulled on his shirt, his every movement hesitant. The swelling to his right hand slowed his untying the ropes binding Taniel's wrists, and through his torn pants Taniel saw Yael's knee and ankle were inflamed to twice the normal size. The boy wouldn't make it more than a mile on foot and Taniel had little chance of going farther. He scanned the banks, heart sinking to see no docks or boats tied along the way. There'd be no easy passage for either of them in following the river upstream to where it flowed from the mountains.

Wading into the river, Taniel tested the water to where it rose to his chest. The temperature was pleasantly cool instead of the icy cold he anticipated, and the current was remarkably easy to walk against. Traveling by river left them dangerously exposed, but there was no waiting for the cover of darkness. Yael needed a healer, and soon.

"Come here," Taniel said.

Yael obeyed without question, only whimpering when Taniel hooked his arms beneath the boy's to carry him so his head stayed above the water. The river buoyed them both, taking the worst of the strain off their battered bodies. Feet sinking into the soft river bottom, Taniel slowly pulled them upstream, toward the eastern mountains, and away from Sevget's hellish sky.

22

No More Games

Two oblong stones twice as tall as Shirin stood on either side of the road leading to Nahr Hasa. One bore arcane inscriptions, the other a carving of a woman. A deer skull covered her face and vines grew at her feet to unfurl upward, encircling her. Antlered skulls, the bones bleached white by the sun, rested before each pillar. Brother Emet signed his forehead and heart as he passed between the two stones, offering an invocation to the Grey Lady. Shirin's skin tingled as she followed him through the markers. The warding sorcery emanating from the pillars fell over her like heavy rain, ensuring she carried no evil.

Nahr Hasa was a village of yellow-grey stone and red roof homes cresting upon low, undulating hills. Memorial stones and a handful of proper graves marked the way into the village, but the blackened sores from funeral pyres scarring fields and the ugly mounds of mass graves were nowhere to be seen.

"Was the Reaping not so terrible here?" Shirin asked.

"No," Brother Emet said. "The eastern lands did not suffer as severely. The villages closer to the Grey Forest where the river's forks surround them were spared entirely."

"Does anyone know why?"

Brother Emet nodded at the pillar behind them featuring the woman wearing the deer skull. "The Grey Lady. Her forest takes in the world's ills and heals them. She protected those nearest her from the Reaping, just as she stopped the eastern blight that birthed the Wastes five hundred years ago."

As a girl, Shirin had heard tales of the lost eastern kingdom that fell to a sorcerer's curse, a mad king's lust for power, or sin-bred demons, depending on who told the story. While the bringer of doom varied, the golden kingdom's fate was always the same: the Wastes were all that remained of its fallen splendor, and the Grey Forest was the barrier keeping the curse and its demons from escaping those unhallowed lands. Shirin had always thought it a far-off story in a far-off place that had no bearing on her life in a quiet fishing village. She'd belonged to the northern mountains and the sea, not the eastern forests cloaked in grey mists and haunted by dark fables. Now, it was her seaside village that felt like a lost myth and the eastern legends were as real as the ground she walked on.

Brother Emet led them to a stone building on the outskirts of Nahr Hasa. Livestock bleated from pens and a charnel stench clung to the butchery. Humming ward-stones ringed a windowless side room. Shirin assumed that was where monsters and dark creatures were turned into talismans. A lump lodged in her throat, imagining Taniel being taken there.

"Why don't you wait outside?" Brother Emet suggested. "I'll ask the butcher about recent, ah ... acquisitions."

Shirin nodded. If Taniel had been killed and delivered here to be harvested, she preferred for Brother Emet to bear the news gently to her and not hear, or worse, see for herself. She kept her gaze on the eastern mountains, dark blue beneath a pale grey sky, and away from the penned, bleating goats awaiting slaughter. After a few minutes, Brother Emet emerged from the butcher's.

"He wasn't brought here," he said.

Shirin placed her hands on her knees to brace against the light-headed relief. "Thank the gods."

"It might've been better if he had been. More than once the butcher has bought cursed men off bone-traders to spare them the fate they were sold for. He says he'll send word to Abbott Mardiros if Taniel ends up at his door."

"Did the butcher hear word of a cursed man coming this way?"

"He said to ask Healer Yasser, the High Mage of Nahr Hasa. That's where he sends the souls fortunate enough to be sold to him. If Taniel survived the journey here, that's where he'll be."

Shirin followed Brother Emet closer than his own shadow through Nahr Hasa's winding streets of shops shaded by bright cloth awnings and painted wooden balconies overlooked by the temple's green tholobate. Chickens clucked in front of homes and the smoky scent of cooking fires drifted through open windows. Stone walls sheltered wealthier residences from the narrow cobblestone way. The streets widened as they sloped upward, the homes became larger, and gardens grew behind their mural-decorated walls.

"Here we are," Brother Emet said. Twin statues of winged, rearing horses flanked the front gate to Healer Yasser's home. The monk rang the bell hanging at the wooden doors. A tall, young man wearing his hair tied in a short ponytail answered.

"Brother Emet!" The youth smiled. "It's been too long."

"A pleasure to see you as always, Eli," Brother Emet said. "I take it Healer Yasser keeps you too busy to make your way to Agr Rav these days."

"It's the trouble in the south," Eli said. "Though I suppose you've seen the worst of it, being closer to Sevget."

"Not so far," Brother Emet said. "But I fear it is trouble that brings us here today. Eli, this is Shirin, and she must speak to Healer Yasser. A life she cares for depends upon it."

Shirin sat on a stone bench in the High Mage's back garden, her hands tightly clenched in anxious waiting. Eli had informed them Healer Yasser was away until evening. He'd gone to seek a hedge-witch who specialized in driving out demons and their influence. A young woman had recently been brought to Yasser's home after surviving a karakin and the mage was concerned for her recovery. Understanding there was little to do besides wait for Yasser's return, Shirin had excused herself to the gardens. Eli and Brother Emet were old friends, so she gave them the privacy to speak to one another unburdened by the awkwardness of introducing a stranger to their long acquaintanceship.

"Oh, I sorry."

Shirin looked up to see a young woman standing on the path curving around a butterfly bush. Her skin was the rich, earthen color of the western people from across the Setareh Sea, her eyes midnight black, and her softly curling hair slipping loose from her long braid completed a look of dark beauty undiminished by the weariness shadowing her eyes and sunken cheeks suggesting too much weight had been lost too quickly. Judging by her clothes—a loose cotton shirt, matching pants, and no shoes—the young lady was a patient of Healer Yasser.

"I no know you here." The woman took an apologetic step back. "I no mean to bother."

"There's no need to go," Shirin said. She was the intruder trespassing onto what must be the young woman's garden retreat. "The tree has shade for the both of us."

The woman gave a shy smile before sitting on the grass. The movement caused her shirt to slip, showing thick scars raking over her shoulder, matching the ones slicing along her forearm. Black veins laced the injuries as if a poison within the wound had stained in its spread.

"Have you been here long?" Shirin asked, wondering if the young woman might know if Taniel had been taken in as another patient.

"Too long," she said.

Shirin frowned. She had an unshakable feeling that she'd seen this woman before, but the where and when eluded her.

"Are you from here?" she asked. The woman was obviously foreign, her accent one Shirin had heard from the western sea traders.

"No. I go out search for my husband," the woman said. "I find demon instead."

"I went out searching for my demon of a husband. I found something far worse."

"What find?"

"That my husband wasn't the monster I thought he was."

"Your husband here with you?"

"No, he started a new life."

"I sorry."

"There's no need to be," Shirin said. "I'm grateful to know the life we had wasn't a false love, but it died in the Reaping."

"You come to Nahr Hasa for new life?"

"No, I'm looking for someone else now."

The woman rubbed her wounded shoulder. "Don't tell Healer

Yasser you looking for someone. He will think you demon-tainted and lock you up."

So this was the young woman Eli spoke of who'd survived a karakin. She didn't seem mad from demonic-taint, but if her scars were indication of how severely the demon had wounded her, it was for the best Healer Yasser had taken her under his protection.

"Shirin," Eli called from the garden steps. "Would you care for tea?"

"Yes, thank you," Shirin said.

The young woman shifted so the tree hid her from the path.

"Would you like to come?" Shirin asked, sympathetic for the poor girl.

"Thank you, no," she said. "I stay here."

Shirin hesitated before returning to the manor. She wouldn't have been so bothered by the woman's unplaced familiarity if it wasn't accompanied by the nagging sureness it had something to do with Taniel. She almost turned to ask the woman if she knew a man named Taniel Sushan, then thought better of it. The demonic scarring was evidence the young lady had more than her fair share of burdens to bear.

Taniel's feet sank into the silty river bottom to catch on hidden roots and rocks. Silver mist rose in tendrils off the water, weaving a heavy veil concealing them from the banks. Taniel assumed it to be Yael's unconscious doing; his long-repressed sorcery escaping to protect him as it had in the burning barn. The boy himself was barely aware of his surroundings. He had stopped responding when Taniel spoke, his head rested limply on Taniel's shoulder, and his face was flushed beneath swollen bruising. Taniel prayed Yael's fever was born from his sorcery breaking beyond his control, not the beating he'd endured. Young sorcerers often fell ill when their gifts got away from them, and Taniel much preferred that be the cause of his illness instead of a head injury.

Yael groaned when Taniel adjusted his hold. The boy was in desperate want of a healer but they were too close to Sevget and Adhar's influence to trust a village along the river. The few times Taniel heard livestock bleating or men's voices from behind the grey mist, he had waded deeper into the river's middle, farther from the shores and the risk of being seen.

They must have been on the water for hours, but Taniel had no way to tell how far they'd traveled. The sun shrouded by silver was his only means for tracking time; the feel of the river's flow was his compass. Twice, Taniel thought he'd gotten confused in the fog and had turned so he forded downstream instead of east. The lazy current felt as though it defied its natural course to carry him upstream, and the water was far too warm for a mountain-born river. He didn't bother pondering if the river's oddities were imagined or another result of Yael's instinctive sorcery. He had no energy to spare on wonder. His legs shook with fatigue, his horns weighed on his aching head, and he tasted Minu's corrupting sorcery on his ragged breaths.

A sudden palsy seized him. Red and black shot over his sight, Yael slid from his spasming grasp, and the last of Taniel's strength guttered, twisting like a candle flame before sputtering out. He collapsed into uncontrolled trembling, helpless to stop his slipping beneath the river's surface. The sensation of a dozen hands pressed upon him, lifting him from the murky waters. He gasped as his head broke the surface. The churning river swelled, pushing him onto the muddy bank.

Taniel coughed. His arms jerked and his legs involuntarily kicked, scoring into the soft ground. Rolling onto his back so he'd not drown in the few inches of muddy water took formidable effort. The river spilled over the banks, nudging him farther onto land. He blinked at the figure kneeling over him masked by the bloody darkness blurring his sight.

"Father?" His father had knelt beside him as he lay dying in Minu's swamp. He'd held him as her curse bled into him and his vision went dark.

"Taniel."

His father had called his name. Begged him not to die. Taniel shivered. He'd felt cold then too, covered in mud, trembling and helpless.

"Taniel." A cool hand cupped his cheek. The power in that touch was ancient, inhuman, and disturbingly similar to Minu's. He closed his eyes. He had no want to see the Demon Witch crouched over him. Too many of his dreams were haunted by that image.

Gentle fingers lifted his chin, encouraging him to look. It wasn't Minu kneeling beside him. The being was made entirely of water in the barest semblance of a feminine human shape. The silver mist eddied around them, visible through the water-being's form.

"She told me of you, but not what she'd done. She has forgotten what we were sent for."

The hand cupping his face reshaped to flow over him. Rivulets ran up his deformed brow, circled his horns, rippled across his twisted ribs and limbs to explore his brokenness.

"It is not as hopeless as you fear."

The water pooled over his eyes. Images flitted like reflections upon a sunlit stream. A path wound through a forest, a deer skull hung on a stone shrine, towering trees arched overhead, and a woman walked beneath the leaves, dark hair braided down her back.

"Find Asherah. Find her, Taniel."

"Taniel? Taniel, can you hear me?"

Yael called him back to his senses. The silver mist was in slow retreat, revealing a reedy river bank, the last of autumn's lilies browned and dying, and the glow of a dock lantern hanging above the sheltering rushes.

"There're homes nearby," Yael said. "I'm going to find help."

Taniel opened his mouth to tell him to keep secret he was from Sevget, say his injuries were from bandits who'd robbed him along the River Road, and warn him not to mention the monster he traveled with. A second palsy snared Taniel, stealing his voice and sinking him into harsh shudders.

"Stay here," Yael said, limping unsteadily through the rushes. "I'll be back."

Taniel forced himself to draw shallow breaths into his seizing lungs. Tainted blood seeped from his tearing skin as the river and sky melted into a haze of corrupted red.

The sun was beginning its western descent in earnest when a weary Healer Yasser returned from his travels. The moment he stepped across the threshold and saw Shirin, whom Eli introduced as a soul seeking aid, he masked his fatigue behind a welcoming smile.

"Forgive me for keeping you waiting, I pray it was not too long," he said, shucking off his cloak. It was old, patched, and a far cry from the finely embroidered robes Shirin expected of a High Mage. "Eli, would you deliver the usual pharmica to the Azimi farm tomorrow? I've set wards to keep ghouls away, but that bite young Pareli suffered has the monster's curse in it." He motioned for Shirin to take a seat by the fire. "Now, my good lady, how may I be of service to you?"

"I'm searching for someone," she said. "We were in Agr Rav when he was abducted and I was hoping by some miracle he made his way here to you. You'd know him if you saw him, he has horns, mismatched eyes, and a severe limp. The curse he carries is worsening, and I must find him soon."

"I've neither heard of nor seen a poor soul such as that," Healer Yasser said. "But I may still be of help. If you have something of his and give me his name, I can guide you to him. Understand, tracking spells are a fickle sorcery. If he's—"

"I know the danger of tracking spells." Shirin rushed to grab Taniel's pack she'd brought with her. Finding his wedding photograph, she handed it to Healer Yasser. "Here. Will this work for the casting?"

The mage stared at the picture. "The young man you're looking for," he said slowly. "What's his name?"

"Taniel Sushan."

"You're sure?"

"Yes, do you know him?" Shirin asked.

"Eli," Healer Yasser said, his eyes locked on the photograph, "find Nesrin for me. The gods have just delivered her from my ignorance."

"*Taniel. Taniel.*" The river lapping at the dark banks whispered his name in a voice as clear and sweet as a mountain spring. Cool hands nudged him, urged him to rise. *"Taniel."*

He remained where he lay in the reeds, tasting the sickness on his breath, smelling the rot of the dying lilies. Minu's corruption writhed like ravenous worms in his chest.

"Taniel?"

He opened his eyes. The river wasn't calling him as it had in his strange half-dream. A child's voice spoke his name. Reeds rustled nearby and he lifted his head.

"Taniel? Taniel?" A girl, no older than nine, skipped through the high grass calling his name in a sing-song rhythm. She turned, saw him, and screamed, tripping to disappear in a flailing of arms, muddy dress, and skinny legs.

He thought to see her scramble to her feet and flee up the hill. Instead, she slowly peered over the reeds, staring at him in wide-eyed wonder.

"Are you Taniel?" she whispered.

He nodded, pressing a hand to his temple to ease the throbbing.

"Yael asked us to find you," she said.

"Where is he?" Taniel asked. "Is he alright?"

"He's at home with Mother. Father and I went out to look for you." She inched closer through the reeds. "I'm sorry I screamed. You scared me."

"I don't blame you. I'd scream too if I saw myself."

"Yael said you had horns, but that you're not a monster." She sat beside him. "You're not scary. Just a little at first." She sucked in a deep breath and bellowed at the top of her little lungs, "Father! Father, I found him!" She resumed whispering. "Are you cursed?"

Taniel nodded.

"Did you used to be human?"

He nodded again.

"If you're cursed, are you going to the Grey Forest?" she asked.

"I'm looking for Master Maqlu," Taniel said.

A man called over the reeds. This time the girl stood to shout.

"Father, I found him! He's over here!" She jumped up and down, waving her arms wildly about.

"For Seraph's sake, Zhalah," the man said from farther down the bank. "What did I tell you about yelling? People are going to think you're half shurala."

"He's hurt! He's looking for Master Maqlu!" She hopped a few more times to show her father where to go before crouching beside Taniel. "Master Maqlu isn't here. He's in Antarr."

"You know where he is?"

"Sure. That's where Father goes to sell his catch."

She touched his horns, tracing her small fingers over his uneven skull in innocent curiosity, her initial fright of him entirely gone.

"Does it hurt?" she asked. He allowed her to lift his left hand. She frowned at the fused fingers and took off her headscarf, using it to wrap his hand as if all it needed was bandaging to be healed.

Reeds rustled and the man stared down at them. He had the leathered face and hands earned from working long hours in the sun. A domed rush-woven hat shaded eyes lined by years, and grey flecked his dark beard.

"Gods above, the world's been a sight crueler to you than most, hasn't it?" he asked.

Taniel coughed up blood in reply.

The man touched a silver knife to Taniel's hand. He nodded in approval upon seeing no reaction.

"My name's Chak," he said, repeating the process with the half dozen talismans he wore looped around his belt and neck, "and that screeching shurala over there is my daughter, Zhalah."

"He's looking for Master Maqlu," Zhalah said.

"I heard you, little monster." Chak did a more practiced inspection than his daughter of Taniel's injury. The lines edging his mouth creased deeper at what he found. "Well, we know we'll make good time on this run. Azariah'll see to it. Can you stand?"

Taniel nodded, and with Chak's help, he found his feet.

"Is Yael alright?" Taniel asked.

"He needs a healer almost as much as you do," Chak said. "I suppose coming from Sevget he's lucky to be alive. We don't let our magic-touched go farther west than here. Not with Wasi Adhar in power."

Chak kept a steady arm around Taniel to guide him from the reeds. A small wooden house stood atop a knoll, smoke unfurled from the stone chimney, a line of hung linens swayed in the breeze, and hens pecked along the dirt path leading to the front porch. A narrow dock extended beyond the reeds' reach where two flat-bottomed boats were moored beneath the glowing lantern.

"I was planning to take a load upriver tomorrow," Chak said, "but if Azariah blesses us, we'll make it to Antarr by night. You're not the first soul she's delivered to our banks."

"And Master Maqlu is there?"

"Yes, though even a fisherman like me can see you need more than a mage's help," Chak said. "You should seek the Grey Lady."

"The gods haven't inspired any reason for me to hold faith in higher powers," Taniel said. "I'll do better seeking help from men than the divine."

Chak snorted. "Who do you think shepherded you here if not the divine?"

"What about Yael?" Taniel asked, not wanting to debate faith with the man who'd shown him only kindness.

"My wife is getting him cleaned up and packing a meal for you both. Seraphs know the boy needs at least six square meals a day for a full month. He's hardly more than skin and bone."

Taniel's legs were too unsteady for him to safely clamber into the boat. Chak helped him down, and the river swelled unnaturally high along the boat's sides to raise it closer to the dock.

"See?" Chak rapped his knuckles three times on the water dragon carved into the dock's post. "Azariah has taken you under her care. Zhalah, untie the boat, then go fetch your mother and the boy."

"Mother!" Zhalah shouted as she unfastened the ropes. "Father's taking Taniel to see the Grey Lady!"

"I said fetch your mother, not shriek at the woman who brought you into this world."

Zhalah raced up the hill. "Mother!"

A woman stepped onto the front porch, shading her eyes from the afternoon sun reflecting off the river.

"What's this I hear about you going off to see another lady?" she asked her husband in mock scolding. Two little boys tailed after her like ducklings. Seeing Taniel, their round eyes went wide.

"Look, Mother, look! He has horns!"

"Don't point, it's rude," their mother said, the boys already hurrying to the dock to get a better look.

"Are you a goblin?" the younger asked.

"Yes," Taniel said. "And I eat little boys who point and don't listen to their mothers."

"What kind of goblin?" the older asked.

"That's alright." The younger reached out his small hand to pat Taniel's horn. "The Grey Lady turns goblins into princes. Father'll take you to her."

"Are you sure you won't wait until tomorrow?" their mother asked. "Get you both a meal and rest before heading upriver?"

"Leaving sooner is better." Chak gestured to the water lapping eagerly at the boat.

"Well, at least get the poor thing a blanket," she said, turning back into the house.

"He's nice for a goblin," the older boy said. The younger nodded in agreement.

"He's not a goblin," Zhalah said. "His name is Taniel."

"What's a Tanny Yell Goblin?"

"Shoo, you little monsters! Shoo!" Chak waved his hands and the children scattered in a frenzy of squealing laughter, well-practiced in the game of fleeing their father's feigned irritation.

"Your family survived the Reaping?" Taniel asked.

"The red veil never touched us. I don't know a single soul east of here who fell ill," Chak said. "The Grey Forest's roots reach far, and this is the Lady's domain. She protects those who shelter in the shadow of her forest."

His wife returned, one arm supporting Yael, the other holding a bundled cloak and a wooden meal box. Yael looked torn between wanting to flee from the woman or collapse into her entirely. The fresh shirt he wore was too large for him, most likely borrowed from Chak, and the oversized cloth made him look deathly frail.

"It gets chilly on the water." The woman handed the cloak and meal box to Taniel.

"Thank you," he said. "Your family is well-versed in unexpected charity."

"Azariah tends our needs," she said. "We're called to do the same for those she brings us."

Both husband and wife helped Yael into the boat. He moved as though his bones were glass and his skin paper.

"Are you alright?" Taniel asked.

He gave a shy nod. The bruising around his eyes failed to hide the redness from crying. Taniel handed him the cloak and the boy hid himself in the folds.

"I'll be back by tomorrow noon." Chak kissed his wife goodbye and took hold of the rope to guide the flatboat upriver. He hardly had to pull. The water pushed on the boat's sides as the current defied its natural flow. The strange presence Taniel sensed on the bank—unnervingly similar to Minu's—thrummed in the river. He leaned over the boat's side to glimpse a serpentine shape undulating below the surface before rippling away.

The air reeks of charred flesh and wood. The crows feasting on the blackened corpses cackle as you walk by. Three wolves tempted from the forest crack burned bones in heavy jaws. Their gold eyes watch you warily, their maws bloody and black. You're glad Kharinah has not descended so far into her savage nature to join them, but you're irritated her wildness has forced you to leave the Wastes. You sensed your daughter running too feral, a consequence of you granting her too much freedom, and your concerns were justified when you stepped from Ha-Ai's dusty ruins into the charred remains of Sevget.

Perhaps Kharinah would've known greater happiness if you had permitted her to be a wolf. She spent most of her childhood undecided on what shape to take, constantly shifting between the two. She wailed for weeks when you decided for her.

She waits for you by the Grey Lady's temple. Vines cover the stone façade and a deer skull sits on a plinth at the entryway. All of Asherah's holy sites have a skull for her to speak through. There are few mortals left who remember that to be the reason for the placement of the bones.

The carved icon of the Seraph has fallen from where it stood atop the temple's doors. It lies cracked upon the stone ground. Wasi Adhar lies beneath, his head collapsed under the statue to spatter like overripe fruit.

"Kharinah, what have you done?" you ask.

"He meant to kill Taniel," your daughter says. She shows remarkable lucidity as she tells how she tracked Taniel to Agr Rav yet was unable to retrieve him when he took sanctuary on the monastery's holy ground. You're unsure if she's lying. You know Kharinah can trespass onto hallowed ground, but there's no telling if she is aware of this. There's very little she reliably understands.

She tells how Taniel was taken to Sevget as a sacrifice to Wasi Adhar who intended to use him as a means to amass the power to defeat you. You almost smile at the irony. It's not the outcome you intended. Adhar brought about his demise long before he had the chance to sully the Grey Lady's name through his rabid zealotry. Yet his being crushed by the icon of the Seraph he worshipped eases the irritation that runs like sun-scorched sand beneath your skin whenever you hear your sister's name.

"There were gentler means of resolving this," you say when Kharinah finishes her tale. "Ones that did not burn an entire town. Ones where Taniel did not escape."

"He didn't escape. The river stole him," she says. "Azariah took him away."

You clench your hands to fists, furious that your sisters insist on interfering in your work. They tolerate wickedness and cannot bear when you take unflinching opposition to the world's evils.

Kharinah senses your annoyance and recoils. Her fear is unnecessary. There's no purpose in punishing her for letting Taniel escape. The bloodlust she inherited from her father blinds her to foresight, but the hunt she inherited from him compensates for those vices. Not even a Seraph can hide a soul from her.

"Find Taniel and bring him home," you say. "No more games."

She cries out as you bind her to your will. Permitting Kharinah some of her usual mischief when you first sent her after Taniel was in error. You allowed her to run too free. Her carelessness almost cost you Taniel and your promise to his father.

"You will not sleep. You will not eat. You will not rest," you say. "You will do nothing else until you bring him to me."

Kharinah's words catch in her throat. Your refusal to allow her anything until she finds her wayward brother includes speech. You expect a silent snarl, a baring of teeth. Instead she looks at you the way she did all those centuries ago when you denied her the choice to be wolf or girl. She slinks away, and if she had a tail, it'd be tuck between her legs. The wolves abandon their feasting to follow, whining and licking her hands. You consider calling her back, softening the discipline through affection, but there is another you must speak to first.

The river snaps at your feet with a viper's cold fury. Azariah does not want you in her waters. She hides what she stole from you. You're unable to sense Taniel despite knowing he is near. No matter. Azariah may shield him from you, but not from Kharinah. Your daughter is neither Seraph nor mortal. Neither human, beast, nor demon. She was supposed to be the perfect balance of all creation. Instead, she exists in defiance of all.

"Azariah," you say, "what have you done?"

She rises from the river in a rush of frothing water, twisting to shape a serpentine creature. The narrow equine head glares down at you from a height towering taller than the nearest trees. Her eyes glow bright and the droplets falling from her flow back into her pellucid form.

"*I spared two souls the consequences of your cruelty.*" Her voice has all the wrath of the harshest rapids.

"That was not your right."

"*Have you not done enough? How many more must suffer until your wrath is satisfied? Until your pride soothed? You would see all creation burn because a man slighted you.*"

"You don't understand." Your sisters have never understood. They have not lived as a mortal. Loved as one. Lost as one. Only you have.

"*I understand better than you. Pretend as you do to higher motivations, we see what you've become.*" Azariah returns to her river, plunging into the waters to throw hostile waves over the banks. "*Nakirah, you are fallen.*"

23

Rooted in Lies

A forbidding silence gripped the river. No frogs sang from the banks. Wrens ceased their flitting through the rushes. The reeds dared not whisper against the other. There was only the water's low murmur and the creak of wood as Chak used the long pole to push the boat upstream. He had the sense to abandon pulling the boat along the river bank and take refuge in the protection of running water.

"Do you see anything?" he asked, dark eyes watching the reeds and woods.

"No." Taniel followed Chak's lead in lowering his voice to a tight whisper. Dusk's nearing was not the source of this hush; the river held its breath in anticipation of a far more sinister coming. The willows swayed without wind, reeds shuddered, and the first touch of the chaotic power heralding Kharinah's approach sank dread into Taniel's chest.

"What is that?" Yael shrank farther into the cloak.

"Pull closer to the bank," Taniel said.

"What for?" Chak asked. Agitated ripples lanced across the river toward their small boat.

"For the demon that'll kill you if you stand between me and her," Taniel said. Accepting Chak's help had put a good man at risk. He wasn't going to further endanger him or Yael.

"I'm not leaving you to be demon prey," Chak said, indignant at the suggestion.

"She'll kill you and Yael if not."

"Running water keeps dark creatures at bay," Chak said. "And once we pass under that bridge"—he used the long pole to point to the stone bridge arching over the river, reflected in the water to create the illusion of a circle—"we're under Master Maqlu's protection. No demon can cross that boundary."

Howling wolves shattered the river's silence, a gust of wind rocked the flat boat, and Taniel felt the manic pulse of Kharinah's dark power. She'd be upon them before they reached the bridge, and he'd be a fool to think the passive protection of a river's running water had the strength to hold her at bay. The wards of Sevget and Tahir's manor had held no influence over her. Not even the divinely blessed power of thresholds had prevented her crossing.

The boat rocked under Taniel shifting to clamber into the river. He'd confront his hunter away from endangering those who'd possessed the courage to help him.

"Don't!" Yael grabbed his arm. The sudden motion dangerously shook the imbalanced boat.

"Both of you stop or you'll put us all in the river!" Chak shoved the pole into Taniel's hands and unholstered the pistol at his belt. "Keep us moving."

"Chak!" Taniel's warning came too late. A whipping wind shrieked through the willows, ripping branches and shredding the river into spitting froth. A dark shape bounded from the trees and across the water as if it were solid ground. The boat pitched under the demon-child's gale and Taniel grabbed the edge to keep himself oriented as they capsized, plunging into the dark river. Claws sank into his arm and his pained scream invited water to flood his throat. Kharinah almost wrenched his shoulder from the socket heaving him from the river onto the bank. The impact knocked the air from his chest leaving him sputtering for breath. She pinned him down, his twisted ribs creaking under her weight, her teeth gnashing in mute madness. A gun boomed and Kharinah staggered to the side. Taniel rolled to hands and knees, coughing up water polluted by blackish blood.

"Let him alone!" Chak leveled the gun. By some miracle, he had gotten him and Yael to the opposite bank while keeping the gunpowder dry.

Kharinah shook herself. The bullet dropped from her back as easily as the river water. A second shot roared and either went wide or had less effect on Kharinah than the first, earning only a sneer. Her charge toward Chak ended in her stumbling to the mud. The demon-child spasmed beneath the blood-red sorcery coiling over her like chains. She screamed soundlessly, thrashing in a vain attempt to escape the enchantment, and her gold eyes wild in panic fixed on Taniel. Her lips shaped what almost looked like a repeating plea. He scrabbled away and she caught him by the ankle. Her iron grip tore his weakened skin, threatening to break his groaning bones.

"Kharinah, stop!"

She ignored him, as indifferent to his clawing at the wet earth as she was a third bullet hitting her squarely in the chest. Wind blistered red and swirled into a portal leading to Minu's manor.

"No! No, don't!" Taniel fought and kicked, unable to break free. "Please!"

She tightened her hold. His ankle bone cracked in her grip. Red pain burst over Taniel's sight as he screamed, and the look Kharinah spared him was one of remorse.

"Don't, please, don't," he begged.

The ground shook, a flash of brilliant sorcery blinded Taniel, and Kharinah released him. Through his swimming vision he saw her dart to the side to avoid a spear of bronze light. Her attacker stepped through a second portal pulsing at the edge of the trees. The man was in his late forties, tall, broad shouldered, and possessed an air of privileged confidence.

"You are not welcome here, demon," Master Maqlu said. "Begone."

Searing bronze sorcery slashed at Kharinah. She whirled away only for her mother's magic to seize her the moment she leapt to attack. She dropped to her knees in soundless, writhing screams, her mother's magic sinking into her like barbs.

Strong hands gripped Taniel, a bronze wind spun a door out of air, and Master Maqlu pulled him through. On the other side of the portal, Taniel saw Kharinah panting on the ground, tears streaming down her face as she reached for him. The way closed, the willows and river disappeared, and Taniel lay gasping in the center of a garden encircled by stone walls. Golden trees swayed under the disturbance of their arrival, and the stone he lay on had the faded stains of numerous magical rites performed upon the circular space.

"Yael and Chak," Taniel hissed through clenched teeth. The break to his ribs was a branding iron in his side. "They're—"

"Dua has them." Master Maqlu gestured across the garden to the second portal closing behind Chak carrying Yael, the two of them led by a young woman. Her black hair was cut short at her chin to frame petite features and large brown eyes.

"Taniel." Dua nodded in greeting, unperturbed she'd just helped pluck them from the clutches of Minu's daughter, or that Taniel's appearance was monstrously changed since last they met.

"Tend the boy," Master Maqlu said. "I'll see to Sushan."

Dua led Chak and Yael into the modest, single-story home as Master Maqlu rested Taniel against the garden wall. In the nearly two years since Taniel last saw Master Maqlu in the halls of Gohar's Arcanum, the mage's appearance had gone mostly unchanged. His head was shaved, silver beard neatly trimmed, and his face was lined from a personality prone to frowning. Yet the time since the Reaping had affected him. He no longer wore the resplendent blue robes of Gohar's High Mage, trading silks for a simple undyed tunic and trousers, belted instead of embroidered. A smear of ash darkened his forehead and metal rings clinked at his wrists—the marks of a penitent guilty of grave sin.

The sorcery glowing in Maqlu's hand pulsed warm where he touched Taniel's arm. The skin that had been tearing like wet paper smoothed and healed. Maqlu gently pressed his hand to Taniel's side. The pain lancing through his ribs ebbed away. Taniel drew in a deep breath, lightheaded from the lifting of the least of his pain, as Maqlu repeated the same process on his ankle.

"By the gods," Master Maqlu said, his hands streaked with Taniel's tainted blood, "what did she do to you?"

Nesrin sat in the living room's corner, preferring to maintain a comfortable distance from Healer Yasser, Eli, and the two strangers come from Agr Rav—the middle-aged woman she met in the garden and a holy brother. They sat close to the fireplace's crackling warmth while the woman named Shirin told her tale. All four of them kept looking at Nesrin for her reaction as Shirin relayed what had happened to

Taniel. How they'd left Gohar and traveled east. How Taniel was hunted by a demon servant of the witch who'd cursed him. Shirin detailed how the witch had deformed him, how desperately in need he was of deliverance from his worsening condition, and how all their previous attempts to find a cure had failed.

Nesrin's heart skipped, thudded, and trembled throughout the tale. She kept her face steady as stone, reluctant to show the slightest emotion with her hosts when they had interpreted changes in her temperament as evidence of the karakin's hold on her. She tensed when Healer Yasser crossed the room to kneel before her.

"Forgive me," he said. She hesitated before allowing him to take hold of her leg and remove the binding from her ankle. Nesrin flexed her foot. The bones felt oddly light now that she was free from the sorcery holding her to the manor grounds. "I never meant—"

"I know you meaning well." She was angry at Yasser, at Eli, and all who'd refused to listen to her. She was furious that everyone from her husband, to old friends, to well-intended strangers insisted on making decisions for her. She swallowed both her anger and injured pride. "And I forgive."

Yasser had taken her into his home, healed her injuries, and done his best to keep her safe from a threat he misunderstood. Holding him in ill-will achieved nothing, and resenting those who had endeavored to help her was poison to the soul.

"But now you help me as I need, and I need you listen," she said. "I want tracking spell. My husband lost and I find him."

"Nesrin, we don't know if Taniel is alive—"

"No. No, you listen. I find him, wherever he go." She had not let walls, wicked men, good intentions, or demons stop her. She would not let death deter her either. "Do tracking spell."

If Taniel was dead and gone to the After then so be it. She would find him there.

Healer Yasser sighed. "Eli, prepare a space and fetch water." Nesrin turned to Shirin, the unassuming woman who'd braved the unknown to see her husband looked after. "Thank you for the watch of my husband."

"When you go to find him, may I accompany you?" she asked. "I'd like to know him safe."

Nesrin nodded. "I think he want to know same for you."

The tracking spell Yasser performed was a more elaborate mirror of the one Iradah the hedgewitch performed in Ethel. The water pitchers were engraved silver instead of clay, the candles decorated, and despite Healer Yasser having tended to her injuries, Nesrin insisted on using a sheet for modesty during the ritual.

"It will take time to set in," he said after the spell was cast and Nesrin dressed. "Days, depending on how far away he is."

A wind whisked fallen leaves to tap the window. Something soft brushed Nesrin's palm. She caught the white anemone flower before it fell to the floor. Heart thrumming high in her throat, she rushed to the front doors, threw them open, and cried a soft sob of gratitude. Small flowers the color of fresh snow bloomed along the walkway and out the gates, leading east.

The lanterns circling the ritual site cast an amber lambency over the courtyard's smooth, ivory-white stone covered by symbols painted in chalk and blood. Master Maqlu crouched outside the runes, his sleeves rolled back like a potter's at his wheel, the veins running from hands through forearms alight with pulsing magic. Small threads of light drifted up from runes humming in harmony with Master Maqlu's spell. Taniel took deep breaths where he lay in the circle's center, wincing as his muscles jumped and twitched under the sorcery's testing explorations. His back was a knot of snarled nerves, the warped bone of his hips groaned, and numbness from lying on the stone held his right leg captive in a tingling vice. The discomfort was nothing. Already Master Maqlu had stopped the blood seeping from his horns, mended the tears in his thinning skin, and lessened his bouts of nausea. Taniel permitted himself to entertain restored hope that he'd at last found release from the worst of Minu's curse.

Master Maqlu frowned and shook his head. "I'll need to try more invasive magics."

"Do what you have to," Taniel said. "It can't be made worse."

"Sushan, the sorcery is woven into your very being." Master Maqlu stepped into the runes. The glow from the sorcery and lanterns cast his features in an ethereal play of shadow and light. "One careless mistake might kill you, and I'd prefer not to have your death on my hands as well."

Taniel flinched, expecting pain when the mage rested one hand on his forehead, the other over his heart. Sorcery flowed over Taniel in soothing waves, slipping through the snarled knots of Minu's workings, careful to explore the corruption while avoiding aggravating it. His heartbeat slowed under Maqlu's influence. His eyelids drooped. Breathing came easier than it had in days. Through half-closed lids he saw Maqlu lift his hand off his chest. A dark, viscous substance clung to his palm, stretching like dough between him and Taniel. Using the rag, Maqlu wiped off the corruption. The red-black substance quivered on the cloth, possessing a life of its own.

He rested his hand on Taniel's chest, chanting in a foreign tongue that Taniel did not understand but was certain he recognized. More viscous rot bubbled up to be pulled away, and its removal left Taniel feeling dizzyingly light. Darkness fluttered at the corners of his vision. In the last moment before drifting down into a lulled trance, he remembered where he'd heard the language Maqlu chanted—it was the same one Kharinah spoke.

Taniel awoke in agony, bucking and flailing to escape the burning.

"Hold him down! Hold him down!"

The hands that grabbed him were searing tongs. Taniel screamed. The pain tearing through him with broken teeth and poisoned claws rivaled that of Minu's reshaping him. He was being ripped apart like he had been then, flesh stripped, bones rendered, his very soul under siege.

"Stop!" Taniel begged as he had begged Minu. "Stop!"

Maqlu placed the corruption-stained rags over Taniel, chanting rapidly in Kharinah's language. A woman's voice joined in and for a terrified moment Taniel thought it was the demon-child. Fear cleared his vision to reveal Dua held him down. She harmonized with her master's recitation, their words cleaving Taniel's skull and turning his bones brittle. He choked, feeling Minu's extracted rot sinking back into him. The agony lessened as the sickness that held him together returned.

Dua helped Taniel roll over to vomit out the dark ichor filling his mouth and nose. She rested a hand on the back of his neck. A cool soothing spread from her touch, gentling the worst of the pain.

"I'm sorry. I thought I could draw it out," Master Maqlu said. "Your curse is a difficult one."

"I noticed." Taniel wiped tears and blood from his face. Crickets sang in the garden and the muffled cries of an infant escaped the home. Those sounds of life felt more foreign to Taniel than the language Master Maqlu shared with Kharinah, belonging to a world he had no place in.

"I'll do what I can to lift it," Maqlu said, "but I don't want to give you false hope."

"I don't expect it to be lifted. Just lessened." Taniel expected no miracles. His finding Maqlu was enough of one.

"Even there I'm uncertain how much I can accomplish. My power cannot stand against Minu's."

"You stood against her before, surely you can do something about her curse."

A strange tension passed over Maqlu's features. "I can handle it from here, Dua, and I believe your youngest charge is calling for you." He waited until Dua had heeded the call of the crying baby and closed the door before speaking. "Sushan, as a Purger, you know how stories change to what people want them to be. I never defeated Minu. I never met her as an adversary. I went to her as an apprentice."

Taniel stared. "What?"

"I didn't know what she was. She hid herself behind a different face and name, and I was young, stupid, too eager to chase rumor of a witch in the north who had mastery of arts lost to time. She taught them to me and I was blinded by that power. It was only years later I discovered who my master truly was. My great battle with her—that was my fleeing her apprenticeship, and her allowing it. I don't know how the story spread of my knowing Minu, or how it twisted into a tale of courage I never earned. I think she cursed me when I abandoned her and planted those seeds of rumor herself. My denying the story of confronting her only spread the lie further until it overshadowed my every true achievement. Any name I made for myself was doomed to be rooted in deceit. Now, if you can, repeat what I just told you."

Taniel did as told, hardly hearing the words. A cold, slippery sickness had settled in his gut at hearing the confidence he'd placed in Maqlu was, and had always been, founded in falsehood.

"You're the first person who's been able to hear me make that confession and not misunderstand." Master Maqlu's smile was bitter. "Anyone I tried to speak the truth to only ever heard me confirm the falsehoods. Forgive me."

"There's nothing to forgive." Taniel understood Master Maqlu's shame. He knew all too well what it was to be seen as something you were not. In a way, Master Maqlu had a worse fate, to be sung a hero all the while knowing he'd accepted the teachings of the dark witch he was praised for defeating.

"Taniel Sushan, there's plenty in need of forgiveness. I allowed myself to become comfortable living under the false tale, and then become too much a coward to correct for it when I was finally called to confront Minu. Before you and your father"—he swallowed, voice thick under the burden of his confession—"before you went north, he came to me. He asked my help. I dismissed him. Like the rest, he believed the tale of my defeating Minu, and I was too ashamed to attempt to tell him the truth I'd given up on. I told your father to bring me evidence before I wasted my time investigating rumor of dark witches. But I knew. I knew he was right, that it was Minu, and I was too much a coward to face her."

"You didn't even try to dissuade my father from going to his death?" Taniel had assumed the ash marking Maqlu's forehead and the metal rings on his forearms were an undeserved penance of him taking honorable responsibility for the Reaping. He'd been wrong, and there was no repentance possible for the High Mage betraying him and his father to their fate.

"Taniel, I'm sorry, I—"

Taniel shifted to put his back to Maqlu. "Go."

There was a pause, then the quiet footsteps of a shamed retreat, and the creak of a door shutting.

Taniel brought his knees to his chest, burying his head in his arms. He wanted to hate the mage for allowing him, his father, and fellow Purgers to go to their ruin. The anger refused to come. All he felt was hollowness. There was nothing Minu had left untainted.

You bury the dead of Sevget. You sink them into the earth. Their flesh will be remolded, recreated to your ends. You will harvest purpose from the destruction your daughter has wrought. One by one, you whisper to them what they are to become while the soil swallows them. The first body is returned to the earth under the eye of a high afternoon sun. Dusk colors the sky by the time the last body slowly sinks into its temporary grave. You save Wasi Adhar's until the end, bidding a more personal farewell to your unwitting disciple.

Kharinah was right to kill him. You would've done so yourself after learning what he intended to do to Taniel. For too long men have thought themselves entitled to steal what is yours. They are determined to repeat the sins of their fathers.

"Perhaps they repeat their wrongs because you don't leave survivors to learn."

Silver light shines behind you. The deer skull laid before the Grey Lady's temple no longer rests on the plinth. It sits atop glowing mist shaped into a cervine body. Its thin legs taper to nothing before they touch the stone.

Asherah's shahavaz, one of the thousands of souls she has bound to her service in death, echoes her voice in all its patronizing condescension. *"It is not only mortals who struggle to learn from past errors."*

"What do you want?" you ask.

"Answer that for yourself, Nakirah. What do you want from all this ruin? How much farther must you fall—"

"Begone." The skull explodes in a burst of crimson wind.

The roots of the Grey Forest have spread beyond tolerance if Asherah is able to send her messengers this far from her trees. When she grew that forest to thwart your first cleansing, you bound her to the woods, trapping her in a prison of leaves and her self-righteous sanctimony. You thought yourself free of her. But Asherah is a poison content to spread slowly. Her forest creeps east to claim the Wastes as her own. Her influence spreads west to turn mortal minds soft and their knees weak to fall in worship of her.

The ground, freshly turned from the buried corpses, shudders under your irritation. You want nothing more than to uproot her wretched woods, and cleanse her from mortal memory. But the forest is one of the few places you dare not recklessly trespass. Instead of fighting the binding you laid upon her, she embraced it. She wove your trapping sorcery into her own power to once again corrupt what was yours. She turned her prison into a fortress, and you created a place where every branch, root, and stir of wind will turn upon you.

24

Reason for Hope

Restlessness hounded Nesrin, nipping at her heels to excite a faster step. She wanted to sprint down the winding path bordered by the white anemones, through the village of red tile roofs nestled between two hills, and into the shadow of the looming eastern mountains. Her legs itched to carry her into the mist-shrouded forest rising from the mountains' roots. Matching her pace to Shirin's conservative gait took terrible effort, and multiple times Nesrin caught herself pulling ahead in her want for haste.

"We'll make it to the village before the rain catches us." Shirin nodded at the swollen clouds threatening to intercept them from the northeast. "There's no need to worry."

"It not worry." Nesrin rubbed the black scars covering her shoulder and arm. "I think it demon-taint. It make me feel like I have fire in feet."

Healer Yasser had been right; Nesrin was infected with vestiges of the karakin's thrall, breeding in her a yearning to leave the safety of warded walls and towns. The mage told her that having someone to truly search for was a fortunate blessing. It gave purpose to her want to wander, lessening the chances of the taint turning to madness.

"Razirah has graced you with her favor," he had said when she and Shirin left Nahr Hasa. "May you continue to walk in her light."

Nesrin did not feel blessed, even as reason and the blooming anemones told her otherwise. She felt sick with unease, and confused by her body aching for rest while her tainted mind urged her to walk on endlessly. Flickers of the visions the karakin had tormented her with lingered like ghosts; Suri stood by the roadside, Taniel's voice whispered her name from an uncrossable distance. She clutched the new talisman hanging around her neck, running her thumb over the silver, willing the visions to fade.

"Are you alright?" Shirin asked.

"I fine, thank you," Nesrin said. Healer Yasser had provided her calming drops to pair with wine should the karakin's influence overwhelm her. She ignored the medicine, deciding to take it only at night to help her sleep, and endure the anxious longing during the day instead of dulling her senses with sedative magic.

The street lanterns were already lit in anticipation of the rainclouds darkening the northeastern sky when Nesrin and Shirin reached the village. A dog barked as they passed by. Chickens clucked at the feet of the woman throwing them crumbs. A man unlatched a front gate, calling out as he approached the small home. Two young children raced out the front door to throw themselves upon him. Nesrin paused to watch the father set down the bag he carried and scoop them up, one under each arm. A woman stood in the doorway, smiling as her husband leaned in to share a greeting kiss.

Longing for what was lost seeped into Nesrin's chest. The month before the Reaping, Taniel had been looking to buy a home. Something small, easy to maintain, and a little outside Gohar. He couldn't bear the thought of raising children in the city, not after he spent his youth roaming forest and field, following the footsteps of his Purger father. Nesrin had held such confidence in that future—a home with children, hearth, and husband—that while she'd worried for Taniel whenever he left for work, she'd never truly thought she'd lose him or the future they'd promised one another.

After the Reaping, she'd spared no thought for the future. She'd lived day to day as a shadow of her former self, narrowing her existence to her daily pilgrimages to the train station until she received word of her husband. The repeating ritual had saved her sanity, yet kept her eyes stubbornly lowered to the well-worn path she walked. Now that she knew Taniel lived, and had a new path to follow, she was forced to raise her gaze to face the cruel possibilities tomorrow threatened, and in so doing realized she could no longer see that promised life.

"Shirin, what you want?" she asked.

"Pardon?" Shirin had also stopped to watch the small family, her lips pressed tight and eyes bright with grief.

"I mean, what you want to do in life? What be there left to do?" Seeing a way forward was impossible when Nesrin's heart so grievously yearned to go back to what should have been.

"I don't know what the future holds. But I do know the gods have never let me stray too far from the path I'm called to walk."

"Which be what?"

"Finding souls in need. My husband was one when I married him, your husband another, and once this is done, I'm sure another lost one will find their way to me."

The first drops of rain darkening the cobblestones encouraged them to hurry to the small inn at the village center. The window shutters were left open, showing the dining area comfortably filled by men sitting at the hearth. Nesrin had heard rumor the eastern lands nearest the Grey Forest were spared the Reaping, but after spending over a year walking Gohar's emptied streets it was strange to see so many people in one place, unburdened by loss and enjoying life's simple pleasures.

Envy coiled in Nesrin's heart, jealous of the men at the hearth, the wife greeting her husband, this village spared from suffering. She shook her head, choosing to see this as reason for hope, not bitterness. There was a better life to be found and these souls had been blessed to receive it.

"Thank you," Nesrin said to Shirin. Gratitude was the best way to escape envy's cruel hold. "For watching over my husband."

"It was the least I could do after what he did for me." By her tone Nesrin knew not to ask for that story. Shirin had visibly shuddered at the memory.

Shirin used the brass ring to knock on the inn's door. Nesrin adjusted the scarf covering her neck to ensure the karakin's scars were safely hidden. She had no desire to test the village's tolerance of demon-tainted travelers. A middle-aged woman with a round face and welcoming smile ushered them in, and Nesrin felt her every muscle tighten in resistance as she crossed the threshold; fighting the karakin's wicked pull for her to wander into the waiting woods. The white anemones decorating small vases on the inn's tables were a heartening reassurance. She walked the right path, even if she was unsure of where it led.

A herd of fallow deer grazed where the Grey Forest's trees met meadow. Taniel watched them from the back porch, an out-of-the-way retreat where he'd not be underfoot while Master Maqlu saw to visitors and other patients. The mage's home rested on the outskirts of Antarr at the doorstep of the Grey Forest, and attracted more supplicants than the village's temple. The unwalled back garden had no clear delineation for where tamed herbs transitioned to the wild fields leading into the forest ablaze with autumn leaves. Mist spun itself around the branches like cobwebs, flowed across the fields in drifting currents, and no matter how proudly the noonday sun shone the grey was never fully banished.

Yael sat beneath a garden dogwood across from Dua, her sleeping infant tightly swaddled to her chest. The bruising covering Yael was gone, his broken bones healed, and only the slicing scars across his arms and neck remained as visible testament to Wasi Adhar's abuse. Master Maqlu was more concerned for Yael's spirit than his physical recovery. He feared even before that final beating, Wasi Adhar had broken his nephew. Strangers, sudden noises, his own shadow—everything frightened Yael. Other than Taniel, he refused to let men near him, and was skittish when he had to be in the same room as Master Maqlu. Only Dua had managed to earn his fragile trust to let her heal his injuries and help him cultivate his long-repressed sorcery.

Yael's brows knitted together as he held his cupped hands in front of him. The silver light glowing in his palm rose like rain drops returning to the heavens. He cast a nervous look toward Dua, who murmured gentle encouragement, earning a shy smile from him. Taniel had more hope than Maqlu for Yael. He was a gentle soul, but gentleness did not mean his spirit lacked strength.

The deer raised their heads, ears and tails flicking as they watched a presence hidden from Taniel's eyes move through the trees. Leaves crunched under unseen feet, ferns rustled, and low branches swayed. Yael shrank behind Dua who rested a reassuring hand on his shoulder, warily watching the disturbed mist swarm where the forest cracked and trembled. The leaves fell still, the branches steadied, and the mists calmed. The deer returned to their grazing, but Dua shepherded Yael inside on the excuse of preparing the midday meal. She paused on the porch beside Taniel. "Will you join us?"

"Thank you, no," he said. He found being left alone on the borders of a forest steeped in ancient sorcery was far more agreeable than being seen by those who sought Master Maqlu's service.

He held his left arm to his chest, the skin tender from Maqlu knitting the splitting flesh back together earlier that morning. Despite Maqlu dedicating every free moment to understanding what Minu had done to him, he was only able to tend the symptoms. The root of the curse was buried beyond his reach. Taniel spent mornings sitting in chalk-drawn runes in the front garden while Maqlu sought to coax Minu's sorcery to give up its secrets. Afternoons were devoted to the library where the mage alternated between taking blood samples, consulting tomes, and resting his hand over Taniel's heart, concentration furrowing his ash-marked brow as he chanted in Kharinah's language.

Attempting more invasive cures for the curse had failed miserably, and Master Maqlu refused to put Taniel through repeated distress, despite Taniel insisting they try. Pain did not frighten him; it was too commonplace in his life to inspire more than dull resignation. Maqlu was unimpressed by his indifference. He claimed their time was better spent working to undo Minu's curse, not mending damage done by recklessly challenging her magic.

A stag lifted his head to look toward Maqlu's home. It snorted, breath pluming in the cool air, then turned to walk into the trees. The herd followed. The deer shared none of the village's healthy respect for the forest. They crossed the boundary as they pleased, while only the boldest or most desperate of men traveled into the trees. Since Master Maqlu had come to Antarr, there'd only been three souls who were beyond his skill to heal. The oldest man made peace with his fate and was buried in the temple's remembrance yard. The other two had ventured into the forest in hopes of meeting the Grey Lady. Neither had returned.

Taniel watched the deer disappear into the mist. He wondered if he ought to follow, act on Chak's advice to find the Grey Lady, and wander into the woods as those two men had done.

The clink of penitential rings announced Maqlu's approach. He sat with a heavy sigh, and Taniel knew what he'd come to say. For the past two days, he'd waited for Master Maqlu to find the words to speak what they both understood. A fourth soul was to be added to those who were beyond his power to save.

"I'm sorry, Taniel." Compassion pulled the corners of Maqlu's mouth into a weary frown. "What Minu did to you, it cannot be undone. Not by my hand, nor any power I wield. To learn enough about what you've suffered would take years. You don't have that long."

"How long do I have?" Taniel's voice was level, as if asking for an opinion on weather or tea. Kharinah had already told him this was his fate—to rot and die, or return to Minu. He'd chosen to flee and had now come to the end of that course.

"Months at the most. It's hard to say, but I'd ..."

"Whatever difficult truth you have to say is nothing worse than what I've already faced," Taniel said.

"I can't be sure how much time you have left, but I expect the degeneration to hasten. I'm surprised you've survived this long."

Taniel nodded, the gesture meant to absolve Master Maqlu of the guilt in his confession. He ascribed far less blame to Maqlu for his inability to save him from Minu's ruining than he did the mage's lapse in courage when he chose not to warn his father from heading to his death. Even there, Taniel lacked the strength to sustain anger. The time he had left was too short to waste on harboring hate for a flawed man who'd dedicated his life to service despite his failings.

"If you went back to her, she'd see you live," Master Maqlu said. "She won't allow death to take what she believes to be hers."

"Would you go back to your former master knowing what she is?" Taniel asked.

"No, but I'd not blame you if you did."

Taniel shook his head. He'd already decided to die as himself, not live to be reshaped in Minu's image.

"Does Antarr's temple take in the ill? Or is there a village nearby that does?" He had no intention of further burdening Maqlu, or distracting him from those in his power to heal. Already he'd wasted too much of the mage's time on a doomed cause.

"I can't spare your fate, but I can slow its onset, and I will do all in my power to ease what is to come. You may stay here. I'll see you are made as comfortable as possible."

"I wouldn't ask that of you."

"Sushan, it may be a matter of weeks until the degeneration reaches a point you cannot take care of yourself. Less if it begins to affect your mind as it has your body."

Taniel swallowed, unable to speak through the emptiness in his chest. He had accepted he was going to die. He had not prepared himself in choosing how to meet this end.

Master Maqlu ran his hand over Taniel's forearm, smoothing the fresh, leaking tears in his skin. "You are welcome here, Taniel Sushan. For as long as you wish to remain."

"Taniel?" Dua knocked softly on the door to his room. "There's dinner."

The mattress groaned under Taniel's awkward shape as he rolled to face the wall, away from the scent of cooking food. The smell of the spiced meat and cabbage stirred currents of nausea in his gut.

"Taniel?"

"I'm not hungry," he said. The guest room would have been cozy for a properly shaped man. He felt restricted by the small space. His worsening coordination made everything feel too cluttered and close to accommodate his clumsiness.

"I can have some brought to you," she offered.

"No, thank you." He hadn't realized how tightly he'd clung to his final strand of hope, not until Master Maqlu's admission severed that fraying thread. Despite reason warning him otherwise, Taniel had believed his suffering, all of Shirin's patient care, and his father's sacrifice was not in vain. He had dared to believe he might walk unburdened by pain, to have his left hand freed from curled contortion. He had permitted himself the hope of seeing Nesrin again, to make amends for his leaving, and be worthy of her.

Rain falling from the dusky sky tapped on the window. The room dimmed under the dwindling daylight, and Taniel failed to rally the muster to light the lamps.

"The gods permit suffering," his father had often said, "but no man is given a greater burden than he can bear."

That was a lie. Taniel had never been able to bear this burden. He had sought to escape its weight for nearly two years, only to learn his pathetic struggles were little more than death throes.

Tears streamed from his clouding eyes. It had all been false. Pointless and for nothing. He wasn't even going to live to see spring. After eighteen months, despair had won its long-waged war against hope, leaving him too lost to do more than hide from the world he was fading from. His ribs ached from his hard breaths and there was no chance of him keeping his weeping quiet.

A second knock sounded on the door. "Taniel?"

"No," he said, unable to voice a more courteous way of telling Master Maqlu he had no want for company.

The door groaned open, the mage ignoring the inelegant request for solitude. Taniel kept his face to the wall as he heard the scrape of Maqlu pulling a wooden chair to the bedside.

"There's no shame in the life you've led." Maqlu rested a gentle hand on his forehead. "And no shame in mourning it."

Memories rose up at his touch—summers warmed by sunlight, childhood days bright with joy, peaceful nights of lying next to Nesrin as they spoke softly to one another. The misery Minu had cursed him to carry lessened, drifting into the distance as the mage encouraged memories of better days forward. Taniel smelled the sea where his father took him in summer. He felt the sand under his feet, racing barefoot down the beach, laughing with a child's unrestrained delight as his father chased him. He heard the krar lyre, felt the beat of the kebero drums as he and Nesrin danced in the square, her joy palpable at hearing music of her home country.

"Rest," Master Maqlu said. The memories guided Taniel into untroubled sleep. "It is more than earned."

Morning's frail gold streamed through the window. Taniel lay in bed, slowly flexing his feet and hands, encouraging his bowstring-taut muscles to loosen and needle-pricked nerves to settle. Master Maqlu had checked on him a little after dawn, Dua had brought him breakfast, and Yael peered in an hour later. Taniel declined their offers to join them for a meal at the table, or in the garden. The day had been busy for Maqlu's residence, patients coming and going, seeking cures or guidance, leaving more whole than when they arrived. Taniel didn't want to see that. He wasn't ready to be reminded of how far he'd fallen. Even more so, he didn't want the visitors to see him, their expressions aghast in horror or awash in pity.

He heard the front door open and Dua welcome the latest arrivals. The women's muffled exchange of polite greetings quickened to eager excitement.

"Taniel," Dua said, "there's someone here to see you."

"Who?" Taniel asked. He prayed the newcomer was Shirin. There'd been no reply yet from the letters he'd sent to Abbott Mardiros asking for word on her and that she be told he was safe in Antarr. He hoped instead of sending a reply, Shirin had sent herself. Rising from the bed stirred the embers settled into his bones. He stumbled, his right leg unprepared to support the movement.

"She says she's your wife."

Taniel blinked. "What?"

Minu's curse had to be affecting his mind. He must've misheard. Nesrin couldn't be here. She was safe in Gohar. Sahak had promised. It wasn't possible—

"Taniel?"

He gaped in stunned disbelief. He'd thought he'd never hear that voice again. Not in this life.

The sound of Nesrin racing down the hall called him to her even as his mind warned him not to answer. She would hate him. The moment she saw him, she'd draw back in disgust. She'd hate him for what he'd become if she did not already for his leaving her.

The bedroom door flew open. Nesrin stopped in the doorway. The smile on her face vanished and her eyes went wide.

"Nesrin." Her name broke on his lips like a prayer he held no faith in being heard. He stood frozen in place, torn between running to her and running away. He'd thought she'd gasp, shriek at the sight of him, or recoil in disgust. But the look on her face could only be described as unimpressed fury.

"That it?" She waved her hand at him.

"That's what?"

"That all? You run from me because this?" Anger flushed her cheeks. "This what you hide from me? Seraphs save me, Taniel! I go looking for you all over, searching everywhere and hearing you be monster and this, this all you have to show me? By gods, I thought you have fangs and demon wings to make such fuss!"

"That wasn't—"

"This"—one hand no longer sufficed. She waved both at him to emphasize her disappointment he was not as monstrous as she anticipated—"this nothing! You come back from taverns to look worse than this!"

"Nesrin—"

"Ah, no! No, no!" Her accent suffocated her words. It always came thicker when she was angry at him. "You no make excuse to me no more. I say this nothing, so this nothing. You have no reason to hide from me. No reason to leave." Tears welled in her eyes. Her chest heaved as she struggled to speak through them. "You had no reason, no reason or right to ... to ..." She wiped her eyes. "You think so small of me? That I care you like this? You think I leave you, so you leave me first?"

"I didn't want you hurt," he said, but his reasons to spare Nesrin from the curse that had claimed him, to be sure she stayed free of Minu and her demon daughter, all of them seemed foolishly selfish when she stood in front of him.

"And you think you leaving not hurt me?"

"You were supposed to be safe in Gohar." He felt a coward, and every bit the monster he appeared to be, seeing how deeply his intentions to spare her suffering had wounded her.

The tears raced thick down her cheeks. "You stupid, stupid man."

He was terrified his touch risked sullying her. Her crying terrified him more. His clumsy hands felt unfit to hold her, and in this twisted form he was unsure of how to bring her closer; but she was graceful as ever, easily finding how to fit into him. A relief impossible to contain turned his breaths ragged, set his arms shaking and head spinning. Broken as he was, holding her felt no less natural than when he was whole.

"I didn't want to hurt you," he said once their shuddering breaths steadied. "I thought—"

"Ah, no, no talk. You be quiet." She buried her face in his chest. "I so mad at you."

"You need to—"

"Shh." She wrapped her arms tighter around him, a gesture he forced his crippled limbs to return.

"I didn't want my suffering to be yours," he said.

"So you make me suffer alone instead of with you?"

"I didn't—"

"Shh."

Unwilling to let her go or allow the smallest distance part them, he inched them toward the bed. She didn't recoil as he feared when he pressed his lips to the top of her head. She curled into him as they sat, indifferent to his uneven limbs and misaligned bones.

"Shh," she said when he started to speak. Her hand took hold of his, uncaring that his fingers were mangled and tipped by black claws. "It wait."

"I'm sorry." He was a fool for thinking the only way to save his wife was to leave the life they had, and he was unspeakably grateful that she'd refused to follow his surrender to wretchedness. She'd held faith, rescuing what he'd despaired in thinking could never survive a world so damaged. "I'm sorry. I'm so sorry."

"Shh." She pressed her finger to his lips. There was no difference in how she looked at him now than she did when she'd kissed him goodbye at Gohar's train station a lifetime ago. "It wait."

25

Into the Woods

Nesrin rested her head on Taniel's chest, listening to the disconcerting stutter of his heart. His breathing came strained even in sleep. Getting him to share a bed with her had been a struggle. He'd swung wildly between the desire to hold her close and push her away, worried about accidentally goring her with his horns or black nails. Even after she showed him how easily that was fixed—stove gloves for his hands and cloth wrapping around the horns—he'd moved gingerly around her, as if afraid his very touch endangered her.

She had failed to hide the karakin scars from him and he'd instantly recognized them for what they were. He was more distraught seeing her healed injuries than she had been receiving them. He only stopped apologizing when she told him she didn't have the patience to tolerate his blaming himself for the injuries.

"It nothing," she had insisted. "Stop fussing or I get mad at you all over again."

He'd smiled then, and hearing Shirin had come as well gave him the confidence to join them for dinner. He ate little, and Master Maqlu telling her it was more than he'd eaten in the last few days was no consolation. Nor was it a comfort when the mage claimed this was the happiest he'd seen her husband.

"Your coming is a greater salve than anything I have to offer," Master Maqlu had said as she helped clear the dinner table.

Nesrin sat up in bed, feeling a warm wetness. A dark stain spread over Taniel's shirt. Lifting the cloth revealed a deep split slowly opening over his ribs. Blood polluted by black leaked from the tear, carrying the sickly smell of rot.

Moving slowly as not to wake him, Nesrin slipped from beneath his arm and hurried down the hall to find Master Maqlu. He had warned her of how frail Taniel was, instructing her to fetch him if anything happened, no matter the hour. Firelight beckoned her down the hall to where Master Maqlu sat beside the hearth, smoking a pipe and bent over a tome thicker than her arm.

"He bleed," Nesrin said, showing her red-spotted hands and shirt.

Taniel held fast to sleep, unstirring when Master Maqlu ran his hand over his side, chanting in a language that set Nesrin's teeth humming.

"What wrong with him?" she asked.

Master Maqlu lifted his hand, checked to be sure Taniel's skin was knitted together, then motioned Nesrin to follow him to the hearth.

"He's dying," he said, relighting his pipe and taking a long pull.

"How we stop it?" she asked.

"I'm sorry, my dear, but we can't. He's too far along. I doubt I could've helped him even if I saw to him sooner. What Minu did to him is far beyond my capacity to heal."

"Then who we take him to? There other sorcerers near Grey Forest, yes? Someone will know."

"Your time is more wisely spent focusing on his comfort in his last days than ushering in his fate faster through travel." Master Maqlu leaned over the chair's arm to feed another log to the fire. "I can slow his degeneration, give him a couple more months and ensure it's less painful."

"There no way to save him?"

"Only the witch who cursed him has the power to spare him death."

"What about Deni Nigist?" Nesrin asked.

"Pardon?"

"Ah ... Forest Queen?" She bit her lip, searching for what the woman of the eastern woods was called in Taniel's language. "Grey Lady. We go to her?"

She knew the stories. The tales had crossed the sea to reach her home country. Deni Nigist was a sorceress, a wise woman, and in some tellings a Seraph who guarded the eastern lands. Her forest was a prison for the wicked ills of the world, and those who braved the woods fraught by fallen creatures to find her were granted a miracle.

Master Maqlu shook his head. "I'd not recommend Taniel travel so far as the market for a legume, let alone into the Grey Forest in search of a legend."

"But she heal him. And you, all magic-touched, you seek cure for the Reaping from her. That why you come here."

"We came here for the forest. There's no—"

"You think she not real?"

"Child, I don't want to get your hopes up over—"

"My question not trick. It only need yes or no. You think she real?"

Master Maqlu sucked on his pipe, dark eyes studying her. "Yes," he said after a pause. "I have reason to think she's real. I believe I saw her once when I first came here. I also believe the tales give her greater beneficence than is wise to believe."

"They say she heal people who come to her."

"For there to be stories there need to be survivors. You hear the rare tales of miracles. Not the countless more of those who disappear into the Grey Forest never to be found. Even the tales boasting happier endings neglect to mention how anyone who enters those woods and has the rare fortune to return does so changed. Not always for the better. Dozens if not hundreds more lives have been lost in vain hopes of finding the Grey Lady than have been saved by her."

Master Maqlu watched her over his pipe. Nesrin got the impression he waited for her to speak. She held her silence, having no words in his language to say.

"Your husband is dying," he said. "You finding him is already a miracle. I caution you not to seek more."

She looked out the window to the Grey Forest. The mist flooding the fields pressed close to the mage's home, and the silver shroud lit bright by a pearl moon reminded her of the anemone flowers, Razirah's white blessing guiding her east to Taniel.

"That for Taniel to choose," she said. "If he seek Grey Lady, that his choice. And if he not seek her, then I go and do for him."

Taniel slogged through the river, the edges of sight distorted by the dream. The ink-black water burned too hot on his skin. Too cold in his bones. The banks were lost behind a thick mist and a voice on the wind whispered from the grey.

Find Asherah. Find her.

The river rose from his waist to his chest. He sensed Kharinah stalking him along the shadowed banks, her fury palpable.

Find Asherah.

White petals bloomed on the black water. The pale anemones flowed together to shape a deer skull animated by silver mist.

Find Asherah. Find her.

Knotted trees below a blood-red sky cast a tangling darkness over him. The river's current carried him into the forest. The water swelled higher to his neck then over his mouth. Thick and clotting, it streamed down his throat—

He woke, vomiting a tarry-blackness. He rolled on his side to clear his airway as a second surge of sickness overcame him. Unable to see through his tears, he heard someone enter the room, summoned by his retching.

Nesrin's hands were gentle and cool, resting on his shoulders as he coughed out the last of the rot.

"Sorry," he said, ashamed she saw him like this.

"I see you be sick all down your front when you come home drunk on Festival of Light," Nesrin said. "Why you think this upset me?"

"I remember you being upset then," he said. Kharinah's hunting presence followed him from the dream. He shivered, checking the window to be sure no golden eyes burned in the night's mist.

"That because you sloppy lover when drunk."

She helped him up, sitting him in the chair as she stripped him out of his shirt and the soiled sheets off the bed. Taniel had wanted to spare her this, tending to a wretched creature who only had hardship and sickness to offer in return.

"Master Maqlu tell me he cannot heal you," she said. "He say your condition only get worse. That you not have much time."

"He's right." Taniel felt sicker at the thought he was doomed to leave Nesrin again. "There's no cure."

She gave a disbelieving huff. "They say to me you dead. Then they say you monster. Now they say you die. They wrong two times, they be wrong again."

"They were right both times. I was dead the moment I ran into that marsh."

Nesrin took his hand, placing his palm over her heart. He felt the gentle rise and fall of her breath. She rested her hand on his chest. "What be that, if not life? If you dead, then I must be too."

"You heard Master Maqlu. This can't be cured."

"I hear him better than you. He say he cannot undo curse. That not mean no one can."

"The Grey Lady is a myth," Taniel said, guessing what Nesrin was thinking.

"Minu the Demon Witch also myth. And they be more stories of Grey Lady than Demon Witch."

"Those stories are never what you hope them to be." Being a Purger meant learning to parse truth from legend, and the tales of the Grey Lady followed the predictable pattern of tales heavily influenced by fable. In all likelihood, there once was a wise woman in the Grey Forest who people came to for healing. After her death, the stories surrounding her had lived on, changing through the centuries until she was misremembered as a spirit or Seraph.

There was undoubtedly an ancient, curative power residing in the mist-veiled trees. Too many verified accounts of healings existed to deny that. Dua's midwife had taken a sickly infant, not expected to survive her first season, into the woods. That child was now a mother herself, but the midwife never spoke of what had happened in the woods. She hardly spoke at all after she braved the trees. Taniel's father told him the story of Purgers he'd known who'd carried a mortally wounded comrade into the forest. They left him there, unable to do more than pray the Grey Lady find him. A month later, the man had walked out of the trees, his injuries healed, and remembering nothing. Too many witnesses confirmed broken people had emerged whole for the tales to be dismissed entirely as legend, but Taniel had no salvation awaiting him in wishful thinking or a healing spring hidden in the leaves. There was no cure to be found in bedtime tales of the Grey Lady. Not for him.

"Master Maqlu say he saw Grey Lady," Nesrin said.

"I'm sure he saw something," Taniel said, "but this land is steeped in old sorcery. That can play tricks on anyone's senses."

"You don't believe in Grey Lady?"

"I don't," he admitted.

"Then what you mean to do? There no cure here, so what? You stay and wait to die?" Nesrin shook her head. "You don't believe in Grey Lady, fine, but I don't believe you give up. I know you, Taniel." She tapped a finger to his chest. "I know this heart, and this say otherwise."

She kissed him. Her touch was warm, breath sweet, and Taniel had no want to repeat his past mistake of leaving her in any way. Nesrin was right. He wasn't going to surrender his last days to deterioration, his senses suffocated by sedatives until he was a wasting shell with nothing left to give besides a final breath.

"I know you, Taniel." Nesrin rested her forehead on his. Her touch was a fierce, rallying cry for him to reject the fate Kharinah claimed was inevitably his. "I give you one hour before you tire of being sitting and sad. And if you wait too long, then I go to Grey Forest, and then you have to come because you no want me go alone."

"One day," he said.

"One day what?"

"Give me one day to pack. Then we'll go."

The one-day delay extended to two as everything Taniel did took twice the time it should. Nesrin was patient with how slowly he moved. The hour he spent in the morning warming stiff muscles to ease the worst of the pain was far more bearable in her company. She worked the ointments into his neck and left hand, alternating between reminding him she was still furious at him for not telling her he was alive, and kissing him. When not tending to him, she and Shirin were at the market, preparing meals for the road, and packing for a month-long journey. Taniel had no intention of venturing so far east that they were ever farther than a few days' distance from one of the many villages bordering the trees. He was wary of traveling too far into the forest. As the son of Sariel Sushan, he understood there were certain lands mortal men were not meant to trespass upon.

Taniel carefully wrapped the tinctures and ointments Master Maqlu had provided. The mage had warned him the medicine's efficacy would wane as his condition worsened, and blessed balms were no substitute for a mage's direct healing.

"You're determined to do this?" Master Maqlu stood in the guest room doorway. He had spent the last two days attempting to dissuade Taniel and Nesrin's leaving. Now, on the morning of their departure, his disapproving frown was replaced by resignation.

"I know you think it's a fool's errand," Taniel said, tying off the small bag dedicated to his medicine.

"No, I think you're beyond the point of foolishness," Master Maqlu said. "What I offer is comfort. You seek hope. I would not make the choice you have, but I never had your courage."

"What you call courage is what my father called idiocy."

"Your father was a good man. He deserved better. You both did."

Nesrin waited for him in the front hall, speaking to Shirin. His wife looked small and overburdened beneath the large pack tied over her shoulders.

"No, I carry," she said, when Taniel reached to take the pack from her. "You already carry too much."

"I'd listen to your wife, Taniel," Shirin said. "She's the sensible one in your marriage."

She and Nesrin had formed a fast friendship over the last few days, and Taniel was tempted to insist his wife remain here in Maqlu's home. Nesrin deserved to live a full life—she need not share his fate. He knew she'd be angered by the suggestion, which was both a deep solace and terrible sorrow.

"Local wisdom claims that only those seeking the Lady should approach the forest," Master Maqlu said, "but I'm sure she'll not mind if Shirin and I see you to the shrine at the border."

A cool morning greeted them, a thin mist curled over the golden carpet of dew-damp leaves, and the air was sweet with autumn. Low, mortarless stone walls divided tamed fields from the wild meadow threatening to overgrow the winding path they followed east to the towering trees.

Shirin's eyes were wet when they reached the forest boundary. A small stone shrine with a deer's skull placed atop stood at the path's end. Ivy twined up the stone, the vibrant green leaves indifferent to autumn's muting presence. The little-used path ending at a shrine before mist-shrouded trees reminded Taniel of the marsh at Beka Valley—how he'd run past the Fen Witch's shrine, ignorant to the fate he rushed to meet. His lips twitched in a humorless smile. Once again, here he was forsaking common sense to plunge into the unknown to seek what was best left alone.

"Thank you," Taniel said to Shirin, "for everything."

She embraced him. "Hold your gratitude until you return."

"And what will you do until then?" he asked. "You'll have to find a better way to spend your days than mothering a monster."

"As I told your wife, monsters in need of mothering have a way of finding me," she said, smoothing his cloak. "I'm sure it won't be too long before another one does. So hurry back before I replace you for good."

She wiped at her eyes as she turned to Nesrin, kissing her on the cheek and exchanging quiet words.

"Seraphs guide you," Master Maqlu said. "Whatever happens, you will find welcome in my home when it comes to pass."

That he directed the farewell to Taniel and the welcome of a return to Nesrin told how the mage believed their journey fated to end.

"You could stay here," Taniel said to his wife, obligated to speak the offer he knew she'd refuse. "I'll come back to you. I always meant to come back to you."

Nesrin took his hand in hers, her resolve unwavering as she led him past the deer skull shrine. "I go where you go."

Taniel had to turn his whole body to look back at Shirin and Master Maqlu. They were less than twenty strides away, yet he felt divided from them by an uncrossable distance. The second time he turned, they and the path were gone, the forest too soon swallowing sign of the world beyond its mist and trees.

Nesrin noticed the change as well. She signed for the Seraph's protection, murmuring a prayer in her native tongue.

"What did Shirin say to you?" Taniel asked.

"That she not want to lose another son, and I am to bring you home. And I promise I will."

Shirin gasped. One moment Taniel and Nesrin moved slowly through the trees, the next only mist remained. She instinctively stepped forward and Master Maqlu rested a restraining hand on her shoulder.

"The forest has claimed them," he said. "They're beyond our reach now."

"Does that mean the Grey Lady will help him?" she asked.

"I pray so."

An anguished screech pierced the morning. The trees shook, and faint tremors in the ground rattled the deer skull atop its plinth.

"What was that?" she asked.

"The Demon Witch's daughter hunts Taniel." Maqlu signed against evil. "Dua has been keeping her out of Antarr. It appears the forest does the same."

The keening shriek came again. The trees replied with an angry groan that snapped like bark and teeth. A thunderous crack shook both earth and sky. A third scream pitched high, and then there was silence.

"Are you sure the demon can't follow them into the forest?" Shirin asked when she found the courage to break the hush.

"No," Maqlu said, "but that Taniel has survived his condition so long and Nesrin found him has me certain they are protected by a greater power."

Shirin plucked one of the white flowers growing along the roadside and placed the bloom beneath the stag's skull. Taniel and Nesrin were beyond her reach, not her prayers. "Gods guide them, and Seraphs keep them safe."

26

Mist and Bones

You stagger, feeling as though your heart has been violently rent from your chest. For the first time in more than half a millennia, you can't feel your daughter. Her feral life that you felt as intimately as you did your own heart and breath is gone.

You tear a portal to where Kharinah last was. The Grey Forest looms, and you taste Asherah's foul sorcery in the air—musty and mud-sodden, like the damp of rotting wood. You see where your daughter forced her way in. The tree trunks are scarred and splintered as if a brutal storm struck only that precise patch of forest.

"Kharinah!" You tug on your will that binds her to you. There is no answer. Her trespass into Asherah's dominion has severed your connection. "Kharinah!"

Already your sister erases the evidence your daughter was here. Small green shoots rise from the blistered earth. The bent trees straighten, their shattered bark smooths, and all trace of your daughter's intrusion is gone.

"Kharinah!" She knew better than to trespass into the forest. You expressly forbade it. You made sure that even in her deepest madness she understood.

The mist snaking across the forest floor rears to swallow the trees—another divide Asherah summons to separate you from your stolen daughter.

"No! No! No!" Your scream cracks stone, splits the earth to reveal the forest's wretched roots. "NO!"

Your wrath turns the air to fire, leaves combust, lightning roars over the ground heaving with your rage. The forest is unmoved. Your daughter is gone to the one place you have no power to protect her.

"This is your doing."

One of Asherah's wretched messengers stands at the forest's edge. Ever the coward, your sister refuses to face you, sending one of her shahavaz sewn from wind, bone, and a dead soul in her stead. Pale light shines from the eyeless sockets of the deer skull. Its insubstantial body is barely discernible from the thickening mist.

"You forced your daughter here." Her voice speaks through the creature. *"You gave her no choice but to follow where the man you broke led."*

"Give her back!" Your second squall of crimson sorcery has no more effect than the first. Fallen leaves become wind-blown embers. Earth breaks on the trees like storm-tossed waves. The forest remains untouched.

"This is your doing. All of this. You cast a reaping upon the world. And now, you face yours." The messenger vanishes, sudden as the twist of candle flame, and the deer skull falls empty onto the dead leaves.

Wind stirred the highest leaves, releasing a golden rain fluttering through the grove of bone-white trees. There was no breeze felt beneath the sheltered, lower branches. No breath stirred the eddying mist or cooled Taniel's burning skin slicked in sweat. The forest floor was still as a grave and just as silent save for Nesrin's soft footsteps and Taniel's shuffling ones. They walked close, hands and arms brushing, unwilling to move farther from the other. The back of Taniel's neck prickled under the certainty that hidden eyes tracked them. A watchful presence dwelled in this part of the woods, forbidding the singing of birds and muting the rustle of falling leaves.

"Taniel." Nesrin pointed to irregular shapes rising from the mossy ground. "There's more."

They had discovered the first skeleton less than an hour after crossing into the Grey Forest. Unlike the deer skulls placed on the shrines at the forest's borders, the remains they'd found half-buried in earth and leaves were human, the bones darkened and weather-worn to where they looked more like roots.

Nesrin had grabbed his arm when they'd found the first skeleton, as if to prevent him from sinking down to join the bones as a horned skull, bent ribs, and twisted limbs decaying into the moss and leaves. Now, she led the way to investigate their latest finding of three more skeletons in the pale grove. No cracks in the bones gave evidence they'd suffered violent ends, and all were laid to rest in a fashion suggesting they'd been tended to in death. The skulls gazed skyward and their hands lay folded over their chests in the position of a body prepared for funeral rites.

Taniel searched the papery bark of the surrounding trees for an engraving or marker to indicate why the bodies had been laid here. More importantly, he searched for a sign showing where he must go to escape sharing their fate.

The mist shrouding the grove shifted and his hip cracked from turning too quickly, convinced he'd seen a figure prowling in the grey—inhuman in movement and unnatural in form. The prickling on the back of his neck crawled down his spine, a warning he'd learned to heed as a Purger.

"What wrong?" Nesrin hurried to him.

He held a finger to his lips, listening to a strange hum lurking behind the forest's quiet. It carried a melodic rhythm and the cold memory of Kharinah singing as she stalked closer. The mists thinned where Taniel thought he saw the figure, revealing nothing more sinister than pale birch. The distant hum fell into silence.

"I'm not sure," he said, "but we shouldn't linger here."

He took a step then staggered from a burst of pain splintering through his leg. He gripped the nearest tree, black nails sinking into the bark, forcing himself to stay standing as he sucked in hard breaths. The hours of walking strained Minu's poorly stitched seams.

"Maybe we rest for little time?" Nesrin asked.

Taniel shook his head. "Not here."

He knew the moment they stopped to rest was the end of his travel for the day. He wasn't ready to surrender to the tired ache in his bones or the fire festering in his joints. Determining how long they'd been walking was difficult. The ever-shifting mist hid distance from him, and the sky—rarely visible through the forest canopy—held unchangingly to the dusky hue of late twilights and early dawns.

"Taniel ..."

"We'll set up camp soon," he said. "I want to find a better place than a boneyard to settle for the night."

He hoped to hear the hush of a stream offering running water's protection, or find a clearing where it was easier to see approaching threats. At the very least he wished to be far from this stretch of bone-strewn forest and the singing presence haunting the trees.

"Those bones," Nesrin said. "Where you think they come from?"

"The people who came to the Grey Forest and didn't return had to end up somewhere," Taniel said.

"Oh. They not find Grey Lady?"

"I guess not."

"You think they find something else? Or something else find them?" She glanced around the trees, her hand hovering near the Purger knife on her belt.

"I don't know," Taniel said. The Grey Lady was not the only strange creature rumored to live in the east. More than once while seeking solitude in Master Maqlu's back garden he'd seen shapes in the trees, their movements too graceful, too indifferent to physical surroundings to belong to a natural beast.

His walking stick struck a hard surface hidden under the soft soil. Knees promising to punish him later, he crouched down, brushing the moss and fallen foliage off the stone. Nesrin joined him, her hands much more efficient at clearing the debris to reveal the carvings.

"That look like Purger ward," she said.

"It does." Taniel traced his fused fingers along the swirling pattern. The edges of the engraving were lost where grass and roots had claimed a stronger hold on the stone, but there was no denying the design bore similarity to the wards he'd been taught. Though he'd never drawn a pattern like this in his work before. The protective wards he used turned away wicked spirits. This stone-cut sigil looked like one meant to summon, similar to the designs decorating Gohar's oldest temples or wayfarer's chapels on the less-traveled roads. He tapped a finger on the rune's center, not recognizing the symbol naming the being it was meant to call forth.

Using his walking stick, Taniel listened for the revealing rap of wood on buried stone to find the perimeters. The slab was far larger than he guessed; at least twice the size of his flat in Gohar. Patches of the pale stone peeked through the carpet of green moss, and stone columns interspersed the trees, disguised by climbing roots and vines.

He ran a hand over the nearest pillar marked by faded engravings. A different kind of skeleton rested here. "I think this was a temple."

"Temple to what?" Nesrin asked.

"A long dead god for a long dead people."

"The people of the Wastes?"

"I don't know." Assured belief belonged to his previous life. This new creature Minu had twisted him into retained little confidence. He was no longer convinced the tales of the eastern kingdom were myth. More and more, he came to think an entire history had been lost in this forest of mist and bones.

Angry crackling disturbed the leaves. Movement too precise to belong to wind cut through the trees, rattling branches. A low lament hummed in the grey. Taniel stepped in front of Nesrin, shielding her from he knew not what.

"What is that?" Nesrin asked. The trees fell suddenly still, but the humming lingered, buzzing in Taniel's ears like concussive ringing.

"Don't you hear it?"

"Hear what?"

"That voice, it's ..." Taniel stopped. The lament had ended, returning them to uncanny silence. He rubbed his temples, unsure if he'd truly heard the humming. Master Maqlu had repeatedly warned that feverish nights and seizures were only the beginning of the curse that had destroyed his body moving to do the same to his mind.

"There's only so much ill-magic one can endure before falling to madness," Master Maqlu had said. "That you've lasted so long is another miracle."

Taniel shook his head. "It's nothing. I must've imagined it."

"This forest have old magic," Nesrin said. "You say it plays trick on senses."

"You didn't hear anything then?"

She tilted her head to the side. "I think I hear water."

Sure enough, Taniel heard running water's faint murmur, leading them down the slope to a wide brook cutting between willow and mossy rocks.

"Go ahead and cross," Taniel said, eager for Nesrin to have running water's purifying power between her and the skeletal grove.

"I help you over," she said.

"No, if I fall it'll take us both down. I'd rather only have to set my clothes out to dry, not yours as well."

Nesrin hesitated before going ahead, picking a graceful path over the stones to the opposite bank. Taniel followed along the stream's bank, searching for a shallower section to wade across. He accepted there was no possibility of him reaching the other side dry. He sought only to minimize how soon he'd have to stop and strip out of his wet clothes to avoid catching chill.

The lament sang out from the trees. He turned, and dread froze his breath. The forest shuddered under a river of mist that darkened from grey to the color of pitch. Branches groaned, contorting in on themselves like men writhing in agony. The blackening mist flowed forth, decaying all it touched. Trees withered under the rot, leaves shriveled as root, bark, and branch succumbed. The rattle of bones joined the singing, and a pale light shone from within the advancing blackness, growing brighter as it followed the decay-laid path.

"Nesrin, run! Don't—" Taniel turned to see his wife and the opposite bank were gone, lost behind an impregnable silver veil.

A small ash tree three strides behind him withered. Its leaves turned to dust as it collapsed to the sickened earth. Taniel plunged into the stream, scrabbling over the slick stones to escape the rot. The decay stopped where the earth met the water's edge, spreading along the banks, wasting ferns and reeds to dust, sending the leaves above him to fall like wind-blown ash. The singing had become a storm inside his soul. He clutched his head in trembling hands. Blood leaked from fresh splits in his skin. His lungs felt on the verge of collapse, his bones groaned at the point of breaking, his frailness unable to tolerate the approaching presence.

The lament ceased, a cool breath stirred his hair, and Taniel looked up. A being he had no name for towered over him. Ashen light rippled from it like moonlight on wind-stirred water. The diaphanous body was vaguely cervine and stood high among the dead, skeletal branches. Its thin legs ended in wisps before touching the ground, and its too-long neck was extended over the stream to peer directly down at him from a face of hollow features better suited to a skull than living creature. The eyes were dark pits, yet there was no denying it gazed at him, and that he was being judged. Taniel held absolutely still, making no attempt to flee, fight, or cower. There were certain beings that there was no challenging. All there was to do was choose how to face them.

The blood trickling from Taniel's horns drifted up so the droplets hovered between him and the spirit. The mist darkened to inky oblivion, the trees wisped into nothingness, and then the world reformed to reveal a scene stolen from memory. The northern swamp of the Beka Valley stretched before him. Guilt slid a thousand blades between his ribs, awakening every old agony of his failure to stop Minu.

Mist swept in, spinning itself to shape Shirin sitting on a fallen log, her face gaunt with grief. She cradled a child's grey corpse. Four more lay at her feet. She stared at Taniel over her dead children, and he felt a thousand more accusing eyes scorch into him, belonging to the countless souls who'd fallen to the Reaping. The black sallow trees of the swamp twisted into the pale stone of Gohar. The city rapidly receded into the west as he turned from the life he thought lost to him and the wife he no longer deserved. Nesrin stood before him on the road.

"You left me," she said. Corrupted veins from a karakin's wound spread from the gaping hole in her chest.

The spirit watched him through it all, the only thing unchanged as scenes born of Taniel's regret and failure formed before him.

Sky and road bled together to show a memory from eight years prior—the train station platform where he'd fought with his father. The words they'd shouted at each other, cruelties neither of them could take back no matter how they wished to later, echoed from the past. Taniel had run off following that fight. His father had gone after him, overlooking a desperate letter begging he investigate strange happenings in a southern farming town.

"*You hold tight to the misery she sowed within you.*" The creature's voice sent a high-pitched ringing through his skull. "*How can you find a way forward when you cling to the guilt of your past?*"

The arched windows of the train station became empty homes, the platform a dirt road strewn by savaged corpses—the scene Taniel and his father arrived to once they reconciled and too late answered the letter. They never spoke of that day despite it haunting the both of them. The village darkened to Tahir's cellar where Taniel had discovered Razban's grisly fate. Another friend he'd failed.

"*You must choose, Taniel.*"

The mist engulfed him in an endless grey. The cold weight of his soddened clothes returned, warm arms wrapped around his chest, and a familiar voice called his name.

"Taniel?"

"She comes for you."

"Taniel?" Nesrin's face came into focus, water dripping from her hair onto him.

He lay sprawled on the stream bank, clothes soaked, skin chilled, and flesh burning where his tainted blood leaked free. His hand shook when he touched her cheek, seeking reassurance she was really there, and not another manifestation of his mistakes.

"Taniel, you hear me?"

"Where is it?" He pushed himself up, arms weak as unleavened dough. The spirit was gone from the opposite bank where the pale grove grew.

"Where what?"

"The creature. Did you see it?"

"I see you fall and not get up," Nesrin said. Her drenched clothes clung to her skin and mud covered her from the effort of pulling him from the stream.

"I'm sorry," he said. His wife may not have seen the silver creature, but surely she'd seen all his failure, seen him for what Minu had revealed him to be.

"What for?"

"I shouldn't have left. Not without seeing you. I'm sorry, I—"

"Taniel, it okay."

"I didn't want to hurt you, I didn't ... I didn't know what to do. It's my fault that she ... it's all my fault. I couldn't stop her and she ..." He hid his face behind his hands, unable to bear her seeing him wearing the skin of his monstrous failure. The Reaping, his father's death,

Suri's, Shirin's children and millions more—all of it was his doing. "Why don't you hate me?"

Nesrin lowered his hands from his face, touching her brow to his. "I only hate you think I see you same way you do."

"I'm sorry," he said again, unable to better confess the severity of his mistakes.

"Taniel, I mad at you, and I be mad for long time. So you need stop apologize so I not feel so bad for being mad at you. Yes?" She waited until he gave a slow nod. "Good. Now, you say you see something? What see? It what make the skeletons?"

"I don't think so," he said. That he and Nesrin were still alive and not fresh corpses laid in the pale grove told him they'd been fortunate in the strange beings they'd encountered thus far.

He sat up straighter, checking to be sure the creature was truly gone. Small green shoots unfurled from the blistered earth of the opposite bank. The pale bark of the withered trees regrew. New leaves bloomed from healed branches. The scent of spring sweetened the air, cleansing the lingering foulness of the mephitic decay.

"Can you see that?" He pointed to the forest's rebirth. He wasn't sure what was real, if Minu's curse tricked his senses, or if the forest revealed itself differently to each soul who walked beneath its leaves.

Nesrin turned to look. Her signing for the Seraph's protection confirmed the changes existed outside Taniel's mind. While the rot had ceased its spread at the stream's edge, the flush of life observed no such boundary. The rebirth crossed the waters, the grass they lay on flowered, leaves not yet fallen flushed to life and new ones unsheathed themselves on branches creaking from the green's rapid spread.

"That be good sign?" Nesrin asked.

"I don't know."

"You think it mean we close to Grey Lady?"

"I don't know."

She helped him to his feet, supporting him for the first ungainly steps as his legs rediscovered their strength. "You need rest," she said.

"Not here." They were too close to the pale grove for him to feel safe from that creature and the visions it brought.

"Then there." She pointed through the trees. "We go there."

Standing stones ringed a small glade. The sea of mist parted in deference to the perfectly circular clearing and not a single leaf lay fallen among the monoliths.

"You think it safe there?" she asked.

"I doubt anywhere in the forest is safe," Taniel said. "But that's most likely the safest place we'll find for now."

Drawing closer, he saw the stone pillars bore symbols similar to the ones found at the buried temple. He walked around the stone ring's perimeter, looking for a carving that warned of a malign force bound within, or a hidden evil to be wary of. He found none, yet he felt an ancient power heavy in the air like humidity heralding a summer storm. It reminded him of the sorcery that thrummed in the halls of Gohar's Arcanum; old, not necessarily harmful, but deserving of respect.

Nesrin gave a tight gasp when Taniel stepped across the stone ring, followed by a sigh when nothing happened and a scolding to be more careful.

"Wait." He held up his hand for her not to follow him in. "Let me check this side."

He repeated the same circling process to examine the ring's interior, not wanting to expose his wife to a hidden malignancy.

"There was stone circle like this not far of my village when I child." She walked alongside him on the outer ring. "The priest say it holy ground. Yaszi Milik he call it, 'God's Mark,' where divine reached down to touch earth, leaving small piece of creation safe from evil."

Taniel kept quiet the argument that his carrying Minu's curse across the stone boundary disproved its ability to keep out evil.

"It safe?" she asked after he completed a third revolution of the ring.

"I don't know." He wished he had more than uncertainty to offer her. He extended his hand to guide her over the boundary. It was more a superstition than proven power, but Taniel hoped his inviting Nesrin into the ring kept him solely responsible for their trespass, sparing her any punishment that might follow.

"You think this be sign Grey Lady near?"

"I think it's evidence there were people here before us," Taniel said. He reached for the pack on her shoulders. She waved him off.

"No, no. I set camp. You sit. You can argue if want, but only if you sit."

Taniel obeyed, and the moment he sat, exhaustion overtook him. He leaned against the nearest pillar to stay upright. The tremble infecting his hands complicated his uncapping the jar of balm Master Maqlu provided to seal his splitting skin. A low moan moved through the forest, too drawn out and rhythmic to belong to the trees or wind. The grass beyond the stone ring shivered. Not a blade stirred within the circle.

"I ... I think I no make fire tonight." Nesrin's voice was level but her posture was taut with nervous tension.

"That's for the best," Taniel agreed. He grunted, hands shaking too hard to get a good grip on the medicinal jar.

"Here." She effortlessly unfastened the lid he struggled to budge. Out of shamed habit, he turned his face from her, tucking his left arm to his chest.

"No." She guided his face to hers. "You no hide from me. Not even in small ways."

Taking his left hand she worked the balm into his fused fingers, then wrist, easing the chronic stiffness.

"Where else hurt?" she asked. He touched his neck, overburdened from holding a crown of heavy horns. She massaged the salve in to grant small relief. "Where else?"

He touched the strained skin over his skull, pulled between a crooked horn and a lopsided ear. Light as her fingers were he flinched under her coaxing the worst of the headache to calm.

"Thank you," he said.

She kissed him. "Where else?"

The air blisters, the ground smokes, but the forest does not yield. You rend the earth into fiery waves that crash upon Asherah's indifferent shore. Not a single leaf is touched by the flame and firebolt you send. The portals you summon to take you to your daughter collapse under silver mist before they can fully form. Her shahavaz prowl the forest's edge, sent by their mistress as a taunt to witness your impotence.

Through the firestorm and rage, you feel a mortal's fragile heartbeat drawing near. You recognize the thrum of his sorcery. After all, it is you who taught him. You quiet the thundering earth and calm the flames snapping with lightning so he may approach unharmed. He shows no hesitation to cross the smoking earth.

"Minu," Maqlu says. Penitential bands on his wrists clink, black ash marks his forehead, and time has left him weary. You pity him. The young man you remember coming to you those short years ago is wasted to a shadow of the greatness he should have been. "Why are you here?"

"To reclaim what is mine."

Maqlu sees the unholy spirits lurking in the forest. His face goes whiter than the skulls they wear.

"Have you never seen the Grey Lady's shahavaz before?" you ask. "Did you never wonder why deer skulls are placed at her shrines?"

"I thought it a superstition," he says.

"She isn't what you think. Or deserving of worship."

"You proved to be something other than what I thought as well."

"Tell me, young one, what gave you the courage to return to me? Has your sheep's frightened bleating driven you from hiding?"

You touch your fingers to his cheek. He stands firm, but you feel his fear; his racing blood, pounding heart, feather-light breath. You feel a familiarity on him as well. Taniel's life is twined into his. The pity you felt for your wayward apprentice sours to displeasure. Maqlu has been tampering with what is yours.

"You should have told me Taniel came to you," you say.

"He's done nothing to deserve that punishment."

You don't rise to his baiting. You knew the moment he fled your guidance he lacked the imagination to understand your vision. "Where is he?"

He nods to the trees where Asherah's shahavaz watch. "He's in her realm now. Beyond your reach."

Maqlu betraying Taniel to your sister is a cold disappointment, but unsurprising. Mortal men are so eager to be led astray.

"That is to be seen." You brush your thumb over his eyes, soft and swift. "But not by you."

He hid your son from you, now you hide the world from him.

His dark eyes go grey then milky white. He cries out in the language you taught him, summoning a shield of bronze sorcery. His power is too little, the defense too late. A wave of your hand banishes his protective spell. He presses his palms to his eyes, groaning desperate enchantments to restore his sight to no avail. Foolish as your errant apprentice is, he still has value. The bonds you hold with Kharinah and Taniel are severed by the Grey Forest; but while Asherah hides them from you, Maqlu's tampering presents an opportunity. His sorcery's lingering influence on Taniel is a thread for you to reclaim your son.

You rest your hand on Maqlu's shoulder. "Be still."

You catch him as he goes limp. Small gasps escape his numbed throat as he struggles to break free of your hold.

You place a finger to his lips. "And be silent."

His protesting moans cease. You hold his hands in yours, tracing Taniel through your apprentice's meddling. A bronze thread, faint yet steady, weaves through the silver mist. Asherah's shahavaz hiss their agitation, powerless to prevent you from using Maqlu as the key to invade their mistress's realm.

Closing your eyes, you follow that thin bronze thread unspooling into the cursed trees.

27

The Grey Lady

Nesrin sat at the entrance to their small tent pitched in the center of the God's Mark, carefully repacking the balms Taniel applied in the morning to ease his pain. Birds sang with easy cheer, shafts of sunlight upon the mist alchemized the silver to golden hues, and the thrum of ancient power rooted in the trees felt more like a gentle hush than the foreboding threat of the previous day.

"It peaceful," she said, unsure of what to make of the forest's serenity.

"The Grey Forest's monsters must be late risers," Taniel said. He walked the inner perimeter of the God's Mark, warming the stiffness from his muscles.

He moved far better than he had yesterday, or any day since they'd reunited in Antarr, and his skin had not split during the night. Nesrin had expected fresh wounds opening on her husband to be the least of their nightly concerns. She'd steeled herself for the dark hours to be fraught with the ghosts of the skeletons they'd found, haunted by the eerie voices that whispered through the leaves, or for the spirit of the pale grove that only Taniel could see to return in want to claim him. She had been prepared to keep a wary vigil through the night like she had when the karakin hunted her. Instead, she'd slept soundly, waking only once to see her husband sleeping as easily as she. She woke again a few hours later to hints of dawn filtering through the tent's pale fabric and Taniel gently stroking her arm from wrist to shoulder. Seeing her awake he'd kissed her, brushing a loose curl from her cheek.

"You think you make nice to me in morning mean I let you stay in bed and be lazy all day?" She'd shifted to rest her head on his chest. "No, I still mad at you. You need get me flowers and bring breakfast in bed for weeks before I let you have lazy day."

His smile had been the first of the day's hopeful signs that whatever healing power the Grey Forest held had taken favor upon Taniel. Nesrin wanted to ask if he noticed the change as well, but was superstitiously afraid that bringing attention to the observed improvements risked revealing them to be wishful thinking. So she offered silent thanks to the gods, and prayed they continue to work through the forest's strange power to bless her husband.

Taniel sat beside her at the tent's entrance. His movements were guarded but he did not wince as he usually did. "I can carry the pack today."

"Maybe we rest here for day," she said. There was no knowing what had granted the small return in his health. It might be his experience with that spirit in the grove, the ancient sorcery of the forest coupling with Maqlu's medicines, or his sheltering in the boundaries of the God's Mark. Nesrin believed the last was the most likely cause, and was reluctant to leave the stone circle. "Or you rest here, I look around. See if there more places like this nearby."

"I don't want you going off alone."

"I go alone for miles to find you. I be fine."

"Tired of my company already?" he teased.

"Oh no, I not let you from my sight ever again. And when I do, I tie you down to be sure you no wander off no more."

His laughter confirmed it was not simply her wishful thinking. He was feeling better.

"I told you, I wanted to spare you—" A violent shudder toppled him to his side. He convulsed as red steamed from his skin.

"Taniel! What wrong?"

Dark spittle hissed through his gritted teeth. "It's her. She's coming."

Nesrin looked wildly about for the demon she imagined Minu to be—a waxen fiend leering to show sharp teeth framed by blood-red lips. Sorcery pulsed hot to her left and a fiery wind spun into a portal, the interior too clouded to clearly see the other side. Silver mist besieged the burning door like crows swarming a hawk. The red wind snapped and crackled, struggling to maintain its shape under the mist's assault.

Taniel screamed. Unseen claws tore into him. His flesh strained as though hooks sunk into him were pulled taut. Blood spurted from the gashes when the magic tugged him sharply toward the portal.

"No!" Nesrin grabbed his arm. Her added weight did little to hinder the force reeling them toward the faltering portal, and Taniel fighting the magic only deepened the wounds it sank into him. She heard his bones creak then snap in punishment for his resistance. His shriek was a blade through her heart.

The sorcery yanked him from her hands. He clawed at the ground, slowing himself just enough to grab hold of a stone pillar.

"Don't come through," he begged. His claws left thin scratches in the stone as inch by inch the witch pulled him closer to the portal. "Don't follow."

A terrible intuition warned Nesrin that once Taniel was taken from the God's Mark, he lost his greatest defense against the dark witch's magic. The silver mist assaulting the portal wouldn't destroy it before Minu stole him through. Nesrin rushed to the tent. Throwing the bedroll and pack to the side, she grabbed the pistol and aimed it at the portal. Through the warring chaos of silver mist and blood-red magic she saw a woman's figure shimmering like a distorted reflection on agitated water.

Nesrin fired three desperate shots. The woman's shape staggered, mist swallowed the portal, and the fiery sorcery collapsed in a thunderous boom that threw Nesrin off her feet. Taniel slumped to the ground, sides heaving, clothes drenched in ink-black blood.

"Oh gods, no. Please, no." Nesrin crawled to his side. Ripping open his shirt revealed lesions cutting to the bone. She pressed the ruined cloth over the deepest. "Don't take him, please don't take him."

"Pack," he said through bloodied lips. "The pack."

She tripped in her haste to grab their travel bag, hurriedly spreading the contents before him. He reached for the jar containing the salve Maqlu provided to heal the splits in his skin. Nesrin uncapped it and set to work liberally applying the ointment over the worst of his injuries.

"Will that be enough?" she asked. She already knew the answer. Torn tissue knitted together but the wounds remained open.

"No." He tried to sit up.

"Don't move. Tell me what need doing."

"Go to the stream. Get as much of the water as you can."

"What for?"

His breaths were wet and weak. "To cleanse her taint. Otherwise the wounds will keep reopening."

Nesrin bit her lip. Taniel needed more than running water and a mage's medicine. "I don't want to leave you," she said.

"It's not far. I'll be here. I promise."

She hesitated at the circle's edge, terrified of leaving only to return and find him dead.

"Nesrin ..." His mismatched eyes found hers, dulling to a distance there was no return from. "This was always the most likely way it would end."

Anger burned through the cold dread holding her in place. A hate she'd never known surged within her, turning her blood to fire, her bones to steel. The witch had stolen her husband, held him from her for over a year, and now she dared to try and steal him again.

"Stay here," she said. She refused to lose Taniel to that witch. "I be back."

You turn the bullet between your fingers, admiring the craftsmanship of the Purger sigil delicately inscribed into the metal. Sorcery sparks around the wound healing below your eye. Bone, muscle, and skin reform. Suffering the pains of flesh is a price you're willing to pay to more closely mirror the mortal form. You spent centuries learning how to shape yourself into a true likeness, not the shadow of flesh and blood your sisters elect. The miseries of the body are small inconveniences compared to its pleasures—and you will know great pleasure when you find the wretch who stopped you from reclaiming your son. Asherah veiled the woman in mist to hide her from you, but you're confident you'll know her when she is found.

Maqlu lies at your feet. The binding you threaded through his veins holds him a quiet captive.

You kneel beside him, running your thumb over his forehead to smear away the penitential ash. "Do you know what Asherah's shahavaz are? They're the souls of the dead who trespassed into her trees. She harvests them. Turns them into abominations."

He cannot see you wave your hand at the silver creatures damned to their frail, insubstantial slavery.

"How many have you sent to her?" you ask. "What lies did you speak to guide Sariel's son into her hands?"

He turns his face from you, ever refusing your teachings.

You leave him lying at the forest's edge. Your binding on him will fade in time. Until then, you'll let the forest decide his fate. The shahavaz watch him. Light glows from the skulls' hollowed eyes. They pace the forest's edge, whispering in voices that are remnants of who they were, starving for the life stolen from them.

There's no visible mark where Kharinah tore into the forest. The trees are healed and unbent, their bark smoothed, their roots unburnt. But you feel traces of her lingering like a scar, and the destructive chaos she leaves in her wake is your means to reopen that into a wound.

You plunge your right hand into the earth. It yields as easily as dry sand to your touch. You'll not abandon your children to Asherah. They'll not be made into pitiful shadows of what they should be.

Your sorcery unfurls westward, singing a summons to the graveyard that was Sevget, and the dead you buried stir. You'd prefer to let them rest longer before waking. They are incomplete in their reshaping, alternating between crawling on four legs and loping on two. Unsure, unsteady creations.

Asherah's shahavaz hiss when you sink your left hand into the earth. This time you do not summon. You release. All the injury and suffering Asherah has forced you to bear, all the hate she bred for you to endure rushes forth. The ground puckers and shrivels like diseased flesh, outlining the buried roots. You bleed your hate into the ground, suffocating those roots until the poison Asherah planted in you is all there is for her forest to absorb. A small, red-black thread snakes up the nearest tree, following the hidden scars left by your daughter's breach, to find the lowest leaf. It shrivels, falls, and is dust before it touches ground.

You smile. You feel the shambling step of Sevget's reborn marching east, sense the fissures you've created in Asherah's defenses widen, and you will know pleasure, great pleasure, in reducing her kingdom to dust.

Taniel pulled himself up to lean against the pillar. The stone cooled his burning skin and the upright position allowed him to draw easier breaths. Stirring the cold embers of his dying faith, he used the blood dripping from his fingers to scrawl a summoning symbol on the stone—the one he'd seen on temple walls, in prayer books, and most recently in the forest ruins. His shaking hand drew an unrecognizable smear of dripping lines. Intent would have to suffice.

"Seraph …" He coughed, then amended the prayer. "Asherah, guide her through life's journeys. Lead her … lead …" His blood-filled lungs drowned his final plea that Nesrin find her way from the forest and not suffer for his failures.

Silver shone through the world's darkening. A humming soothed the arrhythmic gasp of his erratic breath and weakening heart. The spirit of the pale grove circled above the stone ring, its abyssal pits for eyes fixed on Taniel. He understood with the preternatural clarity of a dying man that the creature bore no malevolence. He'd been mistaken in thinking the grove's graveyard was the spirit's hunting grounds and that it intended harm. Yesterday, the lament it sung had been a senseless hum. Now, Taniel was close enough to death to comprehend its meaning; it sang a promise to see lost spirits find rest.

The trees faded to blurs. The taint running from his nose and mouth no longer felt warm. He hardly felt anything at all. A feminine shape flickered in the silver drifting like misting rain from the spirit.

"Nesrin ..." He lost sight of the forest, a woman spoke his name, and then the pale light went out.

Nesrin's trousers were filthy and her sleeves were soaked from her careless haste while filling the water skins in the stream. Her feet flung mud up her back as she raced to the God's Mark. Furious terror pounded in her chest. She wasn't going to lose him. Not to that dark witch, nor to death.

A shimmering radiance slipped through the trees, stretching their shadows long and soft. The light strengthened as she crested the stream's embankment, growing from an eerie brightness to a hum she felt in her teeth. Coming to the top of the rise, she clapped a hand over her mouth to muffle her cry. A monstrous shape hovered above the God's Mark; its body made of luminous mist, its face shaped from death.

She ducked into the trees, one hand clutching the talisman around her neck, the other pressed to her mouth.

"Taniel." She whispered his name through her trembling fingers; a frail prayer that the God's Mark possessed the power to protect him from that creature.

Finding her courage, she peered through the ferns. The spirit descending upon her husband was gone. A woman emerged from mist and shadow to cross into the God's Mark. She moved as silent as night's coming, her steps unhindered by the age lining her features. Years creased the corners of her mouth and framed her eyes, yet no grey flecked her black hair descending in a long braid from a headscarf decorated by green and white beads. Her dress was simple, the blue-grey of a winter's sky, and she looked like any peasant woman to be found in the eastern villages.

Nesrin was unfooled. The woman was only one in appearance, not in nature.

The woman knelt beside Taniel. She felt for his pulse before moving her hands to his arms and chest, exploring the twistings of his bone and flesh. She ran a hand through his hair, sweeping the bloody, sweat-damp locks off his brow. The words she whispered were too quiet for Nesrin to hear. Taniel gave no response. His head was tilted at a limp angle, his eyes half-closed.

Nesrin dug her fingers into the mossy earth, torn between the want to rush to Taniel and fend off this strange woman, the fear that if she so much as moved the woman would disappear along with the last hope of her husband being saved, and the desperation urging her to throw herself at the woman's feet, offering her everything she had to give so long as Taniel lived.

The old woman scooped him into her arms as if he weighed no more than a newborn, cradling him with the tenderness of a mother holding her sleeping son. She leaned her ear to Taniel's lips, then looked to where Nesrin hid.

"Nesrin, there's no cause for fear. And Taniel has no wish to leave until he knows you are with him." She spoke in Nesrin's native tongue. Her voice was the deep groan of ancient trees weathering a storm. "Come."

The command frightened as much as compelled Nesrin to take a timid step forward, but she hesitated to follow as the woman carried Taniel from the God's Mark. She felt like a child—small, vulnerable, and incapable of understanding the events transpiring around her. Taniel reached for her, and that was a calling stronger than her greatest fear. She hurried to take his hand.

"Don't leave." His breath rasped weak from congested lungs. His eyes were clouded. "Please."

She pressed his fingers to her lips; a promise to remain by his side. The woman shifted her hold to rest her hand on Taniel's forehead. His unseeing eyes fell shut and he went still as death.

"What are you doing?" Nesrin asked. Her skin tingled and eyes weighed heavy under the sorcery the woman cast.

"It's alright, child. Your husband will wake."

The answer was too vague for Nesrin's liking. "Are you ... are you the Grey Lady?"

"That is one of my newer names, and I must admit, one I'm not fond of. I am old, but I'd hope never grey. Asherah is the name first given to me and the one I hold most dear."

"Will you help him? Can you save my husband?"

"I can't undo what's been done. Not even we have the power to erase wrongs. But I can be sure he does not suffer so terribly for it."

Again, the vague response left Nesrin feeling as uneasy as when she first saw the Reaping's red spill across the northern sky. She was unable to escape the feeling she was surrendering both her and Taniel to a price they could not pay. "And what do you want for helping him? Please, I'll give you ... I'll do anything. Please."

"Child, there is nothing you can offer that has not already been laid at my feet a thousand times before." There was no menace in Asherah's tone, but her voice sent a chill through Nesrin nonetheless.

"Then what will it take to save him?" she asked. The mist twining about their ankles swelled to their knees like a river sated on spring rain, drowning the trees and ground behind its shroud.

"That is for Taniel to decide, not for me to demand. Now, stay close."

Nesrin held Taniel's hand tight, unwilling to lose him to the grey. Ancient magic filled her lungs, pounded in her ears, and sank its way into her bones. She shut her eyes and clenched her teeth. Her body felt impossibly heavy, she could hardly breathe, and just when she was sure she'd break, the pressure lifted so suddenly it left her gasping under a lightheaded rush. She kept her grip on Taniel's hand as her knees gave way, collapsing to the ground, her vision muddled and spinning.

"What was that?" Nesrin panted. She dug her free hand into the soft earth, seeking an anchor to reclaim her bearings.

"The way is too far to walk by mortal means," Asherah said, pausing to allow her time to recover. "Breathe, child, you'll be alright."

"Walk where?" The dull ringing in Nesrin's ears subsided for her to hear the pleasant hush of falling water. She blinked her spinning vision clear and her mouth fell open, thinking Asherah must have spirited her from the waking world to that of dreams.

The heavy mists they'd moved through were gone. Yellow and white flowers stippled the forest floor thickly covered in creeping woodruff. Towering trees filtered the light slipping through the leaves into a viridescent hue, dappling the mossy trunks that were thicker than Nesrin was tall. Circles of stone pillars stood sheltered within the woods. The structures were twins to the God's Mark she and Taniel took refuge in the night before, except here the white rock was marble-smooth and the engravings in the stone showed none of time's toll.

The vibrant beauty of the forest made Nesrin feel like a wooden doll among porcelain, roughly carved and out of place. She was shamefully clumsy compared to Asherah's inhuman grace as they climbed the gentle hill toward the sound of falling water, slipping on the dew-slicked ground and taking great care to avoid tripping on roots hidden by the lush green. The air warmed from a cool autumn evening to that of a summer's day, the trees thinned, and at the hill's summit Nesrin's breath caught.

"Oh," she whispered. Greater eloquence was lost to wonder.

Waterfalls cascaded from a rise of rock and trees in delicate silver ribbons to form dozens of small pools reflecting the dusky light and canopy to create a landscape of mirrored indigo and gold-tinged green. Smoke snaked up from the clay chimney of a small thatched hut resting in the center of a sprawling glade. Bright fruits hung like precious gems from the garden's trees, sunbirds with flashing plumage flitted among trellises supporting woody vines heavy with harvest, and honeybees circled above blooming herbs. A small herd of deer glanced at Nesrin, tails and ears flicking, before returning to their grazing. The silver, cervine spirits drifting through the trees showed more interest in the new arrivals. They followed on Asherah's heels, crowded close to Taniel with childlike curiosity, or bounded ahead toward the rise of waterfalls.

Nesrin kept hold of her husband's hand as Asherah rested him on the flat rock beside a small pool. The sleep holding him was so deep he barely breathed. Too much time passed between the shallow rise and fall of his chest.

"Get his clothes off," Asherah said.

It took no time for Nesrin to undress him. All his clothes were designed to be easily removed as even dressing was difficult for him. Asherah ran her fingers over his muscles strained like knotted roots at his shoulders, to his chest where they atrophied so his frail skin clung to the shape of his ribs as if the thinnest coating of melted wax had been poured over the bones.

"Oh, child," she said, "what did she do to you?"

She pressed her hand to the ground. The smooth stone shivered, melting into reddish clay at her touch. The remaking rippled out to surround them, and Nesrin's knees sank into the stone softening to soil. Slowly, Asherah pushed her hands into the earth until the mire reached her elbows. Taking fistfuls of clay, she smeared them over Taniel's torso until his chest and abdomen were entirely covered.

"What are you doing?" Nesrin asked.

"His organs are failing." Asherah rested her hands below his sternum. "I can restore them, but it will take time."

She sank her hands slowly through the thick smearing across Taniel's chest, then into his flesh.

Nesrin gasped in distress. "Oh gods, don't!"

"Nesrin, you must trust me to help him."

Horror and hope raged wildly within Nesrin as she watched Asherah's hands sink into her husband as easily as they had the earth. Taniel did not stir. The deathly deep sleep kept him mercifully unaware. She had to look away when Asherah's hands began to move too freely beneath his ribs. She shut her eyes tight against the images conjured by the wet, sucking sounds coming from her husband's chest. A warm dampness soaked into her trousers. Nesrin kept her eyes closed, not wanting to see what it was. She prayed that she'd made the right choice in bringing Taniel here, that he was to be saved and not torn apart again. She offered anything and everything she had so long as it was not her husband she lost.

Taniel coughed. Nesrin opened her eyes, and for a moment, her husband lay so still and silent, Asherah's hands sunk so deep into his chest, she thought he must be dead. Then his chest rose in a breath unfettered by the Demon Witch's mutilations.

Tears streamed down Nesrin's cheeks. She pressed her husband's hand to her forehead, feeling as though it was her lungs that had been freed. Asherah's hands continued to move under Taniel's ribs and each breath he drew came clearer and steadier than his last.

28

All the Lost Souls

Taniel raised his hand to cover his right eye in compliance with the ritual he'd learned worked best to lessen the headache of waking. Slowly opening his left eye, he lowered his hand. A headache was worth Nesrin being the first sight he saw in the morning. She lay curled next to him, sound asleep, her dark hair cast loose over the furs they rested upon.

His wife was the only familiarity in the small hut. A thick layer of dried rush below the bedding separated them from the hard-packed dirt floor of the single room dug into the earth. Clay walls hugged beams supporting a thickly thatched roof, and golden fingers of late morning light reached through a doorless opening. A small alcove bulged off the circular room for a fire pit where low embers breathed their last.

Taniel marveled at how easily his own breath came. The wet rot that had filled his chest the last week was gone, as was the restricting pain like iron shackled his lungs. He sat up and his back spasmed in punishment for him rising too quickly. Moving with greater caution, he pushed the blankets off to reveal a different torso than the one he remembered. His ribs had been realigned. The bones were smoothed into a more natural shape allowing his lungs to take in proper breath, the muscles of his torso no longer felt like moldering rope, and the slashing wounds Minu had torn into him were gone. He frowned at the discoloration mottling his chest and stomach, similar to fading bruises or water stains on parchment.

His frown crumbled into a bitter groan when he saw his left hand remained trapped in its curled contortion. He touched his face and his heart sank. The bulge to his skull was still there, twisting his eye to the side. The horns were there as well, pulling the connecting bones into an unnatural shape. He closed his eyes as the first sparks of the inescapable morning headache ignited beneath his horns. He was still ruined, still broken, still a monster of Minu. Reason told him to be grateful that he'd survived the night, but the despair he'd carried for nearly two years was too close a companion to be so easily abandoned.

"Nesrin." He nudged her shoulder. He was starved for answers and had only vague memories that dissolved to dust at his touch. Last he remembered was seeing a woman coming toward him through the mist, and a lingering sense of surrealness had him wondering if that had been a dream. "Nesrin."

"Let her sleep," a woman said from outside the hut's opening. "Your wife was up until dawn. She's earned her rest."

Curiosity overrode caution, prompting Taniel to rise. There were no clothes in the hut, so he wrapped a blanket around his waist before venturing into the morning. A woman sat beside a large cookfire. She was old, her exact age indeterminable as her face was lined, yet the strength in her movements belonged to that of a far younger woman. Taniel's years as a Purger warned him to tread carefully. The woman only appeared to be one.

"I assume we have you to thank for the hospitality," he said.

"You must not remember much from yesterday," she said. "I'm not surprised. You underwent an ordeal."

She waved her hand over the fire to show his lost memories in the flame—her crouching beside him as he lay dying in the God's Mark, him begging her to see his wife safe, and her promise there was nothing to fear. His insides squirmed when the flames showed her laying him on stone turned to clay, slathering the red over his chest, then reaching through his flesh and bone.

He touched his abdomen. The unnatural discoloration of his flesh was more visible in the morning light. The mottled patches were the same reddish color as the clay.

"You're Asherah?" he asked. "The Grey Lady?"

"Yes."

"Are you a Seraph?"

"Not the first you've met either. Sit and eat, Taniel Sushan." She motioned to the low table by the fire, ladened with bowls of rice, plates of salted meat, eggs, figs and dried dates, pomegranate and cucumber. "The damage my sister wrought upon you cannot be redeemed in a night."

"Minu is your sister?"

"One of the many."

"She's also a Seraph?"

"She is Nakirah, a messenger of revelation, sent to teach mortals the unseen powers."

"I've never heard that name invoked," Taniel said. Nor had he ever seen it written on the walls for temple prayer.

"She strayed from her calling long ago and has led thousands more astray in doing so."

Taniel stared at the woman tending the fire. He'd always assumed the tales of Seraphs wandering the earth were parables of morality. Seraphs were avatars of divine will humanized by icons to give men a tangible name to pray to, not flesh and blood creations. The stories of their intervention, lifting mortals to higher grace, and the darker tales of the divine messengers succumbing to mortal vice were instructions on virtue, not true events.

Asherah's smile was one a mother bestowed an incredulous child. "You pray to the Seraphs, yet you doubt their hand?"

Taniel held her gaze, searching for inhumanness and finding plenty. Eyes blacker and possessing more years than the night met his. He didn't look away, though his skin crawled from the divinity her mortal shape could not cloak. Many of the monsters that imitated human guise could be recognized by their incompleteness. There was something lacking in the way they moved, an emptiness in the eyes, or the absence of flaws in their too-perfect features that rendered them uncanny. Asherah's appearance was not one of incompleteness, but overcompleteness. Her being was too great to be condensed to mortal shape, allowing only the smallest part of her to be shown; the sea held in a glass bottle while losing none of its depth. Taniel shivered. He was not at all reassured to learn divine messengers walked as close to man as legend claimed. Reading of Seraphs in temple writings and praying for their intercessions maintained a comfortable distance between petitioner and divine. Those securities of the detached faith he preferred were obliterated upon meeting Asherah, and he found her presence more unsettling than any monster he'd hunted.

"Does all of this grow in the forest?" Taniel moved the conversation to the safety of simpler subjects. Yet even in the garden the unnatural flourished. The fruit on the orchard trees grew in defiance of season, buds flowered as they pleased, and there was no trace of blemish on root or leaf.

"Not all of it," Asherah said. "Farmers who live near the forest have found they receive strong harvests, so they leave portions of their fields untouched and do not trouble themselves when eggs or animals go missing."

"And if they don't provide you those offerings?"

"Then they do not. They will receive a strong harvest all the same. I'm not a god, Taniel. Their offerings are a kindness, not a demanded tribute, and you are too young to be so cynical."

Taniel split open a pomegranate. "I'm bitter. Not cynical."

"And how do you distinguish the two?"

"A bitter man complains of his sufferings. But only the cynic believes his complaints."

Asherah chuckled and Taniel gave a one-sided smile. Life was endlessly strange that he should find himself casually conversing with a divine messenger in her garden over breakfast.

"That's what my father used to say." He slowly picked out the fruit's red seeds. "He said cynics were cowards hiding behind derision because they lack the courage to see the goodness waiting on the other side of sacrifice."

"Your father was a good man."

"Did you ever meet him?"

"Not directly. But my sister's admiration of him was one of her few displays of reason."

The sorrow of his father's death hollowed Taniel's chest. Fresh images flickered in the fire—his father, Tiran, and Aryeh disappearing into the black sallow trees of the northern marsh. Guilt joined his grief, and the flames twisted to show his father pleading with Minu for Taniel's life, the last sight he'd seen before succumbing to the witch's curse.

"You'll have to let that go, Taniel Sushan," Asherah said. "You cannot escape what Nakirah has done until you stop clinging to the misery her curse is rooted in."

He wiped away tears. "It's not that simple."

"I never said it was simple. Only that it must be done."

"Can you fix me? Make me as I was?"

"No. But I can remake it into a lesser burden. Eat, then join me at the pools when you've had your fill. There is much to do."

She left him at the table, and Taniel moved to sit where he'd not have to see the memories the flames revealed. He picked at his food, troubled that he was able to eat and not have his stomach roil, his throat convulse, and nausea accompany his every bite. He had forgotten what it was like to perform a task so basic as having a meal without being overshadowed by pain. The absence of discomfort made him feel unpleasantly light, as though a part of him was missing. His slow, hesitant bites did not last long. The vestigial discomfort faded as hunger—no longer checked by illness and malformed organs—came rushing in. He tore into the meats, devoured one bowl of rice then another, not waiting to finish chewing one bite before moving to the next. He was glad Asherah had left and no one was there to see him descend upon the food in a mannerless frenzy.

"*Eat slowly.*"

Mouth bulging with boiled eggs, Taniel turned to see a deer's skull watching him. It hovered at eye level upon condensed mist in the meanest shape of a cervine body.

"*You'll make yourself sick.*" It spoke in a dual echo of Asherah's voice and a man's.

He slowed his eating under the spirit's eye, and once he was no longer ruled by hunger, he regained the presence of mind to prepare a bowl for Nesrin. The spirit followed him to the hut, and the sight of the deer skull peering through the doorless entrance was amusingly disturbing.

"The start of my penance. Breakfast in bed, and I'll bring the flowers later." Taniel set the bowl beside Nesrin. She lay on her side, one arm outstretched to where he'd been. He tucked the blankets tighter around her, running his finger over her cheek. "Thank you."

There were no words to adequately convey the gratitude he owed her. Anything he might speak was a shade to how much the hardships she'd unflinchingly endured for him meant.

The spirit nudged his shoulder with its skull.

"Come." More of Asherah's voice than the man's rang through the summons.

The spirit guided him through the trees, drifting slowly over the forest floor in consideration for his limping step, leading him toward the hush of falling water. The large shape looming like a slumbering giant in the mist was revealed to be a rise of rock and tree from which waterfalls tumbled in silver streams to form dozens of tiered pools. Asherah waited at one of the smaller pools sunk into the moss-covered stone.

She gestured to the water. "Step in, and sit down."

He was shy letting the blanket fall away, and cringed in humiliation when she caught his arm to stop him from slipping on the slick stone, steadying him to sit in the pool's center where the water rose to his collarbone. She stepped in after him, and the crystal-clear pool darkened, curdling to mud at her touch. Taniel pressed himself against the stone wall as the changing water became warm and unpleasantly viscous. He flinched under Asherah's hand, remembering all the times he'd seen Minu reach toward him.

"Taniel." Asherah's hand was gentle on his shoulder. "It's alright."

Taniel shook his head, cold sweat sliding down his brow, unable to speak through the fear Minu had poisoned him with. He felt trapped in the clay, and was certain his nightmares of being stuck in mire like this were rooted in a memory lost from the earliest, more terrible days in Minu's care.

"I will not harm you," Asherah promised.

"She told me the same thing." His voice shook under the panic threatening to overwhelm him. Again and again Minu had promised she had no want to cause him pain as she happily turned his every conscious moment into agony. Asherah rested her hand on his chest. Taniel's hammering heart slowed, his breath steadied, and the memories of Minu stealing his humanity loosened their cruel grasp on his mind.

"I'm sorry. For all she's done," she said. "My sisters and I, we have all strayed at one time or another. But Nakirah, she is fallen."

Reaching into the muddied pool, she drew out handfuls of clay.

"Close your eyes," she said and patiently waited for him to find the courage to obey.

He held his breath as she smeared the warm earth over his eyes and forehead, working the clay to his jaw and neck in the smooth, practiced movements of a sculptor. The strokes were shallow to start, tracing over his face and neck, circling the bulging right portion of his skull.

"Your scars run deep," Asherah said. "And not only the ones my sister inflicted upon you."

"There was no avoiding that," Taniel said. He grew up seeing the scars covering his father, Tiran, and Aryeh. In youthful ignorance, he thought them a mark of manhood and looked forward to collecting his own. Upon joining his father in earnest on Purger hunts he'd learned that the physical scars were the shallowest. The ones left on the spirit and mind were the most profound and the hardest to endure.

Asherah's strokes moved from his neck to his shoulders. He hated the feel of her hands making him intensely aware of his total vulnerability, and the clay over his eyes cast him back to the days he spent helplessly blind in Minu's prison.

"Why did you choose to be a Purger?" she asked.

"I'd rather not talk about what my life was," he said. It reminded him too much of all it could never be.

"It will help if you do. Words shape who we are as much as action." Her strokes became slower, deeper, and Taniel was unsure if it was mud or flesh she moved beneath her hands. "Tell me of your father, then."

"I don't think he wanted me to be a Purger," he admitted. Many of his earliest memories were of him traveling with his father to various jobs or waiting for his return. "I was seven when I hunted a hobgoblin that'd been killing chickens in the town where my father was chasing more dangerous quarry. I carried its corpse to the road I knew he was to return on. I waited for hours, and when I finally saw him, I couldn't wait longer." He'd run down the dirt road, the dead monster dragging behind him; the jingle of the six copper pieces he received for killing it was the song of a man wealthy beyond his wildest dreams. "I thought he'd be impressed, but even young as I was, I saw the disappointment he tried to hide. I knew his praise was hollow."

Asherah lifted Taniel's left arm from the clay. She gently flexed his stiff wrist before working the mud along his fused fingers. "Did your father learn to be happy that you followed in his footsteps?"

"My father was never happy." Tiran had told him his father had not been happy since Taniel's mother left. But his father had been proud of him, there was no doubt there. It took Taniel a long time to learn how to read his father's small nods, his rare smiles, and the signs of approval he seldom spoke. Sariel Sushan was not an affectionate man. Praise was scarce, nurturing nonexistent, and as much as Taniel admired his father, he had sworn to be a completely different sort of parent to his own children. He vowed to never leave them guessing to his pride in them. Or love for them. His children would never wonder, as he had, if his father regretted his wife had not taken their son with her when she left. Too many nights Taniel had lain awake, certain his father wished him gone or thought him an unwanted burden. It was not until Taniel turned thirteen that he learned his mother had tried to take him with her when she left. His father had tracked her down and taken him back.

An aching grief rose in the wake of these memories. Everything Taniel had hoped to be, the promises he'd made to be a better father than his, and all his father had sacrificed to give him the chance to do so was gone. There was no miracle to right the course of time to what it should have been.

"Taniel." Asherah clasped his left hand. "You have to let that go."

He took in a steadying breath, and with the exhale he unclenched his fists, releasing the guilt he had held onto in place of what had been lost. Asherah ran her fingers through his. The chronic stiffness in his left hand lessened and the strain of gripping a terrible burden lifted.

She wiped the mud from his eyes. "Look."

He opened his eyes and stared in disbelief at his hand. Tissue no longer knotted the fingers together. His bones felt light as feathers, freed from the snarled pain he had grown accustomed to. Asherah guided his fingers from the half-fist they had been trapped in, aiding them through their proper movements, reminding them how to extend and flex beyond the limited range he had surrendered to.

"Now, you try," she said.

Taniel moved each finger on its own. They were weak from disuse but moved unrestricted by painfully ill-formed flesh. Asherah offered her hand, and when Taniel was able to lace his fingers into hers, he wept.

Dusk's pale violet greeted Nesrin's waking. She rubbed her eyes and smiled, seeing the bundle of snowdrop flowers and valley lilies beside a bowl of rice topped by salted meats and dried fruit. Her smile faltered when she sat up to find the small hut empty.

"Taniel?"

A silver spirit drifted in, slipping into the deer skull by the hearth.

"He's at the pools." It spoke with Asherah's voice. *"Eat before you come. You'll need your strength."*

The skull clattered to the floor and the spirit flitted from the hut, bounding to join two of its fellows in a game of chase that reminded Nesrin of children at play. She rushed through the cold meal, not bothering to change clothes or find shoes before hurrying out. The silver spirits ran with her for a few paces, laughing with unbridled delight, before racing ahead into the mist. The grass was cool beneath her bare feet and the air was heavy with the waterfalls' humid warmth.

She found her husband and Asherah at a lower pool, the water thickened to red mire. The Seraph stood chest deep in the clay, running her hands over Taniel's left arm in slow, deliberate motions. He rested against the smooth rock ledge. His expression—resigned to discomfort—was the one he wore when the Arcanum mages sank needles into his skin to bleed new ink into his warding tattoos.

Seeing her approach, Taniel sat up, then hissed in pain.

"I told you not to move," Asherah said. "Your bones are still setting."

Nesrin sat at the pool's edge so her husband's head rested on her legs instead of rock. "Why you always misbehave when I let you gone from my sight?"

"I was behaving fine until I saw you," he said. "You bring out my worst behaviors."

She saw through his teasing. He was in pain and was too tired to hide it from her.

"How I help?" she asked.

"I'll need you to hold him steady," Asherah said.

"For what?" she asked.

"For me to mend his spine."

Nesrin looked to Taniel who nodded, already having consented to the invasive work.

"It'll be fine," he said. "No worse than what's already been done."

Which almost killed you, Nesrin thought.

Asherah rested her hand over Taniel's eyes. His breathing slowed, and Nesrin shook her head to fight off the sorcery's drowsing effects. After a minute, Asherah lifted her hand, leaving Taniel in that sleep which held him closer to death than waking.

"It's better he not feel what must be done," Asherah said in Nesrin's native tongue. Taking fistfuls of fresh clay, she smeared it over his neck, face, and horns.

"Will he be able to breathe?" Nesrin asked as Asherah thickened the coating. Taniel's chest continued to rise and fall, impossibly finding breath despite the mud masking his mouth and nose.

"Trust me, child. He will wake."

Nesrin repressed a shudder as she slid into the mire. The clay came up to her chest and had the warm, rhythmic pulse of a living body.

Asherah helped her maneuver Taniel so his head and arms fell over Nesrin's shoulders, leaving his back exposed for remolding. Just as she had the night before, Asherah placed her hands on Taniel, pressing through the layers of clay, then into his flesh. Nesrin winced at the scrape of bone being moved. Though the mud was repulsively warm on her skin, the stronger heat emanating from Taniel was nauseating. Her gut lurched in rebellion as the nidorous ill-magic that had taken root in her husband was bled from him. She listened for the beat of his slowed heart, felt the rise and fall of his chest pressed to hers, and did her best to ignore the stomach-churning sounds of Asherah restructuring the internal damage.

Too soon, Nesrin's arms ached, then throbbed from the stress of supporting her husband. She held steady, not allowing the faintest quiver. The ache spread from her arms to her shoulders. She endured, praying for the strength to hold him steady. Tracking the passage of time was impossible. The dusky sky was reluctant to darken to true night and Nesrin's late awakening had her confused as to the hour. She had no idea how long Asherah had been working, or how much longer the Seraph needed to correct the mutilation Taniel had suffered. The strain in Nesrin's shoulders reached her back and hips. She held him steady. Her joints went wooden with stiffness, her muscles burned in want of rest, but her resolve was stone.

"You always were a test of patience," she whispered to her husband. From the beginning, she'd understood marrying a Purger was agreeing to a trial of endurance. Taniel's work took him away for days, weeks, even months at a time; and no matter how many jobs he took on, her worries never lessened.

"I'll be back soon," he'd always said, sealing his vow with a kiss. "I promise."

That departing ritual eased his leaving. Not his absence.

The shifting crack of Taniel's bones was replaced by a soft sucking that reminded Nesrin of feet fording through mud. She felt the strain of holding her husband in her every muscle.

"Come back to me." Her lips brushed Taniel's hair caked in dried clay. "You promised you would."

The forest's strange twilight lightened to what might have been dawn or a reversion of dusk. Exhaustion dulled her mind, urging her to give in to weariness. She held him steady. She knew how to suffer long, aching hours, all the while never knowing if the pain had an end. The last year and a half had been spent under that misery—ignorant of her husband's fate, and unwilling to give up on him.

Asherah ran her hand along Taniel's spine to smooth the clay. "That should do."

Fresh pain shot through Nesrin's arms in protest of her moving to adjust her hold on Taniel. His head fell to rest on her shoulder. The dried clay covering his face was heavily cracked along the outermost layer.

"How much more work needs to be done?" she asked.

"I don't know." Asherah sounded as weary as a mortal woman in her winter years. "Nakirah was indifferent to consequence when she sought to change him. This will take time."

She lifted Taniel from the mud. Nesrin clambered out far less gracefully, slipping twice before successfully heaving herself over the clay-slicked sides. The mud in the depression was no longer a rich red; it had darkened to the black pitch Nesrin had seen infecting Taniel's blood.

Asherah beckoned her to a second pool, the clear waters untainted by clay or corrupted magic.

"This is best done by your hand. You know him better, and he has given himself to you," she said. Untying the sash from her waist, she soaked the fabric in the water, then handed it to Nesrin. "Wipe away the clay to wake him. Remember him as he was as you work, and be patient. You cannot hurry this cleansing."

"What else do I need to do?" Nesrin asked.

"When he wakes, don't let him move until I return for him."

"Where are you going?"

"You and your husband are not the only souls wandering these woods," Asherah said, turning toward the trees. A dozen silver spirits separated from the mist to greet her, swirling in an agitated frenzy like birds battered by fierce winds. Nesrin spun her talisman necklace between her fingers, disliking the uneasiness that followed in the wake of Asherah's departure as much as she disliked the taste of the vague answers the Seraph fed her. Offering a prayer to the gods for guidance, and the patience to accept what she had no power to change, she sat beside her husband, wiping the damp sash over his brow.

"Do you remember when we first met? At that café when you asked me to dinner?" she said. "I thought if I stayed silent, you'd give up and leave. But if I'd known you for more than that minute, I would've known how foolish a thought that was."

He hadn't given up, and it was his determination softened by sincerity that convinced her to accept. Suri had translated all he had said once he left the café. She'd teased Nesrin over the mysterious increase in young men who came in for a coffee over the last month.

"It's only after you started working here that so many come in, and so frequently." Suri had grinned wickedly. She'd been stunned when Nesrin told her she intended to meet Taniel, breaking from her dismissal of all previous flirtations. When Suri asked what had changed Nesrin only shrugged, unable to articulate what it was about Taniel that set him apart.

Nesrin ran the sash over his jawline. He had looked so vulnerably young standing beneath the clock where she agreed to meet him, nervously shifting from foot to foot, hands shoved in his pockets, glancing up and down the pathway. That nervousness vanished the moment he saw her, replaced by warm delight. He had learned a phrase in her native tongue, offering it as he did his arm for her to take.

"Yne ibik ne'ehalu."

The literal translation was "I will take care of you," but the phrase's true meaning failed to easily fit into her husband's imprecise Haeranji. Spoken between strangers, it was one soul recognizing the worth of another, imploring the gift of trust. Between more intimate relations, it was the promise to live in self-sacrifice for the sake of the other.

He repeated the phrase to her at the end of the evening when he walked her home, unbothered by the shabby immigrant neighborhood she lived in, a ramshackle assortment of tenement halls and shanty slums. Her face had burned in embarrassment, unsure of at what point during the evening she began to care what this young man thought of her, and was afraid he'd have no interest in her after seeing she had nothing to offer him. Her face had flushed with a different heat when he kissed her and passed her a napkin from the restaurant they'd dined at. A picture of the clock was drawn above the words "same tomorrow" written in her language.

Nesrin washed the filthy sash in the pool. Silty, red clouds blossomed from the cloth. She had been at the task for over an hour, had yet to reach his skin, and she'd wiped and wrung away an impossible amount of clay. She set down the cloth, using her hands to gently smear off the earthen mask.

She remembered how Taniel had unfailingly walked her to and from work when he wasn't gone on a job. The most ridiculous fight they'd had was when he insisted he accompany her after the physician had specifically instructed him to stay off his sprained ankle for a week. She remembered how he always listened to her confessing the day's petty irritations, or revisited burdensome worries she had told him a dozen times before.

"Come back to me," Nesrin pleaded. She moved her hand over his forehead. Where there had been an unnatural mass of bone, her hands cleared away a clump of damp earth. She pressed her thumb down and felt the shape of a smoothed brow. Hands steady despite her pounding heart, she slowly cleared the clay, resisting the want to claw the mud off him. She heeded Asherah's instructions, recalling Taniel as he had been with each deliberate stroke. She remembered the nights of the Spring Festival spent in Ikdash, the time they visited the Setareh Sea and he told her how dearly he held the memories of his father taking him there. She remembered how he had learned to play songs from her native land on the duduk, restoring a link she feared lost to the music of her childhood.

Nesrin felt the outline of his jaw beneath her hand, smoothed and no longer crooked. A handful of clay yielded to her, freeing his mouth and nose for him to take in a true breath. She cleared the clay over his eyes. They were aligned and reshaped to the face she'd seen at the train station when Taniel had left for the north that final time. He stirred, and she rested her hand to his cheek.

"Yne ibik ne'ehalu," she promised, and kissed him.

The night is moonless, and there are no stars to distinguish the heavens from the ink-painted earth. The hateful mist of the Grey Forest floods from the trees. Ever the coward, Asherah hides behind her grey cloak into which she weaves shadows of what has been lost. Men you counseled move in the mist. Women who came to you for wisdom weep their anguish.

Nakirah. The ghosts of Ha-Ai whisper the name you abandoned in the Wastes. They ask why you abandoned them as well. *Nakirah.*

You sink your hand farther into the ground. Asherah's taunting gives you greater hate to poison her woods. Already you've carved a weeping wound into the trees. The wrath you seed into the earth finds its way into the small fractures left by your daughter. Your hate and her madness breeds a potent curse, and Asherah's kingdom sickens. The trees nearest you are withered. Their bark is blackened, leaves are ash, and the power preventing your trespass is decayed as well. You're sure you could enter now—but you wait. For five hundred years you have been cautious of her forest. You can wait a day longer before you see her uprooted.

Nakirah. Nakirah. The past comes to greater life, shaping into hands that tug at your sleeves, your arms, your hair. You ignore the pathetic conjurings. She'll use any trick, any lie, every deceit to goad you into carelessness.

"It's no lie, Nakirah. *All you see is true.*" She speaks through her death-bound slaves watching from the trees. Their eyes shining from the skulls are the only light piercing the mist, and every silver pinprick is fixed upon you.

Nakirah. Nakirah.

You hear the step of Sevget's reanimated dead shuffling toward you. They drag themselves on beleaguered limbs, longing to return to the earth. Unlike Asherah's sendlings, there is no light in their eyes. They're pitiful creatures of muddy flesh and necessity demands their sacrifice.

"Leave him," you say when three of Sevget's dead crowd Maqlu. They're too close to their previous lives and are envious of the beating heart of the man lying bound.

You don't have the privilege to raise these dead into something more. Instead, you will send them into Asherah's forest. The ground will blister where they tread, the roots beneath shrivel. They will spread your malice through your sister's kingdom and in so doing clear the way for you to enter. The forest will fail, Asherah will fall, and the misguided mortals who erect shrines in her honor will see she is undeserving of worship.

A voice sings from the trees. Sevget's dead tilt their heads in uncanny synchronization to the lament calling to lost souls. The singing beckons them forth and Sevget's dead answer.

"Don't," you warn, but they pay you no heed and lurch into the trees. The violence you expect to greet them—roots ripping free from the earth, branches lashing down to rend the dead limb from limb—does not come. The forest welcomes Sevget's dead. Their steps leave festering wounds on the forest floor, the branches they pass beneath shrivel, and they bring upon the trees the destruction you desired. Yet the lament continues to sing its invitation and the dead pass without resistance into the mist.

"What are you playing at?" you ask the nearest shahavaz, its skull bent low to inspect the poisoned earth.

"*All lost souls belong to me. Has obedience to duty become so foreign to you, you cannot recognize it anymore?*" it says. The light within the skull goes out like pinched candle flame. One by one, its fellow spirits abandon the bone that gives them shape and voice, and fade to wisps. "*I take in the world's wickedness, and you have bred plenty.*"

"You take everything from me." The earth trembles under your fury.

Kharinah, Taniel, all that you love she has stolen from you. The people of Ha-Ai sacrificed your children to her in their rebellion, all because she could not be bothered to look after those who bowed before her icon. She deceived them into paying her favor, left their petitions unanswered, and your children reaped the cost of her indifference.

"You took everything!" Your scream turns the air to fire. The rotted trees burst into blazing pillars.

For too long you have tolerated the sinister spread of her influence. Binding her to the mountains' forest was too merciful. She's a blight that you should have buried in the Wastes.

You stride into the burning woods. The trees groan in their straining to snare you. Roots whip through the soil to drag you into the earth. Her power is nothing to yours. A wave of your hand incinerates the reaching branches. A single word hissed between your gnashing teeth turns the soil to stone to halt the roots. Asherah was always weaker in will. Her refusal to sacrifice for greatness will be her undoing. You fell for her illusion of power and thought you'd forfeit yours if you crossed into her kingdom. You know better now. The forest screams in pained fury as you inflict the agony you have carried for centuries upon it, carving your way through. Asherah will become as intimate with suffering as you have.

29

The Two Seraphs

Taniel's arms were thin, weak and wasted. His atrophied legs were no better. The little muscle he retained had forgotten how to properly move and unfamiliarity troubled his every step. Recovery was slow, and long hours were spent under Asherah's hands as she moved muscle, smoothed bone, and molded his flesh as if he were made of nothing more solid than the clay she used to reshape him.

This morning's work was less intrusive, which meant Taniel was awake to feel her fingers exploring his left shoulder, testing the stability of the joint to ensure the ligaments connected as proper.

"There." Asherah pulled her hand from his flesh. "Rotate your shoulder slowly."

Taniel obliged. No clicking pain greeted the movement.

"How you feel?" Nesrin knelt at the pool's ledge. Her shift, arms, and face were splattered in dried clay. More and more she helped Asherah with removing Minu's curse from Taniel, as more and more Asherah disappeared for longer stretches of time. Entire days often passed without sign or word from the Seraph, and she never revealed to where she went.

"Light," Taniel said. His bones felt disconnected and his limbs unmoored in absence of the grinding stiffness that had held his body together.

He raised his arms for Asherah to lift him from the clay in a practiced dance they'd done a dozen times before. She lay him on the smooth, moss-covered stone.

"That all for day?" Nesrin asked.

Asherah rose from the mud, her movements unhindered by the heavy, clinging mire. "For now. Be sure to stay where you can see the hut," she said as she always did before leaving on one of her absences. "If anything happens, call for me. I will hear."

"Where are you going?" Taniel asked.

"You are not the only soul come to this forest in need." Another of her repeated lines. "Do not wander."

The grey mist swarmed to shroud its mistress, and in a flicker of step and shadow, she was gone. Silver spirits glided from the trees to circle the pools and garden. More of them had flocked to this part of the woods of late. For the last three nights, Taniel had woken to see one standing as a sentinel outside the hut, guarding them from a threat Asherah refused to name.

"There are many strange things in the forest, Taniel Sushan," she said whenever he asked what the spirits watched for.

"She's hiding something," Taniel said.

"You think we in danger?" Nesrin asked.

"Not from her." Evasive as Asherah was in her answers, there was no mystery in her intentions. "Has she said anything to you?"

"Only same she say to you."

Taniel scraped clumps of clay off his skin. He was always concerned more than mud might come away, but Asherah was a far more attentive sculptor than Minu. Her patience in remolding his wretchedness had won his tolerance of her penchant for giving enigmatic non-answers. He owed her more than his life, and was in no place to make demands. There was nothing gained in him obsessing over the trouble that drew Asherah away as there was nothing he could do about it.

Nesrin slung his arm over her shoulder to help him up. Standing unsupported was an inelegant struggle. After realigning his spine, Asherah forbade him from walking for what she claimed was only a week but felt like a month. Nesrin said it felt closer to a year as she had to endure his restless temper. When Asherah at last permitted him to be helped to his feet, walking a hundred feet felt like a hundred miles, leaving him trembling and winded.

His legs shook, unsteady as a newborn fawn's, as Nesrin guided him to one of the pools. The water was a glass mirror of the trees above. Taniel avoided looking into the smooth surface in habit of not wanting to see his reflection.

Nesrin stripped off her filthy shift and slipped into the water. "You come in?"

"In a moment." He was lightheaded from the walk and Asherah's work. Unlike Minu's, Asherah's moldings did not cause him agony. They were, however, disturbingly uncomfortable, and once again he found himself a stranger in his own body. He carefully lowered his legs into the pool, releasing clouds of red clay from his skin. Nesrin dove beneath the water, sending out glimmering ripples to lap over his shins. Tempting as it was to follow her, he remained at the edge, unable to shake the worry he sullied her in sharing the same water. He saw what had become of the pools Asherah first used when remaking him. They were no longer filled by clay or water, but by a reeking, tarry mass. Creeping woodruff and clover slowly grew over those pools, and Asherah forbade them to go near the healing earth.

Nesrin resurfaced. Her dark hair clung to her skin glistening with beading water. The temptation to join her was a physical ache.

"Has Asherah ever told you where she goes?" Taniel asked.

"No, she always be saying same thing. That there other souls in forest and we not go where we not see hut."

Taniel glanced over his shoulder, thrilled he did so by only turning his neck, not his whole body, and that no stabbing pain punished him for the bold movement. The thatched hut and garden were shadowed outlines in the mist, and the ever-burning fire was a beacon to lead them back.

Water lapped on the stone as Nesrin swam to him.

"Come." She took his hand, leading him in. Her feet barely touched the smooth stone while Taniel's shoulders remained above water. The ripples blurred their reflections, hiding his features but not his form. The horns curling from Taniel's head were obvious even in the disturbed water. Asherah had admitted she had no power to remove them.

"My sister wanted you to have them too badly for me to take them away without unraveling you entirely." She had slathered clay onto his neck instead, unknotting the strained tendons and giving the vertebrae stronger structure to support the unnatural weight. There was only so much she could heal. The rest had to be salvaged or suffered.

The water supported Taniel as he waded close to the pool's edge, rediscovering a left shoulder unhindered by a dark witch's crafting, a spine no longer crooked, and legs that bent to allow a proper step instead of dragging stiffly beneath him. Asherah molded him as close as possible to human, but just like the horns, there was an unnaturalness to him she warned was permanent. He was nearly half a foot taller than he had been. His legs bent at an odd angle, his ears belonged to neither man nor goat, and while his right eye was now human in shape and properly set in his skull, Nesrin told him the color was a feral yellow instead of his natural green.

Asherah had freed him from the fatal chains Minu had placed upon him, yet he was still irreparably bound. The Demon Witch's influence was too thoroughly twined into his life. Taniel had asked Asherah if her influence on him bore similar consequences.

"Yes," she had said, and told him the cost of how profoundly she had to root her power in him, that the change was more than physical, and there was a price.

Already tired from the menial exertion of pacing the pool, Taniel retreated to the edge to rest his head on crossed arms.

"What wrong?" Nesrin asked, imitating his pose.

"Asherah says I can't leave," he said.

"Not leave forest?"

"I can't leave the forest's influence. It's too much a part of me."

"How far influence go?"

"Close to Sevget. But she doubts I'll be able to go much farther than Antarr. She advises I not even try."

Nesrin shrugged, far less bothered by this revelation than he was. "I thought we stay in Antarr anyway. You no be able to leave east. Even if not because influence."

"Why not?"

"People hunt you. Everyone frightened now of the things that be different. They think you monster or cursed. But people in Antarr no care you look like this. They not afraid of strange and cursed. They see it too much."

She was right. Even if he wasn't bound to the Grey Forest, he'd be hunted the moment he strayed outside its protection; either to be harvested as Purger Adhar had desired, or simply killed for his appearance being too strange for tolerance. Violent prejudice against the magic-tainted was practiced long before the Reaping, and Minu's curse had inflamed those fears.

"I don't want your life to be lesser because I'm trapped here," Taniel said.

Nesrin splashed water over him. "You not trapped and I not lesser."

Taniel forced a smile. He ought to be grateful. Every breath he took was a gift, but learning he was physically bound to the forest was a spiritual crippling. He had traveled all his life; wanderlust was a need to be sated as much as hunger, and the limits put upon him were a bitter ransom to pay for release from Minu's mutilations. He'd never see Gohar again, the middling plains, or the northern foothills. The Setareh Sea where his father had taken him as a child was only to be found in memory. He had wanted to explore the southern islands, see the celestial lights of the northern skies, and go west to Nesrin's home country to travel the russet plateaus and green valleys she described.

"You be able to stay in one place though?" Nesrin intuited what he struggled to accept. "I think that be hard on you. Even when you dying, you not stay still."

"I think my wandering days are done." He shifted to better show how thin he was. His every rib was visible beneath skin of various earthen shades.

"You get stronger in time. Asherah say this only temporary."

But my being bound is not, Taniel thought. The cost of him living in this world was to lose all save a corner of it.

Nesrin rested her hand on his arm. "You alright?"

"I will be." Dwelling on what was lost only invited in pointless misery. "And those worries are for tomorrow. Not today."

"Then what worry be for today?" She inched closer to him.

"That everything feels disconnected." He flexed his left hand, reminding the weak fingers of their restored mobility. "Asherah says I'll need to relearn basic tasks."

"Like what?" She pressed herself into him. He let her push him so his back rested against the pool's sloping edge.

"Running, lacing my shoes." He pulled her hips up to his. "Buckling belts."

"And?" She ran her hand over his chest. Her fingers traced the fragmented vestiges of the warding tattoo—a few petals of the Wind Daughter's anemone and the vague shape of ram's horns.

"Most everything using my left arm."

"Hmm, what about this? You remember how to do this?" She kissed him long, slow, and deep. His mouth chased hers when she drew back, and she bit her lower lip in a teasing smirk. "Ah, I see you do."

"I'm not so sure. You'll have to remind me again."

After a week of Taniel's incessant begging, Asherah permitted him to walk the forest so long as she was not gone on one of her absences. If Nesrin had her way, he'd never go beyond the pools. She argued he needed to rest, not to indulge his restless meanderings. Asherah had failed to console Nesrin's worries, but convinced her that Taniel's want to wander was necessary. He had to adjust to his new body. The more he used his realigned limbs, the sooner he'd abandon the bad habits formed in his brokenness, relearning what it was to move free from pain's tyranny.

Taniel invited Nesrin to accompany him, but she rarely accepted.

She was reluctant to venture farther than the pools and the hut's clearing. Her wariness was a healthy one. Beautiful as the forest was, it was marked by unnatural presence. Asherah had assured Taniel that he had little to fear from that which also walked through the trees. Her healing him had made him too much a part of the forest, and not even the darkest denizen would dare claim him when he was so bound to its mistress. He was peripherally aware of these beings he shared the forest with, sensing more than seeing their moving through mist and fern. He felt more than heard their whispers rustling leaves, and the ancient power thrumming in every root, rock, and blade of grass was the same rhythm of his beating heart.

Coming to a beech grove brightened by yellow-star weeds, he knelt—more confident in the motion than he'd been the day before—to add the flowers to his wild bouquet. He had no notion for how long it'd been since he and Nesrin first crossed into the woods. Day and night were fleeting hours between long stretches of dusk and dawn, coming and going as they pleased. The uncertainty of time's passage extended Taniel bringing Nesrin flowers as reparation for leaving her in Gohar into an endless penance; one he enjoyed seeing through. Nesrin no longer pretended to be stern when he presented the floral offerings. She smiled as a young girl did when courted.

One of Asherah's silver spirits followed him, fading in and out of the mist, only visible when he paused to look for it. He watched it flit through a ring of tall, pale standing stones. The lithic structures were common sights in the forest surrounding Asherah's hut. Taniel placed his hand over a circular design carved into the stone, reminiscent of the Wind Daughter's anemone that was once tattooed on his chest. He etched the image into his memory to ask Asherah its meaning. She understood the lost language, the same one Master

Maqlu used in his sorcery, and the one spoken by the demon-child in her madness.

Leaves crunched beneath approaching steps. Taniel knew it had to be Nesrin. Asherah moved as soundlessly as light over water.

"Come look at this," he said, examining the carvings decorating the standing stones. "Don't you think—" he froze, the dark presence behind him was terrible in its familiarity.

Kharinah stood ten strides from him. Her cheeks were hollow, her torn clothes were filthy, her golden eyes sunken in sickly shadow, and her hair was a wild tangle better fit for a wolf than woman as was the weak growl rumbling from her throat.

Taniel ran and immediately stumbled. He had barely remastered walking—he had no hope of fleeing. Kharinah cut him off, raising her hands in a pleading gesture. A whistling rasp hissed between her cracked lips.

"What do you want?" he asked. He looked for the silver spirit sent to follow him. It was gone, leaving him alone with the demon-child.

She croaked, hands clenching and unclenching to convey what her lost voice could not, mouth silently shaping a repeating "please, please, please."

"No," he said. "I'm not going back."

Kharinah's cringing timidity vanished. Snake-swift, she lunged, grabbing his horn and pinning him to the ground. Her teeth snapped inches from his face in a starving animal's madness. Minu's magic threaded over her like spider web, barely restraining her from tearing open his throat. Taniel struck out. Blood sprayed from her cheek where his black nails ripped into her. She grinned. The thin red lines on her sickly skin paled as they healed. Cold intelligence replaced her mindless fury. She slashed Taniel across his face in mirror of the wounds he'd inflicted then sank her claws into his left shoulder, mutely laughing at his scream.

"Kharinah!" Asherah's voice cracked like steel on stone.

The demon-child flew off Taniel as if physically struck, sprawling in a ragged heap. Mist flooded forth, a dozen spirits flocked to Taniel, standing between him and the demon-child, and Asherah stepped from the silver storm.

"Forgive me, Taniel," she said. "I meant to find her before she found you."

Kharinah was slow to get to her feet. Blood streamed from her mouth and nose. She bared her teeth, but Minu's magic closing over her throat strangled her words.

"You may speak here," Asherah said, and the crimson threads holding Kharinah dissolved.

She sucked in the miserable breath of a man almost drowned. "Asherah, you've allowed yourself to grow old."

"And you are unchanged," Asherah said. "To no one's betterment."

"You were always critical of me."

"Because you should have been so much more."

Kharinah laughed. "You said I never should've been. It would have been better if I never was."

"A prophecy you chose to live up to."

"Don't pretend I had a choice!"

"There was a choice, Kharinah. It was never easy, but you always ran from it."

"How like you, Aunt. Preaching down at us lesser beings." In Asherah's presence the demon-child no longer looked frightening. She looked worn and sad, like a doll that had been played with too roughly and then discarded.

"What do you hope to achieve here?" Asherah asked.

Kharinah looked to Taniel. "Come home. Please. Mother wants you home."

"You don't have to serve her," Taniel said.

She smiled, joyless and unhinged, tears rolling down her cheeks. "She killed over half the world on a whim and fantasy. What do you think she'll do to me if I truly provoke her?"

He saw it was not only filth clinging to Kharinah; her skin was peeling and dried blood was mixed into the dark grime covering her. She pinched a piece of skin between her claws, tearing it off like a sheet of thin paper.

"As I said, little brother, you were barely put together better than I, and not all of us are deemed worthy of the Grey Lady's favor—" Kharinah snapped her head to Asherah as if suddenly remembering she was there. "It's not fair! Why him? You never helped me! You said I was wrong, all wrong—that I shouldn't be. I begged and begged and you said no. You never helped! You never helped me! It's not fair!"

She keened in her ancient language and the air darkened with her madness. Taniel fell to his knees, covering his ringing ears. Asherah neither denied the accusation nor flinched from the chaos barreling down on her. The feral sorcery shredded the earth, splintered trees, and left the reek of burning flesh in its wake. It only stirred Asherah's hair with the feeble strength of a dying spring breeze.

"It was not my choice to help you, Kharinah," she said. "That was, and always will be yours."

"Don't lie." Kharinah stalked forward. "You always—"

She stopped, staring at the vines twining from the earth to trap her legs. She reached down to touch her finger to an unfurling leaf, and the fury contorting her features crumbled to resignation.

"Oh." She offered no resistance, only a weary sigh, when the feelers encircled her chest and began to pull her into the earth. Taniel drew back. There was a disturbing terror in witnessing her silent surrender. She stared at him as she sank to her waist, said nothing when the earth reached her shoulders, then her neck, and only turned her head up at the very end for a final gasp before disappearing entirely.

The broken trees groaned as they righted themselves. The ones splintered beyond repair followed the demon-child to sink into the soil. Silver spirits pawed at the damaged earth and flowering grass bloomed to close the sore as if Kharinah had never been.

"Did you ... is she dead?" Taniel asked.

"That's up to her." Asherah knelt, resting her hand where Kharinah had stood. "It's long overdue for her to decide what she wants to be."

Your chest caves under the sudden blow of hollowing loss, dropping you to hands and knees. The forest takes advantage of your collapse. Earth flows over your hands in an attempt to pull you into the dark soil. It reaches your shoulders before you regain the sense to burn it to ash. You thought the bond shared between you and your daughter had been severed by the forest, but it had only been weakened. A frail connection survived, unknown to you, until now when it is too late.

You thought you knew pain—finding your children murdered on Asherah's altar, your sisters abandoning, then turning on you—but losing Kharinah is an agony without equal. There are no words. You can only weep, knowing your daughter is forever gone.

Everything. Asherah has always taken everything from you. She swayed the people of Ha-Ai to reject you. Poisoned their minds to build temples to her in replacement of their false gods. She ignored her flock of bleating sheep so it was you who suffered the cruelty of their superstitious greed.

Grief burns through the mortal guise you've worn for centuries. Skin becomes brimstone scales. Your fingers split into talons. The trees shrink as you rise, wings unfurling like smoke.

You will see if you and your sisters are truly undying.

Taniel held Nesrin close. By her breathing he knew she also lay awake listening to the night, sensing the change that had overcome the forest. A corruption fouled the air, tasting of ash and feeling like sand in his throat. Firelight winked off the Purger knife and pistol he kept close to their bed. He prayed he'd not need to use either, doubting a creature that threatened the Grey Forest was to be felled by any blade or bullet.

Nesrin sat up to face the doorless entrance. "You hear that?"

"Hear what?" he asked. The ever-burning fire outside the hut crackled, the waterfalls spilling into pools hissed soft susurrations, crickets chirred in the trees, but through the usual sounds of the night came a thin mewling nearly lost in the dark.

"Is that an animal?" he asked.

"No, that a baby."

Before he could stop her, she was out the door, hurrying in the direction of the feeble cries.

"Nesrin!" He scrambled to his feet, grabbing the Purger knife before giving chase. A dozen different tales of all the evil beings that mimicked an infant's cry warned him not to trust the pitiful wails. A day ago he would've thought it impossible for malevolence to trespass this close to Asherah's garden. Kharinah's coming had shattered that false security, and the night had reclaimed all its dark possibility.

"Nesrin, wait!" He grabbed his wife's arm. "It only sounds like a child; we don't know if it is."

A figure, far larger than an infant, moved in the trees. Taniel pushed Nesrin behind him and raised the knife. Asherah stepped into the fire's ember light, carrying a crying bundle in her arms. Taniel's skin prickled from the wild, ancient magic swaddling the child. His wife shared none of his reservation. She twisted from his grip and rushed forward.

"Is she alright?" she asked.

"No," Asherah said, "but I have hope she will be."

The infant turned her head to show a tuft of dark silky hair, copper skin, and eyes that were drops of gold set on ink-black sclera.

Taniel pulled Nesrin away. "Don't touch it, that's a demon!"

She looked at him as though he were mad. "No, she a baby."

"Don't—" His warning went unheeded. Asherah handed Nesrin the demon-child and his wife readily took her, cradling her with the practiced confidence of a midwife, speaking softly in her native tongue.

Asherah rested a reassuring hand on his arm. "Peace, Taniel. She presents no danger to your wife."

"What did you do to her?" he asked, torn between pity and disgust at the infant Nesrin held. The child turned her head from side to side, rooting, then crying for hunger. Nesrin swayed to rock the child, soothing her wailings to fitful whimpers.

"I gave her a choice," Asherah said. "I admit, I thought it'd take her longer to decide."

"Choice for what?"

"The same as you. A choice to live."

"Does she ..." Taniel paused, the situation was so beyond his experience he wasn't sure how to phrase his concerns. "Does she know what she is? Will she remember?"

"The soul's memories die in infancy so that we might live. She'll have no true knowledge of who she was."

"But she'll still be Kharinah." Physical change did not remake the soul. He had personally experienced that twice over.

"And?"

"She doesn't deserve it."

"Deserve what?"

"Forgiveness," he said, though he heard how little conviction he spoke with. "She doesn't deserve forgiveness."

"Forgiveness is a mercy, and mercy is a virtue only when granted to the undeserving."

You should have killed her, he thought before realizing his bitterness echoed what Kharinah had first said of him.

"I don't take life, Taniel," Asherah said. He wondered if there was anything of his kept secret from the Seraph. In remaking him, she knew him more intimately than Nesrin did. "I heal what is broken, mend the body, and at times the soul. If you wish to see Kharinah pay for her past through death, it shall be you who carries out the deed."

She gestured to the Purger knife, and he felt suddenly ashamed for having it in hand. Nesrin watched him, holding Kharinah to her chest, looking ready to put herself between the child and blade.

"There was a time I shared similar sentiments as yours," Asherah said. "I thought that my blessing was meant only for those who deserved it."

"And?" Taniel set the knife down. Nesrin relaxed.

"Pride led me astray. I weighed their worth and found them wanting. I deemed the many unfit for my favor based on the sins of the few, and a kingdom fell. I was sent to heal, not judge. Far more wretched creatures than my niece have found their way to this forest, and I am called to tend them the same. You came to me broken in body. Kharinah came to me broken in soul. Her need is greater than yours. Do not hold that against her."

"What will you do with her?" he asked.

"Find her a mother. I'm hardly fit to raise a child. Perhaps you know a soul who understands the responsibility it is to raise another."

Taniel did know such a soul. Shirin would not turn away a child in need. Not even a demon-child.

"There's a woman residing at the home of Master Maqlu," he said. "Shirin Basak, she's a mother to all. Even the most wretched of us."

Dozens of Asherah's spirits bounded from the trees into the clearing as if fleeing a predator's hunt. They circled their mistress emitting high, panicked cries. The earth shivered, branches swayed, and for the first time since Taniel met her, Asherah looked troubled. Fear pounded through his veins. There was no mistaking Minu's coming; he'd spent over a year living in dread of sensing her return to the mountain manor.

"Nesrin, take the child into the hut," he said, and was relieved she obeyed without question.

"You should hide as well," Asherah said. "She'll not take kindly to seeing you here."

She waved her hand and the agitated spirits vanished. The forest dimmed in absence of their silver light and the ever-burning fire lacked the strength to banish the coming darkness.

"Does she know I'm here?" Taniel asked.

"Yes."

"Then hiding will do nothing." He cut the Purger blade across his inner arm and scrawled bloody warding runes on the nearest trees. He felt the forest respond to him, sharing his eagerness to hold Minu at bay.

"Save your blood and strength," Asherah said. "She'll not be denied by something so small as warding runes."

"Then how do we stop her?" He ignored the Seraph's advice even as he believed it, continuing to write the patterns on the bark, unable to stand by and do nothing.

"I hope there is the chance to reason with her. There was a time we took one another's counsel."

Taniel went to a third tree. He held none of Asherah's optimism that Minu had a shred of reason left in her. "How close is she?"

"Close. Listen to me, you—"

A monster wreathed in fire roared from the trees. Lightning and flame crackled over the beast's red-black scales, claws the size of horses tore through earth and wood, and Taniel had no time to do more than gape before it was upon them. Jaws three times as long as he was tall snapped closed on Asherah and shook her with limb-shredding violence. Bones snapped, blood sprayed, and the creature tossed the tattered ribbons of her body to the side like unwanted meat.

Taniel stared in frozen shock, barely aware of the viscera dripping off him. The monster turned its wolfish face upon him. Red smoke unfurled from its sinewy legs, its scaled sides heaved then smoothed into skin, and the leathery wings above its ridged back dissolved like misting rain. The creature compressed itself into the false form of a young woman, dark hair tumbling down her back, eyes bright, and skin clear as a summer sky.

Minu wiped the blood from her mouth. "Oh, Taniel. What has she done to you?"

You clench your hands in fury and your heart sinks with sympathy at the sight of the sickly creature Taniel has become. He looks as frail and insubstantial as Asherah's shahavaz she's so reduced him. She's drained him of the life you were carefully weaving into him. You were to make him more, raise him above mortal limitations. Asherah has lessened him to something barely alive. He's deathly thin, his skin a sickly mottling of shades tinged green by this corrupting forest. Worse, you sense the enchantments Asherah has woven into him, forbidding you from forcibly reclaiming him.

You tug gently on the remaining strands that bind him to you. "Come here, Taniel Sushan."

He moves away. "What do you want?"

"You have nothing to fear, not from me." You tug a little harder. He sways before taking another retreating step.

"What do you want?" he repeats.

"I promised your father I'd keep you safe."

"Then leave me here. I can't leave the forest without finding harm."

"Who told you that? Asherah?" His silence is confirmation. You shake your head. What lies and dark dreams has she whispered to turn him against you? "She's not to be trusted."

You touch a rune drawn in blood on one of the trees. It's fresh and unmistakably Taniel's.

"If I didn't know better, I'd think you were trying to keep me away," you tease.

The fear and hate written on his features cannot be his own. Asherah has poisoned his mind.

"I'm not going back," he says.

"Taniel ..." You sigh when he backs farther away. "Whatever she has done to you, I will see you restored."

"Have you not done enough?" Those words reveal how terribly Asherah's influence has infected him.

Nakirah, have you not done enough? Nakirah ... Nakirah ...

The traces of your power that lie buried within Taniel erupt into red veins. He cries out. You silence him with a flick of your hand. No matter how Asherah recreates his image, he will always belong to you. Your sister ensured you cannot come close to him, but she has always been uncreative. You are forbidden from approaching Taniel. He is not forbidden from returning to you.

"Come here, Taniel Sushan."

He's too weak to do more than feebly resist your command. You feel his terror as the red veins force his right foot forward then his left, feel the scream you trap in his throat, but you don't have the time to be gentler in reclaiming him. Seraphs do not die. Asherah will return. You intend to have Taniel safely away before she does.

"Come." As soon as you've rescued him from this wretched forest, you'll ensure he won't stray again. You'll bind him to you as you should have done Kharinah. Sariel Sushan gave him to you, and you gave Sariel your word. "We're going home."

"Taniel, no!" A woman rushes from the hut to grab his arm. Her feet slide over the damp ground as he drags her forward. The spell you have wrapped around his throat chokes off his warning. Tears track down his face. He grits his teeth, the little muscle he has strains in a futile rebellion you'll see corrected.

"Let him go," you warn. You're willing to spare her the last of your patience. She's a frightened child incapable of understanding what she's so stupidly involved herself in. You send a taste of your anger her way. The red pulling Taniel forward flares to scald her hands. She yelps, releases him, and scurries back to the hut. Your approval of her common sense is momentary. She returns to level a Purger's pistol at you in shaking hands.

"Let him go," she echoes your command.

You touch your cheek below the eye where the bullet struck, stopping you from pulling Taniel from Asherah's clutches when you traced him through Maqlu. "It was you."

Kharinah is lost and Taniel almost so, all because of the interference of this miserable mortal.

"It was you!" Fire and wind slices toward that pathetic creature who has done so much unwitting damage.

Taniel's will cleaves through yours, breaking the weakened bonds holding him to you. He tackles the woman to the ground. You rein the burning gale back, not soon enough. A breath of the punishing sorcery catches him. His scream breaks soundlessly on your silencing spell as his skin blisters.

Roots burst forth like black snakes to snarl over him and the woman. They crouch in the middle of the writhing, woody tangle—Taniel holding the woman tight, his skin smoking, his teeth bared at you in unyielding defiance—then the wood closes above them in a sheltering dome.

"*Nakirah, have you not done enough?*" The bloody ribbons of Asherah's mortal body dissolve into mist.

"Have you not taken enough from me?" you ask.

"*I only fix what you destroy. You imprisoned me for it, yet the souls you break still find their way to me.*"

The trees groan. Branches splinter. The forest is unused to their mistress's true form.

"No more of your games. What did you do to my daughter?"

Asherah's sigh is a spring storm, flaying leaves and toppling the weakest trees. "*You refuse to see how far you've fallen, to lose sight of even her.*"

It's only then you hear the screaming of a frightened infant coming from the squalid hut. The wailing is one you know instantly as Kharinah's—a sound you have loved and hated since she first came into the world broken and malformed. It's a cry you heard echoed by your later children in their last, terror-stricken moments before they were sacrificed on unhallowed altars beneath Asherah's idol.

The gods forbade their messengers from interfering with another's calling—there was to be no war or strife among the Seraphs, the first of their creations. Yet, just as the mortals who came after, we are allowed defiance, the chance to err, to fall, and rise above the ruin we wreak.

"Come out, Asherah."

She does, no longer pretending at a mortal guise. Mist plumes under her steps, wind howls with her every breath, and the dark creature that steps from the forest is a knotted nightmare of black limbs and eyes white as death beneath a crown of a thousand twisted branches. Your wings unfurl in smoke, your skin crackles into fiery scales. You lunge with centuries of fury as for the first time in over a millennia, two Seraphs fall to war with the other.

30

What Comes from the Woods

Shirin was certain she had not woken, and only moved from one dream to another. The crimson pall bleeding across the morning sky was the recurring nightmare that had afflicted her since the Reaping. Her throat went dry when she realized it was no dream. The eastern horizon burned red in terrible imitation of the Demon Witch's plague.

She ran barefoot down the hall, calling for Maqlu.

"Out here," he answered from the back porch. Dua had found him a mile north of Antarr on the forest's edge, weak from exposure. She had unraveled the ill-magic holding him captive there to bring him home, but there was nothing she could do to restore his sight. He'd shared little about what had happened to him, ending inquiries with a dismissive hand and saying, "It is done, and this is far more merciful than I deserve."

He sat with hands clasped in his lap, his milk-white gaze fixed to the east. Although he could not see the red dawn, Shirin knew he sensed it.

"What is that?" she asked.

"A meeting that will decide our fates. One we have no say in."

A distant roar shook the ground. A gust of wind, sharp and warm like a dragon's breath, ripped branches off the trembling trees. Master Maqlu offered his hand. Shirin readily accepted the small comfort.

"Don't bother, Dua," he said as the young mage dashed out, blue light rippling like water over her skin. "This is beyond us. If you must act, go to the temple and reassure those who seek refuge there."

"And you?" she asked.

"They'll come here as well, and I'll be here for them when they do."

"Will you be alright?" Dua's devotion to her master had become a daughter's ferocity in protecting her aging father.

"The people need your attention more than I. Tend to them."

Maqlu's calm façade slipped when Dua departed. His hands shook as he signed against evil, murmuring prayers beneath his breath. Where Dua went, Yael was never far behind, and less than a minute later Shirin heard him coming down the hall.

"Where's Dua?" he asked.

"She's waiting for us at the temple." Shirin shaped her face into a soothing smile. "Let's get dressed to join her."

"Is it the Reaping?" Dread shrank Yael's voice to a shaky whisper.

"No, and there's no cause for fear, only gratitude for the Grey Lady's protection." Shirin's stomach writhed at how terrible her lie was. She prayed Yael never discover how little truth it held.

The ground shook as she and Yael made their way through Antarr's streets. Loose roof tiles smashed onto cobblestones, old wooden homes groaned, and dogs howled. There was barely room for them at the temple crowded with frightened souls seeking sanctuary. Dua stood beside the priest at the altar, swaying to calm her squirming infant as she spoke reassurances to the villagers. Most of the temple's supplicants knelt in front of candle offerings and icons, their heads bowed and hands clenched in trembling prayer. Children cried as shrieking gales rattled the windows. Women screamed when a distant roar shook the stone walls and toppled candles. Men cursed, seeing it was not an agitated mist that swirled outside the temple, but the silver spirits of the forest stalking the village streets.

"Have they ever left the woods before?" Shirin asked the white-haired woman standing beside her.

"Yes," she said. "But it is rare, and I've never seen them in such numbers."

A terrible keening screeched like nails dragged over glass. The people screamed, clapping their hands over their ears, and the deer skull on the altar to the Grey Lady cracked in two. The silence that followed the bone's breaking was more horrifying than the shriek. The people held their breath, all of them waiting, none of them knowing for what.

A river watchman was the first to leave, duty compelling him into the mists. A mother followed, her three children hungry and asking for home. One by one, the villagers departed the sacred ground, returning to fields, hearths, and lives, understanding there was little else to do.

"Shall we head home?" Shirin asked Yael.

"Do you think this has to do with Taniel?" He followed close at her heels across the temple's threshold. The noon sun barely penetrated the mist blanketing the square. Lanterns lighting the streets rescued the village from disappearing entirely into the grey gloom, tinged red by the sky's eerie burn.

"I don't know," she lied.

One of the spirits with a deer skull head stepped across their path. It paused, turning its face to Shirin and Yael. Silver glowed behind the eye sockets, one of them partially collapsed from a fissure running through the bone as if it had been violently struck. Shirin was sure she heard it speak her name. She nodded before realizing what she was doing, but the spirit only stared a moment longer before disappearing into the mist.

She wanted to run the rest of the way to Maqlu's home, but false courage was the only protection she had to offer Yael, so she kept her steps steady to mask her mounting fears.

She found Master Maqlu as she'd left him, sitting on the back porch staring east. He held out his hand for her to take and she sat beside him, watching the crimson sky darken to an unnaturally early night. The village lanterns and hearths were kept lit into the midnight hours, and Shirin stayed with Maqlu through his blind vigil, unable to sleep and unwilling to leave him to endure the night alone.

A natural dawn, cold and grey, greeted them. The sky had cooled from its burning, but the eerie silence that had followed the breaking of the temple's skull refused to lift. No birds sang, no deer grazed along the forest's edge, and the people of Antarr sought Maqlu's counsel in hushed tones. He had no answers to give, only words of wisdom and solace. On the second day of mist and silence, people from nearby villages arrived to seek his guidance. They reported similar experiences of red skies, howling winds, and strange spirits coming from the trees. Again, the mage could only offer consolation, and Shirin saw how severely their distress affected him.

"The people came to me as well during the Reaping. They begged my intercession," he told her that second night. "I was powerless to offer them more than empty words, and once again, that's all I have to give."

Twice a day, an hour after sunrise and two before sunset, Shirin braved the fog, wary of the silver eyes that glowed in the grey watching her pass. No one else in Antarr ventured so near the trees, and Shirin thought it more foolish than daring for her to visit the shrine where she'd seen Nesrin and Taniel off. Fractures running from antlers to teeth scarred the deer skull at the border shrine. Shirin lit stalks of incense, praying that this not be a second Reaping and that the mists not take anything more from a world of impoverished souls.

Three days of silence held as if the world was in funereal mourning. The mist was a widow's veil. The quiet a reverent grief. On the third day as Shirin made her afternoon trek to the shrine, she saw a sparrow take flight from the wild fields. The songbird sang, a second answered, and sound sighed free like the release of a long-held breath. The birds' melody was sweet, wind rustled the fire-painted leaves; and it was to that gentle tune of a world restored that the creature came from the forest. It wore a deer's splintered skull and its body was the vaguely cervine shape of the other spirits, though more defined than the ones Shirin had seen before, having the appearance of phantom veins and bones within its silvery form. Leaves crunched beneath its solid step and a small blanketed bundle hung from the skull in a makeshift sling.

Shirin stood as if in a trance. She wasn't frightened by the creature's appearance, nor was she surprised when it stopped an arm's length from her at the trees' edge.

"*Shirin.*" Its voice was a duet of woman and child. "*You are called.*"

The bundle shifted and cried. Shirin reached for the infant without a second thought. Carefully untying the sling, she shushed the child struggling to get free of the swaddling, her little pink mouth open wide in an indignant shriek. By her size and appearance, Shirin guessed the baby to be no more than a week old. Her copper skin was cool, and Shirin held her close to guard her from autumn's chill. She cradled her as the spirit revealed the child's nature, who she had been, who had created her, and all the evils Minu's demon daughter had committed before finding her way to the Grey Lady's realm. It told Shirin what she was asked to do.

"*Will you?*" the spirit asked.

The infant, calmed from her temper, gazed up at Shirin. Her eyes were the same gold on black as the woman who had followed Taniel to The Red Dove Inn. That was the only similarity found in this pathetic, demanding creature squirming feebly in the cloth. There was none of the menace that had chilled Shirin's blood, nor a trace of the malice that had rolled from the woman like thunder over the sea. The infant wriggled one small hand free. Shirin held out her finger for the child to grip. Her tiny nails were black—but so were Taniel's.

"Second chances are never given to the deserving, are they?" She ran her thumb along the infant's cheek, earning a smile.

"*The deserving are rarely in need of second chances,*" the spirit said. "*Will you?*"

Shirin tucked Kharinah's small hand into the blankets. "I will."

The skull was unmoving bone, yet she was sure the creature smiled. "*He said you would. He said you take in broken souls. You walk my lady's way and will be blessed.*"

Shirin's heart leapt. "Do you mean Taniel said that? Did he find the Grey Lady?"

The spirit turned back to the trees. Shirin followed. Need for answers compelled her to cross into the forest.

"Do you know where he is?" she asked.

The spirit's form unspooled into the mist.

"Is he alive?"

The skull fell to the ground, empty and unspeaking.

The last of autumn's leaves fell quickly as if the hastened change in seasons was part of a wanted cleansing. Winter arrived early from the mountains, dusting the village and trees in blue frosts, then burying the roofs in heavy snow. The days were far colder than Shirin had learned to endure in her northern village where the season was tempered by salted southern winds. She no longer yearned for that home or felt the specter of regret haunting the memory of those younger years. The ache in her chest was ever-present, but it was a healed scar, not the gaping wound it had been.

She left Kharinah in Dua's care when she went to pay her respects at the border shrine, the winter too cold to take an infant. Kharina's howls at being left behind were fiercer than a mountain storm. Strange tracks dinted the snow beneath the trees. Their creators were more visible at night when silhouetted against winter's white. They were not the silver spirits that spoke through bone; these were dark beings best ignored as they prowled the snowy forest. A few times she saw them in the trees when she visited the shrine. They watched her as she prayed, and she felt the hunger in their gaze.

"They won't harm you," Master Maqlu had promised. "They stay in the trees. The Grey Lady forbids their leaving."

He melted the snow along the path to allow her easier passage to the shrine. Every day she lit fresh incense, laid evergreen branches before the stone, and prayed that wherever Taniel and Nesrin had been taken, it be to where they were called to go. For all the strange shapes she saw wandering the forest and the odd tracks in the snow, none belonged to Taniel or his wife.

"It may take months, years for them to return," Master Maqlu said. She knew it was out of kindness he refrained from adding, "if they return at all."

Spring was shy in her coming, a maiden reluctant to shed her white dress. When she at last colored the world it was in homage to the season past. Pale anemone bloomed in the wild fields shaded by the Grey Forest.

"Let the white winds guide you, the stars will light your way," Shirin sang "Little Lost Child Found" as she headed to the border shrine.

Kharinah cooed. Music was one of the few ways to calm her squirming when she was tied to Shirin's back. She was a small, spirited child; curious and quick to grow frustrated when she was unable to do things beyond an infant's ability. She screamed when she was denied the solid food Shirin ate, protested the indignity of being swaddled, shrieked in fury when set in her cradle to sleep, but was easily soothed when Shirin sang.

"Wander and I will find you, no matter how far you stray."

The white anemones grew abundantly around the border shrine. Shirin swept the stone clean before setting fresh incense beside the cracked deer skull. A dark shape moved deep in the trees, veiled by mist. Shirin ignored it. Nothing had come out of the forest since the spirit brought her Kharinah, and Shirin had learned to hold faith that the evils the Grey Lady took into her woods did not escape.

"Hear my lullaby, little one, and heed no dark-born fear." She replaced the old flowers with fresh ones. *"Little lost child, you are found, and I will hold you near."*

The shape in the forest grew distinct as it came closer through the spring leaves. Shirin placed a protective hand over Kharinah and took a cautious step from the trees. The creature was tall, and the horns curling from his dark hair added to his towering height. His skin had no consistent color, changing from a natural golden-tawny hue into a clay red, darkening to silt, and tinged by woody green. Shirin stared, thinking he was a forest god become incarnate until she saw the young woman beside him. Hers was the face she recognized.

Shirin pressed her hand to her mouth. "Taniel?"

He grinned. "It wasn't what I expected either. I blame Nesrin, she took too many liberties."

"It get you back for what you did to me," Nesrin said, tapping her fingers on her swelling stomach.

"Oh gods!" Shirin pulled him into a breath-stealing embrace, tears warm on her cheeks.

"I promised I'd come back," he said. A skin-tingling thrum pulsed off him, accompanied by the scent of old earth and new leaves. She held him tighter, uncaring for the strangeness. She'd grown used to strange things living in this village at the forest's edge.

Kharinah screeched at being ignored. Shirin felt Taniel tense. Letting him go, she saw him staring at the infant, his expression unreadable.

"Is that ... how is she?" he asked.

"A terror," Shirin said. "She throws tantrums when I put her to bed, cannot decide if she prefers to be held or set down, and is forever wanting what she cannot have. Much the same as every other child. And I assume she behaves better than yours will if he has the indecency to take after you."

"Ah, I know." Nesrin shook her head. "That why I tell Taniel I hope this one daughter. She can have his horns so long as she have my sense."

Shirin's laugh faltered, seeing a third person waiting in the trees.

The old woman in the peasant's dress, her long dark hair braided down her back, inclined her head when she met Shirin's eye.

"You will be blessed."

The woman's lips had not moved when she echoed what the spirit had told Shirin, and neither Taniel nor Nesrin showed sign they'd heard the promise. A tide of mist flowed through the forest and when the spring breeze swept it away, the woman was gone.

31

Asherah

You come to consciousness slowly. You have been broken so long, and now your physical state reflects what you allowed your spirit to become. You remember what has happened, are aware of where you are, and understand that it will be years, lifetimes, before you wake to where you can move. Earth and root will hold you until then, and I will wait with you. The world has suffered enough for our sins. Yours of passion, mine of negligence. We do not move through time as mortals, yet we both succumbed to its passing. You forgot your calling. I failed mine. The years made it harder, not easier for us to learn that we fought to preserve what was not ours to keep. I erred in growing indifferent. You, too intimate.

The trees above your resting place are black as midnight, their leaves the shade of blood. Their roots twine into the rest of the forest's, and through that interweaving you witness, as I have, the world beyond.

Children play beneath summer's green leaves at the forest's western edge where the mountain rivers flow to the village of Antarr. Two young girls wearing flowers in their braids laugh as they chase birds shaped from silver light. The young man casting the dancing sorcery is no longer ashamed of the scars covering his forearms and neck. One of the girls catches a bird in her clumsy, toddler hands and shrieks in delight as it scatters into butterflies.

The woman the young girls resemble kneads dough on the porch. She watches them with a careful eye to be sure her daughters do not stray too close to the trees. You understand the mother's worry. Even after the forest returned her husband from the edge of death, she is wary of its power, knowing it gives as well as takes. A second heartbeat flutters beneath hers. Her third child is expected in autumn, a son they will name after the grandfather he'll never know.

Taniel sits beside a girl a little older than the two who chase the silver light. Her eyes are molten gold irises set on deepest black. She kicks her legs in nervous energy as if barely repressing the wild urge to run. Her fingers are unsure as she plays a few awkward notes on the woodwind. Taniel's gentle encouragement calms her frustration.

You wonder why he does not hate her. She may not remember her life before, but he does. Yet he shows none of the warranted disgust or fear. She asks him to play. Her childish fidgeting goes still under the music's spell. She hums along. Her remembrance of the tune survives both your attempts to rid Ha-Ai from her memory and her rejecting the life she knew before. There will always be the wildness in her, but the demon's madness is gone, giving her the chance to see it tamed.

The woman she calls "Mother" repairs the dress she tore yesterday climbing the garden trees. A far younger child sleeps soundly in the cradle. The infant inherited the woman's hair and skin tone, and when he wakes, his eyes will match the color of his father's before he was blinded.

The black-barked trees sway as you turn your attention east. Heavy rains batter the mountains' eastern slopes. The deluge abruptly ends where the last leaf of the forest grows, but the roots reaching into the Wastes go farther, far beyond your knowledge before you came to rest here, hidden below the scorched and cursed earth. They have grown to the broken temple of dust and stone where a man prays before the altar. The tree that grows there is small and sturdy, its roots sinking deep into the earth to connect with the forest's.

Farid's skin is pebbled and rough. Your influence upon him ended before the changes you willed were complete, leaving him trapped in a curse he cannot undo. The roots reveal his pain to you, the agony of his warped bones, the burn of his stretched skin, cracked like the barren desert he braved in hopes to make amends for sins that were not his to carry. For seven years he has suffered. It's a moment for you, but an age for a mortal, and you feel all his anguish.

The red leaves above you shiver as you sigh, letting go the hate you have clung so tightly to for half a millennia.

You feel Farid's disbelief when he hears the soft pattering of rain. He runs to the temple's collapsed steps to see groaning clouds sweeping across the Eastern Wastes. Thunder rumbles and the heavens break. The first drops that fall upon him sink into his skin's roughened fissures to smooth his flesh. Cool reprieve finds his bones, releasing him to be as he was made. He falls to his knees weeping in relief.

The earth darkens as for the first time in five hundred years, rains fall in the east.

About the Author

When not reading or writing, S.K. Ehra can be found wandering the woods and, while skittish, is friendly when approached.

You can connect with me at:
https://skehra.com

Also By S.K. Ehra

SHRINE AND SHADOW SERIES

THE FOX AND THE DRAGON

THE CROSSROADS SERIES

CALL FROM THE CROSSROADS

IN THE SERVICE OF SHADOWS

MARKED FOR MADNESS

Made in the USA
Middletown, DE
09 July 2024